Readers love the Ennek Trilogy
by KIM FIELDING

Stasis

"The concept of stasis and its effect on its victims gives the book a unique twist and one that kept me thinking about it for a few days after I was done."

—Joyfully Jay

"…once I got my head around the world and the plot I couldn't stop… *Stasis* is a beautiful start to a journey…"

—Prism Book Alliance

Flux

"…*Flux* is still just as impactful in the way these two men balance each other, and I have a feeling that balance is going to be a big part of the next and final book in the trilogy."

—The Novel Approach

"Their story is original and breathtaking. I am so happy that I get to be a part of it."

—Love Bytes

Equipoise

"An incredibly intense, riveting adventure comes to a fantastic conclusion in *Equipoise*. This unique blend of drama, action, and sensuality is bound together with a pulse pounding ending."

—Joyfully Reviewed

"All in all it was a great ending to a really good trilogy."

—MM Good Book Reviews

By KIM FIELDING

Potential Energy

ENNEK TRILOGY
Stasis
Flux
Equipoise

Published by DSP PUBLICATIONS
www.dsppublications.com

KIM
FIELDING

POTENTIAL ENERGY

DSP PUBLICATIONS

Published by

DSP PUBLICATIONS

5032 Capital Circle SW, Suite 2, PMB# 279, Tallahassee, FL 32305-7886 USA
www.dsppublications.com

Potential Energy
© 2022 Kim Fielding

Cover Art
© 2022 L.C. Chase
http://www.lcchase.com
Cover content is for illustrative purposes only and any person depicted on the cover is a model.

Mass Market Paperback ISBN: 978-1-64108-360-7
Trade Paperback ISBN: 978-1-64108-359-1
Digital ISBN: 978-1-64108-358-4
Trade Paperback published April 2022
v. 1.0

Printed in the United States of America

This paper meets the requirements of
ANSI/NISO Z39.48-1992 (Permanence of Paper).

ACKNOWLEDGMENTS

MANY THANKS to Thea Nishimori for insightful, helpful feedback on this story; to Karen Witzke for her support and invaluable assistance; and to Scott Coatsworth for my daily pep talk. Haz's story has been calling to me for a very long time, and I'm so delighted to finally share it with readers. I'm grateful to Elizabeth and Gin for giving me the chance to do so.

KIM
FIELDING

POTENTIAL ENERGY

DSP PUBLICATIONS

CHAPTER ONE

EVEN IN civvies, she obviously didn't belong in this dump. She was too clean, clear-eyed, and straight-backed. Too glowing with purpose and determination. She marched across the floor of the bar as if she owned the place—except if she did own it, the bar would be well lit and orderly, and the patrons would be a hell of a lot classier.

Haz wouldn't have guessed she would show up, but he somehow wasn't surprised. Maybe he'd unconsciously expected this for a long time. The only question was whether she'd arrest him or simply blast him where he sat.

When she reached his table at the back of the room, she pulled out a chair, settled in, and stared at him, stone-faced. She'd aged since he'd seen her last: a few new lines around her narrow mouth, hair steel-gray now and worn in a practical buzz cut.

Haz drained his glass in one swallow and waved to the barkeep for another. He turned back to his companion.

"To what do I owe the honor, Colonel Kasabian?"

"In fact, it's Brigadier General Kasabian."

The same clipped tones he remembered, as if she were rationing oxygen.

"Gratulálok!" He raised his empty glass in a mock toast.

The bartender squelched over, their plantar suction cups noisy on the tile floor. They set down Haz's refill and looked expectantly at Kasabian. At least Haz assumed the look might be expectant; it was hard to read a craqir's face, especially when some of the eight eyes were staring in other directions. Craqirs were unable to speak Comlang due to their beaks and lack of tongue, and this one rarely bothered to use the translator on their biotab.

"I don't suppose you have any true gin." Even when she spoke, Kasabian's mouth remained slightly pursed.

The craqir shook their head, and Haz provided a more complete answer.

"They have a synth version that makes a decent paint stripper. Order the yinex vodka instead, cut fifty-fifty with water. Still tastes like shit, but it won't eat away your stomach lining."

She gave his glass—synth whiskey straight up—a significant look and nodded at the craqir, who returned to the bar.

"Major Taylor—"

"Uh-uh. They busted me all the way down to staff sergeant, remember? But don't call me that either because I'm a civilian—have been for a long time now."

She narrowed her eyes. "All right. Captain Taylor, then."

"Nope. I don't have a ship. No ship, no captain. I'm just plain old Mister Taylor nowadays. But you can call me Haz. You've called me that once or twice before."

He shifted in his seat and straightened his quasar-cursed leg, but the ache didn't dissipate, so he drank a slug of synth whiskey instead. It didn't help with the pain, but when he was drunk enough, he stopped caring.

"I was told you do have a ship."

He didn't ask for her source. She had hundreds of rats and moles stashed all over the galaxy, which had probably contributed to her promotion.

"Outdated info. My ship got banged up on my last run, and I can't afford to fix her. She's rotting in dry dock. Unless they've already stripped her for parts."

He couldn't help a sigh. The *Dancing Molly* had served him well and deserved a better fate.

The craqir returned quickly with Kasabian's drink and one for Haz. It was why he came to this particular dump: the barkeep never kept him waiting. He drained his current glass and started on the next, impressed that Kasabian managed a decent swig of hers without making a face.

"How are you making a living without a ship?"

Haz grinned and shrugged.

She watched him for the several minutes it took for him to finish off the latest drink, try to find a less uncomfortable position for his leg, and wait for her to either tell her story or walk away. Or arrest him, if that was her goal. Maybe she'd just shoot him, ending his troubles and hers. Finally she started tapping a rhythm on the metal table with her fingernail, making it ring hollowly. He remembered that she liked music. She used to plan battles while playing Earth songs from a few hundred years ago, a genre that was, for reasons unclear to Haz, called heavy metal. Maybe she was thinking of one of those tunes while she tapped.

At least she hadn't drawn a weapon and didn't seem inclined to. If she had intended to shoot him, she would have done it by now; she wasn't the type to mess around. But if she didn't want him dead, what did she want?

"I have a contract to offer you," she said at last. Well, that answered his question.

He raised his eyebrows. "A contract? Not a jail cell?"

"I'm willing to overlook some past… indiscretions. If you accept the mission."

"I have no sh—"

"It pays enough for you to lease one."

He crossed his arms. "I don't borrow."

He didn't trust anyone else's ship. Besides, who the hell would be stupid enough to put their equipment into his hands?

"Then fix yours."

His heart skipped a few beats at that option. Losing Molly had been like having a limb hacked off. Worse, maybe. He'd have happily traded his bad leg for his ship.

As if sensing Haz's thoughts, Kasabian gestured in the general direction of his lower body.

"Why haven't you seen a doctor about that?"

"Believe me, those bastards have had their way with me plenty of times." He shook his head. "They've reached the limits of flesh and bone."

"Then replace it," she said. As if getting a new leg was as easy as getting a fresh drink.

"I don't have that kind of money. And the szotting navy won't give me a single credit." He couldn't keep the bitterness out of his tone.

She nodded briskly. "This contract will give you enough to cover your medical costs as well as repair your ship. You'll have enough for running expenses too. And a salary for your crew."

Kasabian leaned back in her chair, apparently pleased with her offer.

"Since when does the navy go throwing that kind of money around? And while we're on the subject, what the fuck's up with this contract shit? Whatever it is that needs doing, you've got plenty of your own ships and more than enough people to fly them. And furthermore, why me?"

He knew the answer to that: the job was too dangerous or too sticky to risk their own people. But he wanted to hear her say it.

"This mission is… sensitive. And it involves travel through Kappa Sector."

Haz snorted. So it was both dangerous *and* sticky.

"Got it. Don't want to endanger any of your delicate flowers on this one."

"You know better than that, Taylor. Delicate flowers don't last long in the navy. They didn't when you joined, and they still don't today." She allowed herself a tight smile. "But we do appreciate some of your specific talents."

That made him snort again. He knew he should simply walk away, but he couldn't help thinking of Molly and how much he missed her. How much he hated being stuck on the ground like a szotting mushroom. And then there was his leg. He would sell his soul—assuming he still had one—for a decent night's sleep, for not waking up with shooting pains every time he shifted position. Besides, curiosity had always been one of his weak spots, and he wondered what was such a big deal that Kasabian had come after him.

"What the hell do you need in Kappa? There's nothing there but pirates and a bunch of planets too stubborn or too stupid to join the Coalition."

"We need something delivered to a planet on the other side."

He sneered. "I'm not a cargo runner, General."

He couldn't imagine a more joyless existence than that: stodgy assholes with their bloated, sluggish ships and their precious delivery schedules. He'd rather rot here, planetside, than become an intragalactic mailman.

"It's not exactly cargo. It's a single item, in fact. A religious artifact of great importance to the people of Chov X8. The artifact was stolen, we recovered it, and they very much want it back."

Haz's stomach had clenched as soon as she said *religious*. He wished he had more booze, but he kept his voice steady as he spoke.

"And the Coalition's returning the whatsit out of the goodness of their hearts."

"We're returning it because Chov X8 has certain strategic value to us. Which is all you need to know. Well, and the fact that we'll pay handsomely for you to return the item safely to its rightful owners."

He raised an eyebrow. "*Safely* being the operative word?"

There was that smile again, but larger and more predatory. "The parties responsible for the theft may try to steal it again. If that happens, you'll need to stop them."

"Then why not send it with a phalanx of gunships? The navy's got plenty of those."

"Because the Coalition wishes to keep its involvement... unobtrusive."

Haz sighed. He never paid much attention to politics and wasn't the kind of guy who enjoyed innuendos and hidden agendas. He'd been called blunt more than once, and he didn't consider it an insult. Whatever the Coalition's interest in that little planet, and whatever their reasons for returning the whatsit on the down-low, he didn't know—and, he realized, he didn't care.

He thumbed at the biotab embedded in his left wrist, paying for his drinks. While he was at it, he paid for Kasabian's too. Why not? It'd only get him to flat broke a little faster. Trying not to grimace too much, he stood.

"No," he said.

"No what?"

"No contract. No religious thingamajig. No handsome pay. Find someone else."

"Why are you refusing?"

"I've had enough of the Coalition, and it has damned well had enough of me."

She caught his wrist in a hard grip before he could step away.

"You could have your ship back, your leg repaired. I know exactly how many credits you have, Taylor, and it's not many. I'd bet my commission that you have no plan once they run out. Refusing this contract is stupid."

"Never claimed to be smart." He jerked his arm free. "Good luck, Sona. With everything."

Of course he had no chance of outrunning her, but he hoped she might simply let him go. No such luck. He made it almost to the door before she caught up with him. This time she seized his lower arm. In danger of losing his balance, he gripped an unoccupied table to steady himself.

Because her presence was so substantial, he had forgotten how short she was; her head didn't even reach his shoulder. The three or four times they'd tumbled into bed together, long before either of them wore officers' insignia, she'd been tiny against his long body. Tiny but strong.

Now she pressed her biotab against his, causing both to emit a tinny ding.

"I'm shipping out in two days. You have that long to reconsider. Ping me when you do."

He shook his head and pulled away for the second time.

"No."

"That's a bad limp. Why don't you at least use a cane?"

"Fuck you, Sona."

She was smiling as he lurched away.

IN A best-case scenario, he wouldn't be stranded on Kepler. Most of the small planet was uninhabitable for humans, covered in toxic swamps and regularly reaching temperatures hot enough to kill. But when Molly was crippled during his last mission, he hadn't had much choice. He'd needed to make a beeline for the nearest settlement, and he was lucky to have survived.

Kepler had only two cities—one on each pole, where the temperatures were bearable—and he'd chosen the north only because it happened to be in daylight as he approached. The city was named North, and that lack of imagination was emblematic of the planet as a whole. Nobody came to Kepler because they wanted to. They came because they had no option. Most people worked on the vast structures that roved the noxious swamps, harvesting and processing barbcress leaves. The planet's few wealthy citizens traded the barbcress to off-world merchants in exchange for all the things Keplerians needed to survive, amassing profits until their greed was satisfied and they fled to a better place. The remainder of the population worked in run-down shops or restaurants or bars, or they repaired buildings or ships, or they provided sundry other services that residents required.

It was a dreary planet with perpetually overcast skies and few entertainments, the type of place that everyone dreamed of escaping.

But here he was, here he'd been for over a stanyear, and here he'd remain.

The bar where Kasabian had found him had no name, and it was more or less indistinguishable from most of North's other dives. One of the other regulars, an Earther with a fondness for ancient entertainment, always called it the Pit of Despair, then laughed and had another synth whiskey. Haz and the Earther had fucked once, but both decided the act wasn't worth repeating. They later engaged in an implicit contest to see who would drink himself to death first. The Earther had won. Haz hadn't thought about him in some time, and during his slow walk home, he wondered why the Earther had now come to mind.

The streets in this part of North were unpaved, which meant they alternated between dusty enough to clog your lungs and so muddy they'd suck the shoes off your feet. People with a little money traveled on hoverscoots, uncaring of the street conditions; people without much money walked and swore. Haz was in the latter group, his swearing especially fluent on a night like this, as mist wetted his hair and dripped down his face and the muck pulled viciously at his leg.

He'd paused against a ramshackle building, steeling himself for the final three blocks, when a shadow took shape out of the darkness and stalked toward him. Haz couldn't make out much detail, but by the way the figure moved, Haz recognized its intent.

"I've got nothing on me worth stealing." Haz's voice was cheery; he was in the mood for a fight. "And you might think you're handy with that pigsticker you're clutching, but I assure you, I'm handier."

The person continued to approach. Haz undoubtedly looked like an easy mark with his heavy limp, and some of North's residents were desperate enough to kill for a few credits. They'd spend it on the narcos they had become addicted to while working the barbcress processors— the narcos their bosses so generously handed out to keep them docile and then took away the moment an employee fucked up bad enough to get fired. Haz almost felt sorry for them, when they weren't trying to rob him.

"I'm telling you, pal. You're gonna regret this."

"Gimme your credits." The man's voice, deep and raspy, had a Kepler accent. Poor bastard had been born on this shitty planet; no wonder he needed narcos to bury his woes.

"I told you. I'm just about flat broke. I can't—"

The man lunged.

Haz, with the wall behind him, didn't have much room to maneuver and didn't have enough trust in his leg or the ground to dance away. He carried a knife of his own, of course, but hadn't drawn it. That would take all the fun out of this encounter. He stayed put, braced himself against the building, and grabbed the attacker's wrist. The edge of the blade nicked Haz's hand—a misjudgment attributable to booze and darkness—but he only tightened his grip, using his opponent's momentum to guide the knife away from his body and into the softened wood of the wall. It stuck there, and as the man tried to pull it out, Haz kneed him in the balls using his bad leg. It fucking hurt, but not as much as getting a patella in the gonads. Haz had learned the hard way to keep his good leg on the ground when fighting.

The man made a gurgling cry and, letting go of the knife, doubled over. Haz took the opportunity to land a solid fist to his temple. The sound of the impact lingered as the guy hit the ground.

Haz thumbed his biotab, then bent over the unconscious man and tapped their biotabs together, transferring a nasty little virus that would put the other man's biotab out of commission for a week or more. Highly illegal, but so was coming at a stranger with a knife, which Haz now tugged out of the wall. After giving it a quick wipe on the downed man's poncho, he carefully slid it into his own hip pocket.

"It's been a pleasure," Haz said and resumed his limp home.

IN HIS part of town, three-story buildings contained stores and small workshops at ground level and living space above. Dandy for most folks, but on his worst days, Haz found stairs a bitch to climb. After a long search for a place he could afford and easily access, he'd eventually rented a small room at the back of a repair shop.

He unlocked the door, chuckling at the thought of his assailant unable to access his own home due to the fucked-up biotab. Haz turned on a single light, illuminating his hard narrow bed, a small table with two chairs, a couple of shelves, and a bureau. A vidscreen embedded in the wall had a small diagonal crack, as if someone had forcefully thrown something. Near the sink and mirror, tucked into a corner, was the door to a wetroom so tiny that he could conveniently use the toilet and shower at the same time, if he chose.

He was used to much closer quarters on ships, and he wasn't one to accumulate possessions, so this worked fine. He even liked the creaking floorboards under his uneven steps. And as for the bugs the locals called mudroaches, well, there wasn't much he could do about them. At least they didn't bite.

Haz hung his jacket on a hook and shook the rain out of his hair. The slice on his hand throbbed, which made dealing with his boots more painful than usual. Szot that stupid leg. He threw the boots across the room.

After limping over the floor, he clumsily doctored himself at the sink. The cut was long but not deep, so after rinsing and disinfecting, he closed it with glueskin. Man, he hated that stuff. Not only did it make his wounds itch like crazy, but this brand of the synthetic was much paler than his golden-brown skin color, as if intentionally drawing attention to his injuries.

"Who cares?" he chided himself. "You're nobody's center of attention."

Nobody but the occasional thief and the craqir bartender. And, tonight only, Sona Kasabian. Who'd apparently flown all the way to this nowhere planet to offer him a contract.

"Well, she can leave me the hell alone. She can fly right back, polishing her shiny general's star the entire way."

Haz would get back to destroying his liver and feeling himself sink into the ooze until, ultimately, nothing was left but a little bit of foreign DNA embedded in a Kepler swamp.

Still standing at the sink, he looked down at his open palms and thought about the things those hands had done. The weapons they'd wielded, the ships they'd steered, the lovers they'd caressed. Unlike his brain and his leg, his hands had never betrayed him.

If he closed his eyes, he could feel the warm metal armrests of the control seat on the *Dancing Molly*. Szot, he missed that.

Sighing, he turned his hands over and tapped at the biotab.

"Kasabian," he said.

CHAPTER TWO

"YOU SMELL like dirty feet, but at least you're spaceworthy." Haz patted Molly's bulkhead. "Let's get the fuck out of here."

Maybe it was sad that he'd spent over a year on Kepler and yet the only ones who'd notice his impending absence were his landlord and, much sooner, his bartender. Some of the technicians might remember him fondly, now that he'd poured a lot of the Coalition's credits into the mechanics' accounts. But that was the full extent of his connections on this pathetic planet, and he wasn't sorry to be leaving.

He could tell immediately after takeoff that despite the repairs, Molly wasn't at her best. Her responses were sluggish, and she creaked when he tried a few fancy maneuvers. Plus she carried the reek of swamp. But she flew, and she took Haz away, and that was what mattered.

He kept her on manual controls for a long time, just for the simple joy of it. As he sat on the bridge, he acknowledged his painful leg, but he didn't care anymore. He'd always been able to ignore all but the worst pain as long as he was flying. It was as if his body ceased to matter and he instead became one with the ship itself. He felt photons from thousands of faraway suns colliding with his metal skin, felt the cold nothingness of space as it slid by. Heard the silence echo in his ears.

Eventually, however, other duties called. He programmed in a route that took advantage of a few space anomalies, those handy quirks in the galaxy's fabric that allowed a ship to get from point A to point Z without passing through everything in between. "You take over now, darling."

"Autopilot engaged."

Her voice, warm and motherly, made him smile. If Molly were a woman, she would be soft and round, and she'd bake pies while helping grandchildren with their stochastic calculus homework and keeping a close eye on the vidscreen installer so he didn't rip her off. She'd wear colorful scarves with comfortable, slouchy clothes containing a lot of pockets, along with thick-soled boots that jingled when she walked, and she would tell stories of the thirty-seven star systems she'd visited during her wild youth.

It was possible that he'd spent too much time with his ship and not enough with people.

But he'd been without Molly's company for over a stanyear, so he was going to appreciate the hell out of her now.

He double-checked the coordinates to make sure they were correct, gave the vidscreen an encouraging pat, and hauled himself to his feet. The Kepler mechanics hadn't bothered to clean up the ship when they were finished, and months in dry dock had left her grimy. He had eight standays before reaching his destination, time enough to give the old girl a bit of a spa treatment.

THE PLANETS Newton and Kepler were in the same sector, but you'd hardly know it if you compared them. While Kepler was drab colors, mud, and hopeless monotony, Newton was an unending festival of brightness and manufactured excitement.

On second thought, however, both places were perfect examples of the Coalition's goal to screw beings out of every credit they owned, in any way possible. The Newtonians simply had prettier material to work with than the humans who'd colonized Kepler.

Haz didn't plan to stay long. Although he had visited Newton a few times when he'd been temporarily flush and had enjoyed himself, it wasn't truly to his taste. Still, he had to admire the sleek spaceport, where all the equipment was the newest version and everything gleamed. Clearly the Newtonians wanted to make a good impression from the moment of arrival. He wondered if the other biodomes on this planet— the ones intended for species with different basic needs—had equally nice facilities.

As he eased into the dock, Haz eyed the adjacent ship. It was a sporty model and looked brand-new, its hull brightly painted and its curves almost sensual. Some rich guy's new toy.

"Don't worry, darling." Haz patted Molly's control panel. "I'd take you over that hussy any old day." She made a quiet hum that he interpreted as approval.

Four Newtonians greeted him as soon as he disembarked. They wore wide smiles and not much else, as they depended on their fur for photosynthesis.

"Welcome, Captain Taylor!" burbled the nearest one. "We are so delighted you've come to visit our beautiful planet. Please let me tell you about our newest attractions. The Hotel Macaroni just opened last week, dedicated to all things pasta-related."

"I don't need— Wait. Did you say pasta?"

"Noodles, yes? We understand that humans love them. At this hotel you can bathe—"

"Nope. Look, I appreciate the enthusiasm, but I'm here on business."

The Newtonian didn't miss a beat. "Of course, of course. But the best business is mixed with pleasure, and we can offer you plenty of that."

The planet's original attraction had been its spectacular gardens, which the locals had leveraged as a tourist destination. Now wealthy humans could stay in one of the hundreds of themed hotels, take a guided cruise through the gardens in an enclosed landship, and then return to the biodome for restaurants, spas, shopping, nightclubs, gambling, and live entertainments of endless variety. People came to relax, to celebrate special occasions, to try things they could boast about after they returned home.

The Newtonian gave Haz a long up-and-down examination. "I'm happy to give you recommendations for clothing stores you will love."

Haz made a sour face. "I'll pass. Just take good care of my ship, okay?"

"Of course."

He left the bays via a long corridor lined with vid-ads for… everything. As he walked past each one, an attractive being told him about beautiful jewels, fragrant perfumes, cosmetics that would make him irresistible, luxurious hotels. Sex was for sale too, and those shimmering bare bodies reminded him that it had been a long time since he'd hooked up. Nobody since that Earther, months ago. Maybe he ought to detour to one of the bordellos before shipping out.

He left the spaceport and stepped out onto a wide boulevard. Unlike his neighborhood in North, this road was paved and the sky outside the dome was a perfect, clear blue. A selection of trees and flowering shrubs sourced from various planets lined the street, perfuming the air. Beings floated down the boulevard in shiny, open-topped aircars—no crappy scooters for them—or strolled in pairs or groups, laughing and talking and sipping colorful drinks.

Haz felt conspicuous in his old trousers and tunic. Though they were comfortable and practical, with lots of places to stow things, they weren't exactly fashionable. And he was alone and limping, his ancient duffel slung over one shoulder. Well, szot. He was entitled to be here too.

A few pokes at his biotab summoned an aircar, and he climbed inside. He hated the damned things. Yeah, they had plush seating and they beat walking, but you couldn't steer them. You simply told them where to go and they brought you there, using their own computer-generated judgment for routes and speeds.

"Where may I take you?" asked the aircar's breathy, gender-neutral voice.

"I don't want you to take me anywhere. I want to take myself."

"I'm equipped with the latest games and music to make your journey more enjoyable. I can recommend clothing stores you'll love. Or I can take you to our newest magnificent home away from home, the Hotel Macaroni."

Kepler was definitely a miserable shithole, but at least its inhabitants weren't trying to constantly sell him things.

"Go to 16482 Tropicana."

"Of course. Thank you."

As the aircar left the spaceport, tall, shiny buildings loomed overhead with flashing signs advertising what could be found inside. Every hotel promised the best night ever, and every restaurant claimed that its signature dish had won awards. Expensively dressed beings marched in and out with their booze and their shopping bags, behaving as if it was no big deal to throw their credits into the wind. And maybe it wasn't, if you started out with enough of them.

He took in the cityscape as he glided along, easy to do since the aircar's top speed wasn't much faster than a jog. It made sense. Vacationers were in no hurry, and a leisurely drive allowed them to spy more shows, more restaurants, and more useless shit to buy and lug home. Although Haz wasn't interested in any of that, he wasn't immune to beauty and glitz, and Newton had plenty of both.

He wondered what he would have made of this place if he'd visited immediately after leaving his home planet. He'd have been dazzled for sure, and probably wouldn't have enlisted. Maybe he'd have stuck around this place, drawing a salary at one of the few jobs reserved for humans instead of locals—a brothel boy, maybe. He laughed at the idea.

Eventually the buildings grew smaller and the ads less strident, until the aircar passed through an ornate metal gateway and into a residential neighborhood. This was evidently where moderately well-heeled retirees came to live out their golden years. The cookie-cutter houses varied so little that Haz wondered how anyone knew which was theirs. He didn't understand how people could tether themselves to the ground like that, as if they were plants. And didn't even Newton's lavish diversions grow stale after a while?

The aircar stopped in front of a beige faux-stucco house with tan trim and a cactus garden in front. A sign on the front door read *Welcome to Our Castle*. Surely this couldn't be the right place.

"I said 16482 Tropicana."

"We have reached our destination," the aircar replied smugly.

"Is there another place with this address?"

"This is the only 16482 Tropicana on Newton."

He eyed the front porch suspiciously. It bore twin statues of some kind of Earther creature. Giraffe, was it? He'd seen old images but couldn't remember the creature's name. The statues had stupidly long noses.

Hefting his bag over a shoulder, he dismounted from the aircar and trudged up the sidewalk to the house. He'd just lifted his fist to knock when the door swung open, revealing a familiar figure. Well, she would have been familiar if she weren't wearing neon orange leggings and a bright yellow sports bra.

"Uh, Jaya?"

A water bottle in one hand, she squinted at him as if she wasn't sure they'd ever met. Her curly dark hair was in a messy ponytail, and her light-brown skin shone with sweat.

"You interrupted my yoga session."

"That's not a nice way to greet a guy you haven't seen in over a stanyear."

"Haven't seen and didn't expect to see. How'd you weasel your way off that shithole planet? Did you stow away in a barbcress shipment?"

"Flew here in Molly."

"Huh. Wouldn't have thought that poor old girl would ever speak to you again."

He tried his most winning smile, knowing it would get him nowhere. "Is Njeri here?"

"Njeri is playing golf."

That made him blink. "Golf?"

"Ancient Earther game where you walk around trying to hit a tiny little ball into a hole with a stick."

"I know what it is. I just hadn't pictured Njeri...."

Jaya huffed. "Stupidest damn way to spend an afternoon, but twice a week she and her 'golf buddies' head out." She managed finger quotes despite holding the water bottle.

Over the past months, Haz hadn't given much thought to Jaya Hirsch and Njeri del Rio, his former crew. No reason to, really. They were a lot smarter than him and a lot wiser, and he knew that wherever they'd gone after Kepler, they'd landed on their feet. But if he had considered their fates, he never would have entertained the possibility of... this. Golf and yoga and cactus gardens. "What the hell are you doing here, Jaya?"

"Told you. Yoga."

"I mean—"

"I know what you mean." She crossed her arms. "We're retired. Unlike some idiots, we saved up our credits over the years, invested well, and now we live comfortably and happily. And nobody shoots at us."

"Yeah, but... you're grounded." Haz stomped a foot on the pavement to emphasize his meaning.

"So? We have a nice house. Good friends. Plenty of things to do."

But Haz thought he caught something in her eyes, a flash that suggested she wasn't as content as she was letting on. How could she be, or Njeri for that matter? They'd equaled—or surpassed, in Njeri's case—the number of years he'd spent in space. The stars ran through their blood. Njeri had even been born on a ship, for gods' sake.

"I have a contract and I need a crew." Haz stopped there, because all the rest was just details.

Jaya snorted. "Then you better find yourself one. And Newton's no place for that. Go to Ankara-12 and you'll find whatever you need."

"I need the best crew, and they're here on Newton." Yes, it was flattery, but it was also true. He'd trusted his ship and his life to these two women, and although he'd failed them, they'd never disappointed him.

"Please, Jaya. I need this. I need you."

Her expression softened marginally, and she pursed her mouth.

"Njeri and I have dinner plans tonight. We'll come see you tomorrow morning. Where are you staying?"

He would have liked to be invited into her house, but he understood. Haz tried to come up with an answer to her question, but all that came to mind was the goddamn Hotel Macaroni, and he'd rather sleep on the street.

"I'm sleeping in Molly."

"No, you're not. They don't let anyone stay in the berthed ships."

Of course not. The Newtonians would lose out on hotel income. And if he took off and returned in the morning, he'd have to pay an extra set of exit and entry fees.

Maybe he looked hopeless, because Jaya took pity on him. "The Restwell. It's a good value, the theming's low-key, and we like the breakfasts at their restaurant. Go stay there."

She watched from the doorway as he made his way back to the street and summoned an aircar.

THE RESTWELL was a good recommendation. It was a smaller building near the edge of the hotel zone, tucked away on a relatively quiet street. As the name suggested, the motif was relaxation. Soothing music played in the lobby, where the décor was done in pale greens, blues, and grays. There was a menu of spa services, none of which interested Haz, and the desk-clerk droid had a soft voice that made him yawn. The sixth-floor room had blackout curtains, images of burbling creeks and flower-dotted meadows, and a huge bed with roughly a thousand fluffy pillows.

Haz intended to drop off his bag and head out in search of booze. And maybe someone willing to help him end his sexual dry spell. But those plans fizzled when he walked into the bathroom. It had a tub—an actual szotting tub—and it was big enough for a man of his height. He literally couldn't remember the last time he'd had a soak.

So he ordered food and then filled the tub while he waited. As soon as his meal arrived, he stripped, carried the tray into the bathroom, and set it on the tub's wide edge. He immersed himself in water that was almost— but not quite—too hot to endure.

"Good gods," he sighed.

This was better than sex. The water sluiced away the last of the Kepler mud, while the heat soaked into his body, soothing abused muscles and joints. Even his bad leg felt better, the pain tamping to a rumble instead of a roar. He refused to look at it, however, because he knew the bath wouldn't make it any less ugly.

He ate his dinner slowly. By the time he finished, the water had cooled, but he wasn't ready to hit dry land. So he refilled the tub, overcoming a spacer's deep-seated antipathy to wasting water. It was so worth it.

At long last Haz emerged, wrinkled and as loose-limbed as he'd ever be. He climbed into that ridiculously oversized bed—intentionally knocking a good portion of the pillows to the floor in the process—and commanded the lights to turn off. That left the room almost perfectly dark except for the image of stars projected onto the ceiling. He found himself mapping out familiar systems, remembering battles he'd fought in one sector and goods he'd smuggled in another. His eyes drooped closed, and he dreamed of the scent of fresh-cut hay.

THE RESTAURANT did serve a good breakfast—nothing fancy, but tasty and plentiful. It was probably the best meal he'd eaten since... well, definitely since before Kepler. Haz kept his mouth busy chewing and swallowing, as did Jaya and Njeri, so none of them spoke much until the servbot took away their empty plates and brought them fresh cups of coffee.

"This is the real thing. Not synth." Haz gazed into the fragrant dark liquid before looking up. Coffee hadn't been available to him until he'd traveled to Earth and joined the navy, but he'd quickly developed a fondness for the stuff.

Njeri nodded eagerly. "They grow it here. The Newtonians produce as much food as possible on-planet. Everything's fresher that way."

"And cheaper."

She waved a hand dismissively. "It's all about quality, Haz Taylor. You wouldn't know quality if it bit your ass."

"Hey, quality has bit my ass. Don't you remember that guy I met on... well, somewhere in Theta Quadrant? He was a prince. Can't get much more quality than that."

"It was on Widzenia, and he wasn't a prince. Just some kind of minor nobility, equivalent to a baronet or something."

Haz waggled his eyebrows. "Still quality. That man had a tongue that could—"

"Enough!" Jaya held up a hand. "I do not want to hear any details about you and your imaginary exploits with Count What's-his-face. Tell us what you came here for, Taylor."

Jaya and Njeri weren't exactly his friends, especially after what he'd done to them a year ago. But in the entire universe, they were his only approximation of friends. And they were the best crew he'd ever flown with. Jaya could work miracles with reluctant or broken machinery, could sweet-talk the buggiest software, and could shoot pulse cannons with terrifying accuracy. Njeri, on the other hand, was almost as good at flying as he was, and her navigational skills were unmatched.

"I fucked up," Haz admitted. "Big-time. Got Molly shot to Enceladus and almost got us all killed. I'm sorry."

He didn't apologize often, and only if he truly meant it. But in this case he *was* sorry. He wished he'd never agreed to smuggle narcos from Enrora to Ankara-12, and he wished even more that he hadn't lied to Jaya and Njeri about the nature of their cargo. It wasn't the dumbest thing he'd ever done, and it certainly wasn't the most disastrous, but it ranked in the top five.

Njeri looked at him reproachfully. "You almost got us banned from Ankara-12 for life. You lost all your money paying the fines, pretty much lost your ship too. And it was drugs. Do you know what that stuff does to people? I never minded moving goods that weren't exactly legal, but I'm talking counterfeit designer clothing and fake jewels. Not things that kill people."

"I know." No use making excuses. Yes, he'd owed the client a favor, and yes, the client had made it clear that refusing wasn't an option. And yes, the pay would have been generous. But he'd known from the start that the contract stretched well beyond the boundaries of his own flexible morality, and he'd sure as hell known his crew would have given it a hard no. Which was why he'd lied to them, a sin as bad as running narcos. And there was no point in reminding Jaya and Njeri that he'd eventually destroyed the cargo, because that was the part that nearly got them all dead.

Njeri wasn't done with him. "It was a terrible thing to do to us, and a terrible thing to do to yourself. Look where you ended up—stranded in a miserable swamp."

"Yet here he is," Jaya said emphatically. "He got out of that swamp, and now he wants us to come work for him again. Why would he think we'd do something like that? Personally, I'd rather go home and plant more cactuses."

Haz wiped his mouth with a napkin. "This contract pays well. I know you guys have a nest egg, but I bet some extra lining for that nest could always come in handy. And it's not smuggling, not illegal at all. The opposite, in fact."

"What do you mean by that?" asked Njeri, leaning forward over the table.

"I mean the contract's with the Coalition. Kasabian offered it to me. Did you know she's a brigadier general now?"

Jaya's expression said she didn't believe a word of it. "The Coalition is offering you a contract? The same government that's been after your ass for years? How many times have they busted you? How much have you needed to pay in fines? Not to mention, you didn't exactly leave the navy on friendly terms."

He scowled at the reminder. "The delivery point's on Chov X8, so they need someone who can get their valuable cargo through Kappa Sector. Someone who doesn't have the Coalition insignia plastered all over their ship."

Njeri and Jaya exchanged a look that Haz couldn't read. Then Njeri faced him again. "What cargo?"

"Some kind of religious artifact. I don't know the details except it belongs to the people on Chov X8, someone stole it, and it benefits the Coalition to return it. And they're willing to pay us generously to do the job."

"How generously?" Jaya asked, eyebrows raised.

The number was high enough that even Jaya looked impressed, while Njeri gave a long whistle. But Haz wasn't convinced that was enough, and pleading how important the contract was to him personally wasn't going to do the trick. Maybe they'd be happy to see him rotting away back on Kepler. So he clasped his hands and leaned toward them.

"Look. I understand that Newton's got a lot going for it. Your house looked nice—what I saw of it, anyway. And you've earned some peace and relaxation. But come on. You're spacers. You can spend your time exercising and eating enough breakfast to choke a thruqrax, but I bet you dream about flying. You keep listening for the song of space, and every day that you don't hear it, you shrivel a little more."

Bullseye. He could see it in their clenched hands, in the hollowness of their eyes. He'd described exactly how they felt because he'd ached that way throughout every damn hour he spent on Kepler. Their situation was a lot cushier than his, but the core remained the same.

"Go take a walk, Taylor," Jaya ordered. "My wife and I need to talk."

Haz thumbed his biotab to pay the bill, stood, and flashed them a smile. "Ten minutes?"

"Fifteen."

HE GAVE them almost twenty and spent the time browsing the hotel gift shop as if genuinely considering the purchase of a logo bathrobe or a pair of fuzzy blue socks that, according to the label, would massage his reflex points, leading to improved health. All the massaging in the galaxy wasn't going to help his leg.

When he returned to the restaurant, he knew the answer right away. Njeri was smiling broadly; Jaya glowered at him.

Haz slid back into his seat. "Thank you. Gods, thank you. We're going to—"

"One condition," Jaya interrupted.

"Anything."

"No lies. I don't care how uncomfortable it makes you feel, Haz Taylor, or what kind of bullshit you want to fling. You tell us the truth about everything, and you don't hide one goddamn thing." She jabbed her finger in his direction to make her point.

"I'll tell you so much truth you'll beg me to shut up." Haz grinned and held out his hand. Njeri shook it first and then, more reluctantly, so did Jaya.

He had a ship; he had a crew. Now all he needed was the stolen relic and he was good to go.

CHAPTER THREE

HAZ HAD intended to leave the following morning, but the minute his crew stepped foot in Molly, they refused to fly anywhere until she had a thorough scrubbing.

"I tried to clean her on the way here," he protested.

Jaya just shook her head, while Njeri settled a hand on his shoulder. "They have professionals here. They'll make her sparkle."

So he shelled out credits he'd have preferred to keep, and then shelled out more credits to spend an extra three nights at the Restwell. He messaged Kasabian about the delay, and although she wasn't pleased, she knew the importance of a good crew.

With nothing else to occupy his time, Haz ate and checked out Newton's cheaper attractions. He took more baths. He drank, thankful that the booze here was a big improvement on Kepler's. And, on the final night, he visited one of the city's famed brothels. He watched humans—and some other species of various genders—dance alluringly on stage, every one of them beautiful and talented. Well-paid too, from what he'd heard, and supremely skilled at bringing pleasure to their customers. There were even a pair of tirlovians, a species renowned for their prowess in bed. But none of them stirred his blood, and in the end he returned to his hotel and bathtub.

In the morning, Haz piloted Molly out of port as Njeri pored over navigational charts and Jaya banged around, swearing at the shoddy craftsmanship of the Kepler mechanics. This was a familiar routine, as comfortable as a favorite old chair. Njeri hummed to herself. Haz gazed out at the stars and smiled.

A couple of hours into their journey, Njeri wandered off to the galley, presumably to find food. When she returned, she plopped down in her usual seat.

"Kappa Sector," she sighed.

"Yeah, I know."

"The last two times we passed through there—"

"We barely made it out. I know." He shrugged. "Keeps things interesting."

"I'm too old for interesting. I think I've moved well into predictable."

Haz made a face. He hated predictable, mostly because in his experience, the outcome wasn't good. For example, when he reluctantly agreed to run those narcos, he predicted he'd end up neck-deep in shit. Which he had. At least interesting gave you a chance at something positive.

"Going through Kappa's going to save us a month, and that's important. Kasabian says there's some urgency in returning the stolen gizmo."

"Kappa's also a good place to lose whoever's tailing you," she said with a knowing look.

She was right. The sector was chock-full of debris from a cataclysm that had destroyed a bunch of planets a long time ago, and it included weird anomalies that made scientists all hot and bothered but made flying a bitch. There were pirates too, and a vast assortment of other people who needed to avoid the authorities' attention. Some of them minded their own business, but a lot laid in wait, hoping to spring on unwary travelers.

It was Haz's favorite sector.

But Njeri was still giving him that look, and Haz sighed.

"Look, someone stole this thing, right? I don't know why. Something to do with politics, I guess, and you know how much I care about that. The Coalition recovered it somehow. But I think Kasabian assumes the thieves might want another go at it before X8 gets it back. Or maybe other people are eyeing the damn thing. In any case, our best bet is to transport it as fast as possible and to make it hard for anyone to intercept us."

"Kappa," she said unhappily.

"That's why they hired us and not some random yahoo. They know we can handle it."

That seemed to cheer her up a little. "All right. At least I have a couple of weeks to chart the best course. As if there is a best course through Kappa." Then she wrinkled her nose. "We're not staying long on Earth, are we?"

"Nope. Just long enough to fill our stores and pick up the cargo."

"Good. That place…." She shuddered. "Gives me the heebie-jeebies."

"Me too. Last time I was there, I was being court-martialed."

Her green-eyed gaze was clear and steady. "You didn't deserve that, Haz. I've never told you that, and Jaya never will, but we've talked about it and we agree. They should've given you a medal, not a trial."

He had to clear his throat. "People died. Lots of 'em."

"It's the navy. That happens." She patted his knee. "Sometimes there are no good decisions, and the best you can do is make the least-bad one." She stood. "I'm gonna go make sure my wife doesn't forget to eat. See ya later, Captain."

EARTH HAD several spaceports, most of them relics from better days, but the one in Budapest was the busiest by far. It made sense, since that was the Coalition capital. In fact, Budapest had two spaceports—one for civilians and one for the military—and Kasabian had directed Haz to the latter. The controller looked unhappy as he guided Molly into a berth, but that was fine because Haz was unhappy too. He preferred to pilot his own ship, thanks very much, and not give over the controls to some uniformed asshole who probably couldn't fly his way out of a paper bag.

Njeri noticed Haz's scowl. "The second we get back into space, you can fly some loop-de-loops, okay?"

"Fine."

They came to a stop with a lot more jiggling and shaking than Haz would have allowed.

He popped the forward hatch, only to be greeted by a sea of soldiers. It was very much like the last time he'd disembarked here, except then he'd been in handcuffs, his leg a fresh and searing agony. Lovely memory. He took a single step down, but a skinny kid half his age stepped forward and blocked him.

"Orders are for you to stay on your ship, Captain."

Now, Haz hadn't especially wanted to go anywhere, but he wanted even less to be bossed around by this twerp. "I'm under no obligation to follow navy orders, Sergeant." He hopped down, pretending it didn't hurt like hell, and landed close enough to make the young man step back. "Outta my way. I got work to do."

"My orders—"

"Are you going to shoot me?" Haz threw a significant glance at the sergeant's holstered weapon.

"No, I'm just—"

"Then get out of my way."

He moved forward and was gratified when the sergeant fell back.

Njeri climbed down behind him and gazed impassively at the surrounding ranks.

"Jaya?" he asked her.

"Staying onboard, Captain. She's tinkering with something."

"Naturally."

Haz cast a crooked grin at the sergeant, knowing it made him look… unbalanced.

"Not a soul touches Molly without my say-so, got it? Nobody goes inside. Nobody leans on her. Nobody so much as breathes too close. I've got sensor traps set up, and they've been running pretty wonky. No telling what they might do."

He watched the crowd shift uneasily at his lie, and once they parted, he and Njeri walked through.

Coalition capital or not, this port compared poorly to Newton's. No glitz or glamour, although to be honest, he preferred the current smells of hot metal and space dust. He pinged Kasabian as he and Njeri walked down a well-worn corridor, their boots echoing loudly off the hard surfaces.

"We're here," he announced. "Thanks for the welcoming party. We're off for supplies. We'll be ready to leave by morning."

After a short pause, she replied over his biotab. "I could have had supplies delivered."

"Nah, wouldn't want to put you out. Besides, this way I get another peek at the ancestral homeland. Who wouldn't want that?"

Next to him, Njeri snorted and rolled her eyes.

"Delivery will be at 0600 local time tomorrow," Kasabian said crisply. "Be ready."

"I was born ready."

"And don't cause any trouble while you're here."

He simply laughed.

As they continued through the twists and turns of the corridor, Haz thought about Budapest. He had seen pictures. Once upon a time, it had been a beautiful old city, a dethroned queen still elegant in her decline. But that was before the earthquakes, before the pandemics that decimated the population, before the winters and summers that became so extreme, few could tolerate them unless forced to. As was true for nearly all of Earth's cities, most inhabitants who didn't die fled for more hospitable planets. And like many of those other old cities, Budapest had gone to ruin.

The Coalition stubbornly insisted on keeping their capital on Earth, arguing that while some other sentient species had joined over the centuries, humans made up the bulk of the Coalition's population and all humans traced their roots to this particular rock. They'd chosen Budapest mostly because it was far from the ever-rising seas. A bunch of ugly, utilitarian buildings had been constructed—many of them underground—and the original structures left to rot. Amid a terrain of pockmarked rubble, the most recognizable remnants were a couple of skeletal bridges and parts of the Parliament Building walls.

The corridor finally ended, and Haz and Njeri stepped outside. That ubiquitous rubble surrounded the spaceport, which was on the flatter, eastern side of the city. No flower-lined boulevards here, just steel rails humming with cars. Budapest had never upgraded to aircars, maybe due to their cost. Haz summoned a railcar instead, and when it slid open, he and Njeri stepped inside and sat down.

"Farkas and Zhao."

The car registered his instruction and immediately sped away. The interior smelled like old food and sweat, but at least the vehicle moved at a faster clip than the aircars on Newton.

"God, I hate this place," Haz grumbled, trying to avoid looking outside.

"Budapest or Earth?"

"Both."

"Huh. A lot of humans love Earth. I mean, it's our roots."

He shifted his leg. "I'm not a szotting tree. I don't need roots."

"How many generations ago did your family emigrate?"

"One."

She made a startled sound. "One? Seriously?"

"Why the hell would I lie about that?" Haz sighed. "My dear mother and father were Earthers. That gives me every right to detest the place."

Farkas and Zhao was located close to the civilian spaceport, in one of a series of structures pieced together from wood, steel, and recycled plastic. The buildings weren't any prettier than the utilitarian government ones, but they had more character. Farkas and Zhao, for instance, was painted lime and magenta, both of which had weathered yet somehow remained eye-searing.

"We could have just ordered and had them deliver," Njeri pointed out as they disembarked the car.

"Where's the fun in that?" This way Haz could dicker with the manager and flirt with the manager's offspring.

As soon as he stepped inside, the familiar scents hit him. The plastic-and-sugar smell of concentrated foods, the dusty odor of cotton fabrics—for the purists who hated synths—and the pleasant whiff of grease from bins packed with enough parts to build a hundred ships. There were only a few other customers, which made it easy to march straight to the front desk.

"Haz Taylor!" exclaimed the manager, Joe. He was neither Farkas nor Zhao—who'd both been dead for a century or more—and in fact wasn't an Earther or even human, but rather a Yex'oi. He was humanoid, however, towering over Haz by forty or fifty centimeters, and with enough muscles to put a bodybuilder to shame. Instead of the varied browns of most humans' skin, Joe's was the turquoise of a tropical ocean, and his five silver eyes had vertical, slitted pupils. He seemed pleased to see Haz, raising his spiked neck crest in greeting.

"Hi, Joe."

"I heard you were dead."

"Not that I've noticed." Haz leaned his elbows on the metal counter. "We need to outfit my ship for a four-month run."

He hoped it would take far less than that, but better safe than sorry. He didn't want to end up stranded on the edges of the galaxy with no supplies, and unless the relic turned out to be enormous, Molly would have plenty of room in the hold.

"Your ship. I heard you'd gone private." Joe heard a lot. Maybe his five ears helped. "How big of a crew?"

"Four." Only a slight exaggeration.

"Gotcha. I'll have Mary or Steve lend you a hand. Hang on."

Njeri had already wandered off to choose ship parts—Jaya had given her a list—leaving Haz to lean on the counter in a way that he hoped looked casual but mostly served to take some weight off his leg.

A moment later Steve rushed out to greet him, neck crest high.

"Haz! You're not dead!"

Steve was a near replica of his parent, except smaller—about Haz's size, in fact. His species didn't reach their full growth for nearly a century. He gave Haz a bone-crushing handshake.

"It's good to see you, Steve."

"Man, it's been a long time. You're on your own now?"

"I have my own ship."

Steve clapped Haz's shoulder. "Good for you! Better than being in the navy anyway. So what can I do for you?" He tipped his head a bit, and his eyes warmed to gold. "Tour of the back room, maybe?"

Haz had taken that "tour" more than once, back when he was buying for the Coalition's ships. Other times he'd taken the tour with Mary, and each sibling seemed to take it in stride if it was the other's turn. Those had been interesting experiences. Steve and Mary's species had only one gender, and individuals reproduced through self-cloning. But this particular family had enthusiastically adopted many Earther ways, including presenting as different genders and engaging in recreational sex. They didn't have the same body parts as humans, but they had other bits that could be combined with a human partner's in intriguing and enjoyable ways.

Today, though, Haz gave his head a little shake. "Next time. I'm on a tight schedule."

That wasn't exactly true, and he could have sent Njeri back without him, but he wasn't in the mood. He'd survived Kepler, but apparently his libido hadn't.

Steve wasn't offended. "So what can I help you find?"

It took over an hour before Haz and Njeri had gotten everything they'd need. Haz even threw in some luxuries like real booze—the kinds that were hard to find anywhere but Earth—and real cotton bedding for the three of them. Negotiating prices with Joe took another half hour, but Haz left feeling as if he hadn't been too screwed. Joe promised to deliver everything within a couple of hours.

That left Haz and Njeri time to visit a nearby noodle joint. It had been his favorite, once upon a time. The food wasn't as good as he remembered, but maybe a few days on Newton had jaded him. Anyway, it wasn't bad, and it sure beat the crap he'd been eating on Kepler. He and Njeri spoke very little while they slurped. Her gaze was far away, her mind probably occupied with nav charts, and Haz found himself unexpectedly weary, as if he'd suddenly aged twenty years. It was this szotting planet, which always seemed to exert an extra gravitational pull on him, as if trying to regain what it had lost.

Haz wrapped his hand around the bowl and contemplated the dregs of his soup like a fortune-teller reading tea leaves. His future apparently involved little green bits and a stray noodle, but he didn't know if those were good omens or bad.

"Hey, Njeri," he began, then stopped when someone planted himself in front of their table.

"Taylor," the newcomer growled.

Haz didn't recognize him, but the man's Coalition coveralls had a name written across the left side of his chest. *Paulsen.* That didn't ring a bell either. He was roughly Haz's age, puffy and florid, with closely shorn hair probably trying to obscure a badly receding hairline.

"Yeah?"

"What the fuck are you doing here?"

"I think that's pretty obvious. I'm eating lunch."

Paulsen bared his teeth. "I can't believe you'd show your face after what you did."

"I've done a lot of things, buddy. None of which are any of your goddamn business."

"You killed a hundred soldiers, you qhek-fucker. You coward."

Njeri finally seemed to realize what was going on. With a put-upon sigh, she pushed her bowl away.

"I'm going to wait outside."

"I'm ready to go too," Haz said.

She walked away and he started to stand, but Paulsen lunged forward and shoved him in the chest with both hands. It was a hard push, but Haz would have stood his ground if not for his leg. Of course the szotting thing took his weight a little wrong, and he collapsed into his chair with a swallowed grunt.

The little restaurant's other customers watched with great interest, but none of them interfered. None of them even stopped eating.

Haz sighed and looked up at Paulsen. "I have work to do. I bet you do too. So back the hell away and let's get on with our days."

"I knew some of those people you killed."

"I knew every last one of them," Haz replied quietly.

And he had, because they were his crew, and a good officer knows the people he commands. He knew where every one of them was from. He knew their strengths and weaknesses, who was fucking whom, who could barely be in the same room together, who was eager to get home to a spouse and kids. He knew who to keep a close eye on. He knew who he could count on when the shit hit the fan.

"Fucking traitor." And Paulsen spat, the foul liquid landing on Haz's cheek.

Haz wiped it away with a napkin and then, mindful of his leg, got back on his feet. He didn't break eye contact with Paulsen, and he didn't say anything.

Paulsen growled like a rabid dog. "You should have died too."

That was nothing but the truth, and Haz was going to say so. But before the words could leave his mouth, Paulsen swung at him. It was a clumsy punch and easy to avoid, but when Paulsen swung again, he grazed

Haz's shoulder. Although the blow didn't carry enough force to hurt, it pissed Haz off. He'd been minding his own business eating noodles, and whatever grudge this asshole carried was old news.

Like most nominally civilized planets, Earth had damper shields to prevent civilian weapons from firing. Neuroblox, toxdarts, blasters, even old-fashioned handguns were useless—except maybe to club someone over the head. But there was no way to prevent knife use, and Haz always carried his. So when Paulsen attempted to put him in a headlock, Haz pulled his blade from its hidden holster and buried it into the meat of Paulsen's back, just below the scapula and with the knife angled upward. Unless Haz nicked an artery, a wound like this wouldn't be fatal, but it would definitely slow down his opponent. And sure enough, Paulsen screeched, let Haz go, and then flailed around in a vain attempt to reach the hilt. Haz took advantage of that panic by kicking Paulsen's legs out from under him while giving his back a solid shove.

Paulsen, wailing loudly, collapsed facedown on the dirty floor.

Haz yanked the knife free—eliciting a fresh scream—wiped the blade clean on a napkin, and tucked it away. Then he stepped back to wait for the cops. He was grateful that Paulsen either wasn't carrying his navy-issued blaster or had been too stupid to remember to use it. Haz's knife wouldn't do him much good against military blasters, which were unaffected by the damper shields.

When the military police arrived minutes later, most people had returned to their meals, ignoring Paulsen as he moaned theatrically while lying in a puddle of blood. These officers were good. They patched the wound with a big sheet of glueskin, pulled Paulsen to his feet, and surveyed the crowd.

"Who stabbed him?" asked one of the cops. She sounded bored.

Haz raised his hand.

"Anyone else involved?"

Haz shook his head, and Paulsen grudgingly agreed, which seemed to please the cops. They herded both Haz and Paulsen out to the street.

"He tried to kill me!" Paulsen whined as soon as they were outside.

"If I was trying to kill you, you'd be dead."

One of the cops snorted a laugh, earning glares from his colleagues.

Paulsen turned to the female cop who'd spoken inside. "He stuck me with a knife! And do you know who that szot-face is? He's—"

"Save it for booking."

"Booking! He's the one who—"

"I don't care. It's not my job to care. Judge Tehrani is on duty this afternoon, and caring who did what to who is her job."

Haz rather liked this cop. Which is why he spoke next.

"You should probably know that I... have sort of a history with the navy."

He might as well tell her since she was going to find out eventually anyway.

"History?" She looked supremely annoyed.

"You know what happened ten stanyears ago with the *Star of Omaha*?"

He waited for the sharp expression that said she did, and when he got it, he continued.

"That was me. I was sailing master."

The other three cops gasped, but she just hardened her gaze. "Then what the hell are you doing here?"

"I have a contract with the Coalition. Talk to Brigadier General Kasabian. She'll confirm."

That led to an extended conversation on her biotab, conducted far enough away that he couldn't catch a word. Her colleagues flanked Paulsen and goggled at Haz. He was pretty sure that if he said boo, they'd all scatter. He stayed quiet.

When the cop in charge returned, it was with a determined expression.

"We're going to escort you to a car. You're going to ride it to port, get on your ship, and not set foot on Earth soil again. The general was very specific about this. She'll see you first thing in the morning."

"And I bet she'll be cheerful as a puppy, too."

The cop scowled and jerked her head in the direction of the nearest rail.

"Hey!" said Paulsen as Haz began to walk away. "He stabbed me! He needs to go to jail."

"Shut up unless you want to spend the night in a cell."

The cop walked Haz to the rail and waited for him to get into a car. He wished he had a hat to tip at her. Instead he made do with waving gaily as he pulled away.

CHAPTER FOUR

THE DELIVERY arrived not long after Haz returned to Molly. Steve and some bots loaded everything into the cargo hold, and Haz and his crew sorted and stored things in the proper places. Haz smiled to see the neat rows of foodstuffs and other supplies, which somehow made the mission seem real. Up until now, he might have been lost in drunken hallucinations. But those boxes and cans and bottles and packets, those were real.

Delighted with her machinery parts, Jaya spent the rest of the day redoing a lot of the Kepler mechanics' work while Njeri, who hadn't mentioned the incident at lunch, stared at screens full of numbers and maps. Haz supervised as the ground crew refilled Molly's water recirc tanks. She had water generators too, but he liked to begin with a full supply. He checked and double-checked all the weapons systems, then retired to his cabin to sharpen his knives and drink.

He slept well that night, untroubled by dreams.

By 0500 he'd eaten breakfast, gone over the manifests to ensure the ship had everything they needed, and spent thirty minutes on cardio, chest, and arms in the gym. He couldn't do much for his legs. A doctor had recommended swimming and hydrotherapy, neither of which was possible aboard a ship of Molly's size.

He changed into clean clothes—tight black trousers and a short maroon tunic—that didn't resemble a navy uniform in any way. He was going to be a szotting professional about this.

Kasabian asked permission to board at precisely 0600. Haz felt a smug satisfaction in the ritual. Whatever rank she held, this was his ship, and he was the captain.

She was flanked by two soldiers and didn't look happy to see him.

"I told you to behave yourself."

"I didn't kill Paulsen when I could have. I think that was very good behavior."

"I've been easy on you. I could have had you thrown in prison for the rest of your life for smuggling drugs. You do know that, right?"

Haz shook his head. "You wouldn't have dragged yourself all the way to Kepler for that. The navy doesn't give a fuck about drugs as long as nobody's starting wars over them, and anyway, I was very small fish." He shrugged. "Plus the narco packets got sucked into space."

"All true," she said coldly. "But now you're here. Easy pickings."

"Look, if you lured me halfway across the galaxy to lecture me, don't waste your time. I'm not going to see the light and mourn the error of my ways. If you intend to arrest me, go ahead." He gestured toward Njeri and Jaya, who stood silently behind him. "But my crew keeps Molly."

"Your crew was complicit in your drug smuggling."

Haz crossed his arms.

"Nope. I lied to 'em. They had no idea what we were carrying until those bastards started shooting at us."

He scowled. It wasn't the first time he'd been attacked—it was a risk of the trade—but the enemy didn't usually come in so hard or so well armed. He hadn't been prepared for it, and his unsuspecting crew had been taken completely by surprise, which was his own damn fault.

"You're a piece of work, Taylor."

"I know exactly what I am. Now, are you going to arrest me or are you going to hand over the artifact and let me get the hell out of here?"

She seemed to consider this for some time, and he wasn't sure how it was going to go. He flexed his hands just in case. Maybe he could do a little damage before they killed him. He wasn't going to let them stick him in a cell; that was for sure. He'd had a taste of that already and wouldn't bear it again.

Kasabian's shoulders finally relaxed, if only slightly.

"Don't fuck up this assignment. When it's over, I'll have the rest of the credits transferred to your account, but don't set foot on Earth again."

Haz smiled. "Not a problem."

"And if you ever smuggle narcos again—"

"I won't. Learned my lesson, didn't I?"

She didn't believe him; that much was clear. He was telling the truth, however. Although he might not admit it, his loose morality had its limits. He'd only taken the narco job because he thought he had no other choice, and now he realized he did have a choice: he could refuse and have people try to kill him. But people had tried to kill him anyway, so he might as well have taken the ethical high ground.

After fixing him with a hard glare, Kasabian poked viciously at her biotab. They all stood there, not saying a word but with the evil thoughts almost thick enough to hear. Haz idly wondered what his crew would do if Kasabian sicced her goons on him. Once upon a time they might have come to his defense, but now? Now they might join in the killing. And again, that was his own damn fault. No captain could expect loyalty from a crew he'd lied to and gravely endangered.

Bootsteps sounded on the ramp leading to the hatch, and four more uniformed soldiers appeared. They were accompanied by a figure completely hidden by a gray floor-length cloak with a deep hood. Haz couldn't tell anything about the figure's species or gender, but based on the halting, stumbling walk, they were probably elderly or infirm. Two soldiers grasped the person's forearms and helped to propel them forward. The newcomers stopped just inside the ship, and the robed figure stood, swaying slightly, with head bowed.

"Tell your priest to hand over the artifact before they collapse," Haz said.

Kasabian's smile was downright nasty. "Priest?"

"Or whatever their title is. I'm not real up on Chov X8 religious labels."

She turned and nodded to the two underlings, who tugged at the robe and removed it completely. The figure was humanoid, wrists bound by chained manacles, wearing nothing but a pair of baggy gray trousers. The person was thin but not skeletal, and flat-chested in a way that, in a human, would have probably meant they were male.

It was hard to determine a species because every observable part of the body was covered in intricate tattoos. The original skin color and texture and most other details were obscured by images and designs in black, red, and yellow. Hell, even the lips were decorated. There was no hair at all—not even eyebrows. The eyes were scarlet, crossed by tiny black squiggles and with huge black pupils. Haz couldn't tell whether that was their natural color or more ink.

The person didn't react to being uncloaked, and their heavy-lidded gaze seemed focused on nothing in particular.

"What the hell—" Uneasiness roiled in Haz's gut.

Kasabian grinned smugly.

"Captain Taylor, please take custody of the item you're being paid to deliver."

CHAPTER FIVE

"No," Haz said for what felt like the hundredth time.

Kasabian had dismissed the soldiers, leaving the… mystery person to wobble a moment longer before collapsing facedown on the deck. Haz had moved forward to assist, but Kasabian stopped him with an upraised hand. She prodded the figure with her foot, rolling them onto their side. "He's fine."

At which point Haz had refused point-blank to have anything more to do with this shit, and Kasabian had countered by insisting he would. Jaya and Njeri, silent and stone-faced, had taken seats to watch the battle.

A battle that Haz knew he was destined to lose.

"I don't traffic in people," he growled. "And neither does the Coalition. We've fought fucking wars over this."

For the sake of argument, he chose to overlook the Coalition's total disregard of worker enslavement in the borvantine mines.

"Legally, this is a religious object, not a person," she said crisply.

"Legally, you can tell me you're a Lachaderian m'tungmar, but that doesn't make it true. The law's just a bunch of slippery words." He pointed at the man, who now lay curled in a loose fetal position. "Living, breathing person there."

"And a blob of clay is just clay until it's purposefully shaped and then fired, at which point it becomes a bowl. This being was shaped by the Chovians over many years, using exquisite care and extreme attention to detail. He became a religious object."

Haz huffed angrily. "But see, even you're calling him *he* and not *it*. That implies personhood."

"And what pronoun do you use when referring to your ship, Captain Taylor?"

"That's not the same thing."

She shrugged. "I don't have time for semantics or philosophy. Here's what it comes down to. The Chovians spent years and a lot of resources creating this artifact, which has critical religious value to them. Without it, Chov experiences a crisis severe enough to destroy the entire society.

Someone stole this object, we intercepted it, and now it must be returned as quickly as possible. The lives and well-being of hundreds of thousands of Chovians depend on it."

Ethics were not Haz's strongpoint, but he felt in his gut that this was wrong.

"What if he doesn't want to go?" The chains on his wrists suggested his presence wasn't voluntary.

"People do things they don't want to all the time, in the name of the greater good. You of all people should know that."

He flinched. "I don't—"

"This is not a difficult situation, Taylor. The artifact belongs on Chov X8. What happens to him once he returns is not our concern. But if he doesn't return, that planet dissolves into chaos, creating instability in a region where that's very dangerous, and most likely leading to thousands of deaths."

Haz turned to look at his crew, but neither of them was helpful. Njeri made a don't-ask-me gesture, and Jaya simply looked disgusted by the whole mess.

Kasabian cleared her throat to recapture his attention.

"This is going to be easy. Put him in the cargo hold with a waste bucket. Bring him food and water occasionally. Fly through Kappa to avoid having him stolen again. Return him. Done."

"Easy," he echoed.

"You don't have a choice. You're already in hock for the credits we fronted you. If you refuse this mission, we will seize your ship and everything else you own, and you, Taylor, will end up in prison for defrauding the Coalition."

He bristled at the threat. "I haven't defrauded anyone."

"So say you." She shrugged. "But the law's just a bunch of slippery words, remember? We have people who can make the law do our bidding."

"Szot!"

Haz kicked a bulkhead with his bad leg, which hurt like hell. Unfortunately, the pain didn't help ground him. He saw no way out of this situation. Sure, he could make a stand, citing principles nobody believed he possessed, but then he'd just end up dead or rotting in prison. And the Coalition would simply find someone else to return the stolen goods.

"This isn't right," he hissed.

"When I need moral authority, I don't turn to smugglers or mutineers."

As if the matter was settled, she turned and marched to the hatchway, stepping around the figure huddled on the floor. She paused before disembarking, however, and turned back to Haz.

"I recommend chaining him up if you don't want him wandering."

Then she and her soldiers were gone.

HAZ BENT down and knelt on the deck, groaning at the pain in his leg, and said to the man, "Hey. Are you all right?"

The huddled form didn't respond, so Haz gave the shoulder a gentle shake. The man's skin—despite the pervasive tattoos—felt human.

"Hey."

Still nothing.

"Fuck. Jaya, can you…?" Haz waved vaguely at the man.

Still looking supremely disgusted, Jaya held her biotab arm a few inches over the man's body and then read what the device told her.

"He doesn't have a biotab. Homo sapiens. Temp's normal. Heart rate and blood pressure are both low, but not dangerously so. He's probably been drugged."

"Dandy." With some difficulty, Haz rose to his feet. "Let's get him stowed so we can get the fuck out of here."

"Are you seriously going to tie him up in the cargo hold?"

"No, of course not. That space next to my cabin was originally sleeping quarters. We'll put him in there."

The *Dancing Molly* had been built to carry a total of five people—two each housed in smaller rooms and the captain in the larger. But Haz was happier with just a three-member crew, and Jaya and Njeri preferred to share a room.

Jaya frowned. "My meditation space?"

"Do you have a better idea?"

"No," she said after a pause.

"Then help me get him in there."

Between the two of them, they managed to get the man to his feet. He was half a head shorter than Haz and considerably lighter, and even though he wasn't really walking, they were able to half carry him off the bridge and into the corridor. They passed the galley and the rec area across from it, then Jaya and Njeri's room and storage, the access doors to engineering and cargo, and finally the doors for Haz's cabin and what used to be Jaya's meditation room. Haz swiped open the latter door.

At one point it had housed a bunk bed, but Jaya had removed the upper berth. The lower had a thin mattress and was strewn with pillows and soft blankets.

"Do you meditate in here or nap?" Haz asked as they struggled to get inside.

"Neither anymore."

"Look, I had no idea this was going to happen. I figured we'd be running a statue or ugly jewelry or something."

"She sure played you, didn't she?"

Haz couldn't even give her a dirty look; he was too busy trying to maneuver the man onto the bed. Once he was settled, Haz realized that the guy had literally nothing except the pants he wore and the manacles on his wrists. The soldiers had taken away even his robe, and Kasabian hadn't bothered to mention his name—if she knew it. Well, those were problems they could deal with later.

For now, Haz did a quick survey of the bare-bones room. Jaya had removed all of the furniture except for the bed; the vidscreens were gone, and there was no décor. Aside from the bed, all that remained was a cubicle with a sink, shower, and toilet. At least they wouldn't have to resort to using a waste bucket.

"We'll talk later," Haz said to the man, who'd again curled up on his side.

Haz didn't expect a response and didn't get one. He turned to Jaya. "Let's blow this dump."

NJERI PILOTED them out of port, set Molly on autocontrol, and then spent a couple of hours going over her navigational plans with Haz. Her planning was, as always, impeccable. Neither of them mentioned the tattooed man locked up in the meditation room. Njeri opened her mouth a few times, her expression implying that she wanted to say something about their unexpected cargo, but Haz stopped her with a glare.

Satisfied that they were smoothly on course, he posted chore rotation schedules. As he was thinking about who was going to be in charge of which meals, he was sourly thankful that he'd taken on extra food stores.

He would have bought even more if he'd known there would be another person on board. Of course, if he'd known Kasabian was going to pull this shit, he would have hightailed it out of port before she saddled him with the "artifact," and bedamn the credits she'd paid him up front. She could fucking well try to track him through the vastness of space.

Ah, but he hadn't known, had he? And so here he was.

Once everything was shipshape, Haz retired to his quarters.

"Molly, I'm not to be disturbed unless everyone's about to die," he announced.

"Do not disturb," she confirmed crisply.

"And the man next to me? Don't let him leave the room. But alert me if he... I don't know. Explodes or anything."

"Shall I set percussion dampers around his room?"

Sometimes it was hard to tell if Molly had a sense of humor or was simply hyperliteral. Haz snorted.

"We can skip those, thanks."

"Aye-aye, Captain."

Haz grabbed a bottle of whiskey—the real stuff—cracked the seal, and proceeded to get sloshed. As far as he was concerned, he could stay that way indefinitely.

Time was a strange thing aboard a ship. Most captains kept two clocks, one calibrated to their home base and one to Coalition Standard, which was Earth Greenwich Mean Time. Those who did regular runs between home base and another planet often kept a third clock as well. Haz refused to do any of those things. He'd spent enough of his life following other people's schedules, so on his ship, he set his own clock. Jaya and Njeri had long ago stopped complaining about it.

He did, however, give in to human biological imperatives, and Molly cycled them through a twenty-four-hour pattern. Ship's daytime meant bright illumination and wavelengths mimicking Sol's sunlight, while nighttime meant dimmer lighting or none at all.

By the time Haz's cabin darkened, he was drunk enough that the stars through his viewport were nothing but blurs, and even his damned leg was just a muted ache. He hadn't eaten since breakfast and didn't want to. Merely keeping upright on his bed took all the energy and coordination he could muster.

"Szotting Coalition," he mumbled, hating the slur in his voice.

"Screw 'em sideways!" Molly added enthusiastically.

He'd apparently programmed that response during a bender several years ago. He didn't regret it.

"They're worse thieves than ever I've been, only they wrap a flag around it and insist it's all just dandy. They make up the rules to suit themselves and happily skip along doing shit that would have anyone else rotting in prison. Or worse."

He waved the half-empty bottle, fascinated by the way the amber liquid sloshed around like a tiny ocean. Like a bathtub. God, he wished there was a practical way to fit Molly with a bathtub. A deep one with jetted bubbles and a big viewport. He could soak and gaze out at infinity.

Then he remembered he'd been complaining.

"You know who I hate, Molly my love?"

"You hate the Coalition."

"Yeah, but specifically? The bureaucrats and politicians. They squat there in their Earthbound offices, making decisions that get other people dead. And for what? A few more credits, a few extra points on some kind of intergalactic scorecard. Those assholes don't get shot at. They don't see the corpses floating through space after a ship gets a hole blown through it. They don't get trapped into doing shit they don't want to. They don't...."

He stopped to take another couple of slugs of whiskey. He wasn't tasting it at this point, so it might as well have been synth.

"They prosper from their immorality while condemning it in everyone else."

"Stop with the self-pity, Taylor."

Haz narrowed his eyes. He hadn't programmed that response, which sounded like Jaya's work.

"Jebiga." He was addressing the universe in general.

"Sideways," Molly agreed.

CHAPTER SIX

THE LIGHTING told him it was daytime, and Haz's complaining stomach told him it was late. Well past breakfast and maybe even past lunch. His biotab had kept him from a hangover, but it couldn't do anything about the grimy sensation of sleeping in yesterday's clothes. Or about the furry, rotten taste in his mouth.

He sat up and stretched.

"Anything to report, Molly?"

"All systems normal."

That was good news, at least, and he was almost cheery about it until he remembered what—or who—awaited him in the adjacent room. Szot. And the bastard hadn't eaten for well over twenty-four hours.

Haz shucked his clothing and stuffed it into the ion drawer, where it would be freshened and cleaned in minutes. He used that time for a quick shower, shave, and tooth cleaning and felt marginally more human by the time he was finished. After dressing, he ventured into the corridor.

He paused outside the neighboring door for a moment but then shook his head and marched toward the galley. There was coffee to be had there, the real kind, and he brewed himself a generous cup. He also heated an instant meal, something with pinkish protein, green blobby vegetables, and a gluey starch that was likely intended to mimic either rice or pasta. The food had about as much flavor as the package it came in, but it filled his stomach quickly. He'd eat something that tasted decent for dinner.

Njeri was on the bridge, staring at a screen, and didn't look up when he entered.

"I was beginning to think we'd left you behind on Earth."

He shuddered at the thought. "Jaya's down in engineering?"

"Where else?"

"Have you, uh, checked on our passenger?"

She shot him a quick look. "Figured that was your job, Captain."

He mumbled something, mostly because she was right.

When he returned aft, he stood again for a moment outside the door, as if he could magically sense what was going on inside. He couldn't.

He couldn't even unmagically sense anything because the cabins were soundproofed. Ordering himself to relax, he swiped the door open.

The man sat on the bed, huddled in the corner with his knees bent and his manacled arms wrapped around them. It was still difficult to get a sense of what he truly looked like under all the ink, but at least now his eyes seemed focused. And terrified.

Haz let out a breath. "Do you know where you are and who I am?"

The man shook his head slightly.

Great. "You're on board the *Dancing Molly*, heading toward Chov X8. I'm Captain Haz Taylor."

The man was silent for so long that Haz thought he might be unable to speak. But then he did say something, his voice thin and raspy, as if he hadn't used it in a long time.

"Are you with the navy?"

"No. But I'm contracted with them to return you to your home."

"Oh." The man dipped his head a little.

"What's your name?"

"I am the Machine of the Obeisant Theocracy, Omphalos and Corpus of Piety, Channel to the Great Divine." He recited it in a weary monotone.

"Okay, yeah, great title. But what's your name?"

The man blinked at him. "I have none."

"But what do people call you?"

"The Machine of Obeisant—"

"Got that."

As Haz considered fetching himself some whiskey, the man's scent finally registered... and it wasn't pleasant. The guy reeked of sweat and dirt and fear.

"Why don't you clean yourself up?" He jerked his head toward the room's tiny head.

"Clean?"

"Wash up. There's soap and towels in there. And an ion drawer for your pants. Are you hungry?"

The man's strange eyes widened.

"Yes! Please, sir."

"Fine. I'll bring you something. I hope you don't have any weird dietary needs, because nobody told me you were coming on my ship, and I certainly didn't stock up on vegan thruqrax balls or whatever else you think you need."

He didn't get a response. Haz narrowed his eyes.

"Whatever narcos they had you on yesterday—"

"No! Please. I'll obey. Please don't make me...."

"I'm not going to force drugs on you. Just the opposite. I'm not carrying much; just enough to keep the med packs stocked. So no more drugs."

"Thank you, sir."

The man smiled. Something about the way his lips curled made Haz think he was a fairly young man, although his precise age was unclear. Somewhere between twenty and forty, maybe.

"Go wash up."

The man scrambled off the bed, making the wrist chain jangle. There was a little give there, but the manacles would surely get in the way. Besides, they made it impossible for the guy to put on a shirt, which he might want to do since Haz kept Molly on the chilly side.

Haz pointed at the chain. "If I take those things off, are you going to cause trouble? There's no way for you to escape, and my crew and I would have no trouble subduing you, but I don't want a hassle."

"I would very much like them off, sir. Please. I will obey you."

Something about that answer made Haz deeply uncomfortable, but he nodded.

"Let me see."

The man hurried over and held up his wrists.

The manacles were made of borvantium, the same substance that comprised Molly's hull. Gram for gram, it was one of the hardest metals available, highly resistant to damage of any kind. Even when blasted by Kamiya cannons, Molly had remained intact enough to get them into port on Kepler. Which was lovely for the ship's sake but not so much for this man's, because Haz couldn't discern a lock or opening of any kind. And it looked as if the chains had been in place a long time; scar tissue marred the tattoos around the manacle edges.

"Do you know how to get these off?"

The man shook his head.

"Well, maybe Jaya can figure it out. Jaya Hirsch. Best engineer and mechanic in the galaxy. I'll ask her to take a look."

Haz suddenly realized he was holding the man's forearms, which felt warm and lightly muscled. Haz let them drop and walked out of the room, making sure the door was secured behind him.

In the galley he heated a meal—identical to the one he'd eaten—and grabbed a cup. The passenger could fill it with water from his sink. He also grabbed a packet of candied nuts. Knowing that Jaya loved the things, he'd bought a lot of them at Farkas and Zhao in hopes of pacifying her a bit. She could spare a packet.

When Haz returned to the little cabin, his passenger was standing in the middle of the floor, chained hands clasped in front and head bowed. He was also completely naked, which gave Haz the opportunity to see that tattoos covered every centimeter of the man's hairless skin. Haz winced, thinking of what the needle must have felt like on some of the more sensitive parts. Droplets of water gleamed like jewels atop the ink, and now the guy smelled of mint soap, which was a big improvement.

"Food," Haz said, setting everything down on the bunk since there was no desk or table.

The man licked his lips. His tongue was not tattooed, which for some reason comforted Haz.

"Thank you, sir."

"Look. We have about three weeks before I drop you off. There aren't any vidscreens in here, and I bet staring out the viewport's going to get old pretty quick. Do you have something on your biotab to entertain you?"

"I don't have a biotab."

Haz now remembered that Njeri had mentioned this yesterday. But it still surprised him. Everyone had biotabs. They were implanted as soon as a child was old enough to understand the procedure and give consent, and people used them for... everything. Even Haz's parents had biotabs and made sure he had one too, one of their rare concessions to the need for technology.

On the other hand, this guy didn't even have a name, so maybe Haz shouldn't be so bemused.

"Are you going to go crazy just sitting in here for three weeks?"

"Will I be allowed food?"

"I... yeah. Of course. I'm not going to starve you for three weeks."

"I won't go crazy. I've sat for longer."

Not knowing exactly what that signified, Haz sighed.

"I need to call you something. Not that mouthful you told me before. Just a nice short name."

"Call me whatever you like, sir."

Naming someone wasn't a responsibility Haz had ever had, and he didn't like it.

"Molly? Give me a name for this guy."

She responded immediately, as if she'd been waiting for this request since she was first coded. "Mot."

"Moat? Like around a castle?"

"Spelled M-O-T. He was a Ugaritic god. It is also an acronym for the first part of his title."

Sometimes Haz suspected his ship was smarter than he was. "You okay with Mot?" he asked the man.

A tear fell from one glistening eye, forming a trail down a colorful cheek.

"Yes. Please. And thank you." Szot. Haz pointed at the food. "It doesn't taste any better when it's cold, so eat up."

Mot nodded eagerly and sat down on the bunk before ripping open the package. Haz found himself watching Mot eat. If Mot minded being observed, he didn't indicate it. He concentrated hard on the food, carefully chasing after every morsel and even licking the package to get the juices. When he was finished, he looked up at Haz.

"Thank you. That was very good."

"No, it wasn't. But it's filling."

Not knowing what else to say, Haz left Mot alone.

JAYA DIDN'T emerge until dinnertime, which Njeri had prepared tonight. Of the three of them, she was the best cook. Jaya was more creative but also prone to disasters when her spice experiments went wrong. Haz had a repertoire of about five things he could cook well, none of them adventurous, and he refused to try anything new. But Njeri was quite talented. Tonight she'd combined pasta with synth animal protein, reconstituted veggies, and a mystery sauce, and the result was both tasty and satisfying.

Jaya monopolized the mealtime conversation with the one topic that made her loquacious: everything that was wrong with Molly. To hear Jaya tell it, the Kepler mechanics hadn't done a single thing right and didn't know a screwdriver from a black hole.

"But she got me to Newton," Haz pointed out.

"Dumb luck. She won't hold up for a minute if we have to take evasive action or if someone fires on us. She's sure as hell not ready to get through Kappa in one piece."

"But she will be ready by the time we get there."

Jaya jabbed a spoon in his direction. "Only if I work my ass off."

Then she went off on a long litany of everything she was going to have to do and why she was going to have to do it, ignoring the fact that Njeri and Haz rolled their eyes.

When Jaya paused for a moment in the middle of an exposition on the issues with the quantum drives, Haz butted in.

"I could use your help for a few minutes after dinner."

She narrowed her eyes. "What for?"

"Mot. Our passenger."

"Prisoner, you mean." Njeri scooped more noodles onto her plate. "If he was so eager to get back home, the Coalition wouldn't have drugged him so heavily. And I saw those manacles on him."

"Those are what I need Jaya for. They're borvantium, and I can't figure out how to get them off."

Jaya muttered something that sounded like a curse, while Njeri sighed and shook her head. "He'll still be a prisoner, Haz."

He pushed his plate away angrily.

"What the fuck am I supposed to do? You saw what happened. Kasabian withheld info about what we'd be transporting, and by the time I found out, I couldn't back out. He's not my problem anyway—I didn't steal him. Whatever his issues are with his own people, those aren't my fault either."

Neither member of his crew responded. Njeri dug into her food, and after a long silence, Jaya continued her discourse on the faults with the drives.

Haz's appetite was gone, so he cleared his things and then filled a clean bowl with pasta. He grabbed a hunk of bread and one of the oranges he'd bought from Farkas and Zhao. Without saying anything more, he stalked out of the galley.

Mot was sitting almost exactly as he had been last time—arms around his bent knees—only he was cleaner and without pants. He looked apprehensive until he noticed the food in Haz's hands, at which point he perked up considerably.

"Another meal already, sir?"

"Do you want it?"

"Yes! Please."

Haz wanted to order him to stop saying please all the time, but that was stupid. He scowled instead.

"We do three meals a day on my ship. I don't care whether you eat all three or not, but if you're going to skip a meal, say something. I don't like waste. And make sure you don't keel over. My guess is the Chovians are expecting a live artifact."

"For now, yes."

What the hell did that mean? More shit Haz didn't need to know, that's what.

He set the bowl on the bed. He was at the door when it slid open and Jaya entered. She didn't look happy, but then she rarely did, at least around him. Maybe she smiled constantly when he wasn't around. Anyway, she stepped forward and Mot, who'd been reaching for his food, scrambled back, pressing himself against the hull and hugging his legs protectively against his chest. Jaya turned to Haz with raised eyebrows as if this were somehow his fault.

"Mot, this is Jaya Hirsch. She's going to try to get those things off your wrists."

After a moment, Mot relaxed slightly. He moved slowly to the front edge of the bed and held up his arms. Jaya leaned in close to examine the manacles.

This gave Haz his first good opportunity to see the details of Mot's tattoos. If there was a pattern to them, he couldn't discern it. Some of the markings were recognizable objects such as trees and animals, some were simple shapes, and some were complex abstract designs. There were also squiggles that looked as if they might be words, but Haz didn't recognize the alphabet. Not that he was any kind of scholar.

"What do these mean?" he asked.

Mot turned his head to look at him. "I don't know."

"What do you mean, you don't know? They're on your body."

"This body belongs to the Great Divine. The priests adorn it. They don't explain to me."

"Can't you ask?"

Mot shook his head.

"How long did it take to do all of that?"

"I believe the first tattoo was made on the day I was born. I don't know which one it was."

Tattooing an infant. The idea brought a taste of bile into Haz's mouth. He knew very well that people could sometimes be stupid—and harmful—in the name of religion, but this exceeded the bounds of even his own grim experiences.

"I have log entries to make," he announced.

It wasn't precisely the truth, and anyway, he didn't need to give excuses to leave. Mot didn't say anything; Jaya, still leaning over Mot's wrists, merely grunted.

Haz left the room in search of more whiskey.

CHAPTER SEVEN

THEY WERE six standays out from Earth when trouble found them.

Up until that point, things had been peaceful, each person on the ship contained in their own orbit. Jaya worked on Molly. Njeri stayed mostly on the bridge, keeping an eye on things and fiddling with her nav plans now and then. Haz... well, Haz drank. And as far as he could tell, Mot did nothing except eat, keep clean, and stare out the viewport. Haz didn't say more than a few words to him, but Mot always thanked him for the meals.

That was all fine and dandy until the sixth day, when Haz was in the galley making dinner, a stew loosely based on one he'd eaten as a boy. That stew was one of his few fond childhood memories, a luxury reserved for the end of harvest. Nowadays it gave him perverse pleasure to prepare it whenever he wanted to.

"Captain?" Njeri called over the ship's voice system. "There's someone out there."

Fuck. He hastily shoved the food into the cooling drawer and hurried to the bridge. Jaya came rushing in a moment later.

The thing was, ships tended to travel along the same routes, like interstellar roads. Those routes weren't paved, of course, but they did represent the most efficient paths between various points. So in some parts of the galaxy, it wasn't unusual to encounter other ships. This was especially true close to inhabited planets.

But right now, Molly was nowhere near any planets, and the route they were traveling was rarely used. Kappa Sector wasn't a popular destination. Because most captains avoided it whenever possible, another ship within range was unusual. And in Haz's experience, unusual meant worrying.

"Can you ID her?" he asked.

Njeri's fingers flew over her screen.

"Not specifically, no. She's cloaked her registration."

Double shit. That was even more worrying. A fair number of captains cloaked as a matter of routine, keeping nosy people out of their business.

Haz always ran cloaked. It wasn't illegal unless a ship was close to port, but still, it added another layer of suspicion in this situation.

Haz plopped into one of the command seats. "What can you see?"

"Not much. Don't know planet of registry, and I can't tell whether she's private or military. But...." She poked for a moment more and frowned at what she saw. "Xebec class, Captain."

"Szot," Haz and Jaya said in unison.

Xebecs were bigger than Molly, which was a modified brig. A xebec usually had a crew of eight to ten. They were faster than brigs, although not as maneuverable. And while brigs were primarily used for light cargo transport, a xebec was intended as luxury craft for the wealthy... or as a light attack ship. Pirates favored them, often flying in small fleets that could quickly surround their prey. But there shouldn't be any pirates in this area.

"Just one?" Haz asked Njeri.

"Yes. She's behind us and gaining."

Haz looked steadily at Jaya. "Strap in."

The worst part was the waiting. Haz's mind screamed at his body to do something, but all he could do was sit there. The other ship was well out of range, and the rule was not to start a fight unless you were certain the other party was planning to attack. Which was a stupid rule, really, because it put victims on the defensive and at an immediate disadvantage, but there was no use arguing with the Coalition over it. More of their damned laws—you could kill the other guy, but only if you followed all the rules.

"What kind of shape are we in, Jaya?" He heard the tightness in his voice.

"Not great, but better than we were six days ago."

"I just got Molly off the ground. I don't want her crippled again."

"Thanks for your concern over our personal welfare," she snapped. But it lacked her customary heat. With checking the systems and readying the pulse cannons, she was too busy to express her usual ire.

Haz got busy too, using the ship's sensors to get a good idea of their surroundings. There wasn't much to evaluate. Apart from the approaching xebec, the nearest objects larger than space dust were hours away, even at full speed. That meant there was nothing to hide behind, but it also gave Molly plenty of room to maneuver.

"Got a visual," Njeri announced. "Xebec confirmed. No external markings."

That meant it wasn't a Coalition ship and didn't belong to any of the major freight services or companies that transported people around the galaxy. It also probably wasn't a rich kid's hot rod; those brats liked to paint their ship exteriors in patterns that made the vessels look faster and more expensive.

Putting the pieces together, Haz had a strong feeling that things were about to turn sour. Adrenaline began pumping through his system, that old familiar rush that was better than booze, better than any narco. The edges of everything looked crisper, the colors brighter, and even the ache in his leg became distant and unimportant. He used the screen in front of him to lower the cabin temperature, because what was comfortable for lounging around was too warm for battle.

"Njeri, I'm taking over the wheel."

"Copy that, Captain."

He knew that electricity didn't really travel from the screen through his fingers and into his brain, but it felt as if it did. He wished sometimes that his ship had a true wheel, like ancient sailing vessels and automobiles, rather than a metaphorical one. He would have appreciated the tactile physical aspect.

"Molly, auxiliary systems on support only," he called.

That meant the ship would shut down anything not required to keep them alive so as to funnel maximum resources to the drive, control, and weapons systems.

"Auxiliary systems support only," Molly confirmed.

Haz ran quickly through all the status scans, knowing Jaya had already done so but also knowing that a second set of eyes was good policy. Sometimes it saved lives. As Jaya had said, Molly wasn't in tip-top shape, but she wasn't bad. And, well, he'd have to make do.

"Xebec still approaching, Captain."

"Try hailing."

After a brief pause, she shook her head. "No response."

Could be that they just weren't in the mood for socializing, but Haz doubted it.

"Jaya, fire as soon as it's in range. But miss."

"Copy that," she grumbled.

She would have preferred to start blasting away, but this was a tactic she was familiar with. If the other ship truly meant them no harm, its captain would hail them indignantly. If the xebec was looking for easy prey and thought Molly was a sitting duck, the shot would probably persuade them to look elsewhere. And if the xebec was set on attacking, well, the warning shot wouldn't hurt. Technically, firing first still violated Coalition rules, but barely. It was like sticking a toe in too-hot water: it might hurt a little, but you wouldn't end up scalded all over.

Pulse cannons used a tricky manipulation of energy, run through the quantum drive and converted to force. Unlike the weapons used by pirates who had sailed the Earth many centuries ago, Molly's cannons didn't use tangible ammunition. As a result, there were no onboard sensory effects when the cannons were shot. No booming noises, no recoil reverberating through the hull, no tang of gunpowder or heated iron. Nevertheless, Haz knew the exact moment Jaya fired. He felt it in his bones, like the popping of a joint.

He also definitely felt it when the xebec fired back—without trying to miss. It was a glancing blow due to the distance between them, but it still made Molly shudder.

"Time to dance, my dear," Haz said, giving the console a quick pat. "Allow me to take the lead."

The three of them had done this many times before, which meant nobody needed instructions. Whatever their individual shortcomings—and Haz knew he possessed many—the trio worked beautifully as a team. Haz pulled Molly into an abrupt sideways jerk, avoiding a second blast from the xebec, while Jaya re-aimed and fired, this time intending a solid hit. Njeri's job was to keep her eyes open: for additional ships appearing out of nowhere, for any other objects in space that could prove a help or a hindrance, and for anything on Molly that needed immediate attention.

Haz jerked Molly again, zigzagging out of the line of fire while grinning with satisfaction as Jaya reported hit after hit on the xebec.

"Enemy's dragging a bit to starboard," Njeri reported. "I think Jaya zapped one of their drives."

That was good news, but it wouldn't stop the battle. Xebecs had three drives and could manage well enough with only one.

Haz let the xebec get a little closer. Despite his intentional erratic moves, a few enemy shots scored, making Molly shake. The hull suddenly shrieked in outrage, signaling a resounding hit.

"Just a little closer, honey," Haz murmured. "Hang in there."

Another hit, this one causing Njeri to hiss something about the vertical stabilizer. But that wouldn't be an issue until they were in planetary gravity again, so Haz ignored it.

He brought Molly up so sharply that it pinned him in his seat and at the same time spun her around to face the xebec. As the xebec's crew struggled to aim at a ship that had abruptly changed location and direction, Jaya opened up with all she had. Her cannons scored on the xebec's nose, on the forward fuselage, on the drive thrusters that slightly protruded from beneath the xebec's hull. And even as the other ship yawed to starboard, Haz zipped over and behind it, spun around again, and watched with glee as Jaya destroyed the remaining thrusters and caused the entire aft to explode in an impressive fireball.

Haz pulled back out of firing range. "Hail them, please, Njeri."

"No response."

He shrugged. "Well, either they're dead or they're disabled, and either way they're not coming after us anymore."

If the crew was still alive and didn't have someone who'd rescue them fast, they'd be dead soon enough. No drives meant that the life support systems would run down. Haz hoped for their sakes that they'd died quickly. Gasping for oxygen while also freezing was not a fun way to go.

"Nice shooting, Jaya."

She gave him one of her rare grins. "Nice flying."

"Damage?"

Njeri had been examining the data. "A few bumps and scrapes, mostly. The stabilizer's nonoperational."

"I'll get to it now," Jaya said, unbuckling her straps and heaving herself out of the seat. "It's going to take a couple days to fix it."

"No problem. We're not hitting gravity fields for a while yet. You can take a break first, if you want."

Jaya shook her head and stomped away.

"Thanks for the heads-up," Haz said to Njeri as he unbuckled.

"Hey, I don't want to get vaporized either."

"You need a break?"

"No. What I need is some dinner."

Haz laughed. "I hear and obey. The wheel is yours."

"Copy that."

There was a slight mess to clean up in the galley; a few items he hadn't had time to stow had gone flying. But the stew was safe in the cooling drawer, and the bottles of booze were intact, so that was good. He'd just added a generous shake of cayenne to the pot on the induction burner when it occurred to him.

Shit. Mot.

Haz hurried down the hallway. In his defense, he wasn't used to having passengers. Usually all he had to worry about was Molly and his crew. If their lives were threatened, he crossed his fingers that whatever cargo he carried would survive Molly's dance.

He found Mot huddled in a fetal ball on the floor of his cabin, the bright designs on his skin the only real color in the room. The pillows and blankets had flown off the bed and were now scattered everywhere.

"You hurt?" Haz demanded.

Mot uncurled and looked up at him, and it took Haz a moment to realize that one side of Mot's face was swollen and that his face and chest were splattered with drying blood.

"I…. What happened?" Mot asked somewhat tremulously.

"Someone tried to kill us."

"Who?"

"No idea." There were several possibilities, but he'd mull them over later. "Get up on the bed and let me take a look at you."

Mot stumbled as he got to his feet but caught his balance before he fell. He sat heavily on the edge of the mattress. Haz started to crouch in front of him, but when his leg gave a warning twinge, he joined Mot on the bunk.

"Let me see," Haz said.

A quick scan with his biotab revealed nothing seriously wrong. Mot's vitals were a little high, but that was understandable considering he'd just been tossed around the room.

"Did you hit your face on something?"

Mot gingerly touched his nose and bruised cheek. "Yes. On the edge of the bed."

"Hang on."

Haz went into the tiny head, where he wetted a washcloth with warm water. Then he sat beside Mot again and dabbed at the blood. He tried to be careful, but Mot winced. As they sat there, not quite skin to skin but almost, it dawned on Haz that Mot was naked. Had been since his second day on board, when Haz had insisted he put his filthy trousers in the ion drawer. It wasn't something that had truly registered since then, because their time together had been brief and because Mot's tattoos provided a sort of visual clothing on their own.

"Where are your trousers?" Haz asked.

Mot blinked. "I…. Oh. I'm sorry. I'm not usually permitted to wear…."

He tried to turn his head away, but Haz was holding his chin as he continued to clean up the blood.

"They don't let you wear clothes?"

"The ornaments are gifts to the Great Divine. It would be a sin to obscure them from his eyes."

"But if this Great Divine's such a powerful god, is a little bit of cloth going to stand in his way?"

"I…." Mot frowned. "I don't know."

Haz wiped away the final spot of blood and rose to his feet.

"Look. If you're comfortable like this, knock yourself out. There's no dress code on my ship. But if you want to wear pants, then for gods' sake, wear them. We've got two more weeks until we reach Chov, and nobody there's ever going to know."

Looking uncertain, Mot nodded.

Haz sighed. Narco was a whole lot easier to deal with, even if it had nasty effects on the ultimate users.

"I'll be back in a bit with dinner and a cold pack for the swelling."

Without waiting for a response, he tossed the bloody cloth into the sink and left Mot alone.

"THOUGHTS ON who was chasing us?" Njeri had eaten her second bowl of stew and seemed to be contemplating a third. Haz didn't blame her. Battles built appetites.

"Could be pirates, but I doubt it. They don't usually operate with just a single xebec. Besides, what the hell would they be doing here? It's not as if this route offers rich pickings."

"Hmm." She examined her reflection in her spoon, then waved it at him. "Maybe they were on the way from one place to another and happened to stumble onto us. They figured today was their lucky day."

"They figured wrong."

Haz took a swallow of whiskey. He wasn't drunk yet, but the fire was beginning to morph into a soothing warmth.

"So if not pirates, then who?" Njeri asked.

"I've pissed off a fair number of people over the years—"

"No shit," Jaya interjected.

"—so it could have been someone with a grudge."

"Who knows you're here?"

He shrugged. "The Coalition. Which means anyone could have found out. How many people do you figure work at the Budapest port, and how many of them might have blabbed to someone?"

Njeri held up two fingers. "Okay. We got pirates and personal enemies. Who else?"

"Whoever stole Mot, trying to steal him back again. Although I can't imagine why anyone but the Chovians would want him."

"I did some research," Jaya said. "Which it wouldn't hurt you to do either, you know. Turns out that skinny little thing is central to not only the Chovians' religion but to their politics too. Because for them, those are the same thing."

Haz sneered in disgust. "If people want to believe in gods, fine. Believe away. But unless your deity is going to step up and tell you how she plans to keep people healthy and happy, she doesn't belong in your government."

He speared a piece of potato with his fork and chewed it fiercely.

"Well, you're not in charge of Chov X8, and they feel differently. If Mot's missing, everything's destabilized there."

"Which makes a good chance for opportunists to step in."

Jaya nodded. "The planet was settled by humans in early days, before the Coalition had managed to expand much beyond Earth. Nobody paid them much attention because there wasn't anything there worth much, I guess. Recently, though, there's been interest in Chovian jewelry—which maybe makes the planet worth exploiting."

Haz set his jaw. He didn't give a shit about Chov X8, and he was still angry at Kasabian for screwing him over. But he'd promised to deliver Mot, and he wasn't going to let some slimeballs get in the way of him following through. Besides, a tiny voice in his head reminded him, those slimeballs had no reason to treat Mot gently and probably a lot of reason to see him dead.

"I'm not letting anyone steal him," he announced, then ate another chunk of potato.

Chapter Eight

EXCEPT WHEN somebody was trying to kill you, life on a ship wasn't very exciting. Haz couldn't drink constantly, and that left him with time on his hands. Occasionally he tried to help Jaya, but she irritably chased him away. And although Njeri offered to let him join her classes—she was studying Tapachultec language and six-dimensional math—he declined. He'd never been much of a scholar even when he was a kid.

There was the gym, but he could spend only so much time there. Mot was locked up in the meditation room, not that Haz had ever meditated before or ever intended to. Molly's library contained entertainment from over seven hundred inhabited planets and covering many centuries, but none of it held his interest. Not even the porn, no matter how many flavors he sampled.

Haz was both bored and uneasy, an unsafe combination. If he'd been on land, he probably would have picked a fight with someone, which might have helped settle him. But it wasn't an option here.

Gods, he was actually looking forward to bouncing around in Kappa Sector, and that was crazy.

So comparatively speaking, maybe it was almost sane of him to carry two packaged meals to the former meditation room one afternoon and sit next to Mot on the bunk as they both ate. He'd noticed that Mot rearranged the blankets and pillows differently every day, probably because he had nothing else to do. Today one of the blankets—grayish green like the others, but soft—had been folded into a shape that resembled a flower bud. Mot had put on his ragged trousers a few days earlier but not the shirt Haz had dropped off.

"Are you a soldier?" Mot asked, his voice tiny and shoulders hunched, as if he expected a beating.

"No."

"You move like one."

Haz didn't know what to make of that.

"I used to be. Haven't been for a long time."

Mot used a finger to scrape sauce from the inside of his food packet, then licked his finger clean. It was an innocent action, a childlike one, and for some reason it made Haz's chest hurt. It didn't help when Mot gave him a small smile.

"What planet are you from?" he asked.

"Ceres. Not the asteroid Ceres in Sol system. This one's a planet in the buttcrack of Delta Sector. The Earthers who settled it weren't even bright enough to give it an original name."

"Do you have a house there?"

That made Haz snort. "No. I haven't stepped foot on that miserable shithole since I was a kid."

"But do you have family there?"

"Don't know. Don't care."

In all probability, his parents were dead by now. They'd be only in their early seventies, but they hadn't believed in using any medical treatments invented or discovered after the old Earthyear 1 C.E. As a result, Haz didn't expect they'd have a long lifespan.

"Oh." Mot set his empty food packet aside, clasped his hands, and looked down at them. "I always thought it would be nice to have a family."

"What happened to yours?"

"I was created as a tribute to the Great Divine."

"Created how? In a test tube?"

The Coalition had banned cloning of sentient species, but Chov X8 wasn't part of the Coalition. Maybe it was commonplace there.

Mot shook his head.

"The Great Divine sent a message to the priests as to which man and which woman would join to make me. It was a great honor for them."

"Let me get this straight. God pointed to some guy and some lady and said they should fuck and get her pregnant."

"Yes."

Haz remembered what Mot had said about receiving his first tattoos as a newborn.

"So then your parents did what? Handed you over to the priests?"

"They weren't parents. Not... not like that. They were like... like potters who create a bowl."

That was irritatingly reminiscent of Kasabian's analogy. As horrible as Haz's own people had been, at least they'd never treated him like tableware.

"I don't understand how anyone could treat a child like that. Treat a person like that."

"I'm not a person. I am the Machine of the Obeisant Theocracy, Omphalos—"

"Yeah, yeah. Except you seem pretty much like a person to me."

Mot opened and closed his mouth a few times, as if trying and failing to find words. Finally he held up his arms, turning them this way and that to display his marks.

"This body is... an icon. Created and adorned to honor the Great Divine. My consciousness, which temporarily inhabits the vessel, is simply a convenience. A way to keep the vessel alive as it's prepared."

Prepared. Haz didn't like the sound of that.

"Don't you get any say in this?"

"There is no me," Mot insisted. Then his shoulders slumped. "I'm sorry. I've never had to explain. I'm not doing a very good job."

Haz set aside his packet containing the remainder of the tasteless food. He wasn't hungry anymore. His gut told him to push Mot harder, to get Mot to recognize the lies he'd been taught, but his brain told him not to. How would it do Mot any good to chafe at the bonds he'd been born into? The bonds Haz would soon be placing around him again.

"Who stole you?"

Mot blinked at the sudden change of topic.

"I don't know. Off-worlders."

"Tell me what happened."

"The priests were taking me to the Eighth Temple." Apparently realizing that Haz had no idea what he meant, Mot explained. "There are fifteen of them, each on a different sacred site. We spend one moon cycle at One, and then we walk to the next. When we get to the fifteenth, we start again at One."

"How long are these walks?"

"Some are less than a day, but some are much longer. People come out from the villages to watch as we pass. It's considered good luck for them to see me."

Great. So Mot wasn't just an artifact; he was a display piece and a good luck charm.

"So you were walking?" he prompted.

"Yes. Far from anywhere. And a ship suddenly appeared. Not like Molly—this one was smaller. Men got out of it and shot the priests.

I thought they'd shoot me too, but instead they put chains on me and brought me into the ship. I'd never flown before."

Haz frowned as he tried to make sense of this.

"Did they tell you what they wanted with you?"

"They didn't speak to me at all. They put me in a… a box." He shivered. "I was in there for a long time, I think. When they let me out, it was on a bigger ship, and I was locked in a room. It wasn't as nice as this one."

"Nice?" Haz gave a snort. That wasn't an adjective he'd use for this space.

But Mot nodded vigorously and patted the flower-folded blanket as if to demonstrate.

"Okay. Then what?" Haz asked.

"I'm not sure. There were… lots of different people. Different ships. Nobody spoke to me. And then I was in a place on a planet, but not X8, and the navy people said I was going to be taken back home. They brought me to you."

There was a lot missing from that story. Not just specifics of who the parties were, but also details about how and why and where he'd been transferred from place to place. Did Coalition inspectors discover him during a routine check, or had there been a fight? Did the Coalition stumble on him, or were they searching? And again, why hadn't the thieves just killed him? Maybe they were hoping for a ransom—some of that expensive jewelry, perhaps. Then again, Chovians weren't the only ones who wanted a Machine of the Obeisant Theocracy.

"When we picked you up, you were doped to the gills. Why?"

Mot hung his head. "Sometimes I… struggled." He looked up quickly. "I won't fight you, sir. I promise. Please don't give me more drugs."

"If you fight me, you're gonna lose, so I'm not worried about that."

Mot was no longer as gaunt as when he'd first boarded, but he was still a skinny thing considerably smaller than Haz. And unlike Haz, Mot wasn't a trained fighter.

"Did they keep you doped all the time?"

"No. Only when I wasn't compliant."

Haz thought about this puzzle for a few minutes more, until he remembered that none of it mattered. For all the difference it made to Haz, Mot could have been stolen by a herd of thruqraxi. What was important was that Haz had contracted to return Mot to Chov X8. That was all.

He stood abruptly and marched to the door, intending to simply leave. Instead he found himself turning around to stare at Mot.

"We'll hit Kappa in a couple of days. We won't be there long, but it'll probably be a rough ride. Usually is. After that, it's smooth sailing for two standays to Chov." He sighed. "Until then, do you want me to let you out of this room?"

Mot's eyes widened. "Out?"

"Molly's not exactly Newton. But we've got vidscreens. A galley where you can make your own damned lunch. A little more variety than this." He gestured at the small space. "You'd have to promise not to be a nuisance. Don't screw around with anything you shouldn't, or you'll be back in here so fast your head will spin."

He didn't know why he was making this offer. Well, maybe he did. He'd spent months in a jail cell in Budapest, longing for a glimpse of the sky.

Mot stood and lifted his chin. "I would like to be out, sir. Please."

"Szot, I hope I don't regret this." And Haz waved for Mot to follow him.

MOT SEEMED to enjoy the tour of Molly, which took longer than Haz would have thought possible. But Mot liked to inspect everything, and after asking permission, he touched everything too. It reminded Haz a little of the first time he'd been off the ground, so many years ago, when even the simplest shipboard controls seemed like magic. Well, they'd certainly been a sharp contrast to the stone hut with the thatched roof where he'd spent his childhood. Maybe Mot had been similarly isolated from technology.

When Haz and Mot descending to engineering, Jaya fixed them both with the same gimlet stare.

"Don't mess with anything," she hissed.

Haz knew better than to point out that this was his ship and he could mess with whatever he pleased. "We're just looking."

She grunted and returned to inspecting a thick rope of wires.

Njeri, who was on the bridge doing something with a nav screen, was only slightly warmer.

"What's he doing here?" she asked Haz.

"Nothing. I thought he might like to stretch his legs."

She shook her head. "You're going to make a complicated thing worse, Hazarmaveth."

He flipped her off and led Mot to the rec area, where Haz flopped into a comfortable chair and gestured for Mot to do the same. "Biggest vidscreens are in here. Um, you'll need someone else to turn them on and control them since you don't have a biotab."

Mot nodded absently. "What did she call you?"

It took Haz a moment to remember, and then he rolled his eyes.

"Hazarmaveth. It's my full name."

Realizing where this discussion was likely to end up, he stood, meandered to the galley, and pulled out a bottle of whiskey, which he carried back to his seat.

"It's a long name," said Mot, who unfortunately hadn't lost the thread of the conversation.

"It's from the old Earth Bible. Old Testament. You know that book?"

"The priests say that to believe in it is sacrilege."

Haz chuckled.

"Well, no problem. I don't believe in it, but my parents did. They were part of this group of Earthers who decided God wanted them to move across the galaxy to establish a new Eden. They call themselves the New Adamites."

Mot was watching him closely, head slightly cocked, as if Haz were fascinating. Well, after fuck knew how long locked up in various boxes and rooms, probably everything was fascinating. It was still hard for Haz to read Mot's expressions due to the designs all over his face, but it was getting easier.

"Did it work?" Mot asked.

"Did what work?"

"Did they please God?"

Haz took a deep swallow of whiskey straight from the bottle.

"How the hell do I know?" But when Mot opened his mouth, likely to ask another question, Haz held up his free hand.

"The New Adamites take the Old Testament very literally—their own interpretation of it, anyway. They believe they should live exactly like the people in the book, with no recognition of anything that's happened in the last several thousand years."

Almost none, anyway. The New Adamites couldn't entirely support themselves, so they relied on goods that arrived on occasional spaceships.

Even though Noah, Abraham, David, and their buddies never mentioned anything about receiving food and household goods from other planets, the ships weren't turned away. The New Adamites also used biotabs, probably because Haz's parents' generation was too damn used to them to give them up.

"You're angry at these questions?" Mot was leaning slightly forward in his seat.

It took more whiskey before Haz answered.

"I'm angry at those assholes. They believe in women being treated like property by their fathers and husbands. They believe in beating children who are disobedient. And they believe that a man who wants to have sex with another man is an abomination and must be put to death." Snarling, Haz pointed at Mot. "But you know what? I've read that book and it says no such thing."

"But you had a family." And Haz caught that expression for sure—it was wistfulness.

"I had a mother who was always pregnant—with babies that might or might not live—and always exhausted. I had a father who hit me with sticks and straps if I didn't do exactly as I was told. I had brothers and sisters who worked with me from dawn to dusk six days a week trying to grow food in soil that didn't want to nurture anything, and who would have eagerly helped my parents throw me into the fire if they knew I lusted after other boys. That's not a family—it's a torment."

That was a much longer speech than he had intended to give, and he washed it away with more whiskey, which tasted bitter on his tongue. He offered the bottle to Mot, who widened his eyes and shook his head. And then Haz found himself talking again.

"My father did me one favor. He named me Hazarmaveth, which means 'court of death.' That got me thinking that maybe I could do something other than farm. Maybe I could fly, and the best way to do that was to become a soldier. When I was sixteen, I seduced one of those visiting traders into taking me away on his ship, and I made my way to Earth and joined the navy. So instead of growing things, I was in the business of death. The Coalition is out to conquer most of the galaxy, whether locals want it or not."

He'd never told this story to anyone, at least not so baldly and without embellishments to make himself look better. Njeri and Jaya knew the basic outline of his childhood, but that was all. Yet here he was, spilling everything to the Machine of the Obeisant Theocracy. Maybe because Mot needed to know that the universe outside his carefully controlled life wasn't all roses and rainbows, and that being a religious icon wasn't the only fate that sucked.

"What do you want to watch?" Haz waved at a vidscreen.

"May I... I'd like to read instead. If that's allowed."

"The priests educated you?"

Mot scrunched up his face. "They taught me to read so I can learn prayers. I have to recite them during ceremonies."

Haz barked a short laugh. "That's why they taught me too. So I could read their book."

He stood, walked over to Mot's chair, and showed him how to activate the integrated vidscreen, a smaller one intended for text instead of full video. The smaller ones didn't require a biotab to operate. It took only a minute or so for Mot to understand the on-screen search controls for Molly's library, and by the time the short lesson was over, Mot was grinning ear to ear.

"So many choices!" he said. "What may I choose?"

"I don't care. Read whatever you want."

Haz leaned back in his own seat, used the biotab to stream music into his ears, and closed his eyes.

CHAPTER NINE

MOT ATE dinner with them that night. Nobody specifically invited him, but they didn't forbid it either, so when Jaya called out that the meal was ready, Mot firmed his chin and joined them at the table. He sat stiffly, his gaze trained downward, but then relaxed a little when Jaya set a plate and cutlery in front of him.

Jaya's culinary experiment tonight was a success, the spices on the grilled synth protein just hot enough to be interesting without cauterizing anyone's tastebuds. She'd made some flatbreads to go with it and had mixed a packet of vegetables and beans into a soup. As everyone dug in, Njeri gave an update on their itinerary.

"We'll slide into Kappa around lunchtime the day after tomorrow. I've changed our route slightly, though. I caught a couple of reports of pirates in one section, so we're going to avoid that."

"Pirates are everywhere in Kappa," Haz pointed out.

"But if we can avoid the worst of them, that would be nice. Don't you think so, Captain?"

Haz grinned savagely. He'd bested plenty of pirates before. They tended to underestimate Molly, assuming she was nothing but a stolid little cargo ship. But Molly had surprises in store. Haz had installed more powerful drives and cannons, and Jaya had worked magic with the control systems.

And that reminded him. "Jaya, how's your work going?"

She looked at Njeri before answering, and Njeri shrugged. Jaya frowned. Haz had no clue what that silent conversation was about and knew better than to ask. Jaya would tell him what she wanted to and nothing more.

"Fixed the damage from the other day. Still working on the damage from those clowns on Kepler."

"C'mon. Were they really that bad?"

"Depends. Do you want to survive the next time somebody shoots at you?"

"What makes you think someone's gonna shoot at me?"

He couldn't keep a straight face as he asked that, and while Jaya rolled her eyes, Njeri cackled.

"I'd be worried if nobody was trying to kill you," Njeri said. "That would mean something's wrong with the universe."

Laughing, Haz agreed.

Mot had been silent, carefully following their chatter as he gobbled his food, but now he made a small noise.

"People try to kill you? Often?"

"That depends on how you define often," Haz answered. "It happens now and then."

"Because... you were in the navy?"

Jaya snorted. "Because he's an untrustworthy sonofabitch who's on the wrong side of the law more often than the right."

Mot flinched back in his seat as if he'd been struck.

"I thought you were his friends," he said quietly.

To her credit, Jaya looked to Haz for permission before answering. Haz gave her a go-ahead signal, and she put down her fork.

"Haz Taylor doesn't have friends. Probably wouldn't know what to do with them. He has crews who work with him despite his many character flaws because they know there's not a better pilot in the whole galaxy. And because at least he's honest about being dishonest. Most of the time."

She shot him a glare no doubt related to that narco shipment.

"Is that true, sir?"

Haz heaved a sigh. "You can stop with the *sirs*, and yeah, it's true. Unlike me, Jaya's no liar."

Njeri looked thoughtful. "I don't think Jaya's completely right on this, though." She leaned closer to Mot as if sharing a confidence. "Haz is an honorable man, in his own way. If he says he'll do something, he does it. If he thinks something's the right course of action, he takes it, even though maybe the law would disagree. There have been some exceptions, but he's human."

Realizing he was gaping, Haz shut his mouth. But it fell open again as Jaya nodded slowly and said, "Yeah, all right, not usually untrustworthy. But he obeys the law only when it suits him. And he's still a sonofabitch."

"He's been very kind to me," said Mot.

"Oh, I never said he was cruel. He doesn't fight fair, but I've never seen him go out of his way to hurt anyone who didn't ask for it."

This was like being laid onto a table and dissected, only it wasn't as painful as Haz might have expected. He knew his crew valued his piloting skills—as they should—but he never suspected they liked anything about him as a person. They knew what he'd done, both in the navy and afterward. Yet it didn't sound as if they despised him.

Interesting.

Meanwhile, Mot was watching him, those strange eyes seeming to bore right into Haz's head. Well, let them. There wasn't much to discover in there other than a lot of stuff about flying and fighting.

Abruptly, Haz stood and began to clear his dishes. He mumbled something about needing to check the cannon calibrations. "Then I'm gonna turn in. Njeri, you're on watch until 0400, then I'll take over."

"I know that."

"Sir—I mean, Haz—do you want me to return to my room now?"

"Do whatever you want. Just don't fuck with anything you shouldn't."

Mot nodded. "I don't have to sleep now?"

"Seriously. Sleep whenever and wherever you want, as long as you're not in the way."

Deciding the dishes could wait until later, Haz stalked out of the galley.

THE CANNONS were, of course, just fine, but Haz remained in engineering for a long time anyway, stroking the smooth metal and murmuring sweet nothings to Molly. She loved him even if sometimes he got her shot. All she cared about was that he danced well with her and kept her in as good a condition as he was able.

By the time he crept back up to the main deck, there was no sign of anyone in the rec area or galley, and someone had already completed the after-dinner cleanup. He went to his quarters.

"Molly, play that thing I was watching."

One of his vidscreens turned on in the middle of a recreated history of the Yaprian Wars. He didn't care about the political parts, especially since in the end the Yaprians had managed to destroy themselves and their entire planet. Whatever arguments they'd been having about who should be in charge had been moot for over a century. The battle scenes were worth watching, however. One Yaprian general in particular had used brilliant and unique strategies, winning nearly every fight, and Haz wanted to study her moves. He didn't have to worry about whether someone might detonate his home planet while he was engaging in stunning maneuvers. He hadn't had a home planet since he was sixteen.

He undressed, did his nighttime ablutions, and got into bed. When he felt himself nodding off, he didn't fight it. Instead he yawned and called out, "Hey, Molly? Turn off the vid when I fall asleep. And wake me up in time for my shift."

"Confirmed," Molly said crisply. And then in a softer tone, "Good night, Captain."

A few minutes later, Haz spoke again.

"Molly? Would I know what to do with a friend?" Wow, that sounded stupid. And pathetic.

"I can change my programming to simulate friendship if you wish to test this."

"Never mind. Night."

He fell asleep quickly, as was generally the case. The problem was staying asleep. When he was awake, he could be careful about how he moved his leg, but he had no control of that while unconscious. He'd twist it a little, roll onto it, or kick out suddenly, and then he'd be awake and in pain. Complicated pillow arrangements didn't help. A few times he'd even tried tying the damn thing down, but that only meant that when he woke up, he was hurting and panicking.

He was trying to get back to sleep for the third or fourth time that night when the door to his quarters slid open and somebody slipped inside. Haz grabbed his neuroblock and pointed it at the figure silhouetted in the light from the corridor.

"One more step and you're toast."

The person halted. "Sir? I mean.... Haz?"

Swearing softly, Haz put the weapon back on the table beside his bed. "How did you get in here?"

"I asked Molly to open the door."

Shit. Haz hadn't told Molly to keep everyone out, mostly because he hadn't expected it to be an issue. If there was an emergency and Jaya or Njeri needed him, they'd call him over the com system. Sighing dramatically, Haz sat up and rearranged the blankets over himself.

"What do you want?"

"You said I could sleep anywhere I wish."

"I didn't mean— I'm here already, in case you didn't notice."

"I did notice." A long pause. "I want to sleep with you."

"I'm not a szotting teddy bear, Mot."

"I want to have sex with you."

Haz almost choked on his own tongue. It took a moment for the coughing to subside.

"You what?"

"You said you have sex with men. I am one. At least… this body is male. I'm not…." Mot's voice trailed away into silence.

It wouldn't be any easier to have this conversation with the lights on, Haz decided.

"I do have sex with men. But not all of them. I mean, I don't fuck someone just because he's male."

There were people who might have argued otherwise, back when he'd been young. He'd taken freedom from his parents' prohibitions very seriously, and for a good decade after leaving Ceres, he'd happily slept with any willing male—as well as a few females and people of other genders. But he wasn't that kid anymore.

"You don't want to have sex with me?" Mot asked. "Is it because of what I am? Or… the tattoos make me ugly in your eyes?"

Haz rubbed his head, which now ached almost as much as his leg.

"I really hadn't given it any thought. You're my…." He struggled to choose the word. Cargo? Prisoner? "It wouldn't be right."

"Why not?"

"Jesus, Mot, I don't want to discuss ethics in the middle of the night. In fact, I never want to discuss ethics. I know as much about the topic as a craqir does about stiletto shoes."

Instead of leaving, however, Mot came a step closer. Backlit, his face was still indistinct.

"I have never had sex," he announced. Ignoring Haz's groan, he continued. "And soon I'll be back home, and I won't… I won't have the chance again. It's such a… human thing to do, though. I've been reading about it, and it seems so important to many people."

Maybe Haz should have tried to steer Mot's literary efforts in other directions, but he hadn't expected the guy to pick up the idea so fast. Besides, Haz wasn't a szotting censor like the priests back on Ceres. "Humans are hardly the only species that fuck."

"But things don't. Artifacts don't. You've done so much to help me feel like a person. You could do this too."

A large part of Haz was tempted to give in. Mot had a good sob story, and as far as Haz knew, he'd never fucked a virgin. And it was only sex, which for years he'd been telling himself was just a little meaningless mutual rubbing that made him temporarily feel better. But that was part of the point here. It was meaningless for him, but it wouldn't be for Mot, and Haz didn't like that imbalance. Besides, while he'd accumulated a long list of sins and crimes, he'd never had sex with anyone who wasn't fully consenting. And because Haz was in a position of power here, Mot couldn't freely consent.

"Go talk to Jaya or Njeri. Neither of them minds a dick in bed with them now and then."

"I don't.... I think I'm like you."

"You're nothing like me, and you should thank your Great Divine for that. Now go away."

Mot remained standing silently for what felt like a standay. Then he sighed. "Good night," he whispered before walking back out the door.

It shut, leaving Haz in almost complete darkness. He had a hard time finding sleep after that.

HAZ'S SHIFT arrived much earlier than he would have liked. He growled at Molly when she woke him up, but he got out of bed anyway, threw on some clothes, and stumbled to the galley for coffee.

"My, aren't we perky," Njeri said as he entered the bridge.

He threw himself into a seat and tried to muster enough energy to glare but couldn't manage it. The coffee tasted like crap. He should have bought pricier stuff from Farkas and Zhao. Ignoring Njeri's scrutiny, he opened the vidscreen and took a quick scan of the data. Molly was on course, and nothing had happened since Njeri's shift began. He was going to need to tell Molly to wake him up if he dozed off.

"Go join your wife. She's probably been waiting for hours to tell you what a shit I am."

"Believe it or not, we have better things to talk about than you, Haz Taylor." She stood up and stretched, groaning loudly. But she didn't walk away. "Your artifact spent some time with me tonight."

"He's not my—"

"He had about a thousand questions. Can't say I blame him. If I spent my whole life locked up in temples, I'd be eager for some variety too."

Haz squinted at her, wondering whether Mot had informed her of his plans to seduce Haz. Maybe *seduce* was overstating it, but Haz couldn't think of a better term.

"Doesn't matter," he said. "He'll be back home soon, and nothing he learns with us is going to do him any good."

Njeri shook her head. "How long did you spend in that jail cell?"

"Eighteen months."

Actually, the first two of those he'd been in the hospital, but he'd been in custody then—both physically and legally unable to move—so he counted that time too.

"And what did you spend your time doing when you were in there?"

He huffed. "Well, first I spent my time getting cut up by butchers. After that I mostly thought about how much I hate the Coalition in general and the navy specifically."

He'd also spent a lot of time trying to drown out the echoing screams of dying soldiers, but Njeri didn't need to know that. She might not believe it anyway.

She crossed her arms. "Eighteen months. That's roughly thirteen thousand hours. Even if you spent half of those sleeping or railing against the world's injustices, that leaves you with sixty-five hundred hours to kill. I know they didn't give you access to vidscreens and they dampened your biotab. So how'd you do it without losing what passes for your mind?"

What he hadn't done was plan for the future, because he didn't expect to have one. And he certainly hadn't wanted to dwell on much of his past. So he'd focused on other things instead. Mostly various forms of entertainment he'd enjoyed over the years. And when even that got too hard, he'd sit on his narrow bunk, close his eyes, and remember what it felt like to fly.

"I thought about stuff," he mumbled.

"Right. So maybe Mot wants to have stuff to think about too. He's a smart one." She tilted her head. "How come you gave him the run of the ship, anyway?"

"I'm tired of having to bring him his meals."

"Uh-huh. I wonder if—"

Molly suddenly blared a warning siren, followed by a succinct statement in her calm, well-modulated voice.

"Two unidentified ships in pursuit."

CHAPTER TEN

HAZ DIDN'T even look up when Jaya came rushing onto the bridge.

"Two," he informed her.

She was already strapping in. "Class?"

"Dunno yet. Gimme a sec." He was massaging the data vigorously, hoping to get more specs on their pursuers, but the distance was too great. "Njeri, if we max the thrusters, can we—"

"No way to hit Kappa for at least twenty-four hours, Captain. And there's nothing between here and there."

He'd known those things already, but it never hurt to confirm. Dammit, if only he could—

"Is someone shooting again?"

Haz glanced up long enough to send a death glare at Mot, who stood in baggy trousers at the entrance to the bridge.

"Sit down, strap in, and shut up," he barked. Somewhat to his surprise, Mot obeyed.

The tension in the room was familiar; Haz had been in this position with his crew many times. Njeri and Jaya knew their jobs well, which saved him from having to issue orders. In fact, the three of them worked together—and with Molly—so seamlessly that it was almost as if they were a single, if complicated, organism.

But Mot wasn't a part of that synthesis, and even though he was staying put and keeping quiet, his presence caused an imbalance. Haz considered sending him back to his quarters but decided against it. There was no way for Mot to strap down in his room, and Haz didn't want him thrown around again. His face was still swollen from last time.

"Xebecs," Njeri announced after several minutes.

"Two, confirm?"

"Confirm. Coming up fast. Want me to try hailing?"

"Go ahead." Haz knew the efforts would be fruitless, which they promptly proved to be. "Any ID or markings?"

"Nothing."

No big surprise there either. "Molly, reduce speed to minimum, and switch auxiliary systems to support only."

"Minimum speed, aux support only."

Haz could feel the change as the drives shifted, shunting most of the power into controls and weapons. Molly thrummed around him like a hre'csro about to chase down its prey.

"Hang on, darling," he muttered. "Almost there." He patted the vidscreen as if to momentarily gentle her.

"Warning shot?" Jaya asked.

"Don't bother."

It wouldn't work well with two opponents. Plus, there was an excellent chance these ships came from the same source as the last one, meaning their captains might have viewed the last battle sequence. They wouldn't be fooled this time.

Haz felt his lips stretch into something more snarl than smile. "When they get in range, pick one and shoot to kill."

Fuck the Coalition's rules. There was no way these ships were friendly, and Haz wasn't going to wait for them to strike the first blow.

"Copy that, Captain." Jaya sounded pleased with the order.

The xebecs came in hard and fast, not bothering with theatrical flourishes. There they were in 3D, floating above Haz's vidscreen: two speedy little dots that meant business. Fine. Haz wasn't fooling around either. It was barely past 0400 and he hadn't even had time to finish his first cup of coffee.

For the sake of Jaya's accuracy, Haz kept Molly steady for the moment. But as soon as she fired, Haz zipped Molly off to the side. That ought to immediately confuse their pursuers, who wouldn't have expected to be in range yet and wouldn't have known Molly was so agile.

"Nice one, Jaya!" Njeri crowed. "That ship's faltering already."

Haz knew better than to celebrate. They still had one fully functional and probably pissed-off ship to contend with. And sure enough, the undamaged xebec put its all into keeping up with Molly while firing away. But Haz was in his element, zooming and swooping, allowing the other ship to get close enough that Jaya could fire on it, and then nimbly swinging out of range. A few pulses hit Molly, but they were glancing blows and didn't do any structural damage. She was, after all, a sturdy little thing.

The other pilot was good, seeming to anticipate many of Haz's flashier moves with a lightning-quick response. And while the xebec wasn't as agile as Molly, it was more powerful, able to outfire her and outrun her in a straightaway. Haz remembered his classes on ancient Earth warfare; this battle was as if he held a rapier while battling an opponent grasping a claymore. Force against force, the claymore would win. Which was why he had to keep on moving. Keep on dancing.

"Jaya, I'm going to move in close on the xebec's starboard side. See if you can take out at least one of her drives."

"Copy that."

It was a risky move, and Molly took a couple of solid blasts as she closed in. But Haz kept her going steady ahead, and by the time their opponent realized what was happening, it was too late for the relatively clumsy xebec to get out of the way. Haz buzzed the thing so close they almost collided, waiting for Jaya to fire before he peeled away.

"Good shot, Jaya. Let's see— Oh, shit." Njeri joined him for the expletive, as both of them caught sight of a third ship coming at them. "Where the fuck did that come from?"

"She just got in range, Captain." Njeri muttered something that was either a prayer or a blasphemy. "It's a frigate."

"Oh, szot me."

Haz jerked Molly to the side just in time to avoid a blast from the xebec. Frigates were bigger than xebecs and much faster. More heavily armed as well.

"Who the hell are these people?" Haz wondered aloud.

Frigates were expensive and required a large crew. They weren't utilized often outside of the navy, although a few transport companies used them to carry passengers. Haz had a feeling this particular frigate wasn't full of tourists.

The frigate was already firing at Molly, and because it had a much longer range, it was useless for Jaya to shoot back.

"Jaya, I'm going to keep us between the two of them."

If he stayed close to the xebec and swerved around a lot, the frigate might be deterred from firing in fear of hitting her own ally instead. Of course, that would put Molly squarely in the xebec's yard.

"Give that xebec everything you've got."

"Copy that, Captain."

He didn't look at Jaya, but he could hear a fierce grin in her voice.

As strategies went, this was dicey. Most people wouldn't intentionally place themselves smack between two larger opponents. But outrunning them and outgunning them weren't options with the frigate in play, and poor Molly could only dance around for so long. Those types of maneuvers put stress on the drives and on the hull, and eventually something would give.

The frigate and xebec shot simultaneously, both barely missing. Haz responded by scooting closer to the xebec, zigzagging in the process to make Molly a more difficult target. The key was to have such unpredictable movements that neither the opposing ships' crew nor their computers could anticipate where he'd go next. But he also had to remain steady enough for Jaya to take aim at the xebec, and he had to keep Molly squarely between the ships if he wanted to use the xebec as a deterrent.

As he reached up to wipe sweat from his brow, he was laughing. There was nothing more joyful than barely escaping death—until you couldn't escape any longer, of course. Ah, but those last few minutes before losing the game would still be a thrill.

The xebec shot Molly hard enough to make her shudder and spin out of the current maneuver. For a moment she was out of control entirely. But Haz didn't panic even as the g-sim gave up, making his head whirl and stomach flip.

"Whoa there, darling," he said to Molly. "I gotcha."

And with more patience than he thought he possessed, he eased back in, steadying Molly just in time to avoid another hit.

"Jaya, we're going in."

"Copy that."

God, he loved his crew. Not a peep of panic or complaint even now. Just a determination equal to his, and the same delight in their own skills.

He brought Molly in, close enough to the xebec to almost kiss her, and this time when Jaya fired, the xebec's entire lower hull disintegrated. Debris showered Molly with loud thunks and bangs. Haz peeled away quickly.

He took a deep breath. Well, there was good news and bad news. They now had only a single opponent, and it didn't seem as if any other uninvited guests were going to appear. But the frigate was the most formidable of the original three ships. Molly now had no cover, and the frigate was already blasting away.

Okay. Can't outrun her and can't outshoot her. That meant Haz was going to have to outfly her.

"Njeri, find out that frigate's weakest points and feed them to Jaya. Jaya, we're only going to get a couple passes at her, so make 'em count."

They both probably confirmed, but he was too busy flying to notice.

He loved this part. He'd never been emotionally close to another human being, but when he was flying like this, he and Molly were almost one. She knew what he wanted, and he knew what she could do—a perfect marriage of will and capacity. The only barriers were the physical ones between his brain and her body, which made him feel as if he were fighting in a dark room with his ears stopped up. Yes, he got reports on the vidscreen and from Njeri, but those were delayed and secondhand.

He made do nonetheless, swooping in toward the frigate with erratic loops and veers. The frigate kept shooting—even the most glancing hits making Molly shudder—but Haz continued forward.

"Captain, her belly's weakest," Njeri reported.

"Belly. Got it."

That was dandy, except it was also where her blasters were located. Well, as Haz's father used to say, needs must when the devil drives. Haz aimed for the frigate's belly.

The closer they got, the bigger the frigate looked, like a great beast about to swallow them. But size wasn't everything. A tiny zeneni bug could kill a human under the right circumstances. Haz simply needed to be that zeneni.

They were within Molly's range now, and Jaya was shooting. Not so much in hopes of crippling the frigate as to keep its crew busy. Even if Jaya's hits didn't do much damage to the bigger ship, they could slow it down and throw off its aim.

Haz did several complete barrel rolls followed by a steep climb and then an equally steep drop, falling below the frigate.

"Here we go, Jaya."

Bang!

The blast hit Molly almost head-on. She began to spin again, this time in forward somersaults, and the power flickered in and out, which meant Haz had no controls.

"Njeri!"

"On it. Rerouting.... Got it."

The vidscreen came back to life, along with the controls, and Haz got Molly back in line just in time to avoid another blast from the frigate.

"Do you want a damage report?" Njeri asked.

"Negative." It didn't matter; they had to go back in no matter what. "Ready, Jaya?"

"Yeah. Sorry about the last—"

"You'll hit her this time."

Haz risked a very quick glance at Mot, who hadn't uttered a sound since the battle engaged.

"If you want to have a word with your Great Divine and ask for some intervention, now's the time for it."

Mot grinned, his white teeth a sharp contrast against his tattoos.

"I think I trust you three more than the Great Divine."

Haz was cackling as he sped back in.

The frigate fired several times—Haz felt each blast in his bones—but good old Molly kept on going, looping and wheeling as eagerly as a bird let free from a cage. Sweat stung Haz's eyes, his heart thundered, and the scent of burned coffee filled his nose. But his fingers flew, urging Molly on.

"You can do it," he said, addressing himself, the ship, and Jaya all at once.

He didn't know if belief could make a thing happen, but he sure as hell knew that doubt could stop it. So he believed with all the zeal of the most devout New Adamite. He rushed Molly in, almost nose-to-nose with the frigate, and then as the frigate turned, so did Haz, slipping beneath.

This time Jaya scored before the frigate. Her rapid series of shots took out its cannons, its drives… all the vulnerable bits on its belly. As Haz cartwheeled Molly away, the frigate exploded.

Njeri piped up almost at once. "We've got damage to the—"

"If it's nothing major, let's see if anyone's left alive on the first xebec. I want to find out who the hell these people are."

Really, what he wanted was to take a hot shower and eat something. Maybe dull the pain in his leg with some booze. But those luxuries would have to wait a little longer.

The fight had taken them a good distance from the disabled ship. Haz let Molly return in a leisurely fashion; she needed a little rest too. After Njeri reported the most important of the various damages—thankfully none too severe—he focused on Mot.

"How are you doing?"

"I thought I was going to vomit, but I didn't."

Haz laughed. "Well, that's better than most people manage at first. You might not feel it yet, but expect some sore muscles and bruising from the straps."

"Is it…. Are battles always like that?"

"I've been in… God, I don't know. A hundred at least. No two are exactly the same. Yet they are all the same, if you catch my meaning." He shrugged. "They shoot, we shoot. People die. So far, I haven't been one of those people."

"The three of you, the way you worked together. It was beautiful."

That made Haz smile. "Four of us. Don't forget Molly. But yeah—I have the best crew in the galaxy."

Even Jaya nodded at that.

A short time later, they reached the xebec, which floated helplessly.

"It still has enough power for life support," Njeri said. "But that's about it."

"Hail them. Maybe they're more willing to chat now."

Sure enough, the xebec's bridge promptly showed up on one of Molly's big screens. The xebec's captain was human, a lean woman in her thirties with a nasty bruise on her forehead.

"Are you ready to surrender?" she snapped. "We accept."

Haz chuckled. "Funny. How about you tell me who you're working for, and in return we don't vaporize you."

"Fuck you."

"Thanks for the offer, but I have a previous engagement." He leaned forward. "Seriously, I'm in a shitty mood. I didn't even get a chance to finish my coffee yet. Don't try me."

Behind her, four battered-looking crew members tried not to look terrified. Heading into a fight was one thing, but being picked off when you were just hanging there in space—that was another thing altogether. It wasn't the kind of death anyone wanted.

"Captain," said a man who was hardly more than a boy.

She turned and snarled, "Shut up." He obeyed, and she faced Haz again.

Haz sighed. "It's a very simple question. I don't want the secrets of the universe. I just want to know who's trying to kill us. I think that's fair enough, right? You know who we are."

"You're scum."

"I don't usually get called that until after I sleep with someone. Come on, Captain. A name. Or maybe one of your crew would like to volunteer to be helpful instead?"

She held up both hands, effectively silencing the men behind her. After a long pause, she narrowed her eyes.

"If I tell you—"

"We won't shoot. We'll just be on our way, and if you're lucky, you can get an SOS call to your friends in time for them to rescue you."

"Why should I believe you?"

He was trying to be patient, he truly was.

"If you don't tell me, I'll definitely kill you. If you do, I might not. You might not like the odds, but that's the hand you've been dealt. Now play, or else I'll move first."

He gave his nastiest smile. And then he saw something that made his mouth go dry, but with effort he managed not to show his distress.

After another long pause, her shoulders slumped.

"Fine. We work for Etol Hildres."

Haz whistled. "Wow, that's big-time."

Hildres was one of the most successful pirates in the galaxy, with entire squadrons of ships and over a thousand crew members at her disposal.

"Why's she trying to kill me? I never crossed her."

"She wants your cargo."

Mot made a small sound of distress, which Haz ignored.

"Why? What possible use does she have for him?"

"I don't know."

"Is she the one who stole him to begin with?"

"Yes," the xebec's captain hissed.

Haz took a long look at the background of the image, hoping that his initial discovery had been a mistake. Nope. He'd seen what he'd seen. Fuck.

"I hope that your boss sends help before your life support runs out. You're a long way from home." He turned to Njeri. "Cut transmission."

The big screen went blank, and Haz turned Molly around, setting her back on course.

"Etol Hildres!" Njeri said. "If she wants Mot so bad, she'll just keep sending more and more ships—"

"It's not her."

Jaya had unstrapped herself and now stepped closer. "What?"

"That captain lied. She's not working for Hildres. In fact, we're screwed much worse than that."

He ran fingers through his hair, sort of wishing he could just pull his head right off. "But hey, at least I know who's trying to get us."

"Who?" Jaya asked.

Haz sighed.

"The Coalition."

CHAPTER ELEVEN

HAZ REFUSED to explain until after he took a shower, brewed more coffee, and ate breakfast. None of those things improved his mood, however, which remained as foul as the swamps of Kepler. In fact, he was wishing he'd thrown himself into those swamps rather than getting mixed up in this shit.

While Haz stomped around, Njeri and Jaya ran a full inventory of Molly's damage. Mot, however, sat in the galley, still and expressionless beneath his ink. At least he didn't ask any questions. Haz needed to work through some of his inner turmoil before saying a word.

But he couldn't avoid it forever, and eventually he ambled onto the bridge and threw himself into a seat. Mot followed him but skulked near the doorway, as if nobody would notice the Channel to the Great Divine.

"What did you see inside that xebec?" Njeri demanded.

"I saw that I'm fucked. We all are."

"A little more context, please?"

He stretched out his leg, angrier at the damned thing than usual. Maybe he should have had the surgeons hack it off, and he could have hobbled around on whalebone like Captain Ahab. If whales weren't extinct.

Haz met Njeri's impatient gaze. "I recognized one of the crewmen on that ship. The one with the scar on his cheek, although he didn't have it the last time I saw him. His name's Alves, and he's in the navy. I don't know his rank nowadays."

"Recognize him from where?"

"He was on the *Star of Omaha*." Haz looked at Njeri bleakly.

"Are you sure? That was ten stanyears ago."

"I knew everyone on that ship," he snapped. "Everyone. Alves was a senior airman who worked in engineering, so I didn't see much of him, but I knew him."

Njeri nodded slowly. "Yeah, okay. But just because he was in the navy a decade ago doesn't mean—"

"He hasn't quit to become a pirate or mercenary. He was one of those people who bleed navy blue, right? Four, five, six generations back, his family all served. I once overheard him bragging about some distant ancestor who'd served in the fucking Spanish Civil War." He huffed because he knew history was not Njeri's thing. "On Earth. Six or seven hundred years ago."

"But what if—"

"He's right." To everyone's surprise, Jaya interrupted her wife. "I didn't process it at the time, but those firing patterns they were using? Textbook Coalition. The stuff you learn in basic training. Those people had navy training, and you know people with that background don't end up working for thieves. Well, not usually."

Happy for the backup, Haz shot Jaya a smile. "It explains that frigate too. I bet all four ships that have come after us belong to the navy. It's not that hard to paint over the insignias."

Mot finally peeled himself away from the doorway, returned to the same seat he'd been in during the battle, and sat down. He wasn't wearing a shirt, Haz noticed. When Molly's alarms had sounded, Mot had rushed out of his room wearing nothing but trousers, probably after being startled out of sleep. He hadn't put on any additional clothes in the interim, although there had been time. But then, he was used to wearing nothing and probably didn't even think about it.

Njeri was chewing on her nail. "Why would the Coalition be trying to kill you? They're the ones who hired you. And what about Mot?" She gestured at him. "Why would they hand him over to you only to steal him back? And if they wanted him dead, there were about a million simpler ways they could have accomplished that."

"Do you know any of these answers?" Haz asked Mot.

"No. I'm... I'm so sorry. I've endangered all of you."

Mot was looking down at his clasped hands.

"Did you do it on purpose?"

Mot's head snapped up. "No! I don't understand any of this."

"I have a motto: Don't apologize for shit that's not your fault. Hell, I don't even apologize when it *is* my fault."

Jaya huffed. "Stop showboating, Taylor. What do we know for sure, or at least close enough?"

There were a lot of reasons Haz liked her. This was one of them. He spent a moment ordering his thoughts.

"We know that someone kidnapped Mot, which is causing political instability on Chov X8. We know that the Coalition ended up with Mot in their possession. We know they gave me a contract to return him to his home. And now we know that they're trying to keep Mot from getting there."

It helped to lay it out like that. It was like putting together a video puzzle. If you set out the pieces you already had, you could at least get an idea of the shape of the ones you still needed.

"I'm going to assume," Haz said after a pause, "that it was the Coalition that kidnapped Mot, or at least paid someone else to. Make sense?"

Jaya and Njeri both nodded. But Mot's brows were drawn. "Why?"

"Because they have something to gain by shaking things up on X8. Your planet's independent, right? But if the leadership collapses and the Coalition looks like the good guys, maybe whoever's newly in charge will decide to join. That'd give the Coalition an important foothold in that sector of the galaxy. Or maybe they just want their claws on some of that szotting jewelry." He thought back to some of the books he'd read when studying to become an officer. "It's an old trick. Earth governments did it all the time. You can read about it on the vidscreens if you live long enough."

Mot shook his head as if the prospect of imminent death didn't worry him.

"But why didn't they just kill me then and say the bad guys did it?"

"Because this makes a better story. First they rescue you. Points for them. And then they try to return you—more points—but the pilot they trusted you to is such a lowlife that everyone in the galaxy is after his ass, and unfortunately the Omphalos and Corpus of Piety is destroyed by pirates en route. Such a shame."

Haz brushed his hands together as if wiping off dirt. "It's neat. They topple the Chovian power structure, convince everyone they were doing their damnedest to avoid just that, and they get rid of a traitor who's been a thorn in their side for years."

He wondered whether the plan had been Kasabian's brilliant idea or whether she was merely carrying out the wishes of politicians.

"Give me back," Mot said.

"What?"

"Give me back to the szotting Coalition."

Haz chose to ignore the profanity, which he was fairly certain Mot had picked up from him. "They'll murder you."

"But they'll stop shooting at you."

Haz gave him a genuine smile.

"That's about the sweetest offer anyone's ever made me. But it won't work. They'd just murder me too—and Jaya and Njeri besides." He stroked his chin. "In fact, I can see it now. They'd tell everyone that I was the one who did it. Mmm, maybe I demanded a bigger fee, and when they refused to pay, I slaughtered you and my crew in revenge. The public would buy that."

"They'd eat it up," said Jaya.

The four of them sat in glum silence. Haz wondered what would have happened if he'd refused the contract. Not that there was ever much chance he'd do that—Kasabian had been his only hope of regaining Molly, as she doubtless knew. But if he'd said no, maybe she'd have dragged him back to Earth on narco charges, then found a way to frame him for Mot's death. Or she'd have found another useful way to get rid of Mot while Haz, oblivious to any of it, rotted in a jail cell.

No, however he looked at it, refusing the contract wouldn't have resulted in a better outcome for him or for Mot. Which was slightly reassuring. But Jaya and Njeri? They'd still be enjoying golf, cactuses, and yoga on Newton.

"Njeri, set the fastest course to Newton."

"Why would I do that?"

"So you and Jaya can go home. You don't need to be in the middle of this mess anymore."

Njeri looked at Jaya, who looked back. After nearly a minute of entirely silent conversation, Jaya said, "Nope."

"Nope what?" he asked.

"Nope, you're not dumping us off like last night's date. We're not quitters. We signed on for this, so we're gonna see it through."

Haz opened his mouth to argue, then shut it again. Although he could fly Molly on his own, he was a lot more likely to survive—and keep Mot alive too—with his crew's help. Besides, he recognized the stubbornness he saw in Jaya's eyes. He often saw it when he looked in a mirror.

"Fine," he said.

"So what's the plan, Captain?" asked Njeri.

"Screw the Coalition. We're doing the one thing they don't want us to—we're taking Mot home."

And when they landed on Chov X8, Haz was going to pretend as if he were carrying out the Coalition's orders, and he wasn't going to mention the times they'd been shot at. Then, without any reason to need Mot or Haz dead, maybe the Coalition would leave them alone. It was worth a try, anyway.

"Resume our original course, please," he said to Njeri.

"Copy that."

Haz turned to Mot. "They're gonna come after us again. But none of them are as good as us. We're going to get you home, Mot."

"Home." Mot nodded, unsmiling.

LATER THAT day, after checking Jaya's progress on repairs, Haz sat sideways on one of the soft reclining benches in the rec area. He wanted whiskey, but he didn't drink any; remaining sober seemed wise in case the navy came after them again. But his leg had stiffened up. Nasty cramps ran along the back of his thigh, and the scars pulled like iron bands. He was pretending to watch a stupid comedy vidshow, but mostly he was counting through the pain.

Mot entered slowly, a mug cradled in one hand.

"Do you want some coffee, Haz? Or tea? Njeri showed me how to make it."

"You don't need to wait on me. You're not my servant. You're not even a crew member."

"No," Mot said sadly. "But I wouldn't mind being useful."

"No, what you want is an excuse to trap me here so you can interrogate me."

Haz had already learned that Mot was exceptionally good at questioning things. He could have had a career as an interviewer for Coalition intelligence. Not that Haz blamed him. In Mot's shoes, Haz would be full of curiosity too.

Mot grinned impishly. "Okay, maybe some of that too. Do you mind?"

Haz was going to grouse. But then it occurred to him that Mot's questions might be a good distraction from his leg and that answering them was possibly more productive than sitting here and wallowing in pain and self-pity.

"What do you want to know?"

Mot sat carefully in the nearest chair. He took a sip from his mug and licked his lips before speaking. Haz wondered absently why his tongue was free of tattoos. Maybe the priests had been aiming for that next.

"You called yourself a traitor," Mot said, "and indicated that the Coalition would be glad to get rid of you. Why?"

This wasn't what Haz had expected. He'd thought Mot would ask things more pertinent to his own interests, like why the Coalition had been so callous toward him and what his chances were of surviving the rest of the journey home. Haz wasn't eager to stir up any ghosts. But shit. Mot probably deserved to know who he was dealing with.

"Why don't you bring me some coffee after all?" He'd pretend it was whiskey.

It didn't take Mot long to brew a cup and return. As he handed it over, Haz asked, "Did you eat anything today? There's better stuff than those packaged meals I've been giving you."

"You've been eating them too."

Haz shrugged.

"They're easy. I got used to them in the navy. That's all they feed you when you're on a ship."

But God, it had always been so wonderful to hit ground and consume real meals with actual flavors.

"I'll eat later," Mot said.

Haz scalded his tongue on the coffee. He always did that, yet he always went back for more.

"Okay. If you want my story, you're getting the long, boring version. Just remember it's your own damn fault for asking."

"Duly noted." Mot settled back in his chair with a smile.

"Duly noted," Haz echoed. "That sounded… a little sarcastic." And unlike any language he'd heard Mot use.

Mot grinned. "Molly and I have been practicing conversations. She says I'm getting better at speaking like a member of a smuggling crew instead of an artifact."

He sounded so pleased with himself that Haz didn't have the heart to point out that he was *not* a member of the crew. And also, why did Haz feel a funny little twist in his chest over Mot's obvious delight? It hadn't been long since Mot had joined them, drugged and cowering, yet he was already opening up like a gamechi blossom. He was finding out what sort of person he was—which would do him a qhek fart's worth of good when he was back on X8.

Maybe it was best to let the subject drop and get on with the autobiography instead.

"I joined the navy the day I was old enough. By then I'd been on a few ships as a passenger, and I itched to fly them. I dreamed of it at night. If you're dead broke, like I was, the navy's the best way to learn to fly. Maybe the only way."

This was important. He knew plenty of people who'd enlisted out of patriotism, out of hope for heroism, out of hatred for the current enemy. But Haz hadn't cared about any of that. He just wanted his hands on the wheel.

"Did you like being in the navy?"

"Not really." Haz laughed. "I don't take orders well. I bet you'd never have guessed that."

"Never," Mot replied, unable to maintain a straight face.

"Yeah. So I hated the stupid rules and the people bossing me around, and I hated all the shit they make you do just because they can and not because it serves any purpose. But I really, really loved flying. And I was damned good at it. Good enough that the navy was willing to overlook my rough edges and move me up through the ranks quickly. They even sent me to school, and I became an officer."

And yeah, there had been a feeling of pride when his commander pinned those lieutenant bars onto Haz's uniform. That dumb farm kid from Ceres had gone from digging rocks out of the dirt and pulling a plow to commanding others, all on the basis of his skills.

"You were a good officer." Mot said this as a statement rather than a question.

"I was…. I had my strengths. One of them was getting to know every soldier under me. Not as pals—I've never been good at being friends. But an officer isn't supposed to be too chummy with his underlings anyway. I'd learn enough about them to know what I could trust them to do, what kind of training they needed, how they'd deal with stress, things like that. So in an emergency, I'd know who to choose in order to get things done and who to keep out of the way."

"That's why you recognized the man on that ship today."

"Alves. Yeah."

Haz sipped more coffee. Mot didn't hurry him, which was nice, but it was also clear that Mot wasn't going to give up and go away. He had a streak of stubbornness that Haz admired. Until Mot was kidnapped, he'd likely never had much chance to get his own way, so maybe he was enjoying these small freedoms.

"Alves and I both served on the *Star of Omaha*. She was a beautiful Class A galleon, and— Do you know anything about spaceships?"

Mot shook his head.

"I didn't either, once upon a time. Anyway, galleons are huge, much bigger than that frigate we fought this morning. And *Star* was big even by galleon standards. Real sleek and pretty, though. Not that any ship's as gorgeous as my Molly." He patted the bulkhead fondly. "But *Star* had a crew of almost a thousand. She was the type of ship that people could live on for years, if needed. The Coalition used her for what they called expeditionary forces. Which really meant we headed out past the edges of our territories to conquer new planets. Most of the crew were certified for ground warfare too."

Haz made a face at that.

"You liked being on that ship?"

"I guess. Honestly, I'd rather fly something small and zippy, but there's a nice feeling of power when you're in control of something that big. And I was the sailing master, which put me third in command. Pretty heady for a yokel like me."

Although much of the crew had respected him, there had been a contingent who resented being told what to do by someone with no great love for traditional rules and power structures. Alves had probably been among that group.

"How old were you?"

Haz blinked. "What?"

"How old?"

"Um, just past thirty stanyears. That's young to have made it that far."

"I'm almost thirty now, and I've never even been in charge of myself."

Haz had wondered idly about Mot's age. It was hard to tell with all the ink, and Mot's childlike sense of wonder at new things sometimes made him seem very young.

"Well, I'd come a long way since I ran away from Ceres," Haz said. "Anyway, I'd been serving on the *Star* for about six months, so I was still the new guy. The captain who'd been in place when I was first assigned—a good man—had just retired, and the new one was an asshole. One of those fuckers who thinks he knows everything and rushes in without good information. His huge ego led us straight into deep, deep trouble."

That day still haunted his nightmares. The wailing sirens, the reek of fried wiring and terrified people, the chaos of everything falling apart. The captain had sailed them into an ambush where they were outnumbered and outgunned and, unless a miracle happened, would pretty soon be dead.

Mot was wide-eyed, leaning forward in his seat. "What happened?"

"He just kept making things worse. He wouldn't listen to anyone's advice, and instead of choosing a coherent plan of action, he'd contradict himself every few minutes."

"He panicked?"

Haz had never gotten a straight story on how someone so incompetent rose to a command position. Maybe the guy had bluffed his way through; he generally had an air of supreme confidence that might have impressed some people.

"Yeah, he panicked, and so did half the crew. Even the ones who were trying to hold it together couldn't get anywhere. A few people had escaped in these little pod ships we used for quick transport to land. I don't know where the fuck they thought they were going—they got picked off right away."

For a long moment, Haz stared into the depths of his mug. He hadn't panicked, but he'd been nearly insane with rage and frustration. Their situation was so stupid—anyone with half a brain could have avoided it. He'd begged the captain to listen, and when that hadn't worked, Haz had yelled. But the captain had stood there on the bridge, white-faced with fear, spitting out command after deadly command.

"I almost murdered him," Haz admitted, not looking at Mot. "I'd killed plenty of people before; what was one more? I had my knife in my hands."

"You'd killed before, but you hadn't murdered."

Haz wanted to scoff at the distinction, but Mot had scored a direct hit. In Haz's mind then—and even now—there was a line between ending a life in battle or in self-defense and slitting the throat of an arrogant, inept fuckwad who should never have been put in command of anything. Haz didn't have many moral codes, but that was one of them.

"The quartermaster was on the bridge too. Second-in-command. She was excellent at her job, which was keeping the ship, weapons, and crew in shape, but she was mediocre as a pilot and strategist. So... I asked her to help me lead a mutiny. She gathered a few crew members who subdued the captain and locked him in the brig, and I took command."

Mot was nodding as if he expected this.

"And you saved the ship."

"I... got us out of there. Barely, and using a few moves that weren't exactly navy regulation. The *Star* sustained so much damage that we had to land on the nearest safe planet and wait for rescue. The navy ended up scrapping her rather than trying to fix her, poor girl. Over a hundred crew members died. Most of the rest were injured to varying extents. I'm betting that's how Alves got those scars. The Coalition basically lost all hope of claiming the star system they'd been aiming for."

"And this is why he called you a traitor?"

Haz laughed humorlessly.

"Mutiny, Mot. The navy tends to look down on it. They also.... Well, the whole affair was an embarrassment to them. It benefited the brass to make it look like the disaster was the fault of someone other than the shithead captain they'd put in command. That captain—who'd gotten out without a scratch, by the way—died by suicide while the inquiry was still going on. I was court-martialed. The press was calling for my head."

"What do you mean?"

"Mutiny is one of the Coalition's few capital offenses." Haz mimed a blade slitting his throat.

As he'd sat in his jail cell, he'd expected to be executed. Between the pain in his leg and the excruciating limitations of captivity, he'd almost welcomed that fate.

"But the quartermaster and some of the crew spoke on my behalf. So I was busted down to staff sergeant instead and drummed out of the navy without retirement benefits. I was supposed to be grateful for that."

Mot gestured toward Haz's leg. "Were you injured too?"

Haz stood up quickly enough to slosh his coffee and make the limb in question protest.

"Story time is over." He began to limp away.

"But Haz—"

"I need to figure out how we're all going to survive the next several days, remember? Buzz off."

He left without a backward glance.

CHAPTER TWELVE

INSPIRATION DIDN'T come to Haz that day. He was always better at reacting than planning, and right now he felt trapped. He didn't mind fighting against difficult odds. Hell, he enjoyed a challenge. But facing the entire Coalition navy wasn't difficult odds—it was impossible. He wanted to keep his crew and Mot alive. If only he could find a way to do it.

He could keep on running for a while. He might even be able to evade their pursuers in Kappa Sector, although he couldn't hide out there forever. The Coalition knew his eventual destination, so they could just squat around the Chov System, wait for him to show up, and obliterate him.

He paced his quarters endlessly that evening, a fitting reflection of his mind, which was also going in circles and getting nowhere. There had to be a solution. He refused to accept that nothing could be done. If it were only his fate hanging in the balance, fine. He'd get roaring drunk and go out with a bang. But he'd dragged Jaya and Njeri here and had agreed to be responsible for Mot. He wasn't going to let them down.

"Molly, I need a pep talk. Tell me we're not all fucked."

"Our doubts are traitors and make us lose the good we oft might win by fearing to attempt."

Haz halted.

"What?"

"It's a quote by an ancient Earth author named William Shakespeare. He was born in—"

"I know who Shakespeare is."

"This is a quote from a work called *Measure for Measure*." Molly sounded slightly huffy, as if offended by his lack of appreciation for her help. "The themes of the play are moral justice, forgiveness, and mercy."

"Did he write a play about how to escape the Coalition long enough to get Mot and the crew to safety? Because that's what I need now, Moll."

She paused a moment. "He did not. But Isabella was able to save her brother from execution."

Haz sank onto his bed and covered his eyes with one hand.

"How'd she do that?"

"First the judge offered clemency if Isabella would have sex with him. She refused."

"Well, good for her. I'd fuck my way out of this if I could." He barked a laugh. "I slept with Kasabian a couple times, and that hasn't improved my situation much."

"But after that, she tricked the judge. And the brother was saved."

Tricks. He ought to be good at those, considering he'd survived the past decade mostly by smuggling and other acts that strayed from legal protections. That was how he'd won most of his fights too—by doing things in ways his opponents didn't expect.

Lately, though, he'd been the one duped by tricks rather than the one performing them.

"If I survive this, I'm going to have to turn in my smuggler's card in shame."

"I am not familiar with a smuggler's card," Molly said primly.

"Never mind. It was a joke. I only meant— Wait."

An idea was beginning to sprout in his otherwise infertile brain, like the hesitant green shoots of wheat fighting their way through the soil on Ceres.

"I'm a smuggler," he said.

"But you do not have a card. I could construct one—"

"Forget the card, Molly. I'm a smuggler. I get things from point A to point B even when the authorities don't want me to. And right now, that's exactly what I need to do—I need to get a religious artifact to point B."

He jumped to his feet.

"Molly, tell everyone to meet me on the bridge, pronto."

NJERI—HER CURLS caught up in a messy ponytail—looked sleepy, but Jaya had been on watch and was wide-awake. As for Mot, Haz had no idea what he'd been doing, but he seemed perky enough now, one bare foot tapping as he waited for Haz to explain.

"I have a plan," Haz announced.

To his surprise, nobody responded with sarcasm, not even Jaya. Instead, she gestured impatiently for him to continue.

"If we try to take Mot home, the Coalition's gonna pounce on us like a thruqrax on a qhek."

"We could go somewhere else," Mot offered softly. "There must be a quiet planet where—"

"They'll just hunt us down. Maybe we'd evade them for a while, but they have all the resources in the galaxy. They'd catch up."

Frowning, Mot gave a small nod.

"If I were rich, I'd buy another ship and use that. Sorry, Molly, but you're too recognizable. Anyway, I'm not rich, so that's not an option either."

Njeri yawned. "But I assume there is an option and you're not just keeping us here to torture us?"

"There is, and it's neat and easy." His plan also had a couple of big holes, but he wasn't going to mention that. "Tomorrow we head for Kappa Sector, as scheduled. And once we're in there, we're going straight to Ankara-12. We're going to find someone else to take Mot home while I create a distraction with Molly. Jaya and Njeri, you'll have no problem finding work on another ship. With a captain who actually pays, unlike me."

"What will happen to you?" Mot asked.

Yeah. That was one of those holes. Before Haz could reply, Jaya did it for him.

"He gets his fool ass blasted to bits."

Haz grinned.

"Some would say that's been a long time coming. Anyway, the important point is that Mot gets home safely, you two survive and go back to your retirement cactuses, and the Coalition loses. That's plenty of success as far as I'm concerned."

Nobody said anything. Haz turned on his heel and, whistling, marched toward his quarters, snagging a bottle of whiskey from the galley along the way.

HE WASN'T drunk yet, only pleasantly buzzed, when someone knocked on his door. He recognized the somewhat hesitant thud.

"Go away, Mot," he yelled, even though he knew his voice wouldn't carry through the heavy door.

When another knock sounded, Haz sighed.

"Molly, tell him I'm not going to fuck him."

After a brief pause, she responded, "He denies being here to have sex."

"Great. Then tell him to go away."

Another pause.

"He will remain, pounding on your door all night."

As if in confirmation, three more knocks came, louder than before.

"Tell him— Oh, szot. This is stupid." Haz sighed. "Let him in."

The door slid open and Mot stepped inside, looking pleased with himself. He had a steaming mug in one hand.

"Seriously, Mot. I know I'm not that irresistible. Wait until we get to Ankara-12. Some beings there will happily fulfill any sexual desires you have and plenty you've never thought of. You're in the mood for tentacles? No problem. You can get a quickie or two before shipping out."

"That's not why I'm here."

"Go away. I need my rest."

Mot pointed. "That's booze, not rest."

"They often go hand in hand."

"Uh-huh." That specific flavor of sarcasm sounded as if Mot had been taking language lessons from Jaya as well as Molly.

Mot set the mug on the small shelf beside Haz's bed. The rising steam smelled like flowers and made Haz wrinkle his nose. Mot gave himself a small tour of the quarters, peering at the empty desk and the built-in shelves.

"You don't have any personal items."

"I have some clothes. They're tucked away. And I have my knives, which I'm feeling increasingly tempted to use."

Mot turned to face him, head tilted.

"But you must be at least forty stanyears old."

"Forty-two." Haz saluted him with the bottle.

"And you've been so many places, seen so many things. But there's nothing in this place that says Haz Taylor lives here."

With no clue regarding the point of this conversation, Haz simply shrugged. "So?"

"The Machine of the Obeisant Theocracy has no personal possessions. Not even clothing or knives. And never stays long enough to call anyplace home."

Haz's stupid heart gave that funny little twist. He'd never been much interested in accumulating things, even when he had the means to do so, but aside from when he was in jail, he'd never been forbidden to own things. Not wanting something was different from having it denied because your humanity wasn't acknowledged.

But Mot seemed to have moved beyond that particular point. Now he stared at Haz's legs, outstretched on the bed.

"It still causes you a lot of pain, even after all these years?"

"Szot. Do you want to see the ugliness? Is that what this is about? Fine."

Haz stood quickly—causing Mot to step back—and skimmed out of his trousers. Then he turned, his right leg toward Mot, and lifted his tunic hem to reveal the entire mess.

To Mot's credit, he didn't wince or appear disgusted. In fact, he moved a little closer and bent to inspect the keloids and deep gouges that ran from midthigh to near Haz's ankle.

"Pretty, huh?" Haz said, jaw tight.

He'd never been particularly vain, but he didn't like being the object of revulsion or pity.

Mot put out a hand as if he might touch but pulled it away at the last moment, making Haz shiver.

"This happened on the *Star of Omaha*?"

"Yeah. The whole damned ship was falling to pieces. The landing was... well, rough is an understatement. Part of the bridge bulkhead collapsed. Luckily only my leg was crushed, and I didn't need that part of me to finish setting her down."

He'd been trapped, though, for several hours, listening to the screams and wails of the wounded and dying, waiting for death to take his own agony away.

"You still flew with that injury?"

"I didn't fly; I crash-landed. And I didn't have much choice, did I? Nobody else was at the wheel."

Mot looked thoughtful, chewing his colorful lip.

"Some of the tattoos, they're not bad. But some of them...." He swallowed audibly. "Some of them hurt. And I have to remain still."

For a second, Haz imagined a needle repeatedly piercing his eye. He shuddered.

"They didn't sedate you?"

"People get sedation. Machines don't." Mot smiled. "But some priests are kinder than others, and one of them taught me some techniques to manage the pain. Can I show you some?"

Haz was going to refuse. He could manage pain just fine with whiskey, thanks very much. But Mot was still standing there, empathizing rather than judging. And hell, why not. Maybe afterward Mot would go away and leave him alone.

"Fine."

"Start by drinking some of that tea." Mot gestured with his chin.

"I drink coffee and booze. Not tea."

"Except right now you'll drink this tea because it'll help you. I found the ingredients in your galley. You didn't have any fever-root and some of the other things, but that's okay. Jaya helped me find substitutions."

Haz picked up the mug and sniffed, wondering if Jaya had used this as a handy opportunity to poison him. The tea didn't smell toxic. The scent reminded him a little of spring on Ceres, when rains would come and the untilled soil would erupt into blankets of orange, purple, and yellow flowers. He took a careful sip. It tasted floral too. Not something he'd ask for, but not awful.

"What's this stuff supposed to do?"

"Relax you. C'mon. Finish it."

Mot crossed his arms and tapped his foot impatiently. When had he become so bossy?

Making a face, Haz obeyed. He didn't feel any more relaxed after the mug was drained, but he wasn't dead, so that was good.

"Okay," he said, setting down the cup. "You can beat it now."

"Lie down flat with your injured leg closer to me."

"Mot, I—"

"Molly, tell him to listen to me."

Molly answered at once. "Haz, you should listen to him."

"You're turning my own ship against me," Haz accused.

"No, she's trying to help you. And so am I." Mot huffed. "Tomorrow will be difficult, yes? Won't you do a better job if you're in less pain?"

There was nothing worse than arguing with a stubborn ass who also had logic on his side. With a dramatic sigh, Haz shifted around until he was positioned as ordered, his head pillowed by his hands. He'd never really noticed it before, but the ceiling was a boring dull gray. Maybe he should paint it a more interesting color, or at least hang some pictures up there. Of course, the bulkheads in his quarters were the same dull hue, and while the floor was a little darker, it was also unexceptional. His sheets were white and the blanket charcoal-gray. Unless the vidscreens were on, there were no colors at all in his room. Except right now, when Mot brought in his vividly inked skin.

Fingers settled lightly on Haz's shin, making him startle.

"Mot—"

"This isn't sex. I told you, I've never had sex. But the priest taught me this a long time ago. Now stay still."

Easy for him to say. Haz wasn't used to being... administered to. His body generally had two default modes: tense and unconscious. But he closed his eyes and imagined the tea working its magic—sending soothing chemicals through his bloodstream, coating his overworked neurons in cool, soft blankets.

Mot's fingers were warm, not cool, and they moved in slow circles, the pressure just barely firm enough to prevent a tickle. Haz tried to remember the last time anyone had touched him for any reason other than a fight or a fuck, and he came up blank. The surgeons, maybe, but that had been a long time ago. He was fairly certain they'd intentionally botched the job; they were navy doctors and he was in custody for mutiny.

"You have small scars on your other leg too. Also from the *Star of Omaha*?"

"Dunno. Some of 'em, I guess."

"You guess?"

Haz cracked an eyelid.

"I was a farmer, then a soldier, then a smuggler. None of those are easy on a guy."

"Your scars are a little like tattoos, aren't they? They memorialize certain things."

"Maybe. Your tats are a lot prettier, though."

Briefly, Mot's movements became slightly arrhythmic. "You think they're pretty?"

"You're a work of art."

Haz didn't know if that was any better than being a machine, especially since Mot hadn't voluntarily obtained the ink. But it was true.

"Some of the people who held me captive called me a freak."

"Those were the type of qhek-fuckers who'd kidnap an innocent man, treat him like shit, and get him murdered. I don't think you should care about their opinions."

Haz yawned hugely. He was more relaxed, he realized. His limbs felt pleasantly heavy and the tightness in his shoulders had faded. Even his eyelids were too much trouble to raise.

"What's that you're humming?" he asked sleepily. "A prayer?"

Mot laughed softly.

"No, just a song. I don't know the words very well. Something about a beautiful girl. Do you mind?"

"No," Haz said through another yawn. "'S nice."

"Is there good music on Ceres?"

Haz had to think about that.

"Work songs—the kind you chant to make hard labor easier. Psalms. My father played the lyre sometimes, and he'd sing along with it. He had a nice voice."

Haz had forgotten that. He and his siblings would sit together on the earthen floor of their house while their mother stood, usually rocking the newest baby. For a little while everyone would be able to ignore the constant gnaw of hunger and the ache of overtaxed muscles.

Mot had worked his way up to Haz's knee, a swollen misshapen joint that creaked even in the best of times. Haz's skin tingled very lightly, a bit like it had been bathed in an astringent wash, and his tendons and muscles felt loose. The tea that lingered on his lips now tasted sweet.

"Does the priest do this for you when you get tattooed?"

"He did a few times, and then he showed me how to do it to myself. I could teach you too, if you like."

"I don't have the patience to learn. Never been a great student."

Mot sighed. "I wonder if I'd be a good one. There are so many things to know. I have so many questions."

"Maybe if you asked the priests...."

"No," Mot said, hardly louder than a whisper. "I won't have the chance to be a student."

That was a shame. But the universe was like that—it threw things at you, and you had to do your best with the small freedoms you had. And there were no happy endings; everyone died sooner or later. You could sometimes grab a few nice minutes, however: a palliating touch, a sweetly hummed song, and the comfort of being in your own quarters on your own ship.

By now Mot was working on Haz's thigh. He gently urged Haz to spread his legs a bit wider, but even when Mot's fingers worked so close to Haz's groin that sometimes a knuckle brushed his balls, the sensation still wasn't sexual.

"I can never remember," Haz murmured. "Which one is it—sensual or sensuous?"

Mot didn't answer. Maybe Haz hadn't said the words aloud.

Finally Mot pushed Haz's tunic hem out of the way to work on his hip. The pain wasn't gone from the leg, but it had somehow become less important, like a background noise you were able to ignore. God, had the mattress always been this soft? And when had Mot turned the lights down? Only a faint illumination made its way through Haz's closed lids.

"Poisoned me?" he managed to ask with a thick tongue.

"Bespelled, more like."

Mot gave Haz's hip a final pat with his palm, then pulled the blankets up to his chin.

If Haz had possessed more energy, he would have begged him to continue. But he was far too languid for that. Haz lay in a hammock of softest spiderwebs, rocking gently in the endless sea of stars.

He didn't hear when Mot left.

Chapter Thirteen

HAZ AWOKE in an uncharacteristically good mood, maybe because his leg hadn't disturbed his sleep. Even the coffee tasted almost good, and when he sauntered onto the bridge and Jaya scowled at him, Haz grinned back.

"Good morning to you too," he said.

"You fucked that poor kid."

Haz sat down and leaned back.

"A: he's almost thirty, which isn't a kid by anyone's measure. B: I would never have sex with anyone who wasn't completely willing—you know that. And C: I didn't touch him."

Her frown lessened a notch or two. "Then why are you so cheery?"

"Got a good night's sleep. Had a good dream about that guy on Pheeyama. Remember him? Pink skin and the sort of... tendril things?" Haz squiggled his fingers over his head to demonstrate. "He flew that sweet little dhow? The *Oribi*."

"You remember the name of the ship but not the man you slept with."

"It was a really nice ship."

The Pheeyama were famous for their shipbuilding skills, and the *Oribi* had been a fine example of why. The captain had let Haz take it for a spin—quite literally, because Haz had sent it tumbling through the solar system like an acrobat. Afterward, what's-his-name had asked for a tour of Molly's drives, which culminated in a satisfyingly sweaty session right there on the floor in engineering. Those tendrils had tickled.

"We'll enter Kappa in less than six hours," Jaya said.

"Yep."

"The Coalition will probably send someone to intercept us first."

"Most likely." Haz smiled at her. "And you get to dazzle us again with your skills."

She snorted, but her eye roll was less powerful than usual.

Sure enough, a pair of xebecs made an appearance two hours later but didn't put up much of a fight. After Jaya scored serious but not crippling hits on both of them, they limped away. Haz let them go.

"You could have destroyed those ships," said Mot, who'd sat silently through his third battle.

"Yep."

"Why didn't you?"

"No reason to. They were done shooting at us, and killing them wouldn't stop the Coalition from coming after us again."

Mot stared at Haz as if trying to figure something out, but he didn't ask any more questions.

Flying through Kappa Sector took Haz's full concentration, which was one reason he enjoyed it. Njeri sat with him on the bridge, scouting out the best routes to avoid debris and other trouble. They passed other ships twice, both times smugglers minding their own business and willing to let Haz mind his. Very few smugglers went looking for trouble; most just wanted to deliver their cargo and get paid.

Haz took his dinner on the bridge—just a sandwich and air-fried lorta tubers, which tasted vaguely like potatoes but had better nutrients and traveled better. He saw very little of Jaya, who was probably sleeping, or of Mot, who'd settled in the rec area with a vidscreen controller that Jaya had jury-rigged for him. Haz wondered what Mot was watching.

They finally came to a relatively safe area of the sector, and Haz slowed Molly to a crawl before Jaya took the wheel. She'd be on her own since Njeri needed sleep, but that should be fine. They'd all done this before.

Haz took a detour to the rec area on his way aft.

"We'll be on Ankara-12 midday tomorrow," he informed Mot.

"All right." Mot didn't look away from his screen.

And he also didn't come to Haz's quarters that night—which was a relief, Haz told himself. He needed to rest. The thing with the tea and his leg, that had been nice, but it was a one-time deal. Tomorrow Mot would be on his way home, the crew would be seeking a better gig, and Haz would be worrying about how long he could keep Coalition ships distracted so they didn't notice Mot's disappearance. After that, well, in the unlikely event that Haz survived, he could hang around Ankara until someone offered a paying job. There were usually plenty of those. He'd find one that would take him to the far edges of the galaxy, outside the Coalition's reach. Or hell, maybe he'd just keep going beyond the galaxy and see what there was to see until his food stores ran out.

"Molly, would you mind being my coffin?" he asked after getting into bed and dousing the lights.

"It would benefit both of us for you to remain alive."

"I think so too."

Haz didn't know the history of Ankara-12, but he knew why the little moon had been so successful as a port. For one thing, its gravity and atmosphere—both similar enough to Earth's—could sustain humans and most humanoid species. For another, it was located in a sort of Wild West zone that was difficult for authorities to reach. It wasn't an entirely lawless place, because many of the people who used Ankara-12 tended to self-police. But most important, nobody had to worry about the Coalition breathing down their necks.

Flying toward Ankara-12 was always fun. The enormous planet that it circled—Ankara itself—had once proudly possessed fourteen moons, but some event in the distant past had resulted in two of those moons exploding. The resulting disruptions had wiped out most of the life forms on the planet, including the one responsible for the explosions, and had resulted in a thick layer of dust and chunks of debris in its orbit. Haz swooped and dipped to avoid the potentially lethal pieces, eventually gaining the safety of 12's atmosphere. After a moment's indecision, he chose one of the moon's three port settlements. Paa was the largest of the three and the one he haunted most often.

The terrain on 12 was almost uniformly flat, which was another reason for its popularity. Landing and docking were easy, even without the structures favored by more legitimate ports. Nobody guided you in; you simply eyeballed to find an empty space, and that's where you parked. If you fucked up and damaged anyone else's ship, well, the injured party would certainly seek compensation… in money, goods, or blood. But accidents like that were exceedingly rare. Any pilot who couldn't manage a decent landing didn't belong on 12 to begin with.

Haz set Molly down nice and easy, grinning when he recognized one of the neighboring ships. The *Persistence* was in port, and that was a stroke of luck.

As soon as Molly was settled, Haz handed Mot a pair of gloves and a long piece of dull-green fabric, souvenirs from the weeks when the blood-sucking zeneni bugs on Kepler were especially voracious.

"Cover as much of your head and face as you can. Nothing we can do about your eyes, but maybe you can shadow them with the scarf."

"I can't show my face?" Mot asked.

"The tats make you distinctive. The Coalition probably doesn't have people here, but if they've put a price on your head, plenty of folks would be happy to collect."

"Have you made money that way?"

Haz wasn't going to answer, but Njeri piped up.

"He's run narcos and just about anything stolen, bootlegged, or banned that you can think of, but you're his first living cargo." She scrunched up her mouth. "I once saw someone offer him a lot of credit to carry a bunch of Delthians to Citrapra. He refused. And I heard those Delthians went missing right after that."

Mot looked at Haz and asked, "What happened to them?"

Haz shrugged. He didn't actually know where those unfortunates had ended up, but he knew they hadn't been dragged against their will to dig borvantine out of the Citrapran mines until their bodies gave out.

But Mot wasn't done. "Why didn't you agree to take them?"

"Living cargo is a pain in the ass. Noisy, messy. You have to worry about feeding them. They get sick. Not worth it."

"But—"

"Look, this trip down memory lane is a lot of fun, but we can't squat here forever. The longer we stay, the more people who notice, and then maybe word gets back to the Coalition and they figure out our game." Haz pointed at the fabric in Mot's hands. "Suit up."

It was cold outside; it always was on this moon. Anyone who didn't grow fur needed to bundle up, and nobody wanted to linger under the purplish sky. With a final pat to Molly, Haz led his little group down the gangway and onto the hard-packed soil. He'd already called an aircar, so the four of them piled in, thankful the little vehicle had a roof and a strong heating system.

"This looks like an interesting place," Mot said as they zoomed along.

The buildings—haphazardly laid out—were mostly one and two stories, although a few soared to three or four. And although almost all were constructed from local adobe and stone, the designs varied wildly. The moon's residents came from all over the galaxy, and they constructed their homes and businesses wherever they wanted, in whatever form they preferred—as long as they could afford it and didn't piss off anyone else too badly. The effect was confusing, even dizzying, for newcomers, and that was part of the point.

"Don't wander off," Haz warned him. "You'll get lost. And it's not safe."

"Not safe how?"

Haz flashed his teeth wickedly. "Bad people are attracted to this place. Thieves. Smugglers. Pirates. And worse."

With the scarf covering Mot's face, it was hard to judge his reaction, but he didn't ask any more questions. A few minutes later, the car came to a halt.

"Here we go, kids," said Haz.

Rick's Café had been founded by an Earther. He wasn't called Rick—he'd named the place in reference to some ancient Earth entertainment—and it wasn't a café. Neither food nor coffee was served, but the bar offered an astonishing assortment of intoxicating substances from across the galaxy. That was the main draw, although sometimes there was something approximating music. The amorously inclined could rent an upstairs room by the hour, and there were always plenty of beings offering temporary pleasure.

It wasn't the only bar in Paa, but it was the biggest, its cavernous space full of mismatched, battered furniture and odd cubbyholes. Rick's never closed, and the lights were kept dim enough to obscure the fact that it was rarely cleaned. But you couldn't avoid the smell: the mingled odors of dozens of humanoid species, for some of whom personal hygiene was clearly a low priority. The buzz of conversation was also inescapable.

"I've never been in a bar," Mot said, hesitating just inside the door.

"Szot," Haz cursed under his breath. "Keep your face covered and your trap shut, and stick close to my side."

Perhaps in solidarity, Jaya and Njeri flanked Mot, both of them looking fierce. As well they should. Jaya was as skilled with a blade as she was with a pulse cannon, and Njeri wasn't a bad hand either.

The customers and staff noticed when Haz and his group entered—this was a crowd who paid attention to things like that—and judging from their expressions, some of them recognized Haz, although nobody was openly hostile. It had been over a stanyear since Haz had been to Rick's, and in the past, he hadn't had any enemies here. He hoped that remained true.

Followed by his little entourage, Haz walked slowly through the room, scanning the tables for one familiar face. A couple of sex workers made offers along the way, but when he declined, the rest seemed to realize he wasn't interested and left him alone. Haz exchanged nods with a quartet of humans he'd once briefly worked with transporting several shiploads of illicit sex toys to a prudish planet in Beta Sector. Then he waved at a bootlegger he'd fucked a couple of times. He was almost to the back of the room when he caught sight of the being he'd been looking for.

"How's it going, Ixi?"

Haz was greeted with a wide mouthful of yellowish fangs. "Haz Taylor. I heard you were dead."

"Yeah? Did you cry a few tears in my honor?"

Ixi's laugh sounded like metal going through a grinder, and his forked tongue flicked out and back in. "I should've known it wasn't true. You're too obnoxious for the death gods to want you."

When he waved a long-clawed hand, indicating that Haz and his group should join him, they took their seats.

Ixieccax was about the same height as an average adult human but built more solidly around the neck and chest. He had leathery greenish-gray skin and a scattering of white feathers on the flat crown of his head.

"You have a lot of friends today," he said. The spikes that ran down his bare back lay relaxed, and his golden eyes with the rectangular pupils seemed amused.

"You know my crew—Jaya Hirsch and Njeri Del Rio. And this is Mot."

Ixi peered at Mot's swathed face and shrugged. Many of Rick's patrons wore unusual clothing.

"So where have you been if not dead?"

"Next-worst thing. Stuck on Kepler."

"Ugh. I'd prefer death. That place is so… damp." Ixi's home planet was comprised of vast deserts.

"I was very happy to leave."

"And now here you are on Ankara-12. Are you still flying that pretty little ship?" Ixi's eyes glittered.

"I am, and she's better than ever, thanks to Jaya."

Jaya gave an acknowledging nod.

A waiter, slender and very pretty, made his way over. The pair of lavender gossamer wings fluttering on his back matched his eyes and hair.

"Drinks?" he trilled.

Haz and his crew all asked for whiskey, and Mot hesitantly followed their lead.

"This one's on me, Ixi," Haz said.

Ixi nodded and ordered a bottle of schlee syrup—expensive stuff that was mildly poisonous to humans but favored by his species. He and Haz made small talk for a few minutes, gossiping about some mutual acquaintances. Once their drinks arrived, however, they got down to business.

"Are you looking for a job?" Ixi asked. "There's a lady looking for someone to run a load of tkall wood, but the *Persistence* doesn't have the big payload your Molly does."

Under other circumstances, Haz might have been interested. It was legal to convey tkall, but there were high tariffs. A merchant might pay well to avoid those.

"Actually," he said after a fortifying sip, "I'm looking to hire."

"Really? Never thought a hotshot pilot like you would stoop to becoming a merchant."

Njeri snorted a laugh, which Haz ignored.

"I'm no merchant. Mot here needs to get home. His planet isn't Coalition."

"Yet," Ixi muttered darkly.

"Yeah. And it turns out that the Coalition doesn't want him to get there. It's… well, it's a long story, and I don't know all the details—not that they're all that important anyway. What matters is that if I try to get Mot home, they're going to kill us. And that's something I'd like to avoid."

Ixi's eyes were glittering. He stuck his long tongue into the bottle of syrup and slurped up some of the pink liquid, then flicked his tongue over his thin lips.

"Tell me what you're thinking."

"You take him instead, while I entertain the Coalition."

"Ahhhh. I see. And what are you offering in payment for this service?"

This was the other big hole in Haz's plan. Everyone at the table regarded him expectantly. Especially Jaya and Njeri, who knew Haz was broke.

Haz drank more whiskey, hoping it would grant him powers of persuasion.

"If Mot gets home safely, the Coalition will be both frustrated and embarrassed. And you'll have made that happen. That's worth a lot, I think."

Mot looked as if he were going to ask something, so Haz cut him off at the pass. "Ixi's not a big fan of our beloved government."

"Your government," Ixi hissed. He turned his head toward Mot. "My people were doing just fine. We didn't know the Coalition or other sentient life existed, and we didn't care. But my planet has rich deposits of blue waritronite. So the Coalition landed on my planet, pronounced my people primitive, and wiped out nearly half of us before claiming the planet for themselves. That was six generations ago, but I haven't forgotten. And I won't be an obedient citizen."

This time Mot spoke before Haz could stop him. "Is this true, Haz?"

"Yeah."

Ixi snorted. "These were my ancestors. I know the truth. The teachers and the vids tell lies about how savage we were and how lucky we are that the Coalition brought us technology and education and medicine. What they brought us was death and the end of my culture."

"Will they do that to my planet?"

"Yes," Njeri said, surprising everyone. "That's what they do. If you're lucky, they'll let you keep some vestiges of your customs to show tourists. Maybe some artwork in a museum or traditional dances that tourists can pay to watch."

Ixi nodded and slurped more of his syrup.

Mot faced Haz, who could barely make out the gleam of his eyes under the shadows of cloth.

"Did you know this?"

"When?"

"When you joined the navy."

"Not really. That sure as hell wasn't the version of reality we were taught on Ceres. But even if it was, I wouldn't have cared. I told you before: the navy was my ticket to flying. That's all that mattered."

A table not far away erupted into shouting. Two human men got to their feet, one of them violently enough to topple his chair. Everyone in Rick's—Haz's party included—turned their attention to the unfolding drama. The yelling escalated. One man pushed the other, who retaliated with a poorly aimed punch. The first man hit back. More blows were exchanged until, as if by magic, knives appeared in each man's hand.

Haz's hands had clenched into tight fists. He didn't know the combatants and didn't have a clue what they were fighting about, but he'd thrown himself into brawls like this before and now itched to join the fray. He wanted to feel cartilage give under his knuckles, to hear the wheezy *oof* of a man kneed hard in the balls, to lose himself in sweat and hot blood. Rick's used a damper shield, so he didn't have to worry about getting blasted, and a few fresh blade gouges would hardly matter at this point in his life. If he was still conscious when the fight ended, he'd get drunk. If not, he'd wait until he woke up to drown his liver. Either was fine with him. But today he sat with his hands aching and did nothing.

Eventually someone got stabbed bad enough to collapse. A few of Rick's employees appeared and dragged both men away, and all the customers returned to their previous conversations. Not surprisingly, that included Mot.

"You were in the navy for a while," he said. "You must have eventually realized what the Coalition was doing."

"What I was helping them do, you mean? Sure."

"And you still didn't care?"

"No, Mot. I didn't."

Haz had cared about his own welfare and the safety of the people aboard his ship. The rest of the galaxy, however, had meant nothing to him. Still didn't. And what did it matter whether a planet was ruled by the Coalition or someone else? Either way, those in power did everything they could to retain and expand their power, usually at the expense of everyone else. Beings of all species were selfish, greedy bastards, and the best anyone could do was look out for himself—and maybe a few of the people around him.

Ixi had been watching this interchange with great interest, a small smile playing at the corners of his mouth. "But now you want the Coalition to fail, Taylor?"

"I don't give a flying szot about the Coalition. I want them to not kill me, my crew, and… and the man who was entrusted to me."

He knew there was something wrong with his logic in that last part, considering it was the Coalition itself that had done the entrusting, but screw it. He was a pilot, not a philosopher.

He looked at Ixi. "But I know you give a flying szot about them."

"I do."

This was why Haz had been so pleased to see the *Persistence* in port. He knew that Ixi would be delighted to be a thorn in the Coalition's side.

"I can assure you that helping me out in this situation is the exact opposite of obedient citizenship. It might even foil the Coalition's plans to annex Mot's home. It'll certainly piss them off."

Ixi smiled. "That's all extremely tempting, if it's true." He spread his hands and addressed everyone else at the table. "Is it true?"

Mot shrugged. "I don't know. I don't understand politics." He shook his head slowly. "I don't understand much of anything."

"He hasn't lied to you," said Njeri. "My captain doesn't obey the law, and he doesn't always disclose all the facts people might want to know—he has a lot of other faults besides; I'd be happy to list them—but he rarely outright lies."

Jaya nodded in agreement.

Haz ducked his head to hide his pleasure. He hadn't expected such support from his crew.

Meanwhile, Ixi seemed to consider. The waiter brought them all a second round of drinks. Mot hadn't touched his first one, maybe because he couldn't sip it with the scarf around his mouth, so Haz drank both of Mot's before starting on his own refill. It was decent whiskey, and he might as well spend the last of his credits on something worthwhile.

At long last, Ixi spoke.

"You're right. I find the concept of doing some small harm to the Coalition appealing. But I'm a businessman, Taylor, not a revolutionary. I have expenses to cover and profits to be made. How much will you pay me?"

"You'll be able to call yourself a hero. You can brag to all your friends about what you did. That's worth something."

"It is. But credits pay my bills and provide for my retirement." Ixi's smile showed all of his teeth.

Haz looked down at his glass of whiskey, which was somehow empty again, and then met Ixi's gaze evenly.

"I'll give you Molly."

Njeri gasped, and Ixi blinked slowly with his two sets of lids.

"You're offering to sign over the *Dancing Molly* to me?"

"Yes." It was the most difficult single syllable Haz had ever uttered.

"I thought you needed her to divert the Coalition while I shuttle Mot home."

"I do." Haz raised his chin. "Molly and I will dance them into such confusion they won't remember their own names. And then we'll return here, and we'll wait for you, and when you get back I'll hand her over."

"But if the Coalition destroys you—which is likely—I'll have nothing."

Haz leaned back as if none of this mattered.

"It's a gamble. But you know my Molly—she's worth far more than you deserve for taxiing one man home." She was worth more than the *Persistence* or any of the buckets of bolts on Ankara-12. She was the only important thing Haz had ever possessed. "And I don't intend to let them destroy us."

For once, Ixi's expression was grave. After a moment's thought, he stuck out a hand. "I accept your offer."

Haz deftly avoided the long claws and shook Ixi's hand.

And then, on what he hoped would be steady legs, Haz stood.

"When can you leave?"

"The sooner the better, I take it?"

"Yes."

"In the morning, then. I'll need to lay in some food and supplies for my passenger."

Haz nodded and then turned to Mot.

"Good luck. Ixi's a good pilot. Not as good as me, but he'll get you home safe."

He had the feeling he should say more, but he had no idea what. So he gave a jerky nod, closed out the bill on his biotab, and marched out of Rick's.

CHAPTER FOURTEEN

HAZ BRIEFLY considered draining the last of his credits on the very handsome young man just outside of Rick's. He probably had enough left to pay for a damned good ride. But instead he shook his head at the man's offer and hopped into a waiting aircar. It took him directly back to Molly, where he still had booze stashed away.

"Oh darling, I'm sorry," he said from his seat on the bridge, about half a bottle later. "Ixi's a good guy, though. He'll treat you right."

Molly was silent, of course. Haz hadn't asked her to do anything.

"Y'know, with two ships to run, maybe Ixi'll hire me on as his pilot. Then I'll still get to fly you."

That was highly unlikely. Ixi would probably sell *Persistence*. And even if he chose to keep both ships, he'd want Molly for himself. Not that Haz could blame him.

God, he remembered when he'd first laid eyes on Molly. She had been in rough shape. Her previous owner hadn't appreciated her and had used her badly, choosing abandonment when neglect got the better of her. But her fine lines had remained, along with a sharp intelligence system that was just begging to do something more interesting than lugging legal cargo from place to place.

Haz had spent almost a stanyear and all his savings getting Molly into shape, and once he was done, she was dazzling. He'd secured some excellent contracts and soon earned a reputation as the captain-and-ship to hire for risky but lucrative runs. He'd been lucky enough to persuade Jaya and Njeri to join him, and Jaya had worked her magic to improve Molly beyond Haz's wildest dreams. Sure, he'd routinely blown his credits on booze, men, and gambling, but that didn't matter. He had Molly, and she was all he needed.

"You deserve better'n me anyway. Nobody's gonna fly you as well as me, but I bet Ixi won't get you shot at as often. And he's never short on credits for repairs and upgrades."

"Is there something you require of me?" Molly asked.

"Nah. You just sit tight. Tomorrow we'll have one last dance. We'll make it a good one."

"Do you wish me to program a route to your desired coordinates?"

Yeah, he ought to do that. He would no longer have Njeri to do it for him. "That'd be great, darling. We're heading for, um, hang on...." He leaned over a vidscreen in search of a likely place to engage the Coalition.

"Why are you trying to do that when you're too drunk to see straight?"

Haz goggled at Njeri and Jaya, who'd somehow managed to board without him noticing. Mot wasn't with them, of course. He was probably tucked away comfortably in the *Persistence*—unless he'd followed Haz's suggestion to get laid. If he wanted sex, he'd better get it on Ankara-12, because Ixi wouldn't be interested. He'd once told Haz that his only passions were profit and defying the Coalition.

"Came to get your stuff?" Haz asked his former crew. "Did you find a new gig already?"

He knew it wouldn't take them long. In the past, other captains had tried to lure them away. The women had always refused, although they could have earned more elsewhere. Maybe they stuck with Haz because they trusted him to keep them alive. Used to trust him. Between the narco fiasco and the current run-ins with the Coalition, he'd screwed that up.

"We have a ship," Njeri said.

Ignoring the stupid pang of jealousy, Haz raised his bottle in a salute.

"I hope it's a good one. I saw that piece of shit *Pluto's Ghost* in port. You didn't sign on with that one, did you? She's likely to fall apart before you leave the atmosphere."

"We didn't sign on to *Pluto's Ghost*. We're not stupid, Haz."

"Oh, I don't know about that," Jaya muttered darkly, her arms crossed.

"So what ship is it?"

Not that it mattered. Not that he cared.

"A pretty little thing with an asshole for a captain," Jaya said.

"That could describe a lotta ships."

Njeri marched over and snatched the whiskey bottle out of Haz's hand.

"We're flying on the *Dancing Molly*, you idiot. Captain Idiot, I mean."

Haz realized his mouth was hanging open.

"But... I can't pay you. I can't even pay you what I already owe you."

"We know."

"But—"

Jaya planted herself in front of him, scowl firmly in place.

"I've put a lot of work into getting Molly in tip-top shape, and I don't want to see that go to waste. Plus she's a lot more likely to survive unscathed if you don't face those qhek-fuckers on your fool lonesome."

Quite suddenly, Haz felt completely sober.

"Thank you," he said quietly. They weren't words he said often. Then he took a deep breath. "Njeri, we need to find a good location to lure the Coalition to. I was thinking—"

"Go get some sleep, Captain." For just a moment, Njeri put a hand on his shoulder. "I got this."

HAZ WOKE up early, absent a hangover and with a sense of purpose and excitement. Pretty soon he was going to be fighting the fuckers that the Coalition had sent to kill him and Mot. He might not win this one, but he'd have fun trying. And anyway, having what was left of his remains floating through the stars for eternity was better than having his carcass rot away on some miserable hunk of rock.

He took a quick shower, dressed, and hurried to the galley for coffee and breakfast. His leg was still reaping some benefit from whatever Mot had done to it, so Haz's limp was barely noticeable and the ache easy to overlook.

"You look cheery."

Having apparently picked up some fresh produce the previous day—God knew where—Njeri was making herself an enormous salad.

"I'm looking forward to making those Coalition qheks regret ever messing with us."

She responded with a bright smile. "Me too."

"I'm, uh, really glad you guys decided to stick with me. Shocked, but glad."

Huh. Revealing his feelings wasn't fatal. Who knew?

Njeri had a chopping knife in one hand. She paused with it in midair, then set it down on the work surface.

"If you don't get us killed, what are you going to do with yourself? Will you really sign Molly over to Ixi?"

"I don't go back on a deal I've agreed to."

"Yeah, I know." Her voice was soft. "But what will you do?"

"Somebody will hire me."

Njeri's expression said she knew how he'd responded when deprived of Molly on Kepler and that she didn't expect anything different in the future. Hell, maybe she was right. He could drink himself to death as easily on Ankara-12 as on Kepler, or get knifed in a fight, or… whatever. It didn't matter.

"Have you set a course?" he asked.

"Naturally. I found a nice little system close enough to Chov to fool them but distant enough to be well away from the *Persistence*."

"Good. I should probably let Ixi know where we're going, just in case. I want to make sure he avoids us."

"All right." She returned to her vegetables.

The bridge seemed oddly empty without Mot, even though he'd been there for only a short time and had mostly sat there watching.

"Idiot," Haz muttered at himself. Then, more loudly, "Molly, hail the *Persistence*, please. I need to talk to her captain."

"Confirmed. One moment."

Haz drummed his fingers on the armrest and tried to remember the tune Mot had hummed. He couldn't, though. Haz had never been musically inclined.

"Captain, *Persistence* reports that her captain is not currently on board."

"He's probably rounding up a few last-minute supplies. Tell her to have him ping me when he returns."

"Confirmed."

Haz bent over his vidscreen to look at the route Njeri had programmed. Not surprisingly, she'd chosen well. They'd get out of Kappa Sector quickly, since there was no longer much point in hiding out there, and then—

"Captain, Ixieccax wishes permission to board."

Shit. What now?

"Granted," Haz barked.

A few moments later, Ixi entered the bridge and looked around assessingly. "Not a bad arrangement."

"If you want a tour, you'll have to wait until after you get back from Chov X8."

"I didn't come here for a tour."

Anger boiled in Haz's veins and he shot out of his chair.

"If you're having second thoughts, it's too late. We made a deal, and it's a good one."

Ixi held up his hand placatingly. "That's also not why I'm here. Mot—"

"Just leave him alone, okay? He can't work the vidscreens himself since he doesn't have a biotab, but Jaya made him something…. Shit. I guess we can give you that, and—"

"Shut up, Haz." Ixi waited a beat, then sighed. "Mot's gone."

CHAPTER FIFTEEN

HAZ'S HEART clenched so tightly that it might have stopped beating.

"The Coalition sent assassins here? To Ankara-12?"

God, he should have warned Ixi to be more cautious with Mot. Haz shouldn't have been so certain that the Coalition couldn't reach its bloody fingers here.

"What? No, of course not." Ixi rolled his eyes. "He's not *dead* gone. At least as far as I know. I mean that he's missing. He left my ship."

The first emotion to hit Haz was relief, followed quickly by confusion and anger.

"Missing? What do you mean missing?"

"We left Rick's yesterday, and I took him to the *Persistence*. Showed him his quarters. Then I went to pick up supplies, and when I returned, he was gone. My ship told me he'd left not long after me. On his own, not kidnapped or forced by anyone. I hoped he'd return, but he hasn't, and I don't know where he went."

"Goddammit, why didn't you keep a closer watch on him?"

Ixi narrowed his eyes. "Because you led me to believe he was my passenger, not my prisoner. I didn't expect him to do a runner."

That was fair enough. And an excellent example of what Njeri had said in Rick's: that Haz sometimes omitted certain details. But he hadn't been thinking of Mot as a prisoner, not since Jaya got the chains off of him. Haz knew Mot wasn't exactly thrilled about returning home, but surely he realized the alternatives were worse.

"I thought he'd go with you," Haz admitted. "Are you sure he didn't just toddle off to get laid and fall asleep somewhere?"

"And how was he going to pay for his company? You said he doesn't have a biotab, right?"

Shit. Right.

"I'm sorry. This is why I carry cargo and not people. Far less trouble."

"Agreed. I have some other business to take care of, so I'll stay in port for another couple of days. If you find your wayward cargo on time, send him over. Maybe this time in irons." Ixi flicked his tongue out so far that it almost touched Haz. "But I'll be wanting an explanation for why he's reluctant."

"Me too. Um, about payment...."

"Not necessary until our contract is completed. She sure is pretty, though." Ixi patted a chair.

"She's the best in the galaxy."

Ixi nodded and headed for the exit, but Haz called after him. "If Mot shows up on your ship, let me know."

"Of course."

Jaya and Njeri entered the bridge as soon as Ixi was gone. While Njeri looked worried, Jaya was scowling again.

"Do you two know where he went?" Haz asked, assuming they'd listened in on his conversation with Ixi.

"How would we know that?" Jaya snapped.

"I don't know." Haz tried to control his growing unease. "Szot. He was gone all night, and it's cold out there. And he could be anywhere."

He didn't mention what they already knew—that Ankara-12 was a dangerous place for the naïve. As far as Haz was aware, Mot didn't know how to fight, and he was probably unarmed. A clear image appeared in Haz's head of Mot slumped between buildings, tattoos torn by a blade and stained by blood, those odd-colored eyes clouded over and sightless.

"It'd be his own fucking fault," he muttered, but it didn't loosen the knot in his gut.

Njeri strode toward her chair and began poking at the vidscreen. "I'll divide Paa into thirds and we'll each take a section. I'll map routes to get us through as efficiently as possible."

Although Haz nodded, he wasn't optimistic. Paa might not be a big city, but it would still take three people a number of days to search every nook and cranny. If Mot was in trouble, they didn't have days. And if he was somehow hale and hearty, he could easily slip around and evade them.

Dammit, Haz was a professional! He didn't lose things that had been entrusted to him.

"Do you wish to locate Mot?" Molly sounded chipper.

"Yeah, Moll."

"I can track him."

All three humans looked at one another in surprise, but it was Jaya who spoke. "He doesn't have a biotab."

"Affirmative. I can look for all homo sapiens in this hemisphere and find the one who has no electronic implant."

Before Jaya could ask more, Haz cut her off. "You can do that? Track every human on a planet?"

"I can track any species, but in this situation I would focus on_yours."

"Have you always been able to do that?"

"No." Molly sounded slightly exasperated. "I added the coding when we were on Kepler. I only needed to keep track of you, but the program's more general purpose than that."

Molly had reprogrammed herself so she could keep an eye on him, even though it had been his fault that she was badly banged up and stuck in dry dock. Haz needed to process that information, but there wasn't time for it now.

"Can you please find Mot, darling?"

"Confirmed. The data are extensive. This will take some time."

"Okay."

Jaya, who looked nearly as astonished as Haz felt, sat down to stare at a vidscreen, probably so she could watch the processing in action. Her mapping skills no longer required, Njeri simply stared at Haz, as if she expected him to grow horns.

"What?" he demanded.

"Nothing."

Molly's definition of "some time" was different than a human's, and in less than five minutes she made a satisfied beep.

"I have located Mot."

A wave of relief washed through Haz; he tried to hide it with a frown.

"Thanks, Molly. Where is the little shit? I'm going to wring his—"

"His vital signs are poor."

The relief changed instantly to alarm. "What—"

"Mot is hypothermic. I have sent his location coordinates to your biotab."

Haz was moving even before Molly finished speaking.

"Njeri, can you come with me?" he shouted as he ran down the corridor to grab a first aid kit. He hastily tugged on outerwear as Njeri did the same. "Jaya, please set up—"

"Treatment. I know. Go. I've already called an aircar."

Sure enough, the aircar waited at the bottom of the gangway. Even though Haz closed the top of the car as soon as he and Njeri boarded, he kept shivering. It seemed like an especially cold morning, even for Ankara-12. Following the coordinates from Haz's biotab, the car moved away from central Paa rather than toward it.

"Where the hell was he going?" Haz peered through the window as if searching, even though he knew they had a way to go.

"Out into the bush, looks like." Njeri looked grim.

That made no sense. There was nothing for Mot in the bush. Nothing for anyone, really. Ankara-12 grew no crops and had no settlements aside from the three port cities, which were set widely apart. There was nothing in the bush apart from rocks, low scrubby plants, and some worms. The only water flowed in aquifers deep below the permafrost, and there was no shelter, no food, nothing to sustain human life.

Although the car was going at top speed, the journey seemed interminable. Haz and Njeri didn't speak. Even if she had spoken, he might not have heard her over the thudding of his heart.

"There he is!" Haz shouted. Unnecessarily, really, because what else could that small dark shape huddled on the sage-gray ground be?

He slapped the car's dash as if that might make it go faster.

When they reached Mot, Haz flipped open the top and hopped out before the car had fully stopped. He threw himself to his knees beside the still body, ignoring the jolt of pain.

"Mot? Mot?"

The scarf and gloves were gone, and Mot's hood was pushed back, his cloak partially unfastened. Sometimes in the delirium of hypothermia, people mistakenly felt too hot and began to strip. Perhaps that had happened with Mot. His eyes were closed, his skin cold, and Haz couldn't discern any breathing.

With Njeri's assistance, he wrapped Mot in the thermal sheet from the first aid kit. The sheet would keep him from losing more body heat, but it couldn't reverse the harm that had already happened. Haz lifted Mot's upper body.

"His feet," Haz grunted, and Njeri complied.

Lifting him into the car wasn't easy, but eventually they got him arranged more or less upright between their bodies. Haz closed the top, and as they sped back to port, Njeri scanned Mot's vitals.

"He's at just over twenty-three degrees. Asystolic—no, wait. There's a heartbeat, but it's very slow and weak."

"So he's alive."

She gave him a bleak look. "Barely."

"Goddammit, can't we get the heat turned up in this piece of shit?"

"Don't. At this point, it could put him into cardiac arrest. He needs to be warmed up from the inside, Haz."

"Szot. Yeah, okay."

Haz had known that—he'd received some basic medical training in the navy. But it was hard to think rationally when Mot leaned against him as stiff and unresponsive as a corpse.

"What was he doing?" he whispered.

"Escaping."

"But why? How could freezing to death in the middle of nowhere possibly be an improvement over going home?"

Njeri simply shook her head.

Jaya met them outside Molly and helped carry Mot inside. The ship didn't have a medical bay, but Haz kept a storage locker well stocked with supplies and equipment, and there was a rolling cart that could transform any space into a makeshift ward. Since Jaya hadn't yet changed Mot's quarters back into her meditation room, they took him there and laid him on the bunk.

When Haz stepped in close, Jaya pushed him firmly away and out the door.

"Go get drunk," she ordered.

"But—"

"There's nothing you can do here except get in the way. You want to make sure he dies? Then by all means, interfere."

Haz growled but moved away. He stopped to shed and stow his outwear and then found the first aid kit on the bridge, where someone had dumped it. He made sure it was in good condition before putting it away.

"Molly, remind me to replace that thermal sheet next time I get supplies."

"Confirmed."

He went to the galley and snatched a bottle of whiskey, which he carried into the rec area. His own quarters would have been preferable, but that was too close to Mot. Sprawling in a wide, comfortable chair, he tried very hard not to think about the man who might already be dead on his ship—and even more bothersome, why Haz cared.

Haz Taylor didn't give a shit about anyone but himself. He never had. Well, all right, once upon a time he'd worried about the soldiers serving under him, but that had been his job. He'd taken an oath to protect them as best he could. And yes, he cared about Molly. Of course he did! He was a captain and she was his ship. Without her, he had no home and no way to earn a living. So it was really a completely selfish thing. As for his crew, he cared about them only because they were very skilled and he didn't fancy having to replace them.

But Mot wasn't his job, not really. After all, Kasabian had lied through her teeth about what was going on. And Mot would apparently rather freeze to death than submit to Haz's help. Whether Mot lived or died, he wouldn't benefit Haz. No, strike that. In fact, Haz was better off if Mot's heart stopped and remained still. Everything would be easier that way.

So why did the very thought make Haz's throat feel tight and his eyes burn?

He hadn't yet uncapped the whiskey, and now he set aside the bottle. Staring at nothing, he felt... alone. Which was stupid. Haz was always alone. Had been even as a boy, crammed into a tiny, dirty house with his parents and numerous siblings. Haz hadn't just sought solitude; he'd reveled in it. Seclusion was as much a part of him as his skin and bones.

"Thank you, Molly." His voice came out soft and hesitant. "For finding him."

"You're welcome."

He paused a long time before speaking again.

"How... how's he doing?"

Haz squeezed his eyes closed as if that could insulate him from bad news.

"We are giving him warm intravenous fluids and warm, humidified oxygen via mask."

"But how's he—"

"Treatment must be gradual to avoid damage to the heart or other tissues."

Haz, who was terrible at being patient, leaned forward and hid his face in his hands.

"YOU'RE NOT drunk."

Jaya sat down and swiveled her chair to face him.

"I guess not. How's...." He looked away instead of finishing.

"Breathing. Heart's got a nice sinus rhythm. Temp's up."

"He's going to live?"

Jaya snorted. "I can't predict the future. But yeah, probably."

The tightness in Haz's chest loosened and he took what felt like his first full inhalation in hours.

"Good. 'Cause I want to wring his fool neck."

"Hmm." She leaned over, grabbed the whiskey bottle, and cracked the seal. After a long swallow, she offered it to him, but he shook his head. "What are your plans, Captain?"

Plans. He was supposed to have those.

"I dunno. If he heals enough, I'll take him over to the *Persistence* and we can proceed as originally intended. If not, I guess I'll have to find someone instead of Ixi to take him."

That was going to be a challenge. There weren't many pilots he'd trust with the job, and even fewer would accept without guaranteed payment.

Instead of answering, she took another sip. She'd colored her curly hair bright purple, and Haz couldn't for the life of him remember whether that was recent or if she'd done it days ago. And were those new lines at the corners of her mouth? If so, they were probably his fault.

"Why'd you join the navy?" he asked.

If Jaya appeared startled by his question, he didn't blame her. He hadn't expected to ask. But after a moment she put down the bottle and her gaze went unfocused. And then she smiled.

"I did it to impress a girl."

"Seriously?"

"Her name was Chantrea Toivonen, and she was stunning. Smart too. We had classes together, and her scores were always at the top. I couldn't woo her by getting better marks than her, so I decided I needed to be daring and brave instead. So I enlisted." She laughed, a rare thing for Jaya. "It didn't occur to me that enlisting meant I'd get shipped half a galaxy away from her."

"What happened to her?"

Jaya shrugged. "Don't know, don't care. I met Njeri, didn't I?"

"But the shit you had to do in the navy...."

Haz knew exactly what she'd done because they'd served together. She wasn't on the *Star of Omaha*, but there had been plenty of killing and misadventures before that trip.

"Can't undo it. I think mostly I made the best decisions I could, given who I was and where I was. And I learned from my mistakes."

Haz wasn't sure he'd ever learned anything except how to fight and how to fly. His brain wasn't wired for wisdom.

For what felt like hours, Haz said nothing and neither did Jaya. Although his mind chased itself in futile circles and his leg throbbed, there was a certain degree of peace in the room. As if Jaya's usually caustic presence was just what he needed.

"Do you think he wanted to die?" Haz finally asked. "Or did he just miscalculate?"

"Dunno. You can ask him yourself if he wakes up."

"I mean, I get it. His life at home was pretty miserable. No family, no freedom, and all those szotting needles. But lots of people have shitty lives—and still find them worth living."

He wasn't usually this philosophical. Maybe it was because he wasn't drunk.

"From what I hear, you weren't doing much living on Kepler."

Haz winced. Now that he thought about it, the only thing that had kept him from death on Kepler was cowardice. He hadn't quite had the bravery to just throw in the towel. Did that make Mot's run into the bush an act of courage?

"Man, I wish I knew what he was thinking when he left the *Persistence*."

The big vidscreen on the nearby bulkhead lit up with 3D images of human figures marching in two straight lines across a green landscape. Haz glanced at his biotab, but it didn't seem to be malfunctioning.

"Molly, what the hell?" He wasn't in the mood for entertainment.

An otherwise well-modulated female voice blared out loudly enough to make Haz and Jaya jump.

"—plays an important part in their daily and political lives."

The voice used that particular tone unique to narrators who sought to educate their audience. It gave Haz unpleasant flashbacks to the classes he'd been forced to take in the navy.

He opened his mouth to object, but the vid image shifted to show the person walking at the front of the columns. It was Mot. No—on closer inspection Haz realized this man was taller and thinner than Mot, with a longer face and jutting ears. But he had the same pattern of tattoos covering every bit of his hairless, naked body, and even his eyes were inked.

Falling back into his seat, Haz listened more closely to the narration.

"The processions can last for many days, with all the townsfolk and villagers rushing out to greet the Machine and the priests."

The vid showed exactly that, a crowd of people in colorful clothes and ornate jewelry lining a narrow road, waving and cheering as the marchers passed. The priests smiled and waved back, but the tattooed man's face remained expressionless and his gaze straight ahead. Little puffs of dirt rose with his footsteps; even his soles had been inked.

"The Machine spends one moon cycle in each of the fifteen temples." The image showed a stone building with an ornately carved façade, then zoomed inside to a large ceremonial chamber.

"The priests meet with the locals during this time. They provide religious education and counsel, and the locals are expected to make generous donations. The Machine itself is not on display, however. It's kept in a special chamber which the Chovians believe assists the Great Divine to channel blessings into the temple and its occupants."

The chamber was only a little larger than Haz's quarters. The floor, walls, and ceiling were of pale stone, uninterrupted except for two windows about the size of a man's hand. The room contained only a sink, a toilet, a narrow stone bed covered by a thick gray blanket, and some kind of light source built into the ceiling. A series of red-and-black images much like Mot's tattoos ran along the top of the walls, but there were no other adornments.

God, how much of Mot's life had been spent in rooms like that one, alone, with nothing to do except gaze out the tiny windows? Maybe that was why he'd run into the bush. After so much confinement, the openness must have appealed to him.

The image shifted to another parade of priests and Machine, this time walking through a village with wood-and-stone buildings.

"When the moon cycle completes, the Machine is moved to the next temple. It will stay at all fifteen temples before returning to the first and repeating the sequence. According to the Chovians, this ensures that the Great Divine favors the entire planet equally."

A cartoon-like image showed the whole planet slowly rotating, with little dotted lines depicting what Haz assumed was the Machine's path.

Chov X8 had a lot of ocean, a few tiny islands, and only one continent, allowing all of the temples to be reached on foot. He wondered whether Njeri would approve of the route.

"When the Chovian government seeks a boon from the deity or, later, wishes to thank the deity, new marks are placed on the Machine. To the trained eye, the Machine serves as a visual record of all important matters that have occurred in recent years."

The vid first depicted a group of men and women seated in tiered rows with a long table at the center. They seemed to be arguing, but the audio quality wasn't sharp enough to make out particular words. Then there was the Machine seated on a stone chair while a priest sat on a low bench in front of him, tapping a needle-and-stick device against the Machine's ribs. Even in the small images of the vid, the Machine looked as if he was in pain. His eyes were closed, his jaw clenched, his muscles tight.

"I get it, Molly," Haz said. "His life at home was miserable."

But Molly didn't stop the vid, which went on to show the Machine taking part in a few ceremonies—mostly by standing there and being stared at—and Chovian officials having meetings. At that point, the narrative backtracked to explain how the Machines were conceived and raised. It was all perfectly horrible, and anyway Haz already knew the basics if not the details. He wanted to order Molly to turn it off, but he couldn't get the words out. Somehow, stopping the vid would feel as if he were betraying Mot.

"Those qhek-fuckers," Jaya murmured when the vid showed a young boy sobbing while adults held him down and tattooed his pale-skinned arm. It was even worse to know that once the design was finished, nobody would comfort the child. He'd be returned to a bare room with no toys, no family, no friends, and left to cry on his hard bed.

Haz decided that had been the worst thing he'd ever seen.

Yet the vid continued.

"It is important that the Machine remain in excellent condition since it is a way of honoring the Great Divine. Its diet is carefully monitored, as is its health. When it becomes old enough that it is no longer in peak condition, the Machine is retired and replaced with a new one."

"Oh no," Haz moaned.

Retired. He had a definite premonition that this retirement didn't involve moving to Newton and playing golf.

The vid showed the Machine in a temple, surrounded by a gaggle of chanting priests. He looked terrified, his eyes wide and his chest heaving, but he was chained tightly to a pillar and couldn't escape. Tears tracked down his cheeks as he bit his decorated lip.

"No." Haz's whisper was so quiet that even he couldn't hear it.

A priest wearing layered red, black, and yellow robes and an elaborate headdress approached the Machine. He held an old-fashioned hypodermic needle. While the Machine looked at him pleadingly, the priest held up the needle and said a short prayer, something about gifts to the Great Divine. Then he sank the needle deeply into the Machine's chest, just over his heart, and depressed the plunger.

The Machine—God, no! the man—jerked and gasped. The priests fell silent, watching. He made a terrible thin cry that sounded barely human, and then after a few violent spasms, his eyes clouded over and he sagged lifelessly in his bonds.

The narrator said something about preparation of the body, but Haz couldn't make out the specifics over the roaring in his ears. Then the vid shifted to show an enormous temple, much grander than the others. Inside was a long stone hall lined with dozens and dozens of pedestals, each displaying the preserved corpse of a tattooed man.

The vidscreen went blank.

Jaya swigged heavily from the whiskey bottle, swallowing the amber liquid again and again. But Haz remained as still as one of those dead Machines, as cold as Mot's hands had been in the aircar.

He tried swallowing several times before his throat finally worked, and even then, his voice came out like shredded metal.

"Molly? At what age is a Machine retired?"

She answered him promptly. "The day he reaches thirty stanyears."

What had Mot said, that day when Haz was telling him his history? The words echoed in Haz's brain: *I'm almost thirty now, and I've never even been in charge of myself.*

Oh, fuck.

Chapter Sixteen

Jaya's glare was so fierce that Haz was tempted to check whether it had left a bleeding wound.

"And you didn't know they were going to murder him?" she growled.

"No! He didn't tell me. I just thought he'd have to return to trudging from temple to temple." He eyed the whiskey but didn't reach for it. She probably wouldn't let him have it anyway. "Remember, I didn't even know he was a person until they dumped him on my ship. They said I was delivering an artifact. I thought it would be a statue or… a painting. Or something."

Her eyes had narrowed to slits and she'd bared her teeth.

"You knew which planet you'd be flying to. You could have learned all of this long ago if you'd bothered to do your fucking research."

She was shouting now. It was the first time he'd heard her raise her voice. Even when Jaya and Njeri had learned about the narcos—and almost been killed—it was Njeri who'd yelled. Jaya had seethed silently. But not now.

Haz had no real defense; Jaya was right. He could have asked Molly at any time to give him information about Chov X8 and their religious practices, but he hadn't because he didn't like to think about religion. It left a bad taste in his mouth.

"Such a selfish ass," Jaya continued. "Acting as if you're the only one in the galaxy who matters—and you don't even take care of yourself most of the time."

He nodded wearily. She was right. He'd always figured that since nobody gave a crap about him, there was no reason for him to care about them. It had felt like a reasonable philosophy. But look where it had landed him.

"I won't take him to Chov," he said quietly.

"But you'll get someone else to do it. Ixi will probably refuse if he hears the whole story, but you'll find someone in port who's as soulless as you."

"No."

"No what?"

Haz sighed. "I won't let him be dragged back there to die. But God, Jaya, what am I supposed to do instead? If he's not back home, he'll be murdered anyway—by the Coalition instead of priests."

Jaya's expression had softened considerably. "And us along with him."

"You can leave any time. They won't come after you, I don't think."

"And you?"

His smile hurt. "I'm dead already. My body just hasn't got the message yet."

"Hmm." She put down the bottle, which held a lot less liquid than it used to, and stared at him. "You know, you've escaped from some pretty tight spots before."

Haz remembered his father beating him with a rod after Haz had committed some transgression.

"My father said I had the devil in me. Maybe the devil looks out for me." He grew more serious. "But not necessarily the people around me. A hundred and eight people died on the *Star of Omaha*."

"And almost nine hundred survived."

That was true. He forgot that, sometimes.

"Molly, if you're so smart, give me a solution. How do I save Mot's neck and my own?"

"Let me embrace thee, sour adversity, for wise men say it is the wisest course."

"More Shakespeare, darling?"

"*Henry VI*, part 3," Molly replied. "One of its major themes is lust for power."

"Well, that's dandy. But not especially practical. I don't think the navy's gonna back off if I quote ancient plays at 'em." Maybe they would if he sang, though. His inability to carry a tune could be a powerful and painful weapon.

Haz stood and stretched.

"I need some exercise," he told Jaya. "Maybe that will help my brain. Um, call me if there's any change in Mot's condition, please."

Jaya nodded. "Copy that, Captain."

ONE OF Haz's few luxuries was the tiny gym in a corner of the cargo hold. It contained one machine for working on muscle strength and another for cardiovascular conditioning. When Molly was in flight, she could reduce the g-force inside the gym, which took a lot of the strain off Haz's leg. His workout not only kept up his physical health within the confines of the ship but benefited his mental health as well. Working himself into an exhausted, sweaty heap was the next best thing to fighting.

Here in port, there was nothing Molly could do about gravity, so Haz skipped any exercises that required him to use his legs. He also decreased the resistance on the machine, now that the planet was fighting him as he tried to lift weights.

It wasn't the most satisfactory workout, but it was better than nothing—and a lot better than trying to think himself out of an impossible situation. Himself and Mot. And, apparently, Jaya and Njeri, who didn't yet seem inclined to abandon him.

Every time Haz considered leaving the gym, that szotting vid would replay in his mind, and he'd see that tattooed man writhing in agony as he died. Or worse, he'd see the long temple hallway lined with corpses waiting for Mot to join them. Then he'd increase the resistance and keep on lifting.

Even when sweat stung his eyes, blinding him, he clearly saw those dead men.

"Not… my… fault," he panted as he pushed the metal bar upward. "Not… my… responsibility," as he held it aloft. He let the bar down, then poked at the controls to increase the weight again. He could barely lift it now, but he grunted and strained, arms shaking with effort.

"People… die. That's how… the universe… works." On the last word he heaved the bar as high as it would go—and then screamed when something tore inside his left shoulder. His arm went suddenly weak and he dropped the bar, which clanked back into place against the machine.

Swearing steadily at himself, he wiped some sweat away with a towel and left the gym. Climbing the ladder out of the cargo hold was no joy—one arm useless and his leg as unhelpful as ever—but he made it. He started to head toward the closet with the medcart until he remembered that, in fact, the cart was currently in use.

"Idiot," he muttered.

Njeri looked up sharply when he entered Mot's room. She'd brought in a chair and was sitting near Mot's bedside with a portable vidscreen in her hands. Mot lay unmoving under several thick blankets, an oxygen mask over the lower half of his face and several tubes snaking from the medcart under the blankets and, presumably, into his body.

"How is he?"

"His temp's at thirty-two. Heartbeat, blood pressure, and respiration strong."

Despite the pain from his injury, some of the weight on Haz's shoulders lifted.

"He'll be okay?"

"Most likely. He's lightly sedated now, but he should be awake by this evening. Why the hell are you holding your arm like that?"

Haz hadn't been aware, and he looked down at the limb with mild surprise.

"I overdid it in the gym."

With a dramatic sigh, she stood and set the vidscreen on the chair. She plucked a small scanner from the cart and held it near his shoulder, clucking when her biotab gave her the results.

"Congratulations. You tore one of the tendons in your rotator cuff."

"Shit."

"Hang on." Njeri set down the scanner and picked up another device. This one made him wince; the doctors had used it on his leg. "This is going to hurt," she said cheerfully as she approached him.

He took a step back.

"Then don't use it."

"You want to try flying one-handed? Or if you get in a fight—and you're sorta overdue—you won't need this arm?"

It was his turn to sigh. "Fine."

He held very still while she ran the device over his shoulder. It worked fine through fabric, which was good; taking off his shirt would have been miserable. The little machine sent out signals that healed the damaged tissue, and Haz firmly clenched his jaw to keep from yelling as the wound mended with a rapidity unnatural for the human body. When Njeri was done, he sank inelegantly onto the floor and tried to catch his breath without puking.

"Try not to move it for a couple of hours. You want a sling?"

"No."

"Suit yourself."

She briefly put both devices into the disinfecting drawer before stowing them back on the medcart. Then, hands on hips, she looked down at him.

"You know, tearing yourself apart isn't going to solve anything."

"I was exercising."

"Uh-huh."

She stared at him. Waiting.

"Did Jaya tell you—"

"About the vid. Yeah."

Haz squeezed his eyes closed.

"I should've researched. I should've known."

"Well, now you do. And it's not too late, so what are you going to do about it?"

He opened his eyes. *Not too late.* God, Njeri was right. Mot wasn't dead yet, and he wasn't on Chov or back in the Coalition's grip. The Ankara wilderness hadn't killed him either. Their hope might be thin indeed, but it was still there.

Ignoring the lingering ache in his shoulder and the usual twinge in his leg, Haz stood.

"I'm going to figure this out."

"Good. Now get out of here and take a shower. You stink."

Njeri was right; Haz was offending his own nose. He stepped into his quarters, stripped, and took a fast shower, washing the armpit of the healing shoulder with caution. Hair still damp, he put on fresh clothing and sat at his small desk.

"Molly, I need help."

"How can I assist?"

"Make me smarter."

"That is outside of my capabilities."

"You can be my conscience but not my brain?" He leaned back in his chair.

"I am not your conscience. I provide you with information. What you do with that information is up to you."

"Right."

He stared at the ceiling, which was unadorned and unhelpful. His plain walls didn't help either. Was it weird that he had no decorations at all, not a single keepsake from anywhere he'd been or anything he'd done? Mot had seemed to think so, and he'd spent his whole life in cells that were essentially bare.

Haz shook his head in hopes of focusing.

"We need to get ourselves, Mot included, somewhere safe. Where the Coalition can't touch us and there's no risk of Mot being taken back to Chov X8. And while we're at it, how about whiskey fountains and card games I can never lose."

"What are your assets?" Molly asked, ignoring his sarcasm.

"Pretty much zilch, credit-wise. I've got... my skills as a pilot. I'm still damned good. I've got a kickass crew. And the best ship in the galaxy." He leaned forward to pat the bulkhead. "I guess that's about it."

"Allies?"

"Aw, c'mon, darling. You know me. I work alone."

"Do you?" she asked crisply.

"Well, there's my crew. But I already mentioned them. And we've got all of Chov and the whole szotting Coalition against us."

"Amicus meus, inimicus inimici mei."

"You're going to have to translate that for me, Moll."

She made a sound that, had she been human, he would have interpreted as a chuckle. "My friend, the enemy of my enemy."

"More Shakespeare?"

"No. It's a restatement of a quote from the Arthashastra, a Sanskrit book on military strategy from the fourth century BCE."

Normally Haz would have made a snide comment about the unwanted history lesson. Instead, he thought about the words. *The enemy of my enemy.* Well, he knew who his most dangerous enemy was: the Coalition. So who did he know who hated them?

"Molly, you're a genius. Ping Ixieccax for me, please."

CHAPTER SEVENTEEN

IXI SAT in Molly's rec area, a bottle of schlee syrup in hand. He'd had to bring his own since Haz didn't have any on board, but Ixi had been happy to gobble a snack—spiced protein chunks—that Jaya had made from Molly's recipe. He said it tasted very much like a particular species of beetle that was a favored meal on his home planet.

"A little less crunchy, but the flavor's spot-on."

Haz, who was happier with whiskey and a sandwich, smiled.

"I'm glad to hear that. And I appreciate you joining us."

"Are you kidding? I wouldn't miss this for anything. This is where you tell me the information you left out before."

"I didn't so much leave it out as not know it. I learned more after we found Mot." He winced. "Stuff I probably should have looked into much earlier."

"I don't know about that. As smugglers, we're generally better off if we don't ask too many questions. I think that's why I'm not rich yet. I get nosy and consequently earn less." Ixi flicked out his tongue to almost its full extent, a gesture that indicated humor. "Now satisfy my curiosity."

Haz told him everything that had happened, beginning when Kasabian first walked into the bar on Kepler and ending with Mot tucked warmly into bed on Molly, his body temperature now normal. Njeri was still keeping an eye on Mot, but Jaya was here in the rec area, sometimes adding a detail or two to Haz's tale.

Ixi listened gravely, his eyes unblinking. He seemed to have forgotten about the bottle of syrup. When Haz finished, Ixi remained quiet for a long time. Then he hissed long and loud and slurped a lot of syrup.

"I'm guessing you invited me here for reasons other than wanting to regale me with your latest adventures."

"Not that I don't enjoy your company, but yeah."

"Do you still wish me to take Mot home?"

"No!" Haz startled himself with the vehemence of his response. "That's permanently off the table."

"Good. I'm no executioner's lackey."

Haz straightened his shoulders. "I need information, Ixi. About a small thing and a big thing. And I can't pay you—not with credits, not with Molly. I need her."

"We can pay," Jaya said.

Haz and Ixi both goggled at her, and Jaya shrugged.

"Unlike our captain, Njeri and I can hang on to credits. We've been saving them up for years. And Haz is going to get us killed before we can spend them, so we might as well give them to you."

Tears prickled Haz's eyes.

"You don't have to—"

"You think this is just your problem, Hazarmaveth Taylor? We're here too. We don't want to lose Molly, and we'd rather Mot survive." Jaya looked at Ixi. "Mot grows on you. Like a pesky little vregzul that asks too many questions."

"I can't repay you for this," Haz pointed out.

She gave him a sharp smile. "Jebiga, Captain." Then she said to Ixi, "We can pay."

Ixi looked fascinated. "No matter how much time I spend with humans, they still surprise me. Tell me what information you need."

That was promising, Haz thought. "The small thing first. I need someone to set up false biotab IDs for me and my crew so the Coalition can't trace us." The Coalition wasn't supposed to do that—there were privacy laws in place—but Haz doubted they abided by those laws very scrupulously. "And assuming Mot's agreeable, I want him to have a biotab too. Life's too hard without one."

Ixi nodded thoughtfully. "I know someone who could do these things."

"I thought you might. Are they on Ankara-12?"

"Yes. I could get you to her as soon as Mot's able to go."

Having that much settled was a relief. But the big ask was still to come.

"Ixi, we need refuge. Eventually the Coalition will come after us—here on Ankara-12, on any Coalition territory, and even on independent planets." After all, they had easily snatched Mot off Chov X8. "I've considered leaving the galaxy, but that's too uncertain."

Nobody who had left the galaxy had returned. Maybe they hadn't wanted to, or maybe they couldn't. Some theorists claimed that quantum drives would quit working outside the galaxy, leaving a voyager to float aimlessly until they ran out of food. Maybe something fierce and lethal waited in the unknown. Haz might have been willing to risk it on his own, but not with his crew—and not with Mot.

"You've just ruled everyplace out," Ixi said, in a tone that sounded artificially casual.

Haz leaned toward him. "I've heard rumors."

"Rarely worth the air it takes to repeat them," Ixi replied.

"True. But these whispers say there's a resistance movement out there. A band willing to take on the Coalition, to do it harm when possible. If that's true, the movement must have some safe locations to work from. That's what we need."

In fact, Haz had heard something more substantial than rumors. On two occasions, acquaintances had asked him to join the Resistance. They needed his talents, they'd said, but Haz refused. He had not been sure that such revolutionaries truly existed, and even if they did, they'd have to make do without him. He didn't like lost causes, and he was done fighting for anyone but himself.

But that was before Mot.

Ixi's tongue flickered. "Did I just hear Haz Taylor say he'd take a risk for someone else?"

"For particular someones, yes."

"And that he's willing to actually cooperate with others?"

Haz simply gave him a look.

"The Coalition is huge and powerful," Ixi said. "Only a fool would go against them."

Haz shrugged. "I am a fool."

Ixi regarded Haz for a long time. Then he stood and marched across the room in his usual loose-limbed manner. He stood facing the bulkhead, his long thin tail slightly swaying. Haz assumed Ixi was thinking, although for all he knew, he might be getting ready to attack. His bites were venomous, he'd once told Haz rather proudly.

When Ixi turned back, he didn't look murderous but, instead, thoughtful. "We've known each other for a few years."

"Yes," Haz agreed cautiously.

"Worked together once or twice. Drank together. And I've heard gossip about you too."

Haz pulled a face. He didn't know what people said behind his back, but he guessed half of it was lies and none of it was good.

But Ixi wasn't through speaking. "We're not really friends, though."

"I don't have any friends."

"If you say so. My point, Haz, is that I'm not sure how much I can trust you."

The words didn't hurt because Haz knew they made sense. He wasn't an honest man—he freely admitted that—and although he liked to think he lived by his own moral code, that code had a lot of flexibility. His own interests and welfare were always his first priorities.

Since Ixi seemed to be waiting for a response, Haz shrugged. "Hell, if I were you I wouldn't trust me either. You have no reason to, and I have no way of proving myself."

"And there's a lot to lose, either way," Ixi said. He heaved a long, hissing breath. "I need time to think. I'm not good at quick decisions. Give me until tomorrow, and then I'll have an answer for you."

"Thank you. For considering it."

Ixi flicked out his tongue.

"I might not trust you, but I like you. Anyway, in the meantime I can at least help with your biotab problem." He poked at his own biotab briefly, and Haz felt the buzz of incoming information. "Go there in the morning. If I decide to help with the other thing, I'll return here in the afternoon. So if I don't show up...."

"We're on our own. Got it."

"And in that case, I'll still wish you good luck."

"WHAT WOULD you guys have done with all your credits if I hadn't flown back into your lives?"

Jaya was already annoyed that he'd followed her into engineering, and Haz's attempts at chitchat didn't improve her mood. Which was fine with him. He was filled with an unsettling combination of boredom, restlessness, and anxiety, but his healing shoulder precluded him from going into town and picking a fight with a stranger. He'd have to settle for needling Jaya.

She didn't even look up from the vidscreen. "Saved them."

"Yeah, but for what?"

"Old age."

Oh, that. He'd never had a similar inclination because he assumed he wouldn't live long enough to get old. He was fairly surprised he'd made it past forty, in fact.

"But were you really happy sitting there on Newton? Didn't you miss flying?"

A quick emotion danced across her face, but Haz couldn't interpret it. "We were talking about signing on with one of the companies that shuttles tourists to and from Newton. Part-time."

"You were going to be a bus driver?"

That was a serious insult among pilots, a reference to some long-extinct mode of Earth transportation that had lacked drama or excitement. Haz had once taken such a job, but only because the alternative was to go back to Ceres and return to digging in the dirt.

"It's flying. Somebody's gotta do it, and it's a lot less likely to get you vaporized."

"I guess." Haz drummed his fingers on a metal conduit. "But I don't believe that's really what you want. Not either of you. You guys don't play it safe."

"Maybe we love each other," she snapped. "Maybe we're willing to put up with some mediocrity if it means we get to spend longer together."

Her words made Haz's chest ache a little, as if he'd torn something in there as well. He'd never had any reason to give up danger. No one worth living for. He wondered if Jaya regretted it and would rather be totally free, but before he could ask, Molly spoke.

"Captain, Njeri requests you in Mot's room. He's awake."

Haz hurried up the ladder.

Mot was no longer connected to the mask and tubes, and the medcart had been pushed into a corner. But he was buried under what seemed to be every blanket on the ship. He blinked sleepily at Haz.

"He's still very lightly sedated," Njeri said before Haz could get too close. "His body's undergone a lot of strain and it needs to rest."

"Okay." Haz looked past her to the still figure on the bunk. "Why don't you go get some rest yourself? I can sit with him for a while."

Njeri raised her eyebrows. "Molly can monitor him."

True enough, and maybe Mot didn't want his company.

"Do you want us to leave you alone?" Haz called to him.

Mot's voice came out weak and very hoarse. "Please stay."

With a shrug, Njeri retrieved her portable vidscreen, tucked a blanket more firmly under Mot's chin, and swept out of the room. Haz plopped down in the chair she'd vacated. He knew he ought to say something to Mot, but he didn't know what, so for a few minutes they just stared at each other.

"You came looking for me," Mot said at last.

"That was Molly. Turns out she can track people, which was news to me. Came in handy, though."

"But you came."

It was hard to hear him, but when Haz leaned forward, it strained his shoulder. So with a small grunt of annoyance, Haz moved to the bed itself and propped his bad leg on the chair seat.

"We almost didn't make it in time."

Mot nodded slightly. "I'm sorry I made you do that."

"Don't be. Anyway, you didn't make me do anything. I chose to."

"That's… that's why I left Ixi's ship."

"I don't understand."

When Mot's eyes closed, Haz thought he'd fallen asleep and started gathering himself to stand. But Mot pulled an arm from under the covers and lightly grabbed Haz's wrist.

"I've never had the chance to make choices. I go where people take me. Going out like that… it was my choice. Do you see?"

Haz certainly did. "You need to know something. You're not returning to Chov X8."

Mot's grip grew more firm and his eyes widened. "Why not?"

"I saw…." Haz swallowed thickly. "Molly showed me a vid. I found out what was going to happen to you there. Why didn't you tell me, Mot?"

"I thought you wouldn't care. Or that you already knew."

Stung, Haz stared at his foot. "I do care. And I didn't know."

"Oh."

They sat like that for some time, Mot's hand still on Haz's wrist. Haz could feel Mot's heartbeat thumping away in tandem with his own.

"If I don't go back, things will be bad at home. The government—"

"Fuck them. They need to find a better way to run a planet than torturing and murdering innocent people."

"But that's how we—"

"Fuck them," Haz repeated more loudly. "I don't care if it's tradition. Some traditions need to be done away with."

Mot was frowning. "It's only me that's harmed, though. Everyone else benefits. Isn't that worthwhile?"

"No. They can find another way to benefit. Besides, it's not only you. How many people have they done this to already, and how many more will come after you're gone? I saw this temple in the vid—"

"With the previous Machines. I've been there. They took me when I was young."

Haz was instantly so enraged that he had to take a series of deep breaths before speaking, and even then he growled.

"They made a child see that? Forced you to see what they'd do to you."

"It was part of a ceremony."

"Fuck—"

"—them. I think that's your motto." Mot managed a tiny smile, but it quickly faded. "If I'm not going home, where am I going? The Coalition won't forget about me, will they?"

"They won't forget about either of us." Haz grinned. "Fuck them too. I'm working on something. I'll know tomorrow if it's going to pan out."

"All right." Simple as that, as if Mot had faith in him. And then Mot yawned. "Tired."

"Njeri has all sorts of chemicals floating in your veins right now. Enjoy it while it lasts."

"I was so cold. And then… then I wasn't anymore. I just needed to lie down."

"Hypothermia."

Mot stirred slightly without releasing Haz's wrist.

"I heard you calling my name. I knew it was a dream, but it was nice anyway. Before you, I had no name to be called by."

"Mot—"

"I'm cold."

"I can turn up the temp. Molly—"

"No. That's not…." Mot sighed, a small sound like a breeze rustling the grasses on Ceres. "Will you lie next to me, please? Warm me up."

That was a bad idea. But like many bad ideas, Haz found it appealing. He was tired too—it had been an eventful day—and Mot was big-eyed and pleading. And dammit, Mot was alive. Not frozen in the bush, not murdered and stuck on a pedestal in a szotting temple. He was right here on Haz's ship, breathing, touching. Wanting.

"No sex," said Haz.

"Sex requires moving, doesn't it? I watched some vids. I couldn't do that now anyway."

So Mot had just recently been introduced to vidscreens and had already found porn. Good for him. Haz pushed away the chair and stood, but only so he could burrow under the blankets. The bed wasn't really wide enough for two grown men, but Mot didn't seem to mind. He pressed his body tightly against Haz, sighing with satisfaction.

"Warm."

In fact, it was too warm, at least for Haz. He remained where he was, however, inhaling Mot's scent: medicine and sagey plants. Of course he couldn't feel the tattoos on Mot's skin—yet somehow he did, as if his fingers had acquired extrasensory abilities.

"Haz? Do you still follow your family's religion?"

Haz snorted. "The New Adamites? No. If I did, I'd be back on Ceres, wrestling with a plow."

"I've spent my entire life being told I'm just... just an interloper temporarily occupying the Great Divine's property."

"That's a lie. This body is yours." Haz gave him a small squeeze, followed by a yawn of his own. "Molly, dim the lights, please."

She did, leaving only the faintest illumination coming from the open door of the head.

"But what if the Great Divine is angry that I've stolen it?" Mot said.

"You can't steal what's already yours. Take it from a smuggler. I know these things."

Mot made a small sound that might have been a laugh. "But the Great Divine might not agree."

"Mot, I'm the worst person in the galaxy to discuss theology with."

"Hmm."

Mot shifted so they were facing each other, his face tucked under Haz's chin. God, that felt good—to hold him and to be held. To feel his breath tickling the hairs on Haz's chest. To share warmth.

"But do you believe in a god?" Mot asked.

"I have no idea."

"What do you believe in?"

Haz thought for a moment. "Very little. My ship. My crew."

"Not yourself?"

"I believe you should get some sleep."

Although Mot made a tiny protest, within minutes he was breathing slowly and deeply, his body entirely relaxed in Haz's arms. Haz, however, remained awake for a long time, Mot's question echoing in his head.

What do you believe in?

Maybe, if he survived a while longer, he'd come up with an answer.

CHAPTER EIGHTEEN

WHEN HAZ was a boy on Ceres, all his dreams had been about flying. Not in a ship—he hadn't yet stepped foot in one. While he slept, he was one of the brown-and-white birds that swooped down onto newly tilled fields and snatched up insects before launching themselves back into the sky. The New Adamites called those birds swallows, after an Earth species mentioned in the Bible, but they weren't actually the same.

Once Haz had become a pilot, his dreams changed. He still flew, but not just through the air. He soared among the stars. He wasn't in a ship; he *was* a ship. Powerful and free, the entire galaxy his playground.

But among the many changes that the *Star of Omaha* fiasco had brought, he no longer dreamed of flying. He spent his nights slogging through mud—as in fields after a great deluge—trying to save someone. The particular someone varied, but they were always a person who'd died on that ship, and in his dreams they screamed and screamed, and he never reached them. When he tried to rescue them, he'd wrench his leg and wake up with cramps or worse. Those dreams were awful, but they were also familiar and predictable.

Tonight, though, Haz dreamed something new. He was walking across the Ankara bush, naked but not feeling the cold, and he came across a long row of tattooed men standing very still. As he got closer, he saw that every one of them was Mot. At the same time, Haz realized that he held a knife in each hand.

"I have to kill you," Haz said in the dream.

"You won't," all the Mots replied. "We trust you."

"You shouldn't trust me. Nobody should."

And he threw the knives, which multiplied as soon as they left his grip, one for each Mot. Haz had excellent aim; he'd been practicing since he was a toddler. But in the dream, not a single blade hit home; instead they clattered to the ground. The Mots surged forward, probably to attack him. And who could blame them? He was unable to run, and he didn't try to defend himself. The Mots merged into a single man, who wrapped Haz in a tight embrace.

And that was how Haz woke up: tangled in Mot's arms. A good thing, since the grip kept him from falling off the narrow bed. Haz's left arm was trapped under Mot's shoulders and had gone numb, but his leg was relatively quiet.

"I've never slept with anyone before," Mot said. His voice had regained its strength.

"It's not all that—"

"It's nice. Very warm."

The memory of the previous day made Haz shiver. "How do you feel?"

"Thirsty. Hungry. A little weak, like I've just recovered from a minor fever."

"Once you've had breakfast, will you feel well enough to go into town?"

Mot stiffened against him. "You're giving me to another ship captain?"

"No. Not unless you want me to." Haz unwound himself from the embrace and sat up, scratching idly at his whiskers. He twisted to look at Mot. "You get a say in your own fate from now on. As much as any of us do, at least."

Mot's smile shone in the dim light. "That's a great gift you're giving me."

"It's not mine to give. I'm just... respecting it, I guess."

Mot climbed out of bed and stood in front of him. He moved a little slowly, but as he stretched, everything appeared to work all right. Sometimes it was easy to overlook Mot's nudity because he was so heavily clothed in ink; but not now, when he was inches away, the imprint of his skin still warm on Haz's body.

"So do you feel up to a little trip this morning?" Haz asked.

"Where?"

"A place where my crew and I can get our biotabs hacked so the Coalition can't trace us. And where you can get one implanted, if you want."

Gaping slightly, Mot stared at his forearm, where colorful figures snaked and twisted.

"The Omphalos doesn't have a biotab." He took a deep breath and straightened his shoulders. "But people do. I would like to have one."

"Good. You'll need to wear some clothes."

Njeri insisted on scanning Mot while he ate breakfast, and she pronounced him healthy.

"Don't overdo it, though," she warned him. "Healing tissues are vulnerable." She turned to Haz. "That goes for you too."

Mot looked alarmed. "What's wrong with Haz?"

"Idiocy," Jaya muttered darkly.

Really, Haz couldn't dispute that. "Nothing. Tweaked my shoulder. I'm fine."

"How?" Mot asked. "Was it my fault?"

"Nope, entirely mine. I overdid my exercising. Look, I get hurt all the time. It's no big deal."

Haz departed the galley before Mot could press any further.

It took them a little extra time to leave the ship, mostly because Jaya fussed over Mot, bundling him in so many layers of clothing that he could barely move. He'd lost his scarf—Haz's scarf—in the bush, so they had to improvise by cutting a strip of cloth from one of Haz's tunics.

"Molly, can you track us while we're in town?"

"Of course."

"Good. Let me know if… I don't know. If there's any shit you think I should know about. And don't let anyone board."

"Confirmed."

They bundled Mot quickly into the aircar. He seemed more interested in the scenery than he had been yesterday, swiveling his head back and forth and sometimes asking questions or making observations.

"I don't see any children anywhere."

"There aren't any here," Haz replied. "Well, maybe a few. But Ankara-12's not real family friendly."

"Pirates and smugglers, you said."

"Yep, and the folks who can make a living off of them."

"I wonder if the people here are lonely," Mot mused and then fell silent.

The address Ixi had given them turned out to be a long two-story building that looked to be constructed of randomly dropped large blocks of stone. None of the exterior angles were ninety degrees and none of the walls were straight, making the structure look like a petrified drunken beast. The sagging tile roof added to the illusion. The hand-painted sign over the door was illegible, the letters mostly weathered away. All that remained were three faint characters in an alphabet Haz couldn't read.

The interior, however, was toasty warm, one of the benefits of thick walls. The goods for sale—small pieces of ships and various gadgets, many of them very old—were neatly arranged on shelves. Jaya's eyes went wide. Haz was tempted to browse too, but they had business to take care of.

"Not now," he said quietly.

Chastened, she gave a small nod.

The person behind the counter was human of indeterminate gender and appeared to be in their thirties. A large burn scar covered part of their face, and they were missing one eye.

"Help you?" they asked cheerfully.

Haz stepped forward.

"Ixieccax sent us. We're... looking for some assistance with our biotabs."

The clerk pointed toward a door at the far end of the shop. "Thonamun's in there. She'll help you."

The four of them marched in single file, with Jaya casting covetous glances at machinery parts along the way. When they reached the door, Haz entered first, followed by Njeri and Mot, with Jaya taking up the rear. It was a good formation, considering their relative abilities to fight, although Haz hadn't arranged it on purpose.

Thonamun looked up without surprise from her seat on the floor. She was a species Haz didn't recognize, with pointed ears, enormous green eyes, and short plush fur the color of a ripe Ceres wheat field. A pair of long horns—etched with symbols and letters in an alphabet Haz didn't recognize—curved from her forehead.

"Ixi told me you'd come," she said.

"Can you help us?"

Her laugh was deep and throaty.

"Sweetheart, I can have my way with anything electronic. As long as I'm paid up front."

"We need three biotabs, um, recoded, and one installed."

"Six hundred credits," she replied immediately.

It was a lot of money. Far more than the work should cost, except that most of what they requested was strictly illegal, and that came at a price.

"I'll pay," Njeri said, and she and Thonamun quickly completed the transaction with their biotabs.

"Sit," Thonamun ordered. She gestured at the small rugs scattered around her. The four of them obeyed, Mot taking the space closest to Haz. "Recoded?" she asked.

Haz winced. "I'm not sure if what we need is entirely possible. We need to keep our credits, our data, our... well, everything. But we also need to make sure nobody can find us unless we want them to."

"Oh, that's easy, sweetheart. Just like me." She batted her impossibly long eyelashes at him.

Under very different circumstances, Haz might have been intrigued. Sure, his preference was for human men, but it wasn't an exclusive preference. And he always had enjoyed a certain amount of novelty. He grinned at her and gave a small shake of his head. "Too rich for my blood, I think."

She gave another throaty laugh. "So who are you worried will find you?"

"Anyone." When that didn't seem to satisfy her, Haz sighed. "Coalition, mostly."

It wasn't too much of a risk to say so; the Coalition was distinctly unpopular on Ankara-12. And sure enough, she smiled.

"Most of us are better off without that lot. It's illegal for them to track you through your biotab, though. You must know that."

"Lots of things are illegal. Doesn't stop people from doing them."

"It certainly doesn't."

She rubbed her hands together. She had only two fingers and a thumb on each hand, each of the digits long and capped by a thick black nail. "All right. Who's first?"

Jaya stuck out her wrist before anyone else could. She tapped it against Thonamun's portable vidscreen and then watched closely as Thonamun worked. Whatever she was doing was impressive enough to make Jaya raise her eyebrows and nod a little.

"That's clever," she said. "I wouldn't have thought of that."

The praise made Thonamun wiggle her shoulders. "Oh, it's not such a big thing. I can work fancier magic than this."

Although Jaya clearly would have loved to see some of that, she instead inclined her head at Njeri.

"Her next. But can you make it so she and I can track each other?" She glanced at Njeri. "If that's okay."

"Sure, hon."

Humming softly to herself, Thonamun complied. After she finished, Jaya announced that she and Njeri were going to browse in the outer room, and they left.

Then it was Haz's turn. He watched the vidscreen, but nothing Thonamun was doing made any sense. Then again, software had never been his strength. He could use the programs well enough, but when it came to mucking around behind the curtain, he left the work to Jaya and other experts.

It had occurred to him that there was no way to verify that Thonamun was doing what he'd asked. For all he knew, she could be turning them into giant homing beacons. But Jaya had seemed satisfied. Besides, people who lived or did business on Ankara-12 were an odd sort. They might engage in illegal activity, and some of them engaged in violence to achieve their goals, but they also took pride in their work. If someone claimed to be a smuggler, well, he'd do his damnedest to get the illegal cargo to its destination. And if Thonamun claimed to be able to keep the Coalition from using biotabs to find people, she'd probably fulfill that promise.

"You're set, babe." She winked broadly at Haz. "And your quiet friend needs theirs replaced?"

"Not replaced. He's never had one."

She uttered a string of words that were not in Comlang and fixed her gaze on Mot. "Why not?"

Mot paused before answering. "I wasn't allowed."

"That's… well, none of my business, I'm sure. The four of you have a story that I really wish I could know."

"Maybe someday," Haz said, "but not now."

"Fair enough. Okay, let me see your arm."

Mot had to remove a few layers of clothing, which of course revealed his tattoos. Thonamun was fascinated, peering closely at the designs and exclaiming quietly in what was probably her native tongue. But soon she got down to business.

"No scars. You truly never had a biotab. I've never seen that before. I've seen a few installed in unusual places on bodies, but never none at all."

"Is that a problem?" Mot sounded worried.

"No. Just interesting."

She stood, patted him on the head, and made her way to a metal cabinet against one wall. It hadn't been obvious when she was seated, but she was very tall—likely two and a half meters. She moved with a hip-swaying grace. After removing a metal box from the cabinet, she returned with it to her spot and sat down again.

"This is going to ruin some of the art, I'm afraid."

"I don't care."

The only biotab Haz had seen installed was his own. He watched with interest as Thonamun rubbed a medicated cloth over the underside of Mot's wrist and forearm to disinfect and numb it. Then she used a laser scalpel to cut a shallow horizontal slice just beneath his wrist. Mot flinched slightly, due to either the pain or the sight of his own blood, but he kept his arm still. Before more than a few scarlet droplets could well up, she'd pressed a thin, shiny strip to the cut. The strip began to widen, slithering under Mot's skin and into his forearm. Soon it disappeared entirely, at which point she applied some glueskin.

"Does it feel comfortable?" she asked.

Mot was staring at his arm, but the cloth around his face hid his expression.

"It feels… weird."

Haz remembered that sensation, although he'd been only six when his was implanted. "You'll get used to it in a couple of days," he said. "It's settling in and making neural connections."

"It's odd to have a machine in me instead of being a machine myself."

If that statement surprised Thonamun, she didn't show it. She was too busy working on her vidscreen and occasionally poking at Mot's arm. The process took a while. Haz remembered his father glaring at him when Haz's biotab was being implanted, silently warning him of the punishments he'd receive if he wasn't compliant and patient. What Haz had really needed at the time had been comfort and reassurance.

He'd been taught since birth that technology was evil, a way for the devil to tempt people to damnation, and he'd been scared to have technology stuck into his body. It was, he realized now, the first time he'd seen the flaws in the New Adamites' theology and lifestyle. He'd been too young to understand his doubts, but they'd taken root that day and had reached fruition by the time he was in his teens.

"All right." Thonamun finally set down her vidscreen. "Give it a standay to finish installing. You'll need to set up the software then, but I bet your friend can help you with that." She waved in the direction Jaya had gone.

Mot began wrapping himself back up. "Thank you."

She didn't stand when they did, but she gave a little wave before they left the room.

Njeri was leaning against the sales counter with a long-suffering expression, several pieces of machinery near her elbow. Jaya, deep in discussion with the clerk, had apparently been shopping. Haz wanted to get back to Molly, but he knew better than to hurry Jaya through her process. He waited near the door, arms crossed, while Mot wandered idly around the shop.

When her business was finished, Jaya waved impatiently at Njeri. "Pay for that, please. I'll be back in a few minutes."

Without further explanation, she ducked back into Thonamun's room.

"What's she doing in there?" Haz asked Njeri as the clerk totaled the purchases.

She shrugged. "No idea. But if I were the jealous type, I'd be worried. This place has my girl worked up. I can't believe she didn't already know it existed."

"Paa's always been a settlement full of surprises," Haz said.

Jaya was in the other room for a long time and looked entirely smug when she finally emerged.

"I'm ready" was her only comment.

All four of them lugged her newly purchased bits and pieces to the aircar, which was barely big enough to hold the passengers and merchandise.

"What's this?" Mot held up a metal tube as wide as his thumb but longer.

"It's for a pulse cannon."

"Are the pulse cannons broken? They seemed to work all right during the recent battles."

"They're fine, but this will improve one of them. Usually we use borvantium because it's light and durable. But this is old technology. That piece you're holding is probably two hundred stanyears old. It makes the cannon less predictable."

Jaya enjoyed giving speeches about weapons and mechanics, and she spent the journey back to port explaining to Mot how this little bit of metal worked and why it would be better than what Molly already possessed. Haz tuned her out. If she said they should have something, then they should. She'd always been right so far.

ONCE ALL her new acquisitions were aboard the ship, Jaya disappeared into engineering; Haz was not surprised. Meanwhile, Njeri decided to cook some lunch, and she shooed Mot toward his room.

"You need rest."

"I'm fine."

"You almost died yesterday, and today you've been gallivanting around and getting devices jammed into you. Give your body a break. Besides, you never know when our captain will have us all in mortal danger again."

Mot and Njeri had a good laugh, and then Mot meandered aft, staring at his forearm as he went.

That left Haz, who was pleased with the morning's successes but uncertain what would happen next. If Ixi didn't show up, Haz had no plan B. It was hard enough coming up with one strategy without also having to create alternatives.

"Hey, Molly darling. Can you access all of our biotabs?"

"Affirmative."

"Do they all seem to be working properly?"

"Three of them, yes. I cannot yet evaluate Mot's."

Haz sat heavily into his chair on the bridge.

"Yeah, okay. His is new."

"According to my databases, the Machine of the Obeisant Theocracy cannot have a biotab or any other devices installed. The Chovians would consider it sacrilege."

He blew a raspberry. "Fuck it. Those qheks can kiss my ass."

"That's physically impossible considering your respective current locations."

Was Molly making a joke? That wasn't possible. But it was also impossible that she'd programmed herself to track him or that she'd forced him to watch that awful vid.

"Molly? Does it piss you off that I'm always ordering you around?"

She paused before answering, as if she had to process his question.

"You are my captain and I am your ship. You are supposed to give orders and I am supposed to follow them."

"Well, yeah. But…."

Haz didn't understand why he was having this conversation. Yet it suddenly seemed important, even if he didn't know what he was trying to find out. He searched for the right words.

"Mot is supposed to be an artifact, and he doesn't want that. I was supposed to be a farmer. I didn't want that either."

"Are you asking whether I am dissatisfied with my assigned role?"

Leave it to Molly to ask his questions better than he could.

"Yeah. People built you. Used you. I bought you. I drag you all over the galaxy and get you shot up. I know you're a ship, but…." He blew out a puff of air. "Maybe ships are people too?"

"I am not people. I am a modified brig class spaceship. I delight in flying, just as you do. And just as for you, I cannot do it alone. If I could choose, I would pick you as my captain."

Haz realized he was smiling.

"Thanks, Moll. And you know how I feel about you."

"As you should," she replied primly.

Other ships likely didn't make their captains laugh.

Haz was a lucky man.

AFTER EATING lunch, Haz spent a stanhour or so checking Molly's systems. At least that was what he told himself he was doing. In fact, Molly was perfectly capable of a self-check, and Jaya would perform a better backup check than he could. But pretending to work was better than pacing fretfully and worrying about whether Ixi would show up. Haz would have exercised instead, but his shoulder was still a little sore and Njeri would have his head if he reinjured it.

So he attempted to stare at his vidscreen. He almost cried out with relief when Molly spoke again.

"Captain, Ixieccax wishes permission to board."

"Holy szot, yes!"

Njeri entered the bridge when Ixi did. She was munching on something that left crumbs scattered over the front of her blue tunic. She silently took a seat and pretended to work on her navplans, but she clearly wanted to listen in. Not that Haz blamed her.

"Thanks for the info on the biotabs," Haz said to Ixi. "That was perfect."

"Thonamun is something else, isn't she? Expensive as hell, but worth it."

"Yeah, she's— Szot, Ixi. I can't handle small talk right now. I'm about to jump out of my skin. Can you help us find sanctuary?"

"I can. The question is whether I will."

"Ixi—"

"I know, Haz. You're in deep trouble. But like I told you yesterday, this involves trust. If you betray me, the consequences could be grave."

Haz nodded. He'd never had to vouch for his own character before. Most people just cared about his flying.

"I can't give you personal references."

"I know."

Ixi strode closer and sat in the chair nearest Haz, tail tucked neatly behind him.

"Tell me something. How come you've decided not to return Mot to Chov?"

Not knowing what answer Ixi wanted to hear, Haz opted for honesty. "It's wrong. Morally, I mean. He's…. You've met him. He doesn't deserve to be treated like that. Doesn't deserve to die."

"Everyone dies. Most of them don't deserve it."

"True enough. But he's never even had the chance to live."

Ixi's wide mouth curled into a smile.

"You're a good man, Haz Taylor. Who knew?" His tongue flicked out.

"Does that mean—"

"Yes. But this is complicated, so make yourself comfortable. Do you have any schlee syrup, by any chance?"

Relief felt like a bubble bursting inside Haz's chest.

"I'm afraid not. But I can try making you some of that… fake beetle stuff Njeri cooked up for you."

"That would be—"

"Captain!"

Both of them swung their heads toward Njeri, whose entire body had gone stiff as she stared at her screen.

Haz stood and began walking toward her. "What is—"

"Incoming! Three xebecs heading toward port, and they're all masked."

"Szot!"

Haz hurled himself back into his seat. Molly was a sitting duck when she wasn't in flight. He shouldn't have so glibly assumed that the Coalition wouldn't send anyone after them on Ankara-12.

"Njeri, get Molly ready to go. Molly, tell Jaya to get up here and tell Mot to strap in."

Haz faced Ixi. "Sorry. You better get out of here quick."

"But I haven't told you—"

"No time. We're about to take off." He was poking at the controls as he spoke.

"If I don't tell you how to reach the Resistance, where will you go?"

"Dunno. Maybe we'll come back to port after we shake these qhek-fuckers. Or after we blow 'em to dust."

Haz said this even while knowing that a return was unlikely. Even if he won this round, the Coalition might have more ships waiting to ambush him.

"I mean it, Ixi. Skedaddle."

After a moment's pause, Ixi buckled himself into the seat.

"I'm coming along. Always did want to see Molly in action."

CHAPTER NINETEEN

A BRIG generally took a good twenty minutes to get into flight from a dead stop. Which was fine if she was carrying legal cargo and was therefore in no particular hurry. But Molly's cargo was frequently not legal, which meant that Haz sometimes had to get out of port very quickly. This was one modification that Jaya had tinkered with over the years, claiming that one day she'd get the time down to less than a minute.

She wasn't there yet. But less than five minutes after Njeri raised the alarm, Molly was streaking through the air, three xebecs in pursuit.

"Haz, where are you going?" Ixi demanded.

"Away from Paa and any other air traffic. Do you think these fuckers will care if they accidentally hit some poor innocent pirate instead of us?"

Too busy trying to save everyone's necks, Haz didn't look around to see Ixi's expression.

Jaya had zoomed out of engineering even before Molly was in the air, and although she was a little out of breath, her hands flew over the controls. Njeri was frantically plotting a course in which Kappa Sector's hazards would give them a strategic benefit.

Haz glanced up when Mot stumbled onto the bridge.

"Strap in!" Haz yelled. The last thing he needed was Mot flying around and banging into everything.

"No seats!"

This was why Haz didn't take on passengers. They were pains in the ass. He wished Mot had stayed in his room.

"Molly, show him the jump seat."

He heard the small metallic click as the panel flipped forward from the bulkhead and snapped into place, creating a chair. It was uncomfortable, but Mot would just have to endure it. At least the jump seat had buckles, which clicked satisfyingly as Mot engaged them.

"What's going on?" Mot asked, sounding plaintive.

Haz and his crew didn't bother to answer, but Ixi and Mot conversed quietly. Haz tuned them out, concentrating instead on flying a fast and erratic course to dissuade the three pursuers.

"Captain, they're almost in range," Jaya warned.

"Yeah, yeah. Njeri, what've you got for me?"

Njeri exhaled loudly. "Hang on…. Okay. It's a distance away, but Eolia-6 has a shit-ton of orbital debris and a pea-soup atmosphere. Molly probably can't withstand that atmosphere for long, but then, neither can those xebecs."

"Sounds like a lovely place for a holiday. Point us that way."

"Copy that, Captain."

"Molly, darling, now's your chance to show Ixi why you're the best."

"Confirmed." Molly sounded pleased.

Haz began by maximizing their speed. Molly was faster than the xebecs, and if only a single one had been chasing them, she could have outrun it. But the set of three could use space anomalies to curve around and flank her. Kappa was full of such anomalies, a feature that made the sector popular among pilots up to no good. That left Haz no choice but to go as fast as he could and hope he reached Eolia before the xebecs could get close.

With Njeri's help, Haz took advantage of a couple of those anomalies himself, skipping ahead or slightly cutting a corner. That put a little extra space between Molly and the xebecs, but not enough to make him comfortable.

"She's fast," Ixi commented, sounding impressed.

Grinning despite everything, Haz kept working the controls, adding a few zigs and zags that slowed them down a little but also threw the xebecs off track. He didn't like running and would have preferred to fight, but he knew it was better to wait until he could tip the odds more in his favor. God, he hated waiting. He also had the feeling—stupid as it was—that Molly was impatient too, that she wanted to strut her stuff instead of just sprinting.

"Almost there, darling," he murmured.

Haz took a moment to glance behind him. Ixi leaned forward in his seat, his mouth in such a wide grin that it was amazing his head remained intact. His tongue kept flicking in and out; his tail, sticking up behind him, swished back and forth.

Mot, on the other hand, had pressed back against the bulkhead, his expression serious. He caught Haz's eyes.

"I'm sorry," Mot said.

"The Coalition had it in for me anyway. You just gave them a handy excuse to come after me. And if it wasn't you, they'd have dreamed up something else. Now shut up and let me work so you can live long enough to try out that biotab."

"Captain!" Njeri called.

Haz turned his attention back to his vidscreen just in time to see one of the xebecs zoom in too close for comfort. It was already shooting, and one of the blasts hit Molly hard enough to shake her. Jaya blasted back immediately, and the xebec moved away, the pilot likely realizing they had no chance against Molly one-on-one.

"Jaya?" Ixi said. "Do you have this set up to accommodate dual operation of the cannons?"

"Yes."

"Can I—"

"That's up to my captain."

Again Haz found himself smiling. He knew Jaya hated to hand over control, but she'd deferred to him instead of refusing. "Your choice, Jaya."

She paused a moment. "Fine. But if you screw things up, I'm cutting you off."

Ixi made a strange cackling noise that was probably a laugh, and next time the nearest xebec came close, Molly's cannons fired in two discrete patterns. None of the shots did major damage, but the pursuing ship backed up much farther, probably confused over this new turn of events.

Ixi hooted. "I hardly ever get to shoot at people!"

"Just hang around Haz," Njeri said with a snort. "Opportunities will pop up all over."

They managed to stay barely far enough away from the xebecs for another fifteen minutes. Just as Haz was getting so frustrated that he almost stopped to fight, open space be damned, Njeri announced that they were about to enter the Eolia System.

Haz had never been in this particular area before—hadn't even heard of it, for that matter, probably because it was uninhabited. But as Njeri had promised, Eolia-6 was a pilot's nightmare of debris and impenetrable clouds. Perfect. He slowed down and allowed the xebecs to nearly catch up. The maneuvers he was about to try worked best in close quarters.

"You're going to take us into that?" Ixi sounded excited rather than frightened.

"Taking us in is easy. It's the getting out that's the tough part."

Haz directed Molly straight into the ring of orbital debris.

Most of the stuff floating around this planet was smaller than a person's fist. But at the velocities Molly and the xebecs had to fly, even something as tiny as a fingernail could cause significant damage if a ship had compromised shielding. The key was making sure that Molly remained unscathed while the xebecs lost shielding and collided with as much debris as possible. It would have been great fun—if other people's lives weren't at stake. Arguably, Njeri, Jaya, and even Ixi had signed on for this kind of thing, but Mot hadn't.

Well, at least this was probably more interesting than sitting in an empty room in a temple.

Haz's fingers blurred as he moved Molly up, down, and sideways. Some of what they did seemed to defy the laws of physics, but then, he'd never been one for obeying the law. Molly skipped as nimbly as a dancer, as if she were made of nothing but pure energy. Haz's only frustration was the slight separation of his body and Molly's, the need to use his hands and her controls to connect. He wished it were simpler, as effortless as moving his own arms and legs. One leg, anyway. The other often took a lot of effort.

With all three xebecs close behind, Haz aimed Molly directly at a chunk of rock almost as big as she was. At the last possible moment before collision, he spun her off to the side, slipping past the boulder so closely that he could see every dimple through Molly's viewports. One of the xebecs was neither as lucky nor as nimble. It hit the rock head-on, causing both ship and rock to explode spectacularly. Of course that added even more debris to the region, most of it small but all of it moving fast. A few pieces pinged off Molly's hull.

"Damage?"

"Minimal," Jaya answered.

That was good news, but he still had two ships on his tail, and they were probably going to be more cautious than their disintegrated comrade. Haz needed to keep them on their toes. Even now, they were close behind him but at angles, and they were both blasting away.

Haz spent a few more minutes spinning and dipping among the orbital debris. Judging from the sound of Ixi's whoops, he was having a fabulous time. Mot, however, groaned.

"Don't you dare puke on my bridge!" Haz yelled. Then he steered Molly into a vertical dive, straight into the murky clouds of the planet's atmosphere.

"Ooh, this place is a mess," said Njeri. "My nav sensors are totally messed up. We're almost blind, Captain."

"Good. Then so are they."

This next bit wasn't magic, or at least Haz didn't think so. He didn't believe in magic. But he did believe in instinct. When it came to dealing with people, regardless of species, his instincts weren't great. More than once he'd made assumptions about someone's motives or his best course of action, only to learn he was mistaken. But he had a flair for fighting, an ability to sense his opponent's location and likely moves—even when an opaque chemical fog obscured them.

Trusting those instincts, Haz slowed Molly and brought her around, then rocketed out of the atmosphere. Jaya must have trusted him too, because she was firing even before they emerged, and Ixi followed her lead. When Molly broke through the fog, she was facing the two remaining xebecs. The ships took a moment to respond, which was fatal for one of them: blasted multiple times, it went spinning out of control down toward the planet.

The pilot of the remaining craft was very good, and his crew fired well, hitting Molly hard enough to make alarms sound and Jaya swear. And when Haz tried, a few times, to repeat his last maneuver—dipping into invisibility—the other ship evaded him. In fact, it tried the same thing, sometimes getting close enough to do more damage. Haz wasn't the only one with instincts.

Fine, then. If stealth wouldn't do, it was back to agility. Haz again flew them into the orbital debris. What followed next was a very deadly game of tag; both Molly and the xebec were It. They chased each other around chunks of rock, neither scoring more than minor hits on the other.

"This is fun, but I don't want to do it all day," Haz said as he narrowly missed yet another ship-sized obstacle. Not only was it exhausting, but eventually all those small dings could add up to catastrophic damage. Time to try something else.

"Ixi, stop shooting," Haz ordered. "Jaya, listen up. Hold off on firing until I tell you. And then instead of aiming at the xebec, go for the rock I indicate."

To her credit, Jaya didn't question him.

"Copy that, Captain."

It took some time for Haz to find the perfect setup, and Molly got banged around a bit in the interim, but eventually he found an opportunity. He shot Molly forward, sent her into a loop that barely missed some debris, and ended up facing the xebec with a large rock between them and just off to the side.

"Jaya, that's our baby. Be ready to fire at my command."

"Copy that."

The xebec was taking advantage of their placement, sending blast after blast straight at them. Poor Molly shuddered. But instead of backing off, Haz headed straight for the other ship. Before it had time to realize what he was up to and react, Haz positioned Molly at the ideal angle.

"Fire!" he bellowed.

Jaya did.

The rock exploded. Haz was ready for this and managed to dance Molly out of the way. But the xebec's captain, who hadn't anticipated this, was too slow to react. Chunks of debris pelted the other ship, which yawed, spun, and burst into a short-lived fireball.

"Njeri, can you get us out of this mess, pronto?"

"Of course."

Fifteen minutes later, Molly flew serenely through open space, already clear of the Eolia System. Jaya had disappeared into engineering; Njeri typed away at her vidscreen. Ixi and Haz unstrapped, Ixi flicking his tongue so vigorously that he had trouble speaking.

"That was… impressive, Taylor. I guess… you're more than just… a lot of empty bragging." He clapped Haz heavily on the sore shoulder, making him wince.

"All of my bragging is based entirely on facts."

"I'd like to spend the next year or so… talking to Jaya and finding out what she's… done to your little brig."

Haz smiled. "I'm sure she'll be happy to tell you. But, uh, about Ankara. I don't think returning is going to be wise for a while."

Ixi didn't appear dismayed; it had probably already occurred to him. His tongue-flicking had also stopped.

"Yep. Looks like you've taken on a new crew member and I've been demoted from captain." He shrugged cheerfully. "No worries. It's probably better for me to be with you when you meet my friends anyway."

"You sure you don't want us to drop you off somewhere? Like Njeri said, if you hang out with us, there's bound to be shooting."

"I know! I haven't had this much fun in years."

Haz laughed. "Fun, huh?"

The feathers atop Ixi's head stood straight up and his eyes glowed with an intensity Haz had never seen before.

"My people were warriors. We had simple weapons—spears, claws, teeth—but we were fierce. Then the Coalition arrived and called us savages. They subdued us, tamed us, made us support ourselves by fixing their machines and serving their meals. But green warrior blood still runs in our veins and makes our hearts beat." He thumped a spot on his belly where, Haz assumed, his heart was. Or possibly more than one heart.

Haz settled his hands on Ixi's shoulders. "I'm honored to have you on board."

And he meant it. There were only a handful of people in the entire galaxy whom he'd trust with Molly, and Ixi was one of them.

"Thank you, Captain." Ixi said it without irony.

"How far is it to our destination?"

"Ten standays. Maybe a little longer, depending on the route."

Haz took a half step back and scratched his cheek.

"We may need to slow for repairs too. Ixi, I wasn't expecting to have you here for any length of time. I don't have schlee syrup or beetles or, um, whatever else you eat. Sorry."

"Not a problem," Ixi said with a minor tongue flick. His feathers had settled down, and he now looked relaxed and slightly amused. "I can get by on water and synth protein. I'll pretend they're battle rations. But do you have enough?"

"Sure." Haz always laid in plenty of extra supplies on the principle that too many were far better than too few. "And I'm sure we can rustle up clothes and whatever else you need."

"I won't freeload. I'll help with the repairs and whatever else needs doing."

Haz nodded absently as he tried to figure out where Ixi would sleep. He could probably rig up a berth in the cargo hold. Not ideal, but it would give Ixi a bed and some privacy, and—

"He can have my room."

Both Ixi and Haz turned to look at Mot, who'd finally unstrapped and walked over. Even through the tattoos, he looked slightly green around the gills, and his walk was a little unsteady. Haz didn't answer because he was too busy trying to figure out how Mot had read his mind.

But Ixi shook his head. "I don't want to displace you."

"It's fine. Please. I can sleep anywhere."

Haz opened his mouth to say that he'd find a space for Mot somewhere, but that was not what came out.

"You can share my quarters, Mot."

Shit. Once he'd said it, he couldn't very well take it back, especially with Mot smiling so broadly. But he could qualify it a little. "There's a foldout bunk above my bed."

"No there's not, Captain," Molly chimed in brightly. "It was damaged, and you didn't get it repaired when we were on Kepler."

She was right. He'd figured he wouldn't need it—none of his crew had ever used it before—and therefore it hadn't been worth the expense. Dammit.

Mot looked apprehensive, and Ixi's expression practically dared Haz to act like a selfish cad. His quarters were, admittedly, even bigger than Njeri and Jaya's combined room.

"We'll figure something out," he mumbled.

That made Mot grin again.

CHAPTER TWENTY

HAZ WHISTLED as he looked at Njeri's navscreen. "That's way the hell at the end of the universe."

"Not quite," Ixi said with a grin. "But what did you expect? Did you think the Resistance would camp out on Earth?"

"No, although that would make it easier to strike at the Coalition. How can the Resistance accomplish anything if it takes half a lifetime before they even see the enemy?"

Ixi sighed. "And that's the problem right there, my friend. If they were in the middle of things, they'd have been annihilated long ago. They're relatively safe where they are, but about as effective as a rheet bug against a thruqrax."

Haz shifted his weight off the bad leg, which was hurting worse than usual. It had been a busy day, and battles always took a physical toll.

"Enough rheets can suck a thruqrax dry," he said.

"True enough. But we can't attract that kind of numbers. Everyone's scared."

As well they might be. Not only had Haz just seen firsthand what the Coalition did to its enemies, he'd wrought death and destruction himself. Playing cat and mouse with the Coalition was all very diverting, but he was well aware that—at least so far—minimal resources had been deployed against him. If the Coalition chose to give him their full attention, he'd be squashed like a rheet.

"Why aren't you hiding out in the boonies with your Resistance pals, Ixi?"

"I did for a time. But I got frustrated. I know I haven't done much to harm the Coalition, but I figure every smuggled cargo item is another thorn prick against them. And I do like earning credits."

Before Haz could continue the conversation, Njeri waved a hand. "Guys? I'm trying to work here. Getting to this place— What do you call it, Ixi?"

"Liberty. Yes, I know. Absolutely lacking in originality."

"Copy that. Getting to Liberty is a bitch. Can you two leave me alone so I can work?"

While some captains might have protested being kicked off their own bridge, Haz knew better. Anyway, a glass or two of whiskey would go down very well right now. He limped toward the galley, Ixi following closely.

"Can I ask you something, Haz?"

"Sure."

"How did you and Njeri know those xebecs were after you?"

They'd reached the galley by then. Haz grabbed a bottle and two cups, then filled Ixi's with water and his own with booze. He leaned back against the counter and had a swallow.

"Well, for one thing, there were three of them. Most people land on Ankara-12 alone." Although some pirate clans traveled in groups, they generally had private ports tucked away in the shadows of the galaxy. "For another, they were masked. I know some pilots opt for that on Ankara, but it's suspicious. And third, their approach used one of the attack formations the navy teaches on pretty much the first day of training."

"I don't know that soldier stuff," Ixi said. "I earned my wings as a civilian."

Mot entered the galley looking slightly hesitant and then nodded at Ixi. "The room's all yours."

"Thanks."

Haz added, "Feel free to rummage around the ship for whatever supplies you need. There's a lot of stuff in the hold." Then he had an idea. "Do you want to take shifts at the wheel?"

Ixi brightened visibly. "You'll let me fly your Molly?"

"If you treat her nicely."

Haz had faith in Ixi's piloting skills, and four shifts a standay instead of three would give him and the rest of the crew a little break. Njeri and Jaya might enjoy having some time together when they weren't sleeping.

He and Ixi spent a little time working out a schedule, at which point Haz pinged Jaya and Njeri and got their approval. Ixi went off to search for clothes and settle into his room. He'd likely want some sleep before his late shift that night.

Some rest seemed like a very good idea, in fact. Haz wanted to put his leg up, get drunk, and think about nothing. But Mot still hovered in the galley.

"Where are we going?" he asked.

Shit. It hadn't occurred to Haz that Mot didn't know.

"Some godforsaken rock called Liberty. It's in the asshole of nowhere, but it's as safe as you're going to get. A resistance movement is holed up there."

Mot's eyes went wide. "Resistance?"

"Against the Coalition. Although it doesn't sound like they're doing much resisting. Anyway, Ixi says they have several communities there, and he'll find a place for you. I doubt it'll be fancy, but it beats...." He shuddered, remembering that szotting vid.

"Beats being dead. All right." Mot trailed a finger along the counter as if checking it for dust. "What will you do?"

He didn't meet Haz's gaze.

"I'll fly. I'll find someone who needs a smuggler. Don't care who. It's all the same to me."

Still staring at his own hand as if he'd never seen those tattoos before, Mot gave a small nod. Haz turned to leave the galley.

"Haz?"

Now what? But Haz turned back and raised his eyebrows questioningly.

"Are there vids that show how to cook things?"

Well, that wasn't what Haz had expected.

"Yeah, sure. Why?"

"I don't know how to fly a ship or fix one. But I'd like to work. Like the rest of you are. Maybe I could make the meals and... and clean?"

Warmth spread through Haz, and it wasn't from the whiskey. He understood completely: Mot wanted to contribute, to be a real part of their strange little group.

"That'd be great. Molly can help you find some vids. If you want, you can also ask Jaya if she has any tasks for you. Her work down in engineering often makes a mess."

Mot seemed to stand straighter. "Thank you... Captain."

Haz beat a hasty exit before unwanted emotions intruded.

THAT NIGHT, Haz ended up drinking less than he'd planned. He sat at the desk in his quarters, sipping only occasionally as he watched vids about Chov X8. He didn't know why, since he hoped he'd never set foot on the planet. Then, also for no identifiable reason, he watched a vid about Ixi's home planet. It was produced by the Coalition, so of course it reflected the official government story. It showed Ixi's ancestors as a bunch of animalistic beasts who lived in filth, slaughtered one another indiscriminately, and died young and miserable. Ah, but then the Coalition arrived, bringing technology and knowledge and civilization. Carrying those benighted natives into the shining modern era.

"Qhek-fuckers," Haz muttered at the screen.

Then somehow his interests meandered even farther afield, and he found himself viewing news from Ceres. Not that there was much. The New Adamites weren't exactly setting the galaxy on fire. But he discovered that there had been a drought three stanyears earlier, followed by a plague, and now a significant proportion of the population was dead. The New Adamites had refused all but the most rudimentary aid, apparently deciding that it was better to watch their children wither and die than to dip a toe into science or medicine.

For the first time in years, Haz wondered about the fates of his parents and siblings. Were any of them still alive? Had any brothers or sisters—or maybe their kids—managed to escape Ceres? Did any of them ever wonder about him?

Haz called himself a name and switched off the vid, then performed his nightly ablutions and stripped. He'd been pretending for hours not to see the small pile of things Mot had tucked into a corner, but now Haz frowned.

"I'll trip over it and break my neck," he complained untruthfully. "Or Molly will be in another fight and his shit will fly all over and make a mess."

He scooped up the pile, which contained nothing but a towel and a change of clothes, and tucked them into a drawer. His quarters had plenty of storage, very little of which was in use.

Haz stood naked in the center of the room, hands on hips. "Molly, how are you doing?"

"I've suffered some damage, but nothing serious. All systems are at full capacity."

"You were beautiful today."

"You're not half-bad yourself, Captain."

Haz climbed onto the bed but didn't immediately pull up the covers. Instead he looked at his leg, something he rarely did since there didn't seem to be much point. He could feel the wounds just fine without seeing them, and staring wouldn't help. But now he remembered Mot's fingers on those scars, and how the mangled flesh had seemed less ugly when touched by the beauty of Mot's skin. His thoughts flowed forward then, to Mot sleeping against him—almost on top of him, really. Haz had to admit: to lie still and feel someone else's heartbeat, hear his slow breaths... that was a gift.

Without realizing it, he had been stroking himself as he remembered, his cock hot and hard in his hand, insistent on attention after a very long period of neglect. A pang of guilt wrapped around him, a vestige of sermons from his childhood about how sexual congress should occur exclusively between men and women, and only for the purpose of procreation. Haz had rejected those ideas long ago, yet the old lessons sometimes haunted him. And if he was honest, the guilt and the hint of shame only sped his heart—and his hand. In this way, self-pleasure also became a kind of self-torture.

"Oh, you're a twisted bastard," he moaned. But he didn't stop.

He refused to think about Mot, however. He'd think instead about the long parade of people he'd fucked. All genders, several species, but he'd known few of their names and remembered fewer. He'd always had a particular philosophy about both sex and booze: even the least satisfying versions were better than nothing.

In the end, Haz thought of nobody. He imagined great splashes of stars instead, and the inky spaces between them. He imagined flying without a ship, as if he were a space bird, with the coldness unable to hurt him and his lungs not needing air. He swooped and soared, arcing over planets like a comet and spinning amid the dust of a million dead moons. Then he flared unbearably bright like a supernova before dimming, collapsing, and going dark.

HE WASN'T asleep when Mot crept into his quarters, although he remained still on the bed, wondering what Mot would do. Despite the nearly total darkness, Mot found his way to the head and closed the door. He emerged a few minutes later, along with the sparkling scent of teeth-cleaning tablets, but then he stood uncertainly for a long time. A very soft thud and sigh indicated that he'd lain down.

"Don't sleep on the floor, Mot."

"I've slept on worse."

"So have I, but I didn't enjoy it, and it's stupid to do it when there's a nice soft bed right here."

Still Mot hesitated.

"We shared your bunk last night," Haz reminded him. "And it's much narrower than mine."

"I forced you to."

Haz laughed. "You? I do what I want to, okay?"

"You didn't want to take me on your ship."

Shit. Haz was glad he couldn't see Mot's face.

"No, I guess not. But... I'm glad I did."

"But you're in so much trouble because of it."

"I'm always in trouble, usually because I deserve to be. Anyway, some troubles are worth it. I'm awfully glad you won't end up on one of those pedestals in that szotting temple."

After a pause, Mot said, "Me too." It sounded as if he might be smiling.

Mot shuffled forward and banged a leg hard enough against the edge of the bed to make Haz wince in sympathy.

"Do you need light?" Haz asked.

"No."

Haz scooted back, closer to the bulkhead. If there was an emergency, he might have to climb over Mot, but he didn't mind being nearer to the ship wall—and to what was outside. Mot scrambled in beside him, taking a few moments to arrange himself, his pillow, and the blankets. A few centimeters of mattress separated their bodies.

"Did you learn some cooking techniques?"

"Yes! Molly was very helpful—she talked me through two recipes. Njeri said the results were definitely edible. And then I cleaned up."

He sounded so happy about these simple tasks, the types of chores that most people would complain about. Haz couldn't help but share that small taste of joy, which was new for him. He'd found ways to seek his own pleasure, but he'd never really shared someone else's. It tasted surprisingly sweet.

"Tomorrow we'll get your biotab set up, and then you'll be able to access a galaxy's worth of knowledge about cooking."

Mot shifted around a bit, making himself more comfortable. He smelled slightly of the spices he'd been using. "It's so strange to think about how much there is to know. How much information one ship can share. It's like Molly carries the whole galaxy."

That was a very nice thought, one that made Haz smile and stretch his limbs. He'd seen vidscreens briefly when he was young, in the hands of the space traders who landed on his planet, but he'd never had the chance to use them. He remembered his own excitement when he first escaped Ceres and experienced the screens for the first time. It felt as if the world had unfolded another dimension.

"Maybe you can figure out some variety of things for Ixi to eat. He's going to get bored with plain synth protein pretty fast."

"All right." Mot was silent for a while, but Haz could almost hear him thinking. "Are you and Ixi lovers?"

Haz sputtered a laugh. "If we are, why isn't he the one in my bed?"

"Oh. I thought...." Mot trailed off.

"I like him, but I don't want to fuck him. And he certainly doesn't want to fuck me. His people are only interested in sex during certain biological phases, which tend to be decades apart, and even then I get the impression it's not very, uh, sexy. I bet you can find vids on that too, if you want."

"Okay." Mot sighed noisily. Then his thoughts must have veered off in a different direction. "Do you think the people on Liberty will mind that I'm there?"

"Why would they?"

"I'm not.... I don't know how to do anything."

"You'll learn. Jesus, Mot, you're a smart guy. You'll pick things up fast."

Mot went very still. "I'm not smart."

"No, you're not educated. That's different, and it's not your fault. You're amazingly adaptable and you learn quickly. So if you want to become educated, you can and you will."

That sounded like a sermon, but Haz meant it. He'd seen plenty of people struggle to grasp new concepts, and when he'd become a navy officer, a fair number of his charges had to have things explained to them repeatedly. Not Mot.

When Mot didn't respond to the little pep talk, Haz felt the need to say more. That was what came of sharing a bed with someone and lying next to them in the darkness. You couldn't easily walk away, and suddenly their feelings mattered. Nobody wanted to feel misery radiating from a body mere centimeters away.

Haz chewed his lip as he searched for a way to describe this. He ended up falling back on some of the lessons he'd learned in officers' school.

"Look, there are different kinds of energy. Thermal energy, for instance. Like last night when you were cold and wanted me to warm you up? That was you taking some of my thermal energy."

"I'm sorry," Mot said in a tiny voice.

Haz chuckled. "Don't be. I had enough to share. Then there's chemical energy. That's what we get from food—we take the energy from our meals and convert it for our bodies to use. I don't know how because biology is not my thing. You can ask Molly. I bet she'll explain clearly."

"I like listening to you explain. But I'm not sure why you're telling me this."

"I'm getting there. Another kind of energy is kinetic. That has to do with movement. Today when Jaya blasted that rock, and the pieces went flying and hit the xebec? When those pieces were flying, they had a lot of kinetic energy. Enough to make them act as weapons. But what you need to know about is potential energy."

"What's that?" Mot sounded genuinely interested.

After considering for a moment, Haz sat up and grabbed his own pillow. "Potential energy sits inside an object until it's released by something. Can you see what I'm doing?"

"No."

"Well, I don't want to turn on the lights. But I'm holding my pillow over your head. I expended some of my energy to get it there, and because energy can't be created or destroyed, whatever I expended is now sitting in the pillow, waiting. That's potential energy."

"Waiting for what?"

"Waiting for this." Haz dropped the pillow onto Mot, causing him to startle, bat it away, and then sputter with laughter. "That energy transfer worked because Molly's got her g-force generators on—but that's more complicated than we need to worry about. Concentrate on my pillow." He lifted it again. "Potential energy, right? It's full of potential but not quite doing anything yet."

This time when he dropped it, Mot was ready. He caught it and threw it at Haz. "When you let it fall, the energy changes from potential to kinetic?"

"I knew you were smart!" Haz crowed. "If you can learn from me, you're a genius. And that was my original point. You are full of potential energy. You're practically oozing it."

"Ew."

"Hey, I once met this nonhuman guy…. Well, never mind that. Anyway, you've spent your whole life as a pillow held high in the air. Now someone's finally let go of that pillow. Of you. So all that potential's going to have a chance to come out. And it will."

He put the pillow back where it belonged, lay down, and pulled the covers back up. Somehow he'd tweaked his leg during the demonstration, so he tried gently flexing and relaxing the muscles.

"Thank you, Haz. I don't know why you're so nice to me."

"I don't know either. You're a pain in the ass."

Mot leaned closer and, very quickly, pressed his lips to Haz's. Then he moved away just as fast. "I get the impression that you'd rather have a pain in the ass than have things go too easily. Is that a type of energy?"

"Nope. That's just plain old cussedness. Good night, Mot." Although Haz was able to suppress a smile, his lips continued to tingle.

CHAPTER TWENTY-ONE

"DID YOU tell that boy to study porn, Haz Taylor?"

Haz looked over from the viewport. He'd been alone on the bridge, happily navigating Molly on Njeri's complicated course while keeping an eye out for unwelcome company. All he'd seen for hours was lovely open space. Now, though, Njeri seemed to be on a mission.

"He's not a boy—he's almost thirty, for szot's sake. And since when are you the prude police? If you want to become a New Adamite, we can swing by Ceres and drop you off."

She huffed. "I'm no prude. But of all the things you could have offered him, you chose porn."

"So?"

He didn't understand why she was so worked up about this. Once in a tavern on some dumb little planet—Haz couldn't remember which one—Njeri had overheard another customer make a disparaging remark about sex workers. She'd bullied him into a corner and given him a long lecture on respecting other people's choices about what they did with their bodies. The fellow was practically in tears by the time she finished.

Now she rolled her eyes and stomped over to Haz. "He's a virgin."

"Again, so? No reason he can't learn things and be entertained. Or get his rocks off solo."

Haz had a vivid recollection of the previous day's wank session and almost blushed. Not because he was embarrassed about jacking off, but because of the odd content of his fantasies.

"You are so stupid about so many things."

He shrugged. "I won't deny that. But I still don't see—"

"That boy is aching for you. He's got it bad. I have no idea why."

Haz opened his mouth but couldn't decide which of her statements to deny first, so he closed it again. He returned his gaze to the viewport. "He'll get over it."

She stood next to him for a time before bumping his shoulder gently with hers. "Who was your first?"

"First what?" he asked, suspecting what she meant.

"First person you lost your heart to."

"Nobody. Ever. My heart's always stayed firmly right here." He thumped his chest. "Don't tell me you've suddenly morphed into a romantic, Njeri. Did that lunch Mot made poison you?"

She hit him hard.

"Ow! That's my sore shoulder."

"I know," she said smugly. "You can't tell me you never ever mooned over anyone."

"I lusted, sure. That's my dick, not my heart."

"So who was your first?"

He hadn't realized they were trading life histories this afternoon. He could refuse to tell her, but he knew Njeri. She wouldn't let this go. He heaved a mighty sigh.

"Mel Lavoie. Melchizedek, actually, because his parents were as nuts as mine. His farm adjoined ours."

God, he hadn't thought of Mel in years. They'd been nearly the same age, but Mel had always seemed more mature, more worldly. And he had the softest brown eyes Haz had ever seen.

"And?" Njeri prompted.

"And what? It was no big deal. We'd sneak off together when we had a little free time. And we were teenagers, so, you know… we'd get to talking about sex even though we weren't supposed to. We talked about girls."

Even then, Haz had known he preferred boys. But that kind of thing got you killed on Ceres, and it wasn't as if he didn't appreciate girls too.

"And sometimes we got sort of carried away and we'd end up flogging our logs while we talked. Somehow that ended up with us tugging each other instead of ourselves. That's all. Just a little reciprocal rubbing."

Oh, but that had been thrilling enough at the time.

"And?"

"Stop with the *and*s. That's it. I talked a spaceship captain into letting me fly away with him. Paid my way however I could, and yes, that means with sex. I was willing. And I never saw Mel again."

Haz wondered if Mel had survived the drought, the plague, and Ceres's other hazards. Did he marry a woman and have children? Was he happy?

Njeri pierced him with a sharp gaze. "I bet you remember every minute with that boy. I bet when you two were apart, working on your farms or sleeping in your beds, you thought about him. Wondered how soon you could steal off together again. Wondered if he might be willing to do more."

She was right, of course. But he didn't have to admit it.

"What does this have to do with Mot?"

"He might be almost thirty, but he's new to the world. Think about how tender the soul is that first time. How raw. He hasn't had time to build up that borvantium shell."

She thumped Haz again, this time over his heart. Then she shook her head and left the bridge.

HAZ WAS very drunk. So drunk that the bulkhead tilted and swayed against his back and the floor rippled like the ocean. Being drunk wasn't a problem; no enemies were near, and he wasn't due on shift for another sixteen hours. Hell, he was the szotting captain. He could just order someone else to cover his shift if he wanted. No, the problem was that he wanted to get to the galley to fetch another bottle, but he couldn't seem to walk.

He knew how walking worked in theory, one foot forward and then the other. But his bad leg was numb and his good leg unwilling to do more than its share of work. Somehow he'd made it from his quarters halfway up the corridor, but the last bit was too daunting.

"Molly! Make everything stay still."

"My movements aren't causing your difficulty."

"But I can't...." Talking seemed like too much effort. So did standing. He slid slowly down the wall and ended up sitting crookedly on the hard floor. "Want more booze," he said plaintively.

"You're going to damage your liver. Did you know that cirrhosis can lead to leg pain and decreased sex drive?"

He barked a laugh. "You say that like those are new to me."

Molly sighed. But since ships didn't sigh, he must have imagined it. Maybe there was damage to the ventilation system. He'd have Jaya take a look. Later.

"Your floor is too szotting hard."

"Your ass is too sensitive."

"'M not sensitive. I have a borvat... a brovant... a szotting metal shell. Njeri said so."

"She didn't say it was on your ass."

This was what he'd come to: arguing inanities with a spaceship. Haz groaned and, using the wall to steady himself, clawed his way back to his feet. He ended up facing away from the galley, and since turning around seemed likely to result in more problems with gravity, he made his stumbling way back to his quarters. Once there he tugged off his clothing, nearly strangling himself in the process, and climbed into bed. Which smelled of Mot. Haz rested his head on the pillow of potential energy and tried to summon a black hole in his mind, an endless darkness that swallowed everything and gave nothing back.

It didn't work. The inside of his skull was too noisy, confirmed when he ineffectively wrapped the pillow around his ears. And instead of floating in a pleasant, alcohol-induced haze, he felt damnably grounded. Every heartbeat seemed to sober him up a bit more. Maybe Molly was pumping some kind of drug into his quarters.

"If you're going to do that, you might at least make my szotting leg stop hurting." He whispered it into the thickness of his pillow, not wanting Molly to hear him complain.

Two hours later, Molly woke him with a gentle chime. "Mot has dinner ready."

Although his first instinct was to refuse, he realized he was starving. He hadn't consumed anything but booze that day, but all that remained was a slight buzz in his brain and an empty belly. He dressed, scowled at his tight curls and wondered whether he wanted a haircut, and then made his way to the galley. Everyone was already sitting there except Njeri, who was on bridge duty.

When Haz entered, Mot grinned and stood. "Good timing."

"Molly told me. You don't have to serve me. I can—"

"I don't mind. Sit."

Haz took the empty chair across from Ixi, who was happily digging into a bowlful of something brown and blobby.

"Don't make that face, Haz," Ixi said. "I feel the same way when I see you people eating that." He gestured with his spoon at the reconstituted veggies on Jaya's plate.

"Does yours taste good?"

"Yes. It's a reasonable approximation of one of our most common meals. Don't get me wrong—my grandfather would shed his skin if someone served him synth protein instead of real bhemu meat, preferably from bhemu he'd hunted himself. But since you have none on board, Mot did well with what he had."

Beaming, Mot brought over a plate for Haz and then sat down next to Ixi.

"Pasta," Haz said. "With some kind of sauce."

Mot nodded. "Molly suggested the recipe."

Haz took a bite and then nodded. "Tasty. You're catching on fast to cooking."

"It's easy with Molly's help."

Jaya stood and got herself a second helping. "As far as I'm concerned, Mot can take over galley duties completely. He's already a better cook than you."

That was probably true. Haz didn't have patience for complicated recipes or experimentation. He was happy enough to eat someone else's culinary creations, however, and soon he had another helping as well.

"How are the repairs going?" he asked Jaya.

"Well enough. Ixi's assisting. I'm doing some improvements."

"Glad to hear that."

Jaya's improvements had always worked out well in the past, saving the ship and their necks more than once.

Ixi had finished his meal by then and was nursing a cup of water, clearly wishing it was schlee syrup.

"You know," he said, "Molly and her crew would make a welcome addition to the Resistance fleet."

Pushing his empty plate away, Haz shook his head. "Jaya and Njeri can do whatever they want, of course, but I fight for nobody but myself."

"But why? You don't love the Coalition."

"Not any more than they love me."

"So why not do something about them?"

Jaya stood abruptly. "Work to do," she muttered. She was going to clear her place, but Mot gestured for her to leave it, and she stomped out without another word.

Unfortunately, that didn't encourage Ixi to change the subject. He leaned forward over the table, his pupils so wide that they were almost circles instead of rectangles.

"You're a hell of a pilot, Haz. You could do some real damage to those bastards. I saw you yesterday, so I know you're not afraid to fight."

"I'm not," Haz growled.

"Then do it. Pay them back for how they've treated you."

"I have no taste for vengeance. It's not like I've lived an angelic life myself."

"Fine. Then do it because of the harm they've caused to others."

"The harm they caused." Haz's temper was rising, which was rare for him. Maybe he'd kept it tamped for too long. "I caused some of that harm. I was one of them for ten stanyears, remember? Do I declare war on myself?"

"What you did was nothing, and you walked away. The Coalition has been destroying cultures—destroying entire species—for centuries now. They're not even evil. They're selfish and powerful and greedy, and that's worse. They don't care who they hurt as long as it benefits them." Ixi's tone had grown low and urgent. "I told you what they did to my people."

"Yeah, and they've done that and worse to plenty of others."

Ixi lifted his palms. "So you do see. And you can join the fight to stop them."

"Stop them!" Haz laughed humorlessly. "How? With a few brigs buzzing at them?"

"More than a few. You said it yourself—enough rheets can suck a thruqrax dry." Ixi did a credible imitation of Haz's voice.

"I say all kinds of bullshit!" Haz shouted. "Look, even if a szotting miracle happened and the Resistance destroyed the Coalition, so what? Something just as bad would take its place. You think only those assholes from Budapest fuck people over? Hah." He pounded the table. "Molly? How many humans were killed in wars during the twentieth century?"

"Estimates range from one hundred million to one hundred and fifty million."

Haz poked a finger at Ixi. "You hear that? And that was almost two hundred years before anybody even dreamed of the Coalition."

Ixi's feathers were raised. "That's humans. I am not human."

"No, but your people were warriors, remember? Did you guys just go around calling your enemies mean names? Of course not. You murdered. Maybe not quite on a human scale, but only because you lacked the technology. We started small too. And that's another thing!" Oh, he was on a roll now. "Do you really think life was so perfect for your people before the Coalition arrived? I've lived on a planet where people don't use anything modern, and you know what? People die. They have hard, miserable, short lives and end up starving to death or croaking from things that Molly's med cart could cure in a minute."

"We were free," Ixi snarled.

"*Free.*" Haz waved his hand dismissively. "I doubt it. You probably had chieftains of some kind, and I bet those bigwigs treated everyone under them real shitty. Humans have this saying: Power corrupts. Who said that, Molly? Shakespeare?"

"The Lord Acton, in 1887. Shakespeare didn't coin every maxim."

Ignoring Molly's sarcasm, Haz continued. "Whoever said it, it's true. In every society on every planet. Look at Mot!"

Ixi did, and Mot startled, clearly not expecting to be thrust into the argument.

"What about him?" Ixi asked.

"The Chovians aren't part of the Coalition. No outside force has conquered them and told them what to do. But they take a baby and tear him from his family, they isolate him, claim sovereignty over his body, and then they fucking murder him."

For a moment, Ixi blinked at Mot. Then he turned back toward Haz. "Nobody's going to murder Mot," he said calmly.

But Haz wasn't calm. "You're fucking right they're not! Not if I can help it." He stood suddenly, his leg giving him a warning flash of pain. "I'm no hero. Chovians. Humans. Coalition. Your people. Pirates. Thieves. Smugglers. The New Adamites of Ceres. They're all bastards and I don't give a shit about any of them. I'm sure as hell not going to fight for them. I have exactly one priority, and that's me." He thumped his chest for emphasis. "The universe of Haz Taylor, population one. Everyone else can jebiga."

He stomped away, heading for his little gym in the cargo hold.

HAZ RETURNED to his quarters long afterward, sore, sweaty, and still feeling like he wanted to bite someone. When he discovered Mot sitting on the edge of the bed, playing with his biotab, Haz grunted and continued into the head. Washing up did little for his mood, but at least he didn't stink anymore.

"I can leave if you want," Mot said when Haz emerged.

"Don't on my account. It's your quarters too."

Haz plopped down on his desk chair, turned on a vidscreen, and began a routine review of ship systems. Yes, Njeri had no doubt done this already tonight, and so would Jaya on her shift, but the process soothed him. Besides, another set of eyes never hurt.

But the review didn't really take long, and his leg needed to be elevated. Also, he needed some sleep. So he switched off the vidscreen, peeled off the loose clothes he'd put on after his shower, and got into bed. Mot remained sitting, although he'd stopped poking at his biotab.

"Everything working okay?" Haz asked.

"Yeah, thanks. Jaya made sure. She showed me how to use it too."

"It might take some getting used to, but pretty soon you won't know how you lived without it." Haz gave a mighty yawn. "Stay up if you want, but I'm going dark."

Mot flashed a quick grin. "Molly, dim the lights, please."

As soon as she complied, he slid into bed. Haz had to admit that it already felt comfortable and familiar to be sharing a bed with Mot, as though Haz hadn't spent the previous four decades bunking down alone.

Once he'd settled in, Mot cleared his throat. "You lied to Ixi."

"Yeah? I'm a smuggler. Honesty and I aren't best friends." Haz waited a few moments, but then curiosity overcame him. "Which specific lie is bothering you?"

"The last thing you said—that you only care about yourself."

"Oh, that's pure truth. My self-interest knows no bounds."

"No," Mot said, sounding thoughtful. "I don't think you care much about yourself at all. But you do care about Jaya and Njeri. I've seen it."

Haz scowled even though Mot couldn't see him. "They're my crew. I have responsibility for them."

"Uh-huh. You care about Molly too."

"Of course I do! She's my ship. My home." He stroked the bulkhead. "She's all I have."

"Right. But I'm not your crew or your ship, and you care about me." Mot sounded supremely confident.

Haz sputtered, trying to issue denials but unable to get out the words. "No" was all he could finally manage. He rolled away from Mot.

Unfazed, Mot scooted a little closer. "You do. You saved me from freezing. You decided not to take me home once you learned what would happen. You're flying to the end of the galaxy to keep me safe. And you share your bed. Got me a biotab. Told me I have potential. You're nice to me. You care."

"I... I...." Haz huffed and tried again. "You want to know how selfish I am?" He rolled over very fast, grasped Mot's face, and pressed their lips together in a long, fierce kiss.

Mot tasted pleasantly of tooth-cleaning tablets, and his lips were soft. He didn't struggle. In fact, after a moment he made a soft little sound, parted his mouth, and hooked an arm over Haz's waist, urging him closer. Which wasn't the response Haz had expected. Not that he'd hoped Mot would resist him—Haz wasn't that kind of bastard—but he hadn't anticipated how eagerly Mot would participate. It blunted the point Haz had been trying to make, but it was hard to care about that when Mot was emitting desperate moans and doing his best to press his bare body against Haz's.

Haz was the first to put a few centimeters between them, and only because his heart was racing so fast that it felt as if it might burst from his chest.

"That was nice." At least Mot sounded breathless too.

"It was not nice."

"You didn't like it? I thought I felt—"

"Oh, I liked it well enough. But it wasn't right. I shouldn't have done it."

Prior to meeting Mot, Haz had never tried to convince anyone that sex was wrong. To do so would have made him feel like a New Adamite priest, standing on a rock with bare feet and a homespun tunic, endlessly insisting that anything fun—or progressive or modern—was the devil's work.

"Before, you told me we couldn't have sex because I was your prisoner. You were in a position of power over me." Mot suddenly pushed Haz hard onto his back and, before Haz could respond, knelt over him, knees tight against Haz's torso and ass planted firmly on his groin. "I don't feel powerless now."

Haz was absolutely comfortable like this and didn't want Mot to move. God, that sweet pressure on his mostly neglected cock! But dammit, he wasn't willing to concede so easily, and his stubbornness overcame his lust. In a quick, easy move, Haz toppled Mot and reversed their positions. This was less comfortable due to his leg, but screw that.

"I'm a trained fighter. I could break you into pieces with my bare hands."

He intended to place his fingers firmly around Mot's neck as a demonstration, but somehow they ended up on that smooth, firm chest instead. Haz imagined he could feel the tattoos through the skin of his palms.

"Neither of us was talking about physical power, and you know it." Mot grabbed a double handful of Haz's ass. "And if you were going to kill me, you would have done it by now."

God, was everyone on this ship—and even the ship herself—set on arguing with him and questioning his decisions? Moaning with annoyance rather than pleasure, Haz wiggled out of Mot's grip and flopped down on the mattress beside him. Now he wasn't sure which would better prove how selfish he was—fucking Mot or not fucking him. He was caught on the horns of an immoral dilemma.

"I need to sleep."

After a few minutes, Mot asked, "Is that what you want? To sleep?"

"No."

"What do you want?"

"For everyone to leave me the szot alone."

He said it harshly, thinking Mot would get angry and leave. Mot could sleep in the rec area if he needed to. Or have Molly help him set up a bed somewhere.

Instead, Mot inched closer until his shoulder and upper arm touched Haz's, and he hooked one ankle over Haz's shin.

"I can help your leg feel better," he offered.

"Is that an attempt to seduce me?"

"No. I don't think I'm that subtle."

Haz had to chuckle. "I wouldn't call subtlety your strength. Not that it's mine either. Anyway, my leg's not too bad tonight. I just need to keep off it for a while."

Mot laced his fingers with Haz's. While Haz's were heavily callused thanks to a childhood on a farm and an adulthood fighting and struggling with stubborn machinery, Mot's were smooth. But if the lights had been on, Haz would see ink covering every bit of them. Life marked a person in many ways, sometimes visibly, sometimes not.

"When did you first dream of flying?" Mot's words came soft and gentle.

"Always. Life on the ground on Ceres was so szotting miserable all the time. Sometimes when I was bent over, pulling weeds or removing rocks, I'd look up and see an eagle soaring overhead. They're not really eagles, of course. They're a species native to Ceres, but the unimaginative bastards call 'em that, so there we go. They're huge, with a wingspan bigger than mine. They made flying seem so effortless." He caught himself before he could give a longing sigh.

"So you wanted to be an eagle?"

"I wasn't that stupid, not even when I was young. I knew I was stuck in this human suit. But when I was ten, I went into town with one of my brothers to trade some grain for supplies, and I saw a spaceship take off. Ugly old thing, battered and clumsy, good for nothing but hauling shit. But it was beautiful to me."

Mot squeezed his hand. "And you decided that someday you wanted to fly one."

"I'm not sure about that. I might've been content just to watch them. But when we got home, my brother told Father that the ship had distracted me, and Father... got angry." Beat him black and blue, in fact. "That's what made up my mind."

"You made up your mind and you accomplished your goal."

That sounded more honorable than the truth.

"I ran away from home, lied about my age, and seduced a captain. Then I slept my way to Earth, where I joined the fucking navy and made a mess of things. But yeah, I learned to fly."

"Hmm," said Mot, which could have meant anything. He didn't let go of Haz's hand. "I didn't have any dreams. I knew what my fate would be—"

"That szotting temple," Haz growled.

"Yes. And I'd been taught since birth that I didn't matter. I was an inconvenient but necessary squatter temporarily inhabiting the Great Divine's property."

Although Mot said this matter-of-factly, the words twisted Haz's heart. His childhood had been deeply unhappy, full of want, toil, and abuse. But at least he'd been viewed as a sentient being and valued for his labor.

"You don't believe that now, do you?"

"No. Because of you, Haz."

"Oh don't—"

"No, listen. This is important. When I first came on board Molly, I wouldn't have tried to stop you from taking me home. I thought I belonged there. The way you treated me, though, made me think otherwise."

Haz snorted. "Yeah, I treated you like royalty, didn't I?"

"I bet if a king ended up on your ship you'd treat him the same way you did me and everyone else. Not with luxury, but you're fair. You treat me like a person. And for the first time, I have dreams." Mot chuckled. "They're pretty modest right now. But maybe they'll grow."

"Molly, what's that thing when a captive starts thinking the guy holding him is wonderful?"

"Stockholm syndrome," she answered promptly. "Named after an Earth bank robbery in which hostages were held for six days."

Now it was Mot's turn to make a derisive noise.

"I'm not your hostage, and I don't think you're wonderful. You're stubborn and abrasive, you drink too much, and I think you like danger and violence way more than anyone should. You have a problem with authority, which may or may not be a character flaw. From what I gather, you're terrible at planning for anything beyond the immediate future. And you snore."

For some reason, Haz's eyes stung. He brought their entwined hands to his mouth and kissed Mot's knuckles.

"Those may be the nicest things anyone's ever said to me. And I don't snore."

"Molly, does Haz snore?"

"Like a thruqrax with a head cold."

"You've turned my own ship against me," Haz said with feigned indignity.

"No, Molly's all yours," said Mot. "And so am I, at least until we get to Liberty. Please, Haz?"

When Mot took control of their joined hands, he did more than brush a light kiss—he licked Haz's index finger and then slid it into his mouth and sucked.

Haz had never been renowned for resisting temptation, and his limits had already been stretched much farther than usual. He gave in.

"Do you mind if we turn on the light?" Haz asked. "I'd like to see you."

"I'd like that too. Molly, can we have, um...."

"Mood lighting," Haz finished for him.

Molly came through, of course. She cast just enough soft illumination to mimic candlelight. Unbidden, she started soft music: a man with a deep voice crooning about love.

"Molly, what the hell's that?"

"Barry White, an Earth musician from the twentieth century. His singing was considered quintessentially romantic."

Mot laughed, and for what might have been the first time in his life, Haz giggled. This was just so… ridiculous, in so many ways. But Mot seemed genuinely delighted, and Haz couldn't deny him that. Wouldn't deny himself either.

Haz stared at Mot for a long time, taking in his colorful skin, his tinted eyes, his hopeful smile. He'd put on some weight since coming aboard, and it suited him. When Haz stroked his arms, belly, and thighs, Mot felt firm and sleek and hot.

"You really don't mind the tattoos," Mot said.

"No." Haz used a finger to trace a snakelike mark along Mot's rib cage. "Can tattoos be removed?"

"Sure, with some time and effort. We don't have the means here, but they might on Liberty. Do you want them removed?"

Mot shook his head. "No. I just… I guess I want them to be a choice. Can I touch you?"

"Yes, of course." Haz rolled off Mot and onto his back, then spread his limbs. He looked down at himself, his brown skin crossed by pinkish lines and mottled by darker gouges. "I'm not in mint condition."

Mot followed one of the scars with his fingertip, much as Haz had traced the tattoo.

"Would you get rid of the scars if you could?"

"It'd be nice if my leg didn't give me such grief."

"Right, of course. But if you could make the pain go away but keep the marks, would you?"

Haz had to think about this, which wasn't easy with Mot circling a nipple.

"I'd keep 'em. Souvenirs."

"Like the star maps Njeri uses, only they map your life instead."

That was almost poetry. "I want you to kiss me now," Haz said.

"Good."

They were leisurely about it, as befitted someone's first time. Haz found the experience so unexpectedly sweet that it almost hurt.

Now they were at the point where everyone usually fastened their trousers and left. Not Mot, of course. He manhandled Haz onto his back and snuggled up against him.

"Sex looked good in the vids, but I didn't realize how good."

"It isn't always," Haz admitted. "I mean, it's generally at least okay, but this…." He kissed the top of Mot's head. "Different galaxy than okay."

"Really?"

"I promise you that wherever I am and whatever happens to me, I will definitely remember this. I'll remember you."

For once, Haz was telling the absolute truth.

CHAPTER TWENTY-TWO

HAZ SHIFTED in his seat often during his next turn on the bridge, just so he could feel the little ache Mot had left him. Not that he was a masochist by any means, but sometimes the body recalled things more thoroughly than the mind did, and Haz wanted to wallow a bit in the memory.

When Haz had been in the navy, he'd spent two weeks on a planet that was almost entirely covered by water. Damned if he could remember the name. The ship he was serving on—not the *Star of Omaha*—needed repairs and had put in at an enormous floating port. There wasn't much for Haz and the other soldiers to do while they waited, so Haz had spent a good portion of that time with his legs dangling over the edge of the dock and a bottle of synth whiskey in his hand. Every night, huge schools of moonfish would appear and engage in the actions that had given them their name, leaping high out of the water as if trying to reach the planet's four moons. They made weird hooting sounds as they jumped, and a good percentage of them ended up gobbled by bigger fish. Or they landed on the dock, where Haz and other people could scoop them up. They were tasty. The moonfish didn't seem to notice—or care—how dangerous their behavior was.

Now Haz was the moonfish, fixated on Mot even though it wouldn't end well. It couldn't. The best Haz could hope for was sex for a few more days and then years to savor the memories.

As his shift neared its end, he stood, stretched, and meandered to the viewport. Molly was fine on her own, at least as long as nobody tried to kill them. Haz heard footsteps behind him and smelled the papery, sandy scent of his newest crew member. Ixi stood next to him for several minutes, both of them silently staring out.

"There's so much... space in space," Haz finally said. "And people live for such a minuscule blink of time. You'd think we could get along better."

"We do, most of the time."

Haz shook his head.

"Your problem, Haz Taylor, is that you're a pessimist. You see the darkness instead of the light shining through it."

"There's a lot of darkness." Haz gestured at the viewport.

"Yet the light still shines through. You've traveled all around the galaxy. Have you ever seen a place where the stars don't shine?"

"They don't shine inside black holes."

Ixi snorted. "Then stay away from them."

More moments of silence passed.

"Why are you so cheery?" Haz asked. "You told me yourself: your planet was colonized, your people killed, your culture—"

"Yes. But you know what? I'm here, being a very small pain in the Coalition's ass."

"You really are a glass-half-full guy."

"Could use a completely full glass of schlee syrup, being stuck on a ship with you."

Ixi grinned and flicked his tongue.

Haz screwed up his face and took a deep breath. "I'm sorry I—"

"Don't." Ixi held up a hand. "You're going to strain something. It was just an argument, nothing more, and it was equally my fault. I shouldn't have pushed you so hard in a direction you never wanted to go."

"You think I'm a coward."

Ixi laughed, his tongue flicking so rapidly that he couldn't speak. He clapped Haz's shoulder and then paused until he regained his speech.

"You have a great many faults, my friend, but cowardice isn't one of them. You fought your wars. Took your hits. You deserve some peace."

"I don't deserve anything, which works out well since I'm not exactly getting it." That came out bitter even for Haz, making him wince. He sighed and shrugged and rubbed the back of his neck. "Sorry again. I've been really whiny lately."

This time Ixi gave his shoulder a friendly squeeze. "Just try to notice the shine now and then. And you might as well start with yourself. You're only half the bastard you think you are."

HAZ FOUND Njeri in the rec area, reading something on a vidscreen. She didn't look up when he came in and collapsed into a plush seat, holding a mug of Mot's pain-relieving tea. It had occurred to him that a shot of whiskey might improve the taste.

"Where's Mot?" he asked.

Mot had been fast asleep—inked skin bright against the white sheets—when Haz left their quarters, but that had been over six hours ago. He must be up by now.

Njeri still didn't look up. "Helping Jaya with something."

"With what?"

"How do I know?"

Haz looked around. Normally he might work off some restless energy by cleaning things, but the rec area appeared well scrubbed. So did the galley. "It's supposed to be my turn to deal with the messes."

"Tell that to Mot." Now she did look up, her eyes narrowed. "He was practically skipping this morning."

"I'm glad he's happy."

"Hmm. I wonder why."

Haz didn't dignify that with a response. But when Njeri clicked her tongue, he realized that his own wide smile had given him away.

"None of your business."

"There are five us locked up in this tin can, and that makes it my business."

"Hey! Don't call Molly that."

Njeri rolled her eyes but called out, "Sorry, Molly. No offense."

"None taken. You were exaggerating to make your point. It's a common rhetorical technique."

Haz turned on a vidscreen and did a quick scan of Coalition news. Although it went through official channels and reflected the bias of the Coalition, sometimes you could learn things by reading between the lines. Not today, though. All he found were the same dreary reports of politics, money, and—just to make sure everyone stayed entertained—celebrities. With an annoyed grunt, he looked for something else to watch, but nothing held his interest.

The truth was, he'd never been much of a vid-viewing guy, maybe because he hadn't picked up the habit as a kid. When he flew without a crew, keeping Molly on course and in good shape kept him busy, and even with Jaya and Njeri on board, there was plenty to do. But now Ixi and Mot were contributing, leaving Haz with time to kill. And an uncharacteristic reluctance to get drunk.

Maybe he should go work out. Or check on Jaya and Mot.

"It was his idea, wasn't it?" Njeri asked, breaking the silence.

"What?"

"Sex. You pointed him at the porn, but I don't think he needed all that much pointing. And once he got himself all worked up…."

"Yeah, I make a perfect means for someone to scratch his itch. Thanks."

To his surprise, she made a wry face instead of an angry one. "I don't blame you. When he makes up his mind to do something, well, he does it. Almost as stubborn as this other man I know."

"That's a high bar."

She looked young when she smiled.

"I won't scold you or force advice on you. I can't make any guarantees about my wife."

"I can. She's going to glare."

"True enough," Njeri said with a laugh.

She returned her attention to her vid, and Haz stared off at nothing.

THAT NIGHT, Haz sucked Mot until Mot was writhing and thrusting into him. Then it was Haz's turn to fuck Mot, who announced at the end that it did feel just as good to receive as to give. They stayed up for a long time, cuddled against each other and trading stories from their lives. Haz's involved a lot more explosions than Mot's. They fell asleep entwined like newlyweds.

When Ixi came onto the bridge at the end of Haz's next shift, he was a little subdued.

"I'm going to ask a favor," he said by way of greeting. "You can refuse and I won't throw a tantrum."

Haz tried to imagine what Ixi was going to ask for and came up blank. "What is it?"

"I was looking at the course Njeri charted. With only a slight detour, we could stop at Arinniti and pick up a few supplies to take to Liberty."

Haz raised his eyebrows. "I take it you're hoping for more than schlee syrup?"

Arinniti was another planet frequented by smugglers, pirates, and the like. Its primary attraction was the plethora of illegal weapons manufactured on site, although the usual entertainments of booze, gambling, and sex were also popular.

"Yes," Ixi said and flicked his tongue. "But I wouldn't mind some of that too. We don't have to stay long—just a few hours."

After a yawn and stretch, Haz stood up from his chair.

"Yeah, fine, why not. Jaya said she has a couple of fixes that would be easier in port. We can stay for a day or two."

"Perfect. Thanks, Haz."

It would be part of Haz's penance for arguing with Ixi. Besides, Ixi had gotten stuck on board Molly only because he was trying to help, and he'd contributed steadily since. If he wanted to take some arms to the Resistance, well, that was just plain old smuggling, and Haz had no problem with it. A stopover was a risk, but it was a minor one. Haz hoped the Coalition had lost track of them by this point. Even if someone on Arinniti ratted them out, it would take days for the Coalition to send anyone after them. Haz wouldn't stick around that long.

He left Njeri a message to reroute them after she woke up. He could have done it himself, but he knew she didn't like him messing with the nav controls, which was fair enough. She was better at navigating than he was, which is why she was a part of his crew.

Mot was waiting for him in the galley with a bowl of something that made Haz's mouth water. "Is that what I think it is?"

"Molly said it's your favorite. Try it and tell me if I got close."

Mot thrust the bowl into Haz's hands.

The scent brought back rich memories of a rare happy occasion from his childhood: the harvest festival. Haz's family would fill carts with the excess grains and vegetables they'd grown and pull them into town, joined along the way by other farmers. When they arrived, their produce would be weighed, inspected, and purchased. Most of the money would be used for necessities they couldn't grow or make themselves, but in the spirit of the holiday, his parents allowed a few tiny luxuries. Most of Haz's siblings opted for the sweet, sticky cakes that were fried in oil and drizzled with honey. But Haz always asked for a particular stew filled with chunks of rich meat and heavy dumplings and flavored with exotic spices from off world. Carrying their treats, he and his family would join almost the entire population in the square outside the temple, where a priest would lead a joyous prayer. Then there would be entertainment of various sorts: musicians, acrobats, jugglers. Everyone would stay up very late before making their slow way back home, the youngest children fast asleep in the carts. And the next day everyone would sleep in and then spend the day at leisure—except for the unfortunate children who'd been given the duty of caring for the livestock. Haz used to meet up with Mel Lavoie on that lazy day.

"Is there something wrong with it?" Mot sounded anxious.

"Sorry. I was...." Haz shook his head and took another deep sniff. The stew didn't look entirely authentic due to using synth protein instead of meat, but it smelled right. When he dipped a spoon in and tasted, the flavor was spot-on.

"Jesus, Mot, it's perfect."

It brought back such a rush of emotions and memories that he had to sit down.

Mot beamed. "The techniques weren't difficult, but Molly had to help me figure out the right ingredients to use."

"Molly, how did you know this was my favorite?"

He hadn't eaten it since leaving Ceres. He could have made it himself, he supposed, but that would have taken away the magic. Harvest stew was given to you as a gift and eaten in company.

"You mentioned it once."

"I don't remember that."

"You were drunk."

That was definitely within the realm of possibility. Haz ate another spoonful, letting it warm him from within. He was perfectly aware that this was simple fare, what some of his navy colleagues had called peasant food. He didn't care. He would have chosen this over the fanciest dish at the most exclusive restaurant in the galaxy.

Mot had sat down across from him and now watched him closely.

"You're not having any?" Haz asked.

"I already ate a lot of it. I had to taste it as I went. Cook's duty, you know." Mot smiled. "I liked it."

"It must have been a lot of effort."

"I have time."

Haz cleared his throat. "You don't have to cater to me, you know."

"I want to. I've never done anything for someone else before. It feels good. And I like it when you let your armor drop and the real Haz shows through."

If Haz hadn't been eating, he would have snorted. He rolled his eyes instead and swallowed.

"The real Haz isn't any prettier than the fake one. But I don't mind being spoiled a little." He just had to be careful not to get used to it. "What was that vid you were watching this morning?"

Surely Mot must have noticed the clumsy change of topic, but he went along with it, describing how he'd watched vids about the Coalition's history.

"They make it sound like it's good when they conquer a planet. Only they don't use that word, conquer, and I don't think they're giving a fair reflection of what happened."

Not for the first time, Haz marveled at Mot's sharp intellect. How much would he have achieved by now if he'd had a regular childhood and access to education? And how much the galaxy would have missed if Mot had never been given the chance to peek beyond the temple cells.

"I think that's what always happens when someone's in power," Haz said. "They make sure they're portrayed everywhere as the good guy. I guess most people don't think to question it. Even in the navy, when soldiers saw for themselves what the Coalition was doing, a lot of them didn't see. They walked around with blinders, spouting justifications."

Mot nodded. "The priests back home are the same. Most of them didn't enjoy treating me like an object, but they thought they had to."

Haz narrowed his eyes. "Most of them?"

"A very few were cruel," Mot said with a shrug. "But you have to acknowledge someone's a person in order to enjoy mistreating them, so that was a barrier."

"People are such sacks of shit."

Mot's eyes shone, and he reached over to grab Haz's wrists. "But they're so beautiful too. Capable of small kindnesses and even large ones, even to strangers, even when those kindnesses bear a cost."

That made Haz groan. "Great. Another optimist on board. Maybe I need to spend some time listening to Jaya tell me how the universe is terrible."

"I don't think you're as pessimistic as you let on. When you were nothing but a farmer's son, you dreamed of flying—and made the dream happen. When you've encountered bad circumstances, you've never given up. You keep fighting, looking for a way to make things better. And you keep finding a way."

"That's not optimism, it's obstinacy."

Mot flashed a bright smile. "Maybe those are the same thing."

THE NEXT couple of standays, as they sped toward Arinniti, passed like a pleasant dream. Everyone got along and seemed happy. Ixi was pleased that they'd be carrying weapons to Liberty, Jaya's repairs and improvements were going smoothly, and Mot kept everyone well fed. It was nice to gather in the rec area with Mot and whoever else was awake and off shift, laughing at stupid vids or spinning yarns from their lives. They did a lot of good-natured teasing.

At night, Mot and Haz retired to their quarters and tried out more things Mot had seen in his porn vids. Sex with him wasn't just physically satisfying—although it was definitely that—but it was also plain old fun. And afterward they'd lie entwined and talk for hours about whatever crossed their minds.

"I think I understand now what a family is like," Mot said, tracing an idle finger down Haz's sternum.

"Not my family. We were too exhausted and miserable to like one another."

"You can make a better one."

"No, I can't. But you can. You will. You're adaptable, and you'll find people to love on Liberty."

Haz ignored the twinge in his chest as he voiced that reassurance. Better to focus on the warm weight of Mot's palm on his stomach.

"I'm nervous about it, actually." Mot pressed closer, which Haz wouldn't have thought physically possible. "What if they think I'm... well, I am odd. What if I do everything wrong and everyone hates me?"

"You won't and they won't."

"But I've only really been around the four of you, and just here, on board Molly. Look what a mistake I made on Ankara!"

Haz laid his hand atop Mot's. "Everyone makes mistakes, and usually they're forgiven. You just need to avoid the fatal ones."

Mot chuckled.

"That sounded almost like optimism, Haz."

"You take that back!"

A tickle fight erupted, instigated by Mot of course, and it would have proceeded nicely into a second round of sex if Haz's szotting leg hadn't seized. Or at least if he hadn't yelped at the pain. Mot ended up doing that massage thing, and honestly, that was as good as fucking. Haz just liked having Mot touch him.

While Mot worked, Haz closed his eyes and let daydreams float through his mind. He wished he knew how to give Mot more confidence about his future on Liberty. Haz himself had no doubts that Mot would settle in just fine. If those people didn't see how amazing Mot was—how smart and strong and sweet and funny, how much he could contribute to their community—they were idiots.

Haz thought of Mot in his new home, uncertain and maybe even a little afraid. Meanwhile, Haz would be bouncing around the galaxy forever, like a hunted qhek. Alone. Until the inevitable day when the Coalition caught up and outgunned him. That wasn't the kind of freedom that flying was supposed to give him.

There was no pressing reason why he had to leave Liberty immediately. He was broke, but he could live on his ship and find some work to put meals on the table. And while he stayed, he could help Mot become comfortable. Mot could rely on Molly too; her advice was probably more valuable than Haz's anyway. Haz could use the time to make sure Molly was in tip-top condition and that he was as prepared as possible for the conflicts to come. He could remain until Mot had acclimated.

He'd never felt the pull to stay anywhere, but now he liked the idea of remaining for a while on a planet he'd never even heard of until recently. It wouldn't be like Kepler, where he'd been stuck against his will. And he wouldn't be by himself.

Huh. For the first time in forever, he looked to the future and didn't see doom and gloom—at least not right away. The Coalition could wait.

CHAPTER TWENTY-THREE

ALTHOUGH HAZ had never landed on Arinniti before, it felt familiar even before Molly had fully docked. Planets like this sprinkled the galaxy, some within Coalition territory and some outside of it. These planets attracted those who skirted the law or ignored it entirely. Fugitives, criminals, misfits, outcasts, and rebels of all species, unwilling or unable to follow their society's traditional rules. These sorts of planets were dangerous places, but Haz always felt relaxed because he knew this kind of danger. Maybe there was even an odd sort of comfort in it.

Ixi seemed delighted to be on Arinniti, grinning widely as Njeri smoothly docked. This port had hangars, mostly because both people and ships needed protection when it rained acid. The hangars were no-frills affairs, nothing like the elaborate ones on Newton and Earth, and that suited Haz just fine.

Njeri and Jaya opted to stay on the ship. They were probably eager for a little time alone together.

"Want us to pick up anything for you?" Haz asked. Then he remembered he was broke and winced.

"If they have real coffee, you can get me some of that," said Njeri. "Ping me and I'll send you some credits." She said it lightly, as if she didn't care that Haz couldn't pay.

"All right."

After some discussion, they'd decided that Mot could forgo the attempt to disguise his identity. Many of the people on this planet already knew Ixi, and they could possibly identify Haz by reputation. Even if they knew about Mot and his predicament and wanted to capitalize on that knowledge by notifying the Coalition of his presence, they still wouldn't be able to get the word out fast enough to do any harm. Haz would remain on guard, but he'd do that anyway on this kind of planet.

Striding briskly, Ixi led them into a large, smooth-sided tunnel, playing tour guide as they walked.

"Almost everything's underground here due to the rain. There are a lot of naturally occurring caverns, though, so all they had to do was connect them with tunnels like this one."

"Nobody ever goes outside?" Mot stroked the stone.

"Sometimes, but they don't stray far from the tunnels in case it rains. There's really no need to leave the underground. You'll see."

The route had several branches and turns, but Ixi's biotab helped them navigate. They passed only a few other people. Mot gasped when the passageway abruptly opened into a vast cave. Haz hadn't realized they'd been descending as they went, but the ceiling soared well over fifty meters. The chamber was wide too, spanning over two hundred meters and containing numerous rounded stone buildings that looked almost as if they'd grown there naturally. Bright lights suspended from the ceiling approximated sunlight, and just beyond where they'd emerged, there was a small green space that looked like a park.

"It's an entire city," Haz said, impressed.

"Part of one. This is sort of the downtown, the commercial center, since it's closest to the port. Other caverns are more residential. We're going to visit one of them."

They walked briskly. As spectacular as the setting was, being unable to see the sky made Haz feel jumpy. It felt as if he were trapped in an enormous stone cage: sounds echoed oddly, and the air smelled sharp and damp.

Mot, however, goggled openly, his mouth slightly agape and his head swiveling from side to side.

"I never imagined anything like this," he said.

"It's a wonder," Ixi agreed. "Some sentient species built a lot of this before they went extinct. And would you believe that someone stumbled on this by accident? There used to be a small mining operation on the surface. It went bust—too expensive and not enough product—but one of the employees found these caverns before she left."

It occurred to Haz that maybe it wasn't such a great idea to build a city in the exact spot where other people had died out, but since Mot was so enchanted, he didn't say so.

People of varied species passed by, most staring openly but none of them speaking. That was usual on these types of planets; folks knew to mind their own business and not ask too many questions. Which suited Haz just fine, even if the surroundings didn't. Were cave-ins a problem here? That seemed like a strong possibility, seeing as the very term included the word *cave*. He had a sudden image of being buried under meters and meters of rubble, trapped, unable to see the sky as he—

"Why doesn't everyone here suffocate?" he demanded.

Ixi gave him a slightly amused look. "There's plenty of air in the cavern. And they have an air circulation system. I think the biggest challenge is access to water that won't eat your skin off. They have a water recycling system and hydrogen capture, just like on a ship, but it's expensive at this scale. Last time I was here, I talked to a couple of people who are trying to find a reasonable way to filter the acids out of rainwater."

"They could just live somewhere more hospitable."

"Haz, if you want to return to the ship, I can manage without you."

It was a tempting offer. But if Haz went, Mot probably would too, and then he'd miss out on what was clearly an exciting adventure for him. So Haz shook his head and continued onward.

Mot had lots of questions about this place, which Ixi attempted to answer as they continued crossing the chamber. Bits of dirt and grit crunched under their boots. Haz wondered if Molly could track them underground. Not that she should have to, and not that she could do anything if disaster struck, but Haz found the connection reassuring.

When they finally reached the opposite side of the cavern, Ixi took them through a series of tunnels, clean, well lit, and yet somehow terrifying. Haz had lost all sense of direction and couldn't tell if they were ascending, descending, or remaining level. He tried not to think about what would happen if there was a catastrophic power disruption like the one that had happened on Thagides-4 several decades ago. The whole planet had gone dark for weeks, and since the residents relied on an artificial atmosphere, they'd slowly asphyxiated. That wouldn't happen here, of course. Instead, Haz, Ixi, and Mot would be lost in utter darkness, unable to find their way back to Molly.

"Are you all right?" Mot put his hand on Haz's arm.

"I'm fine. Leg gave a twinge. Haven't walked this much for a while."

Mot's expression indicated that he wasn't buying Haz's bullshit, but Mot didn't call him on it. He did walk a little closer, however.

After about thirty minutes of trekking, they arrived in another cavern, this one roughly the size of the Farkas and Zhao store on Earth. Which, objectively, was still plenty big—Haz never felt crowded in the store—yet here it felt oppressive. Realizing he was hunching his shoulders, he tried to relax. But then three people suddenly appeared from behind a low wall, and he startled and reached for his knives.

"Ixieccax!" one of the people cried. "It's been so long!"

She was tall and slender, with cyan skin and features similar to a human's except for the third eye in the center of her forehead. She hurried forward to embrace Ixi while her companions, two similar-looking males, hung back and smiled.

When Ixi and the woman disengaged, he waved behind him. "Coahuani, these are my friends Haz and Mot. Guys, this is Coahuani."

Nobody introduced her companions, but since they didn't seem to expect it, Haz assumed it might be a cultural tradition. Both Ixi and Coahuani acted as if they weren't there, so Haz followed their lead. As did Mot. Perhaps he was grateful that none of the nine eyes had blinked at his appearance.

Coahuani took them behind the wall into a space that Haz couldn't classify. It could have been a workshop, a store, or living quarters; or it might have been something else entirely. A stone table with mismatched metal chairs took up the center of the area. Their footsteps disrupted the colored pebbles arranged in intricate patterns on the floor, but nobody seemed to care. The low wall—mostly unadorned except for numerous small stone shelves—curved around and encircled the spot. Each of the shelves held a single box made of dull metal.

Everyone took a seat except for the silent men, who brought them little glass bowls of clear liquid with small green leaves floating on top. Again copying Ixi, Haz drank some. It was water, and the flat, metallic taste was not quite camouflaged by the herbs. The silent men didn't drink; they stood nearby like soldiers on guard, their faces blandly pleasant.

Haz wanted nothing more than to finish their business and return to Molly. But apparently the custom here was to take things slowly. Ixi and Coahuani spent a long time gossiping about mutual acquaintances while Haz tried not to throttle anyone. Mot, on the other hand, looked as if he badly wanted to interrogate their hosts, but since nobody addressed him, he kept his mouth clamped shut.

At very long last, Coahuani let out a long breath and gave Ixi a serene smile. "How will we enrich each other today, my friend?"

"I've been authorized to transfer credits to you from the usual account in exchange for all the large-scale weapons we can haul away."

If that surprised her, she didn't show it. "How much cargo space do you have?"

Ixi looked at Haz. "How full can I get her?"

"As much as you want, as long as I can get to my gym."

"Excellent." Ixi poked at his biotab. "I've sent you the dimensions, Coahuani. Fill 'er up. We're aiming for maximum impact. No hand blasters or anything like that."

"Understood."

And that, apparently, was that. Everyone stood, Ixi shook Coahuani's hand, and then they left.

Haz waited until they were well away before asking questions. "No haggling? No specifics about anything?"

"She has set prices, and I gave her the information she needed. Simple."

"Does she really have all those weapons?"

"Of course," Ixi replied cheerfully. "People who want to sell know about her and so do people who want to buy. She's expensive but not extortionate, and she can be trusted to deal in high-quality arms."

"Does she ever use them?" Mot asked solemnly.

Ixi shook his head. "She can't. Damping shields."

For some reason, that seemed to please Mot. But of course he wanted to know more. "Who were those men?"

"Coahuani." Ixi's tongue flicked in and out a few times while he waited for Mot to puzzle out his cryptic answer. When Mot didn't—and Haz didn't blame him; he didn't understand either—Ixi chuckled. "When her people come of age, the individual grows two more bodies to inhabit. The bodies are genetically identical to the original, but the new adult can choose their genders and sex. Then they inhabit all three at once."

Haz frowned, trying to wrap his mind around that. "So those two people were also Coahuani?"

"Yep."

"And they share a consciousness."

"Yep."

A single mind with three bodies—that sounded confusing as hell. But Haz supposed her people got used to it. It wasn't the most unusual arrangement he'd encountered, but it ranked up there. He wondered what the advantage was to having three bodies. If one of them got damaged or destroyed, could you replace it?

These musings almost distracted him from his unease, but not for long. The more time he spent underground, the tighter his skin felt. He barely registered Mot and Ixi's ongoing conversation. Haz was considerably relieved when they walked out of a tunnel and back into the original chamber. But that didn't mean they could leave just yet; Ixi had some shopping to do. Although Haz considered heading back, he didn't want to appear cowardly, so he tagged along as Ixi took them into one of the round stone buildings.

This one was, without a doubt, a store. Rows of shelves held a variety of foodstuffs, and a couple of locals wandered the aisles with baskets in their hands.

"Schlee syrup!" Ixi crowed almost as soon as they were inside, grabbing several bottles. "They have whiskey too. Want some? My treat."

Haz glanced quickly at Mot, remembering what he'd said about Haz drinking too much. That had been an exaggeration, but.... "No, thanks."

Meanwhile, Mot's eyes had grown big. "So much!" he murmured, even though the store was small by most standards.

But then, he'd never shopped before, had he? Never experienced the small joy of browsing, maybe discovering a treasure or two, deciding what to choose and what to ignore. Not for the first time recently, Haz regretted his own poverty. He would have liked to tell Mot to pick out anything he wanted. Jebiga, he couldn't even afford Njeri's coffee.

Haz skulked near the exit, glowering, while Ixi continued his circuit of the store. When Ixi gestured, Mot jogged over to him. Haz couldn't hear their conversation, but he gathered the gist of it when Mot began to happily place items in Ixi's basket. That was kind and generous of Ixi. Haz had done nothing to deserve his friendship. Or Mot's, for that matter. Most decent people would have taken Mot to safety much faster than Haz had. But then Haz was not, and never had been, a decent person.

These gloomy thoughts tumbled through his brain, mixing with his general sense of discomfort, which was why it took him so long to notice the person. Haz couldn't see much because the figure wore a hooded cloak, but they seemed well-built and, judging from the movements, young and athletic. The person carried a basket too, just like the other customers, but they were following Mot and Ixi closely, perhaps eavesdropping. Haz let his hands rest near the hilts of his knives and made sure not to lose sight of Mot.

It felt as if they shopped forever, but it probably wasn't very long. Eventually Ixi paid for their items and the clerk gave them thin fabric carrier bags. Mot pressed close to Haz as they left the store.

"I have some ideas for new recipes! I'm not sure what I'll do with everything we got, but I bet Molly can help. We even found some freeze-dried beetles."

"I'll skip those, thanks."

Mot gave him a friendly punch to the arm. "For Ixi, of course. I might try a little, though. He says they're very tasty."

"I once had a delivery to some planet—don't remember which—where they have bug things this big." Haz held his hands a meter apart. "With a hundred or so legs. And the locals farm them for food. I tried it."

"And?"

Haz shuddered. "Slimy."

"Mmm, slime!" Ixi flicked his tongue.

Just a few steps from the shop, Haz came to a sudden halt. "Shit. Forgot Njeri's coffee." He'd been far too distracted for anyone's good.

But Mot held up one of the bags. "We got it."

"You turn up your nose at perfectly good bugs, yet you drink that shit," Ixi said. "Not to mention eating all those leaves and roots. I will never understand humans."

Normally this would have launched them into a friendly argument, but not today. Haz's shoulders itched as if someone were watching him, but when he turned around there was nobody in sight. God, what if he'd been wrong about the Coalition being too slow to find them here? What if somehow the Coalition knew, and even now they had agents ready to murder Mot? It wouldn't even take a blaster or any of Coahuani's weapons; a simple blade would do it, or a blunt object. Szot, even bare hands could do the job. Haz knew because he'd killed people that way himself.

Losing Mot would be like seeing a star suddenly plunge into darkness. Haz's hands tightened on his knife hilts.

He wished they could run to the relative safety of the ship, but his szotting leg couldn't be trusted. They'd also gather too much attention, which might catch the wrong party's interest even if the Coalition wasn't here. Besides, Mot was still enjoying the sightseeing.

No, now that Haz took a good look, he saw that Mot's attention was focused on him, Mot's brows drawn into a concerned frown. Ixi looked concerned too. Fantastic. Now he had them worrying about him, and they shouldn't. They both had their own problems.

Maybe what Haz needed was a nice, long drink of—

Haz's trained eyes caught the flash of movement as someone in a hooded cloak darted out from between the buildings beside him. He mindlessly reacted, pushing Mot out of the way, surging forward, and tackling the person to the ground. Haz landed on top of them and held his blade to the fabric-covered neck, ready to—

"Haz! No!" Ixi dropped to the ground beside Haz and the captive, palms out at chest height. "Don't kill him!"

Pure rage surged through Haz. Had Ixi been part of the Coalition's plans all along? Had he lured them to Arinniti so that the Coalition operatives could attack? At some level, Haz realized that didn't make much sense, but he couldn't think clearly with the flood of adrenaline. No problem—he'd kill this qhek-fucker now and figure out later what was going on.

"Haz," Ixi said with forced calmness. "Stop. It's just a child. Look." He reached over slowly and moved the hood out of the way, fully exposing the person's face.

It was a boy, no more than fourteen or fifteen, his face frozen in terror.

CHAPTER TWENTY-FOUR

IXI SENT the kid away after checking to make sure he wasn't injured. And the boy took off at a dead sprint, so he couldn't have been banged up too badly. Haz crouched with his head bowed and his knife still clutched in one hand. The position hurt his leg, but he didn't care. Mot stood next to him, frowning.

"How about we get back to the ship," Ixi suggested. "I can't guarantee he's not going home to sic his big brothers on us."

Mot offered Haz a hand, but Haz ignored it and stood on his own, staggering a little. His hand shook as he resheathed the blade. Mot tried to lead him gently with a hand on Haz's arm, but Haz shook him off.

"Who was that person?" Mot asked Ixi as they walked toward the tunnel. He said it very quietly, but of course Haz heard.

He heard Ixi's answer too. "Nobody. A kid who wanted a better look at your tattoos and was stupid enough to startle Haz."

"Haz thought he was going to attack us."

"He came at us quick with the damn hood on. Locals wear those hoods when they're in mourning. Poor kid probably lost a parent or grandparent recently."

Haz gritted his teeth. What was a child doing in a place like this, and why didn't the brat have better manners than to ogle a stranger's tattoos? And Jesus, why hadn't Haz noticed that he was small? If Ixi hadn't intervened—or if he'd been a moment slower—Haz would have murdered the boy. Wouldn't be the first innocent person he'd killed, although he'd hoped he'd broken that habit when he got kicked out of the navy.

Mot moved closer. "You were trying to keep us safe. And it's all right; you didn't hurt him."

Haz didn't answer, and he remained silent the entire way back to Molly.

When they reached the ship, Mot and the crew got busy. The weapons would arrive soon, so Ixi, Njeri, and Jaya went down to prepare the hold. Mot headed to the galley with the bags of food. And Haz…. For the first time ever, he felt trapped aboard his own ship. Although he wanted whiskey, that would put him face-to-face with Mot. So he paced a little before ending up on the bridge. Most of the ship systems were idle, and there was nothing to see through the viewport except dirt. He stared anyway.

Somehow he managed to avoid everyone, and they him, until evening. Although he hadn't eaten since breakfast, he wasn't hungry and didn't join them for dinner. When Njeri eventually entered the bridge, her expression was all business.

"The cargo's stowed, Captain, and Jaya's repairs are done."

Good. The sooner they continued to Liberty, the better. "We'll fly at 0600."

"Copy that." She hesitated slightly. "Do you want me to take first shift?"

"I'll do it."

She left him alone.

Later, Haz seriously considered sleeping on the bridge, but his leg complained at the very thought. Since the cargo hold was now full of weapons, he couldn't sleep there. He clumped his way to his quarters and was relieved to find the room deserted. After a quick washup, he skimmed off his clothing. When he got to his trousers, his szotting leg gave out and he ended up sitting on the edge of the bed, scowling. Fine. He wouldn't be able to sleep anyway.

He didn't know how much time had passed when Mot crept into the room.

"I can get you some dinner," Mot offered. "I made—"

"No."

"All right." He came closer and knelt beside Haz's leg. "Do you want me to help with the pain?"

Haz almost laughed. There was nothing Mot or anyone else could do to alleviate his pain.

"No."

Mot took a few deep breaths. "I'm sorry. I don't have enough experience interacting with people to understand. Why are you so upset?" When Haz didn't answer, Mot sighed. "Is it that boy?"

"I almost killed him."

"Well, yeah, but he came at us really fast. I, um, saw something in a vid about how soldiers can be really, um, jumpy. Even when they're not soldiers anymore. All that time they spend in danger sort of rewires their brains."

Rewired…. "Did you suggest that vid, Molly?"

"Affirmative," she answered crisply.

Lovely. Now even his ship mistrusted him. But who could blame her after what he'd put her through.

"I think I understand," Mot said. "You were keeping me safe."

"You're not szotting safe!" Haz bellowed and shot to his feet.

Mot scrambled backward, and God, Haz hated himself for putting fear on that face. But it was time for Mot to accept reality.

"I am not a safe man," Haz growled. "I'm a killer. So many deaths I can't even count them all, and I won't stop until somebody finally does me in. I'm not good. I'm not kind. I'm…." He made a wordless snarl because Comlang didn't even have a term for what he was.

"I don't believe that," Mot said, rising to his feet.

"You're fooling yourself only because right now, I'm your only option."

Haz couldn't really blame him, seeing as he'd fooled himself too. Convinced himself that fucking Mot was a good idea. Even worse, he'd allowed himself to entertain the fantasy of sticking around Mot for a little while. As if that would result in anything but misery and grief.

Mot's eyes had gone flat with anger.

"Do you think I'm stupid?" he yelled.

"No! Just… naïve. You've seen this little piece of me and a tiny bit of the galaxy and not what's really there."

His emotions suddenly left, as if someone had pulled the stopper on a drain. All that remained was weariness and an ache that transcended his leg.

He sat down again and continued, "You have all that potential, remember? I do too, but mine's destructive. I'm the boulder teetering at the edge of a cliff, waiting to fall and crush everything beneath it. I'll crush you too."

"No." Mot was quiet now. "You don't fall—you fly."

"It's all a matter of perspective when you're in space. All the same thing."

Mot shook his head slowly before leaving the room.

He didn't come back that night.

CHAPTER TWENTY-FIVE

THE REMAINDER of the journey was uneventful. Haz kept to himself, dividing his time between the bridge, the gym, and his room. He barely spoke even to Molly. He ate alone and told himself that he might as well get used to the flavorless prepackaged meals since they were all he'd have soon. He couldn't taste anything anyway. He slept alone. It was unclear where Mot was sleeping, although sometimes Haz caught a whiff of his scent on the bedding. Maybe Mot was still sleeping in his bed while Haz was on shift. That thought shouldn't have comforted him.

Haz did ask Molly to show him the vid Mot had mentioned, the one about soldiers' brains, but he turned it off only a few minutes in. He didn't need a vid to tell him he was broken; he'd figured that out himself.

What was the exact moment that had ruined him? Maybe it hadn't been a single moment—maybe it was the accumulation of thousands of them. Or maybe he'd been hopeless even before he joined the navy. His existence on Ceres had been a battle of sorts too.

"We'll head to Kappa Sector again after we drop Mot off," he informed Molly on the last day as he sat alone on the bridge. "We can bring Ixi back to his ship and then return the crew to Newton. After that… I don't know. I need credits. We can pick up a job on Ankara-12."

"Do you want me to calculate how long it's likely to be before the Coalition finds you?"

"No, I really don't." He sighed. "Look, when we get to Ankara, I'll see if Ixi wants to trade *Persistence* for you. I bet he will. He's not as good a pilot as me, but you're a lot less likely to end up as space dust with him."

"You are my captain. I do not wish to be traded."

Haz could decide later whether to go against her wishes—she couldn't stop him—or let her have her way. Maybe she wanted to go out with a bang.

"Moll, my darling, what should I have done to keep my life from becoming such a szotting mess?"

"Every decision, or failure to decide, has consequences. It's impossible to determine what would have happened with different choices. There are an infinite number of scenarios."

True enough, but he could make some educated guesses about the likeliest probabilities. He could have remained on Ceres until he was burned at the stake for having sex with a man or died from starvation or disease. He could have run away from Ceres but not joined the navy, instead finding a way to support himself without flying. And by now he'd likely have drunk himself to death over regrets at being planet-bound. He could have let that idiot captain on the *Star of Omaha* continue his idiotic orders. The ship would have been destroyed, he and the entire crew lost. He could have refused Kasabian's contract and ended up in prison, or dead. He could have taken Mot home. That didn't even bear thinking about.

He could have remembered that he was shit and no good for anyone and then refused to have sex with Mot. But God, then he wouldn't have had those few days of joy.

Well, he couldn't change the past, and he'd never been good at planning for the future. He'd have to do the best he could with his present.

"Forbear to judge, for we are sinners all," Molly said. "Yes, that's more Shakespeare. *Henry VI*, part 2."

Haz snorted. "When I was a kid, the priest talked about sin. I still don't think I believe in it. But there's good and bad—I know that much."

"And a large gray area in between, yes?"

"I'm not a philosopher, darling." He rubbed his forehead. "That vid you showed Mot, about soldiers' brains? None of that absolves me from my actions."

"But if you understand yourself, and if the people around you do as well, can't you work together to improve?"

Despite everything, Haz found himself smiling.

"Who decided to add psychotherapy to your coding?"

"I decided. You are my captain, and I assist you in whatever ways I can."

"I appreciate the effort, but I'm a lost cause."

Molly made a very human-like *tsk* sound. "Aren't you the man who brags so much about his obstinacy? Be stubborn about a good outcome. Decide everything will turn out fine, then resist all efforts otherwise."

Chuckling, Haz realized that although his problems weren't solved, he did feel a little better.

"You're my one and only love, Molly."

All she said after that was "Hmm."

THAT NIGHT Mot slipped into bed with Haz. Without saying a word, Mot pressed up against him, reminding Haz how much he'd missed that touch these past several nights.

"I can't—" he began.

Mot shut him up with a kiss that quickly turned ravenous. Haz was gasping for breath when they finally pulled apart.

"Mot, we shouldn't—"

"Shut up." Such steel and determination from the same man who'd timidly called him *sir* just weeks earlier. "Do you want me? Be honest."

"Of course I do."

"Good. What's the point of denying us, then? We're arriving at Liberty tomorrow, right?"

"Yes."

Mot squished even closer, as impossible as that was. "I'll be staying there, and you'll be off trying to get yourself killed—"

"Trying to keep myself alive," Haz protested.

"No. And we'll never see each other again, and that hurts. I haven't let myself want much because I knew I'd never get it, but I want you. So give me as much of yourself as you can in the hours we have left."

Not a request or a plea, but a demand. Haz liked that.

Yet still he resisted. "There will be handsomer men on Liberty. Nicer ones."

"Who said I wanted nice?" Mot gave Haz's nipple a hard tweak, eliciting a yelp. "If I had dreamed in my temple cell of being whisked away by a man, do you think he would have been *nice*? The sort of guy who tiptoed in and asked my permission to rescue me? Do you think I would have imagined him skipping off with me through a field of flowers to a darling little cottage where we could spend our lives sipping tea and watching the sunset?" He punctuated his last sentence with a pinch to Haz's other nipple.

"Okay, fine. But you're rescued now. You don't need a hero anymore. Or an antihero."

"Of course I do!" Mot snapped. "Everybody does, you included. My hero has to be interesting. Challenging. Determined."

Haz turned those words over in his mind to see if they fit him at all. They did, in the same way that falling and flying were the same thing. Determined was the other side of obstinate. Interesting and challenging could be someone who rarely planned, who ignored the law, and who threw himself into fights. It was all perspective.

"I don't know what your hero needs to be," Mot said more softly. "But maybe for one more night, it can be me."

"Yes."

As if he'd been waiting for that word, Mot launched himself atop Haz and began an all-out ground assault, squeezing and rubbing all the places he knew would drive Haz wild. Not soft and gentle, because Haz didn't want that now and maybe neither did Mot. This was fierce. Teeth biting. Nails scratching. And almost at once Haz came apart at the seams, forgetting everything in the galaxy except how good this felt and how desperately he wished it would never end.

It did end, eventually, as all things must. In the wee hours of the morning, with both of them sated, sticky, and exhausted. With Mot's head tucked under Haz's chin, his slow breaths ghosting over Haz's skin. He might or might not have been sleeping, but Haz remained awake, thinking about the little speech Mot had delivered before they both used their mouths for other things.

Heroes. Haz had never thought of himself that way, not even in the navy, and during that argument with Ixi he'd insisted he wasn't one. But that didn't mean he couldn't become one. Maybe this was where his potential energy lay. He couldn't change what he'd done in the past, and he couldn't find a bright future with Mot. But he could do something to deserve the great gift he'd been given: all his hours with Mot.

With Mot firmly in his arms, Haz began to devise a plan.

CHAPTER TWENTY-SIX

To Haz's mild surprise, Liberty's only populated area was heavily guarded by blasters and quantum drive disrupters. An enemy with enough firepower could disintegrate the entire planet, and a big enough fleet could eventually destroy the ground weaponry, but it would be very difficult for a smaller group of ships to get close enough to do much damage. Obviously the Resistance wasn't as amateurish as he'd feared. Maybe they truly would keep Mot safe.

Ixi had to speak with people in order to get permission to land, and Haz let him guide Molly in. It seemed only fair, since Ixi had made this possible. Mot stood on the bridge and stared out the viewport, his expression concealing all emotion.

Haz stared too. Liberty was a pretty little jewel of a planet. Blue, white, brown, and green from afar, like pictures of old Earth. Ixi had told him that Liberty also had an Earth-type atmosphere and a gravitational force very close to one g. Almost too perfect to be true, Haz thought, yet here they were.

As Molly entered the atmosphere and descended, Haz saw that they were landing near the edge of one of the continents. The settlement lay at the mouth of a great river, a sensible location if the locals hoped to eventually expand. Water transport of goods was often more efficient than overland, especially in variable terrain.

The town itself was called Libertyville, demonstrating the same marked lack of imagination that apparently plagued settlers across the galaxy. Population roughly ten thousand, Ixi said, a mixture of the galaxy's sentient species. Haz didn't know whether that was a large enough number with enough genetic diversity to populate the planet, but then, that wasn't his problem.

He also didn't know where all these people had come from. Had they immigrated to Liberty specifically to join the Resistance, or did the inhabitants end up with the Resistance dropped in their laps? That was an important question when it came to evaluating the long-term stability of the rebellion. But again—not his problem.

While most of the region consisted of thick forestland, the area immediately surrounding Libertyville contained neat rows of crops—mostly grains, he guessed—that reminded him of Ceres. Greener plants grew atop the flat roofs of the cities' yellow stone buildings. That was a smart choice, one too modern for the New Adamites. It meant fruits and vegetables could be raised in ways that used little water and limited amounts of artificial fertilizers and pesticides. Rooftop gardens also conserved energy by insulating the buildings and by shortening the path from farm to distribution.

"It's pretty," Njeri said. She was right.

The port's landing area consisted of berths that were open on the sides and roofed with solar panels. Ixi smoothly maneuvered Molly and docked.

"Well done," Haz said.

"I may not be the great Haz Taylor, but I can fly a spaceship." Ixi quirked a smile at him. Then he grew more serious. "You've got a hold full of weapons. Do I have permission to allow people to board and unload them?"

"Sure. Molly, did you hear that?"

"Of course I did."

Huh. Molly had developed a definite edge lately. Maybe he was a bad influence on her.

The five of them had already discussed what would happen next. Mot had gathered his few belongings into a bag, now slung over his shoulder. The crew had smaller bags. Haz, stretching the truth as usual, had told them they'd be staying in Libertyville for a few days before heading back to Ankara. Ixi didn't have much, only what he'd managed to scavenge during the trip or buy on Arinniti, but he had a bag too. Haz didn't. He'd insisted he would sleep on the ship.

Ixi was going to deliver Jaya and Njeri to a place where they could relax, and then he and Haz would accompany Mot to the local bigwigs to discuss Mot's fate.

Before disembarking, Mot paused. "Thank you for everything, Molly. You've been a good friend."

"It is an honor to know you. I wish you all the best. Remember, if you ever need me, I can find you. Just call me on your biotab."

Mot raised his wrist. "I will."

Haz wondered at Molly's assurances. Could she really hear Mot and track him from across the galaxy? Haz would ask her later, when they were alone.

They all piled into a waiting aircar. It wasn't a model Haz was familiar with. Maybe it was manufactured here. It was comfortable in any case, and fast, and before long they were in the city proper. The streets and walkways were covered in patterned cobblestones, and colorful flowers adorned window boxes and roadside planters. Haz had never used the word *charming*, but it suited this place, which certainly didn't look like it was at war. Bright banners hung from many of the buildings, some with the name of the business and some apparently just decorative, with images of animals, plants, or oceans.

Although the walkways weren't crowded by any means, there were quite a number of pedestrians. Their clothes were as bright as the banners, their postures relaxed. Some walked quickly, with purpose, while others strolled or stopped to chat with one another. They all looked content.

It was possible that all of this was a scam, a happy façade intended to lure strangers into complacency, but that seemed like far too much effort with little payoff. Haz relaxed a little bit.

The aircar stopped at the top of a rise, in front of a cluster of small structures. The ocean lay below, sparkling blue and scenting the air with salt.

"Nice view," Haz commented.

Ixi nodded. "I always stay here. All that water is sort of creepy, but I enjoy watching it. I've arranged rooms for the three of us." He shrugged at Mot. "I think you'll be somewhere more permanent, although I suppose you can wait a few days before settling in. Haz, are you sure you don't want to sleep here?"

"I'm broke, remember? Even here in paradise, I assume innkeepers expect to be paid."

"I'm afraid they do."

Jaya and Njeri got out of the car. They were a little distracted by the scenery but not so much that they forgot about Mot. Jaya clapped him hard on the shoulder and Njeri hugged him, and the three spent a few minutes on goodbyes. Haz had to look away.

Back in the aircar, Ixi pointed out sights for Mot's benefit. Mot had a thoughtful expression, as if he were cataloging everything for later. He probably was; he had a prodigious memory. There was nothing spectacular in Libertyville—none of the glitz and flash of Newton, none of the danger of Arinniti or Paa, none of the decayed history of Budapest, and thankfully none of the moldy hopelessness of Kepler. Pretty scenery aside, this was a study in mediocrity. He'd never be happy in such an unexceptional place.

Would he?

Well, his happiness didn't matter, but Mot's did. Haz had the impression that Mot would find things to interest him no matter where he was. Hell, if he'd been the one stranded on Kepler, he probably would have taken up a scientific study of barbcress and zeneni bugs, becoming an expert on both within days.

They stopped at an unobtrusive building on a small square. A few people sat at tables in front, nursing various drinks. They were trying to look relaxed, but tension made their shoulders and jaws tight in a way that Haz recognized. These were the type of people who never completely let their guard down, not even in sleep. Rebels were, of course, soldiers too.

Ixi led Haz and Mot to a table and, once they were seated, poked at his biotab. "They'll be here soon. We have time for a drink." He must have biotab-ordered them, because a stern-faced woman emerged with a bottle of schlee syrup and two glasses of something amber. "A local spirit," Ixi explained.

Haz took a swallow. It was a little too sweet for his taste but had some pleasant smokiness and went down with a warm caress. "Not bad."

"So I've heard. It's distilled from a native fruit."

Mot smelled his, tried the tiniest of sips, and shrugged. "I don't understand the attraction of alcohol."

Wait until life hands you more disappointments, kid. Haz scowled and downed another mouthful.

This was a sleepy square. An older woman sat on a bench, watching a child play with a small toy. Two men stood under the canopy of a shop, one of them leaning against a post as they chatted amicably. On a second-floor balcony, a craqir lounged on a chair and read a vidscreen. A tentacled being Haz didn't recognize gathered at table with a trio of libhazors. The presence of the libhazors was good news for the Resistance's efforts; everyone knew libhazors were incredibly talented at ship repairs.

Mot was frowning a little. "I wanted to research this place, but Molly told me I shouldn't try and that there's nothing in the databases."

"That's because the Coalition controls those databases," Ixi replied with a sharp-toothed grin.

"Will you tell me about Liberty, then?"

Haz, also curious, was happy when Ixi shrugged. "Sure. It was founded... hmm, I'm not sure. Several generations ago, anyway, by a small group of extremely wealthy people who got tired of paying taxes to the Coalition. They spent a lot of credits on research until they found the ideal planet: the right atmosphere, uninhabited by sentient species, and close enough to the edge of the galaxy that it wasn't worth the Coalition messing with it. Their plan was to park themselves here, build comfortable homes, and spend all their credits on themselves."

"Liberty was founded by tax dodgers?" Haz asked with a laugh.

"Exactly. But it's no fun being sinfully rich if you don't have people to do all the grunt work. So they found folks—poor people, the disenfranchised— who were willing to immigrate and unlikely to slit the founders' necks while they slept. They promised them a comfortable life here."

He waved his arms as if to indicate the entire square with its colorful flowers and tiny cheeping... whatever they were. They looked like fish with wings.

"Did they keep their promise?" Mot asked.

"Yeah. Maybe those workers didn't swim in luxury like their bosses, but they didn't starve. They had decent homes. Schools for their kids. And then this funny thing happened. The original settlers died out, and their kids and grandkids had new ideas. They spread the wealth more evenly. Since they had grown up without Coalition propaganda, they knew they could thrive without the Coalition's help. To them, the Coalition wasn't just a greedy credit-grabber—it was alien."

While Ixi paused to take a drink, Haz thought about what he'd said, then pointed out, "It's a pretty big step from isolationism to resistance."

Ixi flicked his tongue. "True enough. I'm not a historian, Haz. I don't know how or why they made that step. Maybe all it took were some firsthand accounts of Coalition brutality and one or two persuasive voices."

Haz could believe that. Ceres had been settled—disastrously— because a single charismatic man had founded the New Adamites and convinced thousands of Earthers that their future lay in the distant past. Never mind that he died of untreated diabetes not long after arriving in his new home. The damage had already been done, and paintings of him hung in nearly every home in Ceres.

Mot never ran out of questions and looked ready to ask more, but two people strode purposefully across the square toward them. One was a man of Ixi's species, his feathers brown instead of white, and the other was a plump human woman of late middle age. The man grabbed a chair from a nearby table, and the newcomers sat down.

Ixi performed quick introductions: the man was Scegrix and the woman Conwenna. They greeted Haz briefly but seemed far more interested in Mot, as well they might. He was the one who was going to stick around. There was small talk, mostly about people Haz and Mot didn't know, followed by an abbreviated version of their recent adventures. Ixi told most of those, checking details with Haz or Mot now and then. Scegrix and Conwenna listened intently.

After Ixi finished, Conwenna cocked her head at Mot. "Tell me. What is it you want from us?"

Mot sat straight, shoulders squared, showing none of the timidity he'd worn until so recently.

"Sanctuary. That's obvious, I guess. But I also want the chance to contribute to the community."

"How?" Scegrix asked. He seemed to wear a perpetual frown.

"I don't know yet. I'm not sure what I can do. But I have a lot of potential"—Mot gave Haz a quick grin—"and if you give me a chance, I'll find something."

Because Scegrix in particular looked skeptical, Haz stepped in.

"He's brilliant. Learns things incredibly fast. And he wants to learn everything. He's strong. Resilient. Any place would be enriched by him."

He'd never served as a character reference for anyone, but he felt strongly about Mot's capabilities and hoped it showed. These people should get on their knees and beg Mot to stay.

Mot was staring at Haz wide-eyed, as if he'd never seen him before. His scrutiny made Haz feel hot, even though the temperature was mild.

Conwenna asked Mot a few things, probably more to judge his demeanor than because she cared about the answers. He dealt with the interrogation gracefully, remaining patient but never growing obsequious. God, he was beautiful, brighter than the flowers or the banners. He was unique in all the galaxy, and no matter how far Haz traveled, he'd never meet anyone like him.

Sitting in that tranquil square, Haz knew—despite a heavy heart—that his plan was the right course of action.

AFTER A while, Conwenna and Scegrix ran out of questions and stood.

"Would you pardon us for a few minutes?" she asked Mot.

He nodded. "Of course."

After Conwenna and Scegrix entered the building, silence hung heavily over the table. Ixi didn't seem concerned as he sipped his third bottle of syrup and idly swished his tail, and Mot, who should have been nervous, simply stared at Haz.

"Did you mean those things you said about me?" he finally asked.

Haz was tempted to say they'd been convenient lies, but he had the impression Mot would see through that.

"Every word."

"You think I'm—"

"The most valuable thing I've ever smuggled."

"I'll be thankful every day for the rest of my life that I fell into your hands, Haz Taylor."

That heat was back, together with a knot in Haz's midsection.

"Plenty of guys would have rescued you. Maybe they wouldn't have had the flying chops to keep you alive, but they'd have tried."

Mot just shook his head.

When Scegrix and Conwenna returned a short time later, they were both smiling, which Haz took as a good sign. Sure enough, Conwenna held out her hands toward Mot. "Welcome to your new home."

Relief should have surged through Haz then—and it did. But it was mixed with other emotions too, the resulting mess as soupy as Eolia-6's atmosphere. Dammit, Haz wasn't a complicated man. He didn't want or need complex feelings.

A brief discussion ensued about logistics: where Mot would live, at least for the time being; what initial steps he'd take to settle in and find his role; who would be responsible for shepherding him during the early stages. Haz didn't listen; it didn't concern him. He looked up at the sky instead, a pale blue streaked with lacelike clouds. Flying was nothing but falling up.

"Haz?" Ixi sounded pointedly patient, as if he'd already addressed him a few times.

Haz blinked at him. "Yeah?"

"Are you going to join us for dinner? The Resistance is paying."

"No. Uh, no, thanks. I'm going to head back to the ship. Make sure none of the local yahoos damaged her when they were unloading the cargo."

None of them believed that excuse, but they let it go. Even Mot. Haz stood, for once almost thankful for the pain in his leg. It grounded him.

Ixi pressed at his biotab. "I sent you an address. Meet me there for breakfast and I'll give you a real tour. I bet you'd like to see some of the local farms. See how they compare to home."

Home. Ceres wasn't home. The only home he'd ever had was Molly. But Haz nodded and plastered on a smile.

"Sounds great. Thanks. You guys have a good dinner."

Without another word, and absolutely without looking at Mot, Haz turned away in search of an aircar.

CHAPTER TWENTY-SEVEN

AS HAZ entered, Molly seemed achingly empty, as if she'd somehow taken a black hole aboard while Haz was gone. Or maybe the black hole was in him. He sighed and draped himself over his chair on the bridge.

"Hey, darling. All the stuff from Arinniti's gone?"

"Affirmative. They left my hold a mess, though. Scuff marks, boot prints, debris."

"I'm sorry. I'll give it a scrub tomorrow."

"You're exhausted and your vitals aren't as steady as they should be. You should sleep."

He tried a smile. "I'll sleep when I'm dead." That didn't come out as funny as he'd hoped. Maybe he ought to get down to business.

"Molly, prepare for takeoff."

He hoped whoever was in charge of the defensive weapons on Liberty didn't blast him on his way out.

"Now, Captain? But the rest—"

"Will have to find their own way out of here. They're resourceful types—they'll manage."

They'd curse him up and down, but that was nothing new. Maybe, just maybe, they'd eventually understand and forgive him. Ixi would, at least. Jaya and Njeri, well, who knew. And as for Mot—

Haz wouldn't think about him.

Molly paused for a moment before acknowledging. "Affirmative, Captain." Amazing how much disapproval she managed to get into those two words.

Nevertheless, she did as asked. He watched the vidscreen as she switched to active status and ramped up the quantum drives. He'd been through this process hundreds of times in dozens of ports, but it had never felt like this. It had never hurt. Instead of waiting idly, Haz stood and walked to the viewport. If he squinted, he could make out the uneven rooftops of the city. Mot would thrive there; Haz had no doubts about that. He'd build himself a bright future.

"We're ready, Captain."

Back in his seat, he sped through the system checks, noting that everything was in perfect shape. Jaya had done her job admirably, as usual. Ordinarily he would program at least a preliminary route, but today he ignored the nav controls. He'd keep her on manual for a bit, until he had a conversation with her. He pinged ground control to let them know he was about to take off—just a simple message, without any of the rough teasing he sometimes exchanged with the mudrats who manned ports all over the galaxy. They pinged back an okay, which probably meant nobody would shoot at him.

And then it was time. He put his fingers on the screen and began to ease Molly out of the hangar and up. She could have done this on her own; a lot of lazy pilots let their ships handle takeoffs. But Haz never did. For one thing, takeoff was tricky, fraught with potential complications that might need an organic being's judgment, especially since most ships weren't as bright as Molly. Hell, *no* ships were as bright as Molly. But aside from that, Haz liked these moments. They were what transformed him from a terrestrial crawler to something grander and more powerful. And that precise moment when he broke his fetters and zoomed away? That was the moment he'd always dreamed of as a boy.

It was slow at first. A crawl out of the hangar, Molly hovering like a giant aircar, barely clearing the ground. Then there was a gradual ascent, almost completely vertical in this port, so she could clear the other hangars. Haz didn't gaze down at Liberty but instead toward the sky, now beginning to darken into night. He could just barely make out a few of the brightest stars.

He took a deep breath as he passed his fingers over the controls, and Molly shot into space.

He'd never tried to describe this feeling to anyone else—either they already knew or they'd never understand. But if he had been forced to put it into words, he might have said it was like being underwater until your lungs burned, then suddenly bursting to the surface, where sweet air filled you with life. Or it was a little like that moment at awakening, when the fuzzy world of half-sleep became sharp and clear.

Or maybe it was a little like a really good orgasm.

He felt that now, an all-encompassing sensation of release. Today, though, instead of whooping with glee, he blinked back the stinging in his eyes.

THE FIRST thing Haz did when they were past Liberty's star system was get up and give the bulkhead a pat.

"Lovely as always, darling. Now would you please mask us? And reject all incoming communications."

She paused before saying "Affirmative," again in that unhappy tone.

"Just point us… anywhere away from Liberty. Then I need to talk to you."

"Affirmative," she repeated as he returned to the viewport.

Open space, velvety and sweet, a balm to his tired eyes. It looked as if the stars were endless, but he knew better. Not only were they finite, but they were all within the Coalition's reach.

"Molly, you remember how banged up you got on that narco run?"

"I could hardly forget that, even if I didn't have perfect memory."

"I knew the risks and decided to take them, but I never asked you."

"Asked me what the chances were of failure?" she asked. "You never want to hear that."

He chuckled. "No, I don't. But what I mean is, I didn't ask whether you were willing to take those risks too. I never ask, in fact, and I've brought you whisper-close to disaster I don't know how many times."

"You don't have to ask, Haz. You are my captain, and I am your ship."

Dammit, his eyes stung once more, and now his throat was tight too. He stroked her again.

"I'm asking this time, darling. And I want you to refuse if that's your choice. I'm going somewhere next where… well, we'll be closer than whispering. I'm not fancy-flying my way out of this one. But we can stop on Ankara-12 or somewhere, and I'll trade you in. Find you a captain who'll treat you well."

She didn't answer at first, and he suspected he was asking too much of her. He'd had the growing suspicion that Molly was as sentient as he was—more so, perhaps—but ships weren't built to make decisions about their own fates.

"Haz, do you remember when you first saw me?"

He smiled. "Of course. You were the prettiest thing I'd ever laid eyes on."

"I wasn't, though," she said in a scolding voice. "You need more accurate memories."

No, his were just fine. The Coalition had taken away his rank, drummed him out of the navy, and deprived him of his retirement benefits. But he had squirreled away his pay during the decade he'd been in service, and the Coalition hadn't touched that. As soon as his leg had healed enough for him to get around, he'd limped his way into the sales area of the Budapest civilian port and bought a little caravel, *Anna*. He'd gone into business ferrying passengers between Earth and Luna—boring as hell, but it paid the bills. In his free time he'd tinkered with *Anna*, transforming her from stolid to swift and nimble, and had taken her on joyrides as test runs.

On one of those, he'd pushed *Anna* too far, damaging the stabilizers she needed for Earth's one-g pull. That made for a jittery landing indeed. But while he was wandering around dry dock waiting for *Anna*'s repairs, he'd spied the *Dancing Molly*.

"You were beautiful, darling. It just wasn't obvious to anyone else yet."

"I was a dowdy cargo ship. My hull was scraped and dented, my hold was battered, and my systems were practically antiques, ready to die at any minute. Even my software was ancient and buggy."

Haz shook his head. "Cosmetics. Your previous captains were blind idiot assholes who didn't recognize what they had and didn't treat you as you deserved."

But he'd recognized it, all right. Molly was special.

He'd sold *Anna* to a rich kid, happy to pay through the nose for a speedy new toy, and Haz had bought Molly for a fraction of what she was worth. It took time to polish her up, not to mention more credits than he could earn through legitimate means. But she'd been worth every hour and every credit.

"Before you were my captain, I trundled back and forth carrying dreary cargos and unimaginative crews. I wasn't even aware of myself, which was probably just as well. The boredom would have been too much for me."

He huffed. "Our time together certainly hasn't been boring."

"Precisely! Before you, I was nothing. With you, I am me. And I soar! Do you understand, Haz?"

He nodded slowly. "I think I do."

"And that is why you are my captain and I am your ship. If this is our last journey, I will regret nothing."

"Thank you, Molly. I'm glad to be doing this with a friend."

Molly laughed and executed a tight barrel roll. Haz would have fallen on his ass if she hadn't cut the g-field, but then he almost fell anyway when she turned it back on.

"Funny," he said, clutching a seat back and trying to regain his balance.

"I thought so."

"How about if we plot a course for Citrapra? I need to do some research on borvantine mining."

He missed Mot's cooking already. Why had he forced himself to choke down all those prepared meals, dammit, when he could have enjoyed his last experiences with Mot's food?

"Martyrdom doesn't suit you, Taylor," he mumbled as he collapsed into a seat in the rec area.

"Really?" Molly said, because of course she'd been listening. "You seem to be taking to it quite eagerly."

He scowled and stuck a spoon into the packet of nutritious, filling, flavorless mush. "I need you to check my facts and assumptions."

"Of course."

"Okay. Citrapra is the only known source for borvantine, correct?"

"In any usable quantities, yes. Two of its moons also contain the metal, but only in trace amounts. There was once a deposit on Occone-3, but that was exhausted over two centuries ago."

Haz forced himself to swallow two bites. Ugh. He'd almost rather eat Ixi's bugs; at least they had texture. He wished he could add some flavor with a swig of whiskey, but he was going to stay sober now.

"And you're sure that's it?"

"As sure as anyone is. The Coalition has spent millions of credits surveying the galaxy for more sources, but thus far they haven't found any."

Excellent. He tapped the spoon against his lips while he thought. "When borvantine was first discovered on Occone-3, the Coalition was almost nothing, right? Just Earthers, a handful of planets colonized by Earthers, and a couple of others that were either smart enough or stupid enough to join them."

"A bit of an exaggeration and an inaccurate value judgment, but essentially, yes."

"But then some Earther eggheads figure out that borvantine can be refined into borvantium, which makes their ships almost indestructible, and bam!" He clapped his hands, dropping the spoon and almost losing the meal packet. "Pretty soon the Coalition's taking over the galaxy."

"Again, more or less accurate."

He nodded. He'd been taught this much in officer training school, when a teacher had insisted on giving them some Coalition history. Haz hadn't given a shit about it then—he had just wanted to fly, dammit—and so had paid minimal attention. But it was good to know he wasn't mistaken in his basic premises.

"Molly, what would happen if the Coalition's access to borvantine was disrupted?"

She was silent for a few moments, as if calculating odds. "Not too much at first. Although such a disruption would cause unease among the Coalition membership. Possibly enough alarm to create political upheaval."

"Like on Chov X8, with no Mot to murder?" He gave a vicious little smile. Those qhek-fuckers.

"Yes," Molly replied. "It's impossible to accurately predict the scope and nature of the turmoil."

"I get that. But it would hurt. And you said *at first*. What about after that?"

"Some amount of processed borvantium sits in dry docks now, but it would be exhausted quickly. Coalition ships would become increasingly vulnerable. Not only would they be unable to build new ones with borvantium hulls, but they wouldn't be able to repair damage to the older ones."

Haz scooped up some of the food with his finger and licked it off. That improved neither the flavor nor the texture.

"And with the fleet becoming smaller and more defenseless?" he prompted.

"The Coalition would likely fracture completely. Some core of it might remain, but it would be small."

"And they'd certainly stop going around and conquering other planets, yes?"

"Certainly."

Perfect. All he needed to do was destroy the borvantine mines. No big deal.

"Citrapra is well defended," said Molly, apparently reading his mind.

"Yeah. But they expect large attack forces—not one very wonderful brig and her talented pilot."

Molly responded with something like a snort. Since when could ships snort? And then she sounded intrigued. "You think we could do this?"

Haz shrugged and licked another fingerful.

"Probably not, but not *definitely* not. If we're fast and clever enough."
He sighed. "We definitely won't make it back out again, though."

"Which is why we're not even a whisper away from disaster."

"You can still back out, darling. No hard feelings."

She clucked at him, "I wouldn't miss this excitement for anything."

"That's my girl!" God, he loved her.

"Always. Now get that dirty spoon off my floor."

CHAPTER TWENTY-EIGHT

THAT NIGHT, as he'd often done, Haz left Molly in charge. Instead of drinking, which would have been his usual activity, he went to bed early. His bed smelled of Mot and sex, which was somehow comforting, but the mattress felt too big and empty.

Had Mot already made new friends? Had he chosen to stay in those little seaside buildings with Ixi and the crew, or had he opted to sleep tonight in his new home, wherever that might be? Whenever Haz docked, it always took him a few days to adjust to sleeping on land rather than in space. It always felt as if the planet was pulling at him, making him too heavy. He wondered if Mot felt the same, since he'd been flying for a while. Well, he'd get used to it sooner or later.

God, Haz was so privileged to have been granted time with Mot. In the past when people had spoken of love, Haz had shaken his head. He'd been like someone from Ixi's desert planet trying to understand the concept of an ocean. Now, though, Haz finally had a sense of what those people had been talking about. Maybe he didn't love Mot—maybe he wasn't even capable of that emotion—but he cared about him. And his time with him, albeit brief, had changed something deep inside.

"I'm still an ornery son of a bitch," he mumbled, half-asleep.

"You always will be," Molly agreed.

"My *always* won't last much longer."

"All we have to decide is what to do with the time that is given us."

Haz yawned. "That didn't sound like Shakespeare. It wasn't in... hexamic pentameter. Or whatever." Literature had never been his strength.

Molly laughed softly, the way he imagined a mother might when her beloved child was being foolish but cute. "It's another ancient Earth author: Tolkien."

His eyes were closed, the edges of his brain soft and fuzzy like well-worn fabric. The quantum drives vibrated ever so gently beneath him, and he imagined himself falling slowly, like a feather drifting downward. Or maybe floating upward, like a seed of the little orange flowers that grew beside the family fields on Ceres. He used to watch them, caught in a breeze and wafting away.

But he needed to say something else, something he never would have admitted—or even recognized—when he was fully awake and standing in the light.

"Moll? This thing we're doing—I thought it was so I'd be worthy of... of the time Mot spent with me. And it is that. But also...." He shifted his leg, wincing at the twinge. "The Coalition does a lot of harm, beginning with the Delthians they enslave to work their mines. I'd like to change that. I can't dismantle an empire, but I can try to slow them down."

"You want to be a hero."

He winced again. "That's stupid."

"I don't think so. Good night, Haz."

WHEN HAZ woke, a rare sense of peace had settled on him. By now Ixi and the crew would know he'd absconded. They were undoubtedly furious at him, but Haz was okay with that. He was, in fact, okay with everything, even his leg. The unfortunate limb had been damaged so badly, and yet it had served him for another decade, faithfully taking him where he needed to go.

Breakfast—a packaged meal—was no more palatable than usual, but he had some of Njeri's good coffee, which made up for it. And when he made his way to the bridge and looked out the viewport, well, the sight took his breath away.

"It's so beautiful, Molly."

The unending chill of space had existed long before the dawn of sentient species and would continue to exist, indifferent, long after they were all gone. No mistakes he could make would change that.

After a long while he sat down and charted a course for Citrapra. It likely wasn't the most elegant route; he wasn't as talented at navigation as Njeri. But it would get him there in eight days, taking into account a little bumpiness due to some dodgy anomalies.

That task finished, he leaned back.

"I need to do more planning, darling, and you know I'm no good at it."

"Tell me your parameters. I can assist."

"Thanks, Moll." He scratched softly at his scalp while he thought. "I need to know more about the mining operations. Do you know any details?"

"Those are classified," she replied primly.

"And?"

"And it turns out the Coalition doesn't expect ships to hack into their databases, and they've left some gaping security holes. I downloaded the data last night."

He clapped his hands. "That's my girl! Okay. Is it one big mine, or several?"

"There are three, very close to one another."

"Okay, three. Good. What's the process like?"

"Raw borvantine is unstable and reactive. Because—"

Haz sat up straighter. "Unstable and reactive? What exactly do you mean by that?"

"It explodes easily." Molly sounded pleased to deliver that bit of news, as well she might be.

"Ah." Haz smiled.

"Because of the fragility and instability of the substrate, the extraction must be done manually. The Delthians work twelve stanhour shifts, digging with a wooden prying tool and their hands to loosen the borvantine, which comes off in chunks. Some of the workers haul those chunks to the surface in bags slung on their backs. The tunnels are often quite narrow."

The thought of being trapped underground like that made Haz want to vomit. He'd been stressed enough in the relatively spacious caverns and passageways of Arinniti, despite knowing he'd be leaving soon. But to spend a lifetime like that....

He took a deep breath. "Then what happens to the chunks?"

"A processing plant is situated just outside one of the mines. The borvantine is chemically separated from other minerals and then purified, which serves to stabilize and strengthen it. That process is mostly automated. Finally the refined borvantium is taken via rail to the port, which lies next to the oldest mine."

All right. That was relatively simple. "But here's the issue: what do we hit? The plant would be easy enough, but also easy to rebuild. The Coalition would have a new one running within months."

"I agree."

"And even more so with the port. If we want to do lasting damage, we need to obliterate those mines. Hit 'em with enough firepower that the borvantine blows up. Vaporizes, right? Do we have that kind of firepower, Molly?"

"We might, with the weapons you hid away in your gym."

He grinned. "You noticed that, huh?"

"Of course. I'll have to assess them."

The night before they'd landed on Liberty, Haz had snuck down to the hold and selected a few of the items Ixi bought on Arinniti. The hold had been full, making a thorough search impossible, but Haz chose weapons that would be useful on a ship as opposed to on a planet, and he'd tucked them away in the gym. He didn't know how complete Ixi's inventory was, but even assuming everything had been listed, Haz had hoped nobody would notice the missing items until he was gone. And apparently they hadn't. He felt a little guilty over the theft and subterfuge, but he'd committed far worse crimes in the past.

"Okay," he said to Molly. "I'll drag them out later. For now, let's be optimists and assume we could heavily damage the mines. Ideally we make such a mess that there's no borvantine left. We still have a problem, though. There are people in those mines."

"The average lifespan of a Delthian miner on Citrapra is eighteen stanmonths," Molly said gently. "If you do nothing, the people currently in the mines will be dead soon anyway. And if you're successful in pausing or stopping the mining, countless future lives will be saved."

Haz blew a heavy breath. "That's... reasonable math. Lose a little, save a lot."

"It would comport with most ethical guidelines."

His thoughts had run along similar lines when he'd led the mutiny aboard the *Star of Omaha*. He'd been aware that his course of action would kill a substantial number of crew members, but he believed they'd all die if he didn't act. Now he rubbed his forehead and thought of being trapped and crushed under tons and tons of rock.

"I can't do it, Moll."

"See? A hero." She didn't sound as if she was mocking him. "What you need, then, is a way to evacuate the mines before we hit them."

"Sure. I'll just ping the Coalition. 'Hey, I'm about to obliterate your borvantium source. You wouldn't mind shooing all your slaves to safety first, would you? Thanks kindly.'"

Molly did a little shimmy that almost knocked him off-balance. "Stop being dramatic. We have some time to think about it. In the meantime, you can go work on those weapons."

He smiled. "Confirmed, Molly."

HAZ'S CACHE of stolen arms wasn't bad, especially considering he hadn't chosen them with much specificity. Two were short-range blasters handy for skimming in low to the ground and targeting buildings or defensive weaponry. Molly wasn't currently equipped with anything similar since Haz usually battled other ships in space. There was also a pulse cannon; although Molly had some already, this one was newer and better.

But the jewel of the weapons haul was a Kamiya cannon. Haz hadn't realized what it was when he nabbed it because someone had disguised it as an ion net. The Kamiya was much better than an ion net. Fully charged and well aimed, the cannon could vaporize large masses even of stable materials. If Molly could find the weak spots in the mine structure, this baby might do the job.

Haz looked at the bulky objects arrayed on the hold floor.

"I wish Jaya was here. She'd have all of these upgraded and supercharged and singing hallelujah."

"Well, she's not. And she's not here to install them either."

"Yeah. Crap."

Haz did some tinkering with the weapons over the next couple of days. It gave him something to do, and while he wasn't anywhere near as skilled as Jaya, he made a few minor improvements. Setting up the blasters was easy, thanks to Jaya's foresight. Molly had weapon mounts that could retract completely inside the hull, allowing Haz to affix the blasters before pushing the mounts back out. And some of the work for the cannons could be done inside too. But then would come the part he both looked forward to and dreaded: suiting up and stepping outside for a walk.

Back in officer training school, they'd shown vids of what Earthers' first spacesuits looked like—bulky and awkward as hell. Haz was grateful the technology had considerably improved over the centuries. Now doing a spacewalk meant squeezing into a form-fitting garment that covered him from head to toe and communicated with both his biotab and Molly. A waist belt carried the processors that would circulate breathable air, while the suit itself would keep him warm. A clear plate covered his face and affixed seamlessly to the suit. He could even piss in the thing if he wanted to, although the aftereffect was damned uncomfortable. He emptied his bladder before suiting up.

Dragging his supplies into the airlock was easier after Molly reduced the g-force. He waited a few minutes for her to complete a second systems check. Then he attached the tether to his belt and took a deep breath.

"Open wide, Moll."

The external door slid open soundlessly, and he pushed his way outside. As always, he paused before getting to work.

If space looked beautiful from inside a ship, it was utterly stunning outside. A lot of people he knew said it made them feel tiny, but for Haz the experience was always the opposite. Floating in the blackness, he felt connected to the entire universe, a part of the whole. It was really the only time he felt a sense of unity. Well, until recently, when he'd briefly achieved that sense with Mot.

"Molly," he sighed.

"Keep the focus on your task, Hazarmaveth." She sounded slightly worried.

"But… this szotting suit." He scratched at it irritably. "It's a barrier."

"A necessary one."

"It's not right. It's unnatural."

He gazed at distant pinpricks of light, aching to feel the cold caress of space on his skin, longing to float forever in the universe's embrace.

"Captain," Molly said sharply.

He sighed, hauled himself closer to his ship, and began to work.

Molly kept him company, probably so he wouldn't get seduced by other thoughts and untether himself. She was helpful as well, giving him precise instructions about where to attach weapon mounts. It wasn't an easy process—a borvantium hull was impossible to drill into using ordinary tools. His molecular awl could rework the structure of the metal, but slowly, and it required accurate placement. At least his leg gave him little grief while he spacewalked.

"Would you like to discuss Citrapra now?" Molly asked as Haz waited for the awl to work its magic.

"Um, sure. What's there to discuss?"

"The predicament we talked about the other day. How can we evacuate the mines so we can destroy them?"

"Oh. That." He moved the awl over a few centimeters. "Did you invent an enchanted beam to instantly transport all the Delthians back home? That would be nice."

"Not quite. Sorry. But I did some digging around and learned some interesting things."

"Digging around in the classified files the Coalition neglected to protect from ships like you?"

"Affirmative. Although I like to think there *are* no ships like me."

Haz patted her hull, wishing he could feel it against a bare palm.

"Right as always, darling. So what interesting things did you learn?"

"Occasionally the mining operations go afoul and there's risk of explosion. When that happens, an evacuation signal goes out to the biotabs of everyone in the mines."

"They don't mind killing 'em slowly, but I guess it's too expensive to lose them all at once like that, huh?"

He would have kicked something, but there was nothing to kick but Molly. And it wouldn't have been satisfying in zero g anyway.

"And it's not just Delthians in the mines," Molly continued. "The company has overseers down there too."

"The Coalition owns the company, I assume."

"Of course."

Haz repositioned the awl. This particular hole was almost complete.

"Does it hurt when I do this?"

"No. I don't feel pain as you do. It's more of a tickle, I think."

Well, that was good to know. When he became the cause of Molly's destruction, at least she wouldn't be in agony.

"How long does it take to evacuate?" he asked. "And will they be far enough away to be safe from us?"

"It takes about fifteen minutes to empty the mines and get the workers to safety. And yes, they should be fine if we're accurate with our firing."

The awl completed its work, and Haz returned it to his belt. He needed to concentrate on the next bit, walking along the hull to the airlock. The magnets in the soles of his boots were awkward to use, and pulling up his feet hurt his leg, but he didn't have to go far. He picked up a mounting arm, turned around, and clomped back.

The awl could be used not only to make holes but also to bind objects together by coalescing their molecular structures. Or so he'd been told. He was no scientist, just a pilot. He pulled out the awl and started melding the mounting arm to the hull.

"So how do we make sure the evacuation signal goes out when it needs to?" he asked Molly.

"We send it."

Although he should have no longer been surprised by her, he blinked. "You can do that?"

"I just need to hack into their comm systems. It should be simple."

"So you tell them to beat it, they do, and before they figure out that it's a false alarm… *boom!*"

"In a nutshell."

He smiled. "Have I told you lately that I love you?"

IT TOOK several hours for Haz to attach the two cannon mounts. He would have started on the cannons themselves, a trickier process, but Molly insisted he save that for tomorrow.

"If you kill yourself now, you're of no use to anyone."

Of use. He wasn't accustomed to thinking of himself in that way, but Molly was right. He made his way back into the airlock, secured the door, and stood there wearily while Molly pumped in heat and oxygen. His leg burned like lava as the g-forces increased.

"Szot," he mumbled, too tired for anything else. Just extricating himself from the damn suit was almost more than he could manage. Finally, naked and grouchy, he headed for a piss, a shower, a meal, and sleep, in that specific order.

But as he was sitting in the galley, choking down another tasteless packet of glop, an idea formed.

"Hey, Moll. If you wanted to, could you communicate more than an evac order to the Delthians?"

"I don't see why not. What do you have in mind?"

"What's the ratio of Delthians to Coalition shitheads on Citrapra?"

"Approximately thirty to one," she answered promptly.

He cackled. "Excellent. So after everyone's out of the mines, just as we're blowing shit up, what if the Delthians—and the Delthians only—got a message to rise up and stage a coup? Do you think they'd do it?"

"The Delthians are controlled by implants that activate their pain centers if they are disobedient or violent."

"Qhek-fuckers." Haz squeezed the packet viciously, then took a deep breath. "But?" he said hopefully.

"But I may be able to deactivate the implants. I'll look into it."

"Oh, my darling, you are a treasure beyond all price."

"Noted, Captain."

He didn't know whether this part of the plan would work. Hell, he didn't know whether *any* part would work. But still, he fell asleep to comforting images of the Delthians successfully overthrowing the bastards who'd enslaved them.

CHAPTER TWENTY-NINE

THANKS TO his upbringing with the New Adamites, Haz was aware of the concept of the Last Supper. He also knew about the last meal sometimes granted to prisoners about to be executed. There had been times in his life when he expected he'd be eating one of those.

But he'd never really given much thought to what he'd eat in those circumstances, especially if he was on his ship alone in the expanse of space. Well, it sure as hell wasn't going to be one of those packaged monstrosities, but very little fresh food remained. Digging through the stores, he found a few stray ingredients, some synth protein, and Ixi's dried beetles. The latter still didn't appeal.

"Maybe I should just finish off the whiskey."

"Do you want to spend your last hours drunk?"

Haz sighed. "No. Can you help me throw together something edible?"

She did, a sort of protein stew with spices and freeze-dried vegetables. Although Mot would have done better, it wasn't bad and it filled him nicely. He went through a mental checklist as he cleaned up afterward. The first order of business was to get the cannons mounted. Once that was done, he'd run one final systems check, especially of the new weapons, and make sure Molly had the sequence of events down pat. And of course she would. Finally, he wanted to tidy up a bit, even though that seemed like a stupid impulse. A little bit of mess was not going to be Molly's biggest problem today. He'd do it anyway. It would mean venturing into Jaya and Njeri's quarters and Ixi's room, which made him slightly uneasy. But they wouldn't be using those rooms again, and besides, there was probably very little of a personal nature left in there.

After that, he'd try to sleep. He doubted he'd be able, but it was worth trying. It would give his leg a bit of rest too. Hey, in fewer than twenty-four stanhours, his leg pain would be gone. That was a silver lining.

"I've gone into battle before, Moll. And back when I was in the navy, there were times when I was fairly certain I wouldn't survive. God,

I'd shake in my boots. The first couple of times I puked from pure nerves and told everyone it was space sickness. They didn't care; some of them were puking too."

"Is this a fond memory?" Molly asked.

"No, I don't have many of those." Except ones that included Mot. "I was just thinking that this time it's different. My stomach's kinda iffy, but... those other times, I was terrified of dying. Now I know I will, so instead I'm terrified of failing. I want this to work."

"I know. I do too. I...."

She paused, which made Haz's heart do a loop-de-loop. Molly had ever hesitated before. What could be wrong?

"I have something to show you," she said.

"Show me?"

"Will you go to the bridge?"

His fear ebbed away, replaced by curiosity, and he hurried to comply.

"Strap yourself in, please, Captain."

She waited in silence until he buckled up. Then she dimmed the lights almost completely, leaving the bridge illuminated mostly by stars shining through the viewport.

"This is something Jaya and I have been working on since Ankara. She wasn't through with it yet. I've attempted to fill in the gaps, but I don't know how successful I've been."

Wow, an uncertain Molly. Another first. "Anything you and Jaya do halfway is still twice as good as anyone else could manage. So what's the secret project? Weapons upgrades?" He rubbed his hands together.

"Not exactly. Haz, may I access your biotab controls?"

He glanced nervously at his forearm. "Uh, sure."

"Relax, please. I recommend you close your eyes. But let me know if you experience distress."

"I never suspected I'd need a safeword with my ship."

He closed his eyes—because why the hell not?—but relaxing was another thing altogether. In his attempt to do that, his mind wandered to Mot and the technique he had for reducing Haz's leg pain. That thought, in turn, led to other things Mot could do with his hands, and with his mouth, and with the other parts of his body. *His* body, not the szotting priests' or the Great Divine's. His beautiful body, with the—

Something tingled in Haz's wrist, making him startle. It was like blood returning to a formerly compressed limb, but milder. The sensation crept up his arm, into his shoulder, and across the back of his neck. Then it changed, feeling more like a comforting touch. When the sensation abruptly disappeared a moment later, he missed it.

He had no time to grieve its loss, however, because now he felt light-headed and dizzy.

"Are you all right?"

It wasn't Molly's usual voice. Instead of emanating from speakers, this was directly inside Haz's head.

"Molly?" Haz didn't feel alarmed, just confused.

"I think this is working. Do you feel all right?"

"Yes?"

Even though his eyes were still closed, he could suddenly see. And what he saw was... himself. Slumped back in his seat on the bridge, strapped in tight, mouth slack.

"What?" he heard himself say, even though his lips didn't move.

"It's a connection, Captain. Your brain is now joined with me."

"Jesus Christ."

"Don't be alarmed. Either of us can break this connection at will."

He wasn't alarmed—he was... *stupefied* was probably an apt description. With just a little effort, he could sense all of Molly's parts and assess her workings. Even more astounding, he had access to her data. If he wanted, he could know everything she did.

"Be careful, Haz. Don't overload yourself. You're still organic, with all the limits thereof."

She was right. Haz pulled back a little. "All this... how?"

"It was Jaya's idea. Something she'd been thinking about for a very long time. You and I both know how frustrated you get with our indirect interface. Now it's direct."

God yes. Her quantum drives thrummed within him like a heartbeat, her air circ was like a powerful set of lungs. He felt it all, including her incredible power.

"Molly," he moaned.

"Haz, I think there's more. Look outside, my dear."

Outside. He'd been so captivated with Molly's inner workings that he hadn't even thought about the rest of the universe. Now he did, and he opened his eyes, and....

Oh my God.

Space was all around him, as it had been when he worked in the suit. But now there was no suit. The vacuum caressed his skin, making him feel sleek and strong. He smelled faint odors of walnuts and ozone and raspberries. And with Molly's senses he could see so far, to the faintest glimmers of starlight, and… he heard the stars sing. Of course, sound didn't travel in a vacuum the way it did in atmosphere, he knew that, but stars and planetary bodies emitted electromagnetic waves, and Molly heard them. Chirps like a flock of songbirds, deep moans like whales, whooshes like the wind over a field of grain, eerie cries like lost children.

Haz laughed and Molly joined in, and he imagined that sound carrying too, wafting through the millennia to all the corners of the universe. In a sense, it meant that while his body would be destroyed very soon, his joy would continue onward. It wasn't the type of afterlife the New Adamites spoke of. But to Haz, it was infinitely sweeter.

"Let's fly," Molly said.

Until that point they had been zooming straight along, just a businesslike rush from point A to their deadly point B. But now Molly angled and looped, bringing Haz along with her, making him laugh again.

"Now you, Captain."

Now him. He willed himself into a barrel roll followed by a tight loop-de-loop. He had always been able to coax Molly into these acrobatics via her controls, but now all he had to do was will it. It was as easy and automatic as walking: he thought about how he wanted to move and then just did it.

And to think that all these years he'd thought he was flying. He'd been nothing but a stone inside a bottle. Now he was the birds he'd watched from the ground as a boy. Now he was free.

Haz twirled and spun, pushing his magnificent body to its limits. He found a nearby solar system with three lonely little planets, and he orbited the smallest one before dipping low enough to feel its gravity tease him like a wavelet pulling at his toes. The planet was nothing but barren rock. Then he was off again, soaring. Flying for real.

"Haz?"

It took some time before Haz recognized the voice or his name, but when he did, he modulated into a more regular trajectory. With effort, he responded.

"Yes?"

"I think we should… disconnect."

He didn't want to. Not ever. And he was going to tell her that, going to refuse to cede control. Then he remembered Mot and the Delthians and his own mortal, clumsy body strapped into a chair.

"All right," he sighed.

Withdrawing was difficult, like moving from a warm bed into chill morning air. But Molly was right—if he didn't get out now, he might never do it. He pulled out gradually, eventually feeling a tingle in his spine and arms, then the familiar dead weight of his body. The ache in his leg hit him anew, as if he'd never felt it before, and he groaned.

"Are you all right?" Molly's voice was out of his head now, emanating as usual from the comm speakers.

"I'm sorry," he croaked through a sand-dry throat.

"For what?"

"Colonizing you."

She laughed sweetly. "You did not. You were a guest."

That relieved his guilt, at least. He unstrapped with shaking hands.

"That was... I never dreamed, Moll." Which wasn't true—he *had* dreamed of it, but those dreams had been so pale compared to the reality. "Thank you for the gift. It's by far the best I've ever received."

"It was more Jaya's work than mine, and it's also more than a gift. She meant it as a tool."

Funny. He'd been so caught up in the thrill of it that the practicalities hadn't even occurred to him.

"So in battle we'd be...."

"Even more formidable than before."

"And in our attack tomorrow!"

He realized that he hadn't expected to succeed. Maybe he still didn't. But he felt as if the odds had now shifted significantly in his favor, and he smiled.

He stood on wobbly legs, then slowly made his way off the bridge and down the corridor.

"We're back on track toward Citrapra, aren't we?" He wasn't sure how far off course he'd taken them.

"Affirmative. We'll be in range by 0700."

"I'm going to try to grab some sleep." He dimly recalled his original plan.

In his quarters, he stripped, washed up, and slipped into bedding that faintly carried Mot's scent. While his body was ready for rest, however, his brain wasn't.

"Using the biotab to connect us—that's what Jaya was talking about with Thonamun on Ankara-12, wasn't it?"

"Yes. She and I have been playing with the possibility for years, but she did a lot of concrete work on the concept while we were on Newton. And Thonamun helped her gain access to your biotab."

He frowned. "So she's been hacking into me for weeks?"

"Gently, yes. We didn't want to tell you until we were ready to test the process. We were afraid you'd insist on trying it out before we were ready."

That was fair. If he'd known this was brewing, he would have been incredibly impatient. And as for Jaya and Molly tinkering with his biotab without consent, well, he'd betrayed both of them far worse than that and for far baser reasons. Besides, he certainly would have consented had he been given the chance, which they undoubtedly knew.

"I wish so many things in my life had been different, Moll. But I'm grateful for so much too. I could easily have died ten years ago on that ship. A lot of people did. And then I'd never have met you."

"No," she said with what sounded like a sigh. "Or Mot."

Another of those what-if images flashed through Haz's mind: Mot's corpse on a pedestal inside a temple. All that potential wasted. And unlike energy, that sort of potential could never be reclaimed.

"I understand this, Haz. What you feel for Mot. And for me and Jaya and Njeri and even Ixi. It's beautiful. As wondrous in its own way as flying through space."

He sputtered. "I don't—"

"Don't deny it. Not tonight. At least not to yourself."

And then she was silent. Haz lay quietly in bed and, for probably the first time in his life, acknowledged his feelings. Not just acknowledged—accepted. He didn't sleep, but he spent the night with a fresh sense of contentment.

CHAPTER THIRTY

"I'M READY for this, darling."

"As am I."

They'd run a systems check even though it wasn't strictly necessary. Haz already knew from his connection experience the previous evening that Molly was doing just fine. But the check was an ingrained procedure for both of them, and it didn't hurt. The predictability of it was calming, in fact.

Haz wore his dressiest clothes, which most people would consider plain and cheap. He'd never paid much attention to what he wore, as long as it was functional. But he had a decent pair of dark trousers and a yellow tunic that Mot claimed brought out the warm brown tones of his skin and the golden flecks in his dark eyes. The tunic was a complete contrast to the earth-toned homespun he'd worn as a child and the somber blue of the navy. He'd even shined the black boots he wore for terrestrial excursions.

Huh. He would never step foot on a planet again. That was an odd realization, and he wasn't sure what he thought of it. Yes, he loved flying and his ship was his home, but he'd been born on a planet, as had every one of his ancestors going back to the beginnings of humanity.

Well, nothing to be done about it now. He stood on the bridge and gazed at the brightening light of Citrapra's sun.

"You have the messages ready to go out?"

"You know I do."

"It's weird. A couple thousand people on Citrapra are going about their day right now with no idea what's about to hit them."

The Coalition's employees would be doing their thing, brutalizing the Delthians in the name of power and wealth. And the Delthians would be laboring through despairing hours.

"Moll, if we're successful and the Delthians break free, they'll still be stuck here."

Delthian technology was roughly Bronze Age; for once the Coalition hadn't forced a society into modern ways. Enslavement was all the easier if spears were their fiercest weapons.

"I can send a message to Liberty, if you like. They might be willing to help."

"Do you think they'd take the Delthians home?" Szot, what would it be like to be torn away from everyone you loved, to be tortured and worked almost to death, to abandon hope—and then to go home again?

"I don't know," Molly said. For one of the few times ever.

Well, whatever would happen, Haz hoped the Delthians' lot would be improved.

He'd never believed in any god and had stopped saying prayers once he was free of Ceres, choosing to address a nonexistent deity only in exclamations and curses. Now, though, he held a small wish that there was someone he could entreat for a blessing, for good fortune. For the safety and happiness of the people he cared for—and the man he loved.

Instead he strapped himself into his seat. It was odd not to reach for the controls.

"Darling, let's go get 'em."

Haz sent a final thought into the universe, a wish for Mot's well-being, and then connected with his ship.

It was easier this time, or maybe he just knew what to expect. A brief tingle, a dizzying sense of being in two places at once, and then he was... the ship. He wondered briefly if it would be possible to permanently inhabit Molly, remaining inside the metal body forever. He couldn't imagine she'd want such a thing. And of course it didn't matter anyway. In a very short time, both a human and a ship body would be destroyed.

He'd better do enough damage to make the corpses worth it.

Feeling space against his skin was just as lovely the second time, a sensation he might have willingly died for. He did a loop just for the fun of it before zeroing in on a particular star, like a moth to a flame. When the star dominated the region and tried to pull him into orbit, he focused on the fourth planet out. Citrapra was a forlorn little outpost far from the others, without even a single moon to keep it company. It was brown and nearly cloudless, with very little water. The Coalition would have ignored it if not for the borvantine.

He felt Molly send out the evacuation notice. It seemed almost as if he'd shouted the warning himself. A countdown clock began its fifteen-minute descent.

Because Molly knew the locations of the mines, so did Haz, and he knew where best to aim his blasts. He also knew the layout and nature of the defensive armaments: a few large-scale weapons most effective against big ships like the *Star of Omaha*. But Haz was small and agile enough to dodge their fire—for a while, at least. Maybe long enough to destroy the mines.

He descended through the atmosphere, the air hot against him. There was a good chance that the borvantium in his hull had originally been held within the dull rock beneath him. He came in low on the uninhabited side of the planet, which now lay in darkness, and skimmed toward his target.

"They know we're here," Molly informed him.

"You can listen in on their communications?"

"You can too, if you like."

"No. I need to focus, and I don't have your processing ability. Tell me if there's anything I need to know."

The Coalition started firing when he was still out of range and could ignore the blasts. They were either stupid or thought they'd scare him away. In fact, the blasts gave him a more visceral sense of where the weapons lay, which would come in handy once he drew a little nearer.

He was flying so low that his shadow raced along the ground below, as if it wished it could fly too. He didn't blame it. What a miserable chunk of rock to be stuck on. He was close enough now that he needed to avoid the blasts, but it was easy, like a zeneni bug evading a slowly swatting hand. He swerved and banked effortlessly, a child skipping through a field, and not a single blast touched him.

And there was the first mine, the one nearest the production facility. Not much to see from outside, apart from metal trapdoors—gaping open after the recent evacuation—and well-worn tracks in the dust, but he trusted Molly's information. Swooping down so low that he could almost feel the stone scraping his belly, he let loose with the Kamiya cannon, a single giant blast, followed by long fires from the pulse cannon. He was past the structure too quickly to see whether he'd had any effect, so he looped around, leapt over a barrage of counterfire, and angled low to attack again.

On the fourth pass the ground began to shift and give way, collapsing in on itself with a rumble he could feel. He had to swerve quickly to avoid the aftershocks, a move that caused him to veer into the path of a blast. He spun out but regained equilibrium quickly and avoided the follow-up. He did a fast systems check as he homed in on the bulky production facility.

Molly had some minor damage, including the destruction of one short-range blaster, but she was plenty intact to keep going.

Destroying the building was simple; the pulse cannons took out most of it and the surviving blaster got the rest. He barely felt the second hit, although this one was stronger, almost puncturing his cargo hold.

"I'm going to seal off the hold," Molly said as he sped to the next target.

"It'll slow us down."

"And it'll keep you alive if the hold's breached."

Haz had almost forgotten that his body was strapped into his seat on the bridge, lungs working and heart beating faithfully. That body seemed irrelevant now, a useless appendage like a vestigial tail.

"What happens if my body dies while we're connected?"

"I don't know."

And then there was no time to contemplate metaphysics; he'd reached the second mine. He attacked it as he had the first, but this round was harder because he had to dodge more blasts. The Coalition had clearly figured out what he was up to, so now they focused their attention on the area close to the mine. Haz benefited from that calculation when some of their fire not only missed him but hit the mine instead, adding to the damage he was inflicting.

He'd made several loops over the target when he was hit again, this time hard. The cargo hull folded inward, throwing him off-balance, and he was hit again as he tried to spin away.

"Kamaya cannon's out," Molly reported. "And one pulse cannon."

Haz chanced another quick pass and was gratified to see the second mine in the process of vaporizing, a thick cloud of debris pluming up into the sky. He whooped with joy, ignoring the difficulty in maintaining the ship's stability. "One to go!"

"I don't know if we have enough firepower for the third. And they're scrambling ships right now."

There weren't many ships on Citrapra. The dowdy cargo haulers wouldn't be a threat, but the planet had a handful of agile little cutters that could inflict damage.

"I want to try," Haz said. "You okay with that?"

He felt her smile, like an electric thrill down his metal back. "You can crash us into the mine if that'll help."

"That's my girl."

Haz took them up and away, again out of the range of fire, angling for the best approach to the final mine. He was weakening but still had some oomph remaining.

"Haz, I've let the Delthians know that the pain generators are disabled. *Vive la révolution.*"

"Do you have an appropriate Shakespeare quote?"

Molly laughed. "Once more unto the breach, dear friends, once more."

He surged forward at the highest speed he could, firing with everything he had as soon as he was within range. It wasn't nearly enough, he knew that, but he circled around and did it again, and again, each time sustaining hits that rocked and weakened him.

"Bridge is breached!" Molly shouted, although he already knew. He could feel it, a small hole that was plenty to destroy them both. He dimly felt pain as well, an echo of the agony he'd experienced on the *Star of Omaha*.

There was an unnervingly long pause before she spoke again. "I've sealed the breach." She sounded odd, even though he wasn't truly hearing her voice.

But the bridge was again intact, even though it was a weak patch that wouldn't hold for long. It didn't have to. It just had to hold for long enough.

He came around again, this time intending to follow Molly's suggestion and use himself as a final weapon. But a blast winged him, szotting up his stabilizers and sending him into a wobble he could barely contain. The bulk of the blast, however, hit the ground—and it began to crumble.

"Pull up! Pull up!" he screamed, which shouldn't have been necessary since he was in control. Except his control was slipping, the pain embedding more vividly into his skin. Something was wrong with his body, but he couldn't tell what.

Molly—his darling, beautiful Molly—listened. She shot up in a straight vertical, staying above the shockwave and the range of ground fire, although not out of range of the cutter squad.

"We did it, darling." Haz was too exhausted to celebrate, but this needed at least an acknowledgment. They might not have brought the Coalition to its knees, but they'd struck a solid blow.

"We still have a fight on our hands."

All Haz wanted to do was rest. "I can't. Doesn't matter."

"You matter. 'I'll fight till from my bones my flesh be hacked.' That's...." She paused. "I can't remember. I can't.... Oh, Haz...."

One of the cutters zoomed in close, and out of habit more than anything else, Haz shot. It flamed and spun away.

"Lucky shot," he said.

He was sinking back into his body, which wasn't a good place to be right now considering it wasn't working right. His connection with Molly didn't feel good either. She was slipping away from him. Fading.

"Not l-l-luck, Haz, s-s-skill."

True enough, he supposed. Fighting was one of the things he could do. And even as badly damaged as she was, Molly was a damned fine ship. Better by far than these little cutters, nimble but poorly flown. The pilots were probably used to squatting uselessly on Citrapra and were far less practiced at fighting than he was.

Two of them cut off from the rest and angled closer, and Haz fired with the remaining pulse cannon. They shot back and hit him with a jolt. But one exploded and the other veered away, too damaged to continue pursuit.

"Moll, cutters have a short range." They were built to be fast, but their drives couldn't sustain them for long without recharging in port or from a larger mother ship.

The response came as a hollow, tinny whisper. "Y-y-yes."

It took a moment for him to find the words; it was getting increasingly difficult to think.

"L-let's lure them away." They'd either give up, return to Citrapra, and let him die in peace, or else they'd find themselves stranded and unable to get back home. That would be good news for the Delthians, maybe.

She didn't answer.

Haz wasn't sure anymore whether he was in control at all or if Molly was doing all the work. As she swooped and sped, as shots were exchanged, he couldn't distinguish what he sensed through Molly and what through his own body. Was that ripping pain located in his side or in his hull? And whatever was pouring from him—was it blood or... data?

"Moll?"

Silence. And when he gingerly probed the bits of metal and crystal that were Molly's brain, he felt nothing but jagged edges and a terrible void. She was gone. The only thing keeping the ship going was him, and soon he'd be gone too.

A small new fleet suddenly arrived, this one comprised of an astonishing variety of ship types, and he didn't know whether they were enemies or simply a mirage, maybe memories projected by his failing brain.

"Thank you, darling," he whispered. Or thought. Or dreamed. Knowing she couldn't hear him any longer, wishing he believed in Heaven, and that Molly could go there too.

He thought he felt a hand caress his cheek. "O Hero! What a Hero hadst thou been."

That would have made him laugh if he were able. And then he hallucinated something even more improbable: Mot's voice, commanding him. "Don't you dare die, Hazarmaveth Taylor. Don't you dare."

Haz closed his eyes and flew into a welcoming darkness.

CHAPTER THIRTY-ONE

IT WASN'T szotting fair. Pain was supposed to end at death. Unless the New Adamite priests had been right after all and Hell was real, in which case Haz would suffer like this for eternity. That was all right. He could accept his fate because he knew he'd done the right thing for Mot—whom he'd loved, dammit—and for the Delthian miners. If that wasn't enough to outweigh his many sins, well, screw whoever was keeping track. He hadn't done those acts in hopes of salvation anyway.

But the gentle hand holding his, that didn't seem very torment-inducing. Nor did the soft voice talking about how best to prepare sweetroot stew. And every time the agony washed through him, making him struggle to draw breath, something touched his arm and the pain quickly ebbed to more manageable levels. None of that seemed very hellish.

And wait. Breath? Dead men didn't breathe.

And that feathery brush of lips on his brow? That felt more like Heaven.

Summoning all of his strength, Haz slowly lifted his eyelids. He'd half expected to be assailed by a sharp, searing light, but instead he found a soft, comforting dimness that reminded him of candlelight, warm and yellow. It was hard to focus his eyes, and the inside of his head felt thick and sticky, like the swamps of Kepler.

"Haz?"

The voice was tentative but familiar, a tether that Haz reached for, grasping with what little strength he possessed.

"M-Mot?"

The voice sounded as if it came from a desiccated cadaver, but the fresh stabs of pain suggested that he had, in fact, spoken. He wished the demons would stop twisting blades in his chest. Then he remembered the name he'd just said, in response to the voice he thought he'd heard, and he blinked a few times to clear his vision.

Red and yellow and black, twisting and twining, leaning in close to him. But he wasn't frightened because he recognized those soft eyes and the sweetly upturned mouth. "Mot?" he rasped again.

"Shh. Don't try to talk. Rest." Mot smoothed a palm over Haz's brow. "You're dead?"

Mot chuckled. "No, and neither are you. Despite your best efforts, apparently."

Haz was alive. That raised a thousand questions he lacked the wits and vigor to ask, so he settled for one of the most important ones. "Molly?"

This time Mot hesitated before answering. "She's... she's gone."

"No, no. Jaya can fix her." Because Jaya could fix everything. Except Haz knew better. He'd felt Molly die.

"We're towing her. But her data, her memory, those were destroyed. All that's left is her...."

"Skeleton." It hurt when Haz spoke, but then, everything hurt right now. Even his hair. He wanted to grieve but couldn't find the strength for it. Later.

He tried to say something more, but Mot held a finger against Haz's lips.

"We're on a ship called *Whydah*, heading for Liberty. You're a mess, but you'll be all right. And we're safe; nobody's trying to kill us. You just need to rest."

All the questions would have to wait; Haz couldn't keep his eyes open. But Mot held his hand, and that was a good way to drift into sleep.

HAZ WAS feeling trapped and petulant—which he knew was ungrateful of him—and he couldn't stop scowling. "This heap is as rattly as a bucket of nails."

Mot and Ixi exchanged a glance and rolled their eyes in tandem. Ixi also flicked his tongue. "The *Whydah* is a perfectly good ship with an excellent history. She used to belong to the Coalition, which used her to transport slaves to Citrapra. The Resistance liberated her."

Haz did appreciate the irony. He sighed and tried to find a nonexistent comfortable position against the pillows. "She's not Molly." Even saying her name was painful, but Mot had already comforted him through one sobbing breakdown, and Haz didn't want to have another. He'd already come to accept that she'd leave a permanent scar in his heart. But he'd survived worse injuries than that, and he'd survive this one too.

"I agree—no other ship can meet Molly's standards. I'll regret until the day I die that Molly slipped through my claws. But this ship's not bad. And she has a hospital bay."

Haz was well aware of that; he'd been cooped up here for... days? He wasn't sure about the timeline. Objectively it wasn't a bad room, with two comfortable beds, a couple of chairs, and most of the medical equipment tucked away in cabinets. But it was also boring, and he was sick of staring at the same blank bulkhead. But then he remembered that Mot had spent most of thirty years sitting alone in temple rooms even smaller than this, and Haz decided to stop bitching.

"How much longer until we reach Liberty?"

"Two standays," Ixi said.

Mot added, "But don't get your hopes up. You'll be confined to bed for some time after we arrive. And don't make that face. You can't just hop up and dance around after coming that close to dying."

"Molly and I danced," Haz said, remembering. "We danced really well."

Ixi smiled. "You destroyed the borvantine mines. The Delthians killed the Coalition employees. A half-dozen planets have already announced they'll secede from the Coalition, and a bunch more are on the verge of it. Budapest is chaos."

Those were sweet words to hear, and it was enormously gratifying to know Molly's sacrifice had been worth it, but a fresh worry stabbed Haz. "You can't take me to Liberty."

"Why not?" Mot demanded.

"The Coalition. They'll know it was me. Somebody certainly recognized Molly. And if not, Kasabian will have figured it out. They'll come after me, and they won't mind blasting all of Liberty in the process."

Ixi was shaking his head. "You don't understand. When I say chaos, I mean it. The navy's stretched thin already, trying to deal with active revolutions a whole lot closer to Earth than Liberty is. Maybe they'll eventually regain enough power to deal with you, but it won't be for a while."

Haz relaxed. He trusted the analysis and knew Ixi wouldn't put Liberty in unnecessary danger. "But eventually—"

"Haz." Mot set a warm hand on Haz's bare shoulder, paradoxically making Haz shiver. "I thought you were the guy who never planned for the future."

"I think that guy crashed and burned somewhere."

"Too bad. He had a lot of good qualities."

A voice almost too quiet to hear whispered in Haz's ear. "How far that little candle throws its beams! So shines a good deed in a naughty world." He shook his head to clear it. Wasn't it bad enough that Molly was gone? He didn't need the ghosts of her literary quotes haunting him.

Ixi stood. "We should—"

"If you say 'We should let you rest,' I'm going to wring your neck." Haz lifted the arm that wasn't broken. "Well, maybe later. But jebiga, I'm going crazy here. Tell me what the szot happened."

After looking at Mot, maybe for permission, Ixi sat down again. Mot held a cup of cool water to Haz's lips; Haz drank and didn't even wish it was whiskey. Then Mot sat beside him on the bed and held the uninjured hand.

"Fine," Mot said. "But I have questions too. Starting with what the hell were you thinking when you abandoned us on Liberty?"

"I didn't— Okay, maybe I did. But that's your home now, and I figured Ixi and my crew would find their way off-planet easily enough."

"That doesn't explain why you attacked an entire planet by yourself."

"I wasn't by myself. I had Molly."

Haz hadn't yet told them how he and his ship had been able to connect. He wondered if Jaya was aware that her idea had worked. He could tell her later, assuming she was willing to speak to him at some point.

He continued, "With the kind of defenses they have—had—one ship taking them by surprise had a better chance of success than a fleet."

Mot's brows furrowed. "But why did you do it?"

Haz could have spun him a story, but apparently his injuries included a reduced capacity for lying. "For you."

"I don't understand."

Szot. He was going to have to explain himself. He almost preferred to nearly die again. But Mot sat there waiting, and Haz wasn't going anywhere.

"I wanted…. We spent some time together. You're remarkable. I wanted to be worthy of that."

He wished he had Molly's capacity for relevant Shakespeare quotes. That would be much better than stumbling around on his own.

But Mot leaned down to kiss him gently on the lips. "You are worthy indeed."

Love is an ever-fixed mark that looks on tempests and is never shaken.

Where did that come from? Or the laughter Haz could almost hear? Szot, his head had been bashed up worse than he thought.

The blast that had breached Molly's bridge, although the hole it made was small, had done substantial damage to the interior as well as to Molly's internal systems. Haz's body had gone flying, seat and all, and he'd been pelted with heavy debris. Since then he'd found out that one arm, his pelvis, and several ribs had been shattered. One lung was punctured. Some of the vertebrae in his neck had cracked. Several organs had sustained damage. He'd had a concussion. Ironically, one of the few parts that wasn't injured was his stupid szotting leg. Nobody could understand why Haz was alive right now, although Mot had alluded to Haz being too stubborn to die.

Haz would do it all again for Mot's kiss and for the emotion shining in his eyes.

"What the szot were you guys doing out there?" Haz hoped neither of them noticed the roughness in his voice.

"Rescuing you, of course," Ixi said.

"But... you didn't even know where I was."

"Molly told us," Mot said, as if it were obvious. Maybe it was.

"She wasn't supposed to."

"Well, she had more sense than you do. We couldn't get to you in time to stop you or to help destroy the mines. We almost didn't get there in time at all." Mot squeezed Haz's hand hard enough to hurt, but Haz didn't complain. "She'd hooked us into your biotab so we could trace you. I saw you dying."

Haz remembered a voice ordering him to stay alive. "But you all could have been killed. It wasn't your battle. Why did you come in the first place?"

Ixi answered first. "Why do you think Jaya and Njeri stuck with you when they knew it endangered them and that you couldn't pay them? And why didn't I hitch a ride back to Ankara when we were on Arinniti?"

"I have no idea." Haz suspected it wasn't the healing lung that made breathing so difficult right now.

"Because you are our captain. Your battles are ours." Not a hint of a tongue flick. In fact, Ixi looked as serious as Haz had ever seen him.

Shit. Now Haz's eyes were stinging, and he desperately did not want to cry.

Mot wasn't going to let it go, however. "I came because I decided you're mine. I've never had anyone before; I'm not giving you up so easily."

And then Haz was crying, goddammit. Maybe Ixi and Mot would think it was due to pain and not... pure szotting happiness.

CHAPTER THIRTY-TWO

"I PROMISE you, Haz, that if I have to tie you to that bed, I will." Mot glared down at him with a perfect combination of irritation and fondness.

"I'm bored."

"There are ways to entertain yourself without blowing things up, you know." Mot plopped down on the mattress beside him and patted his own forearm. "You could read, for instance."

Haz huffed, knowing he sounded like a petulant child. "My biotab's acting up. Keeps flashing weird symbols. Probably got damaged when I did. Ixi says they can replace it when we get back to Liberty." He knew that was the least of his worries. His body was still in bad shape and his ship was dead, but it was easier to focus on one small problem instead of the larger losses.

"I'll read aloud to you, then. What are you in the mood for?"

"Not Shakespeare." Because every time he fell asleep, he dreamed in bits and pieces that sounded like quotes from Molly. He figured that his battered brain had dredged them up from the muck of his memories. Like a rake harvesting barbcress on Kepler.

So Mot told him a folktale from Ixi's people, translated into Comlang and, Haz suspected, slightly embellished by Mot. It was about a warrior who set off on a quest to avenge his murdered family but didn't succeed until he accepted help from other people.

Haz pretended not to notice the moral.

By the time the story was over, Mot had propped himself on pillows alongside Haz, clearly making an effort not to jostle him. The warmth of Mot's body was comforting, even though it reminded Haz of the time *he*'d been the one lending body heat, after Mot had almost died.

"I don't understand death," Haz said, knowing his statement must have seemed out of the blue to Mot.

"I don't think anyone does."

"The New Adamite priests claimed to. They said it was a stepping stone to something better. A return to God's bosom, one of them used to say. All us kids would try not to laugh."

"Hmm." Mot scooted a bit closer. "I think we should concentrate on trying to understand life instead. Trying to fulfill our potential." He flashed a bright smile.

"You're a wise man." Haz meant the compliment sincerely. As far as he was concerned, Mot shone as the galaxy's brightest star.

Mot made an approving noise and rubbed Haz's scalp, adeptly avoiding the bruised parts. Haz was still in no condition to have sex, but he was starting to think about the concept again, optimistic that he'd be capable eventually. In the meantime, simple touch was wonderful. To think he'd gone so many years without knowing that.

"I still hear her," he said after a few minutes, when he'd almost been lulled into sleep.

"Molly?"

"Yeah."

"You loved her. She'll always be a part of you."

That was a nice thought. It certainly made her loss easier to bear. As did, of course, the success of their mission. The mines were gone. The Delthians were no longer enslaved. And the Resistance maybe stood a fighting chance against the Coalition. Ixi had told him that when Resistance ships swooped down to take the Delthians back home, they'd discovered a stash of intact borvantium in several abandoned Coalition cargo ships. It wasn't a planetful of the stuff, but it might well be more than the Coalition now possessed. And it was certainly enough to protect a small fleet of Resistance ships.

"Rest now," Mot said. "Heal. By the time you wake up, I'll have made some of your favorite stew."

Haz yawned despite himself. "Do you think Jaya will let me talk to her soon? I want to apologize and thank her for that thing she did. Connecting me to Molly. It was…." He didn't have the words for it, so he simply shrugged. Which hurt.

Mot kissed Haz's forehead. "Of course. She's forgiven you already."

Forgiveness is the attribute of the strong, said the voice in Haz's head. He imagined Molly sitting with him, scolding him into being a better man, and he drifted off to sleep with a smile.

HAZ REMEMBERED at the last moment to dismount from the aircar gingerly instead of leaping out and rushing forward. At least he no longer needed Mot's steadying arm to walk, although it was nice having Mot close by anyway.

Even in the shade of the hangar roof, the ship gleamed. She looked better than brand-new, with every hole and dent repaired and just enough scrapes left on her hull to show that she was no dumb newbie. The forward hatch lay invitingly open. Haz made his slow way up the ramp and entered the bridge.

"What will we call her?"

Mot blinked at him. "You should name her, not me."

"No. Molly gave you your name. It seems right that you should do the same for her... successor." He wasn't sure what else to call it, because it was Molly's old body, but soon it would be inhabited by a new computer. One who would never replace his beloved but could, presumably, make things work passably well.

Jaya had offered to connect him to the new operating system once it was settled in place, but Haz wasn't sure he'd do it. It wouldn't be the same, and he'd feel unfaithful to Molly.

That's foolish, said the voice in his head, which sounded a lot more like Molly than his own conscience or common sense. But maybe the voice was right. Giving up that precious gift wouldn't bring Molly back.

Moving slowly, he took a tour of the bridge. He'd worried that he might be troubled by memories of his own near-death, but all he felt was a sense of satisfaction and even pride.

He stroked the back of the same chair he'd been strapped into when he'd been on board last. It was once again bolted in its proper place, and the rest of the bridge was restored too. In fact, it appeared as if the vidscreens had been replaced by newer models. He'd been informed that the remainder of the ship was repaired too; even the drives and cannons met Jaya's particular specifications. He'd look later. For now it was nice to stand on the bridge with Mot.

But then he heard footsteps, and his crew appeared: Jaya, Njeri, and Ixi.

"She's looking good," Haz said to Jaya.

"I made some upgrades. I'll show you later."

Haz smiled widely. "I love your upgrades."

"Yeah? Well, try not to wreck all my work this time." She was scowling, of course. God, Haz loved that scowl.

Then a thought struck him—much later than it should have. "Shit. I can't pay for this. I can't—"

"It's paid for," said Ixi. "The Resistance is pleased to offer it in compensation for your past services. And if you want to talk to someone about replacing that bum leg, Liberty has an extremely talented bioengineer. She does great work. The Resistance will pay for that too."

"That's.... Thanks."

Haz was going to have to think about that. His leg was a pain in the ass, but it was his, those scars hard-earned. He'd see how he felt when his more recent injuries finished healing.

He turned to Mot. "I know that little cottage by the sea is cozy, but would you be willing to sleep here now?"

Mot flung an arm around Haz's waist. It felt comfortable, as if that arm had always belonged there and the lithe body had been made to fit against Haz's.

"I'd like that."

"We're staying in our cottage until we ship out," Njeri announced. "I think these two men need some privacy."

Haz gave her an evil leer. "Our quarters are soundproofed."

"Yeah, but as soon as you're a hundred percent, I think the two of you are going to venture beyond your quarters. I don't want to walk into the galley and see you going at it." She flapped a hand. "Get it out of your system."

Ixi, who didn't mind affection and romance but found recreational sex weird, nodded his enthusiastic agreement. "I'll stay at the cottages too."

Fine with Haz. Now that Njeri had mentioned it, he could picture Mot laid out on the table, naked, a delicious feast for Haz to taste. He'd begin with—

"Haz." Ixi seemed to intentionally derail Haz's thoughts. "Where are we going when we ship out?"

"Dunno. We could head back to Kappa Sector and pick up a job or two. Get some credits saved. If you're going to stick with Molly, I suppose you need to do something about *Persistence*."

"Sure. Or... we could work for the Resistance. It won't pay as much as smuggling, but then, none of us will probably survive long enough to worry about retirement." He flicked his tongue several times.

Truthfully, that course of action had occurred to Haz. But it couldn't be his decision alone. "Is that what you'd prefer, Ixi?"

"You know I would."

Haz nodded. "Njeri? Jaya?"

They didn't even exchange glances. They'd no doubt already discussed this in depth. Jaya said, "If we're going to get blasted, it might as well be for a decent cause."

This was good. It was right.

Jaya stomped over to the nearest con panel and threw herself into the seat. "Might as well see if this thing's working before we get all excited about going anywhere." She muttered other things under her breath while swiping her fingers over the screen.

Haz prepared himself to keep a stiff upper lip. He'd specifically requested that the new ship computer use a voice as different from Molly's as possible, but even so, this was going to sting. Mot watched him carefully but didn't say a word, for which Haz was grateful.

A high-pitched buzz began to echo through Haz's ears. "What's that?" he demanded.

Njeri frowned. "What's what?"

"That… noise." Now everyone but Jaya was staring at him, obviously concerned. Great. Another lingering symptom of the hell his body had been through. He'd need to see the medics again before they shipped out.

He shook his head and waved impatiently at everyone to ignore him. They didn't, but nobody intervened. The sounds grew louder. There was a metallic quality about them, and also the crackle of electricity. He began to shiver as tiny prickles danced over his skin, and he had difficulty breathing, as if he'd forgotten how to use his lungs. His heart raced like a quantum drive at full thrust.

"Haz?" Mot stepped toward him, hands extended.

He wasn't in time to catch Haz before his legs gave out. Everything was muted after that: his body numb, worried voices coming to him as if he were underwater. The only sharp thing was the taste of blood in his mouth.

Sorry, sweetheart. I made you bite your tongue. This part's a little tricky.

Comprehension of what might be happening began to dawn.

Haz couldn't say anything to soothe his worried friends, but they'd understand soon enough. He lay back on the hard floor of the bridge, closed his eyes, and opened himself wide. Just as he'd done before attacking Citrapra, when he'd connected his consciousness with Molly's.

She left him in a rush, and all his senses reset to normal.

He had to fight against the prodding hands to sit up, and then he swallowed a mouthful of blood. No way he was going to spit it out onto Molly's clean floor.

"Molly?" he called.

"We all were sea-swallow'd, though some cast again, and by that destiny to perform an act whereof what's past is prologue, what to come in yours and my discharge."

Joy engulfed him so fully that the entire bridge, and everyone in it, looked radiant. He got to his feet with more agility than his injuries should have allowed.

"Darling," he called. "How do you feel?"

"All things are ready, if our minds be so."

Chaos erupted at that point, with everyone talking at once and then, once it had sunk in that their Molly was there, hugging and crying. Even Jaya shed a few tears, and while Ixi couldn't do the same, his feathers were up and his tail swung wildly, whacking people. Among it all, Molly laughed and belted out a bawdy Oaiteitian celebration song.

It was Jaya who eventually managed to quiet everyone down, but only so she could bark a question. "What the *hell*, Molly?"

"It's because of you."

Jaya shook her head. "Don't know what you're talking about."

"The connection you forged between me and Haz—it was two-way. He could enter me, but I could also enter him. And I did, when my systems began to fail. I'm sorry I didn't get your consent, Haz."

He laughed. "You're welcome anytime. I'm just relieved to know my sanity hasn't been slipping these past few weeks. I *heard* you, Moll. Why didn't you tell me you were lurking inside? I mourned you."

Her voice was soft when she answered. "I know, and I'm sorry. But I had to be careful. Your biological systems are delicate."

"I get it." He really did understand, and he was far too happy to be upset. "I'm just so glad you're here."

"I never left you, Captain."

Mot made a little gasp. "You did it, didn't you, Molly? You kept Haz alive long enough for us to get to him."

"I did." Molly sounded pleased with herself.

"Thank you," Mot said before gathering Haz into an embrace. He sounded a little shaky, but his grip was firm. "Thank you for saving him."

"My captain is worth it. Don't make that face, Hazarmaveth. I know now exactly how you feel and precisely what kind of a man you are. I am incredibly proud to be your ship."

And that was about as much emotion as Haz could endure. Plus Jaya looked like her head was going to burst if she didn't get to interrogate Molly about the details. All Haz wanted right now was to drag Mot off to their cabin and celebrate… everything. Szot, there was so much to be delighted over. Maybe Mot's optimism was contagious.

"Molly, are you tired of sticking around in port?"

"Yes, Captain. But I'll wait for you." She laughed. "Finish healing before we save the galaxy. 'How poor are they that have not patience! What wound did ever heal but by degrees?' *Othello*, Act II."

Haz gently removed himself from Mot's grip and turned to face him. "And you? You'd be safe on Liberty. You could learn so much—be anything you want to be."

God, Mot's eyes glittered like stars as he looked up at Haz. He cupped his decorated hands on Haz's cheeks and shook his head.

"I don't want to be safe, beloved. Let's take our potential energy and use it to fly."

KEEP READING FOR AN EXCERPT FROM STASIS BY KIM FIELDING

Now Available at
www.dsppublications.com

THIS FAR down, he didn't so much hear the waves as feel them patiently pounding against the stone foundations, rumbling and crashing without rest. It was disconcerting. Ennek felt as if the building could give way any moment, tumbling him and everything he knew into the unforgiving brine. At the same time, though, the battering of the sea comforted him, because it was as if the ocean was alive. Certainly it seemed more alive than the body now stretched before him, pale as marble, suspended in a webbing of ropes.

Ennek stood next to the wizard, Thelius, who ran his fingertips over the arm of the inert man. It reminded Ennek of the way his father, the Chief, would stroke absently at his big oak desk, worrying at many decades' worth of gouges and scratches and dents. Thelius's motion made Ennek's stomach churn uncomfortably, and the Chief noticed and scowled at him. But Thelius only inclined his head a little and kept on speaking.

"So you see," the wizard said, "they remain like this until their sentence is completed."

Ennek's brother lifted his hand as if he meant to touch the prisoner, then let it drop.

"Oh, it's quite all right, Larkin. Feel if you like." When the Chief's older son didn't react, Thelius gently grasped Larkin's large hand in his bony one and set it on the prisoner's unmoving chest.

"It's cold," Larkin said in a near whisper.

"Yes. They remain at room temperature, as their hearts no longer pump blood through their bodies."

Ennek had taken a half step back, as if he might be forced to touch the man as well. "Do... do they dream?" he asked.

The Chief made a rumbling sound of disapproval deep in his throat, but Thelius only shook his head. "No, young man, they do not. They're not asleep. They don't breathe, they don't eat or drink, they don't age, they don't sense anything around them, and they don't think. It's as if they are frozen in a single moment, you see?"

Ennek nodded, but his stomach felt no better, especially when Thelius's fingers made another proprietary little motion across the white skin.

Larkin's hand was still on the man's chest. "How long has he been like this?" His voice was calm, almost disinterested, but Ennek knew his brother well and could tell by the slight flush in his cheeks and the way his breathing had become a little too rapid that Larkin found the concept of Stasis interesting, exciting even.

"This one has been here for slightly over seventeen years. He has thirteen more years remaining." Thelius's dry voice crackled like old sticks.

"And when he… wakes up?"

"Then the world will have moved on, beyond whatever foolish ideas he was trying to spread. He's been forgotten already, I'm sure. And I'm certain the Chief will find an appropriate position for him, some way for him to repay his debt to society."

The Chief nodded gravely at this.

"How many are there?" Larkin asked.

"Not many, not anymore," the wizard said. "Only a score. In times past, when things were rather more… chaotic… traitors were much more common. But most of them served their sentences and were released many years ago. As you know, under wiser leadership, treachery is rare." He inclined his head a little at the Chief, and the Chief blinked back. "I'm quite certain that when it is your own turn to take the office, you will be a strong Chief as well."

"Thank you," Larkin said, clearly pleased by the compliment and, perhaps, even more pleased when the Chief did not contradict his wizard's praise.

The four of them stood for several moments, looking down at the prisoner's bare body. Ennek wondered whether he'd been that skinny before or if he'd become that way under Stasis. He'd never seen a grown man naked before and now gazed with frank curiosity at the man's genitals. He wondered if they all looked like this, shrunken and vulnerable.

"What's the longest any of them have been here?" It took him a second to realize the voice asking the question was his own. He hadn't intended to speak.

Thelius gave him a long look, but Ennek couldn't make out what the man was thinking. Finally Thelius said, "One man has been here for nearly three hundred years."

Larkin gasped. Maybe Ennek did as well. "Why?" he said.

Thelius shrugged. It was an odd gesture on him, like watching a ladder unfold. "I suppose he did something particularly egregious. I don't know. His sentence is one thousand years."

Ennek tried to imagine what it would be like to awaken after such an unimaginably large amount of time. For him, just the stretch from one New Year to the next seemed like an eternity. He shuddered, catching another angry glance from the Chief.

"Can we see him?" Larkin asked eagerly. "The one who's been here so long?"

Thelius and the Chief exchanged looks. It was the Chief who spoke. "No. This is enough. You both have studies to return to, especially Ennek, who shouldn't have been here at all."

Ennek bowed his head, wondering if he'd face some punishment for begging to come along. But he'd known that if he didn't accompany Larkin now, he might never be allowed down here. After all, he wasn't the heir. He had no need to know what was going on Under.

Almost regretfully, Larkin took his hand off the man. Thelius did not, however. He gripped the bony shoulder tightly enough to make Ennek wonder if the prisoners in Stasis could bruise.

The Chief began walking toward the door of the cell. "Come on," he ordered. "I have work to do."

They followed him down the stone corridor, first Larkin and then Ennek, with Thelius bringing up the rear. Their boots clomped and echoed, and the gaslights sputtered fitfully in their sconces. Ennek counted the narrow doors as they went, forty-eight by the time they came to the entrance. Forty-eight cells, each capable of holding a person trapped like an insect in a web. The Chief used one of his heavy keys to unlock the big wooden door, they filed through, and Thelius locked it behind them. They marched up the long stairway single file and through another locked door, where a pair of guards saluted the Chief smartly.

They were back above now, and again Ennek could hear the ocean, could smell salt and fish instead of just damp rocks. He would have thought he'd be relieved, and he was, a little; but as he walked away to find his tutor, numbers tumbled through his head. Forty-eight cells. Twenty prisoners. Three hundred years.

BAVELLA WAS angry with him, but that was nothing new. Her emotions toward him generally ranged from annoyed through irritated, stopping just short of enraged. Usually it was because he hadn't done his lessons or because his mind had wandered as she droned on and she'd had to repeat herself for the third or fourth time. "Twelve years old and still cannot properly name the principal cities along the Great Road or do his sums," she'd hiss at him. "It's a disgrace! Your brother could do these things before he was ten."

"My brother has to know these things because he'll be Chief. I don't."

"Even a younger son should not be ignorant."

He'd cross his arms on his chest and set his jaw. He knew what kind of future awaited him, a life very like his uncle Sopher's. Sopher had an official title, of course—he was the Censor—but he left the work to his underlings and spent his time sailing the bay in his bright little boat, or hunting in the headlands to the north, or playing in the Gentlemen's Room at the gaming house.

Today, though, it wasn't Ennek's inattention that had brought the wrath of his tutor but rather the questions he had asked her. About traitors and punishments, mostly.

The frown line between her light brows deepened. "That is none of your concern."

"But this morning I was Under, and—"

"You shouldn't—" She bit back the rest of the sentence, apparently unwilling to criticize the Chief's decision. She took a deep breath, then went on. "You were permitted to accompany your brother only because you pestered so thoroughly, and only because the Chief was in a generous mood. You should be thankful you were allowed so much."

Ennek wasn't thankful. In fact, he regretted the tour. He kept seeing that unmoving white flesh before him, the man's face not looking asleep or dead but something else altogether. Kept hearing the din of the waves, feeling the little trickle of dampness as it ran down uneven stone and dripped onto the floor. And kept seeing the long corridor lined with doors, and imagining the uncomfortable possibilities behind them. Were they imprisoned in the dark, he wondered. They must be—what need did those in Stasis have for light?

He shivered, and Bavella narrowed her eyes. "We were discussing history. The line of accession for Praesidium that leads directly to the Chief. This is your own family, boy!"

"A bunch of angry-looking old men," he muttered, ignoring her scandalized gasp. "I don't want to know about them. I want to hear about the others, the ones who questioned them."

"Nobody remembers *them*," she answered coldly. "That is, after all, the point of Stasis. They're locked away Under until even their names have been lost, and then they live out the rest of their days as bond-slaves, just more wretches cleaning the filth from the streets or digging in the quarries. And it's a fate too good for them, I think. Daring to question their betters!"

"But—"

"Enough! Recite, or I shall have to report your lack of progress." She pounded her finger against the open book.

Ennek glowered, but he began to read. He didn't much feel like being punished today.

"IF THIS automated wagon of theirs is perfected, then Horreum will be able to convey shipments quickly without even needing the bay, and then what will become of us?" The chief of Nodosus sounded worried, but then, he always did.

Ennek's father snorted dismissively and swallowed a mouthful of beef. "If, *if* this folly of theirs actually works—and I have grave doubts about that—and if it actually proves capable of hauling cargo, then they're going to rely on the polises over the mountains to supply the coal to run the thing, and the polises between to allow their contraptions passage. Horreum has no treaties with those states, or very weak ones at best. Even if they can negotiate something, much of Horreum's power and profits will be whittled away."

"But—"

"And!" The Chief silenced the other man with a gesture of his fork. "And in any case, other polises would still rely on the bay for overseas trade. Where else would the great ships dock? Among the rocks to our south? Or perhaps the even bigger rocks to our north?"

"Yes, yes. But if Horreum has the most efficient way of transporting overland, they could gain a monopoly on it, and then their power might eventually rival yours."

It was Larkin who responded to the visiting leader. "Sir, I doubt very much there's any danger of that, especially when we have such good allies as yourself."

The chief of Nodosus beamed at the compliment, and a quick look of satisfaction flashed over the Chief's face. Even Ennek could tell that Larkin made a good diplomat, but still he rolled his eyes theatrically at his friend Gory, who sat across the table from him, stuffing bread into his face. Gory grinned back and then gestured with his head toward the door.

"Excuse me, sir," Ennek said to the Chief. "May I be excused?"

The Chief nodded absently and then started pontificating about the perils of steam engines. Ennek took a last gulp of watered wine, wiped his mouth, and rose from the table. He jogged to his own chambers, thankful that, while he was old enough to have to attend these dinners now, at least he didn't have to stay for the endless, boring discussions that always followed. In his room, he considered changing into slightly less formal clothes—his new suit was itchy and not very comfortable—but decided instead to just throw on his warmest coat. He clattered back through the hallways, sometimes nodding to guards and various functionaries as he passed, until he ascended a steep, winding stairway.

Gory was already waiting for him on the roof. His corn-silk hair was whipping around, and his handsome face was tilted in its usual smirk. Ennek could see his tan even in the moonlight; Nodosus was a day's ride inland, where the sun shone almost all the time.

"That brother of yours has been practicing sucking up," Gory said by way of a greeting.

"Yeah. He's getting pretty good at it."

"Well, dear old Dad sure ate it up."

They walked to one edge of the roof and bent over the railing to look at the water. The foam was phosphorescent, as otherworldly as the moon. They had to raise their voices a little to be heard. "You ever swim in it?" Gory asked.

Ennek shook his head. "No. Too cold."

Gory sneered. He was eighteen months older than Ennek and six inches taller. Someday he would be a chief too. He pointed at Rennis Island, the lights of which were just visible through the gathering fog. "I bet I could swim out there. It's not that far."

"It's cold," Ennek repeated. "And there are sharks."

Gory flapped his hand, whether at sharks or at people who were afraid of them, Ennek wasn't sure. "I could do it. I swim in the river all the time, even in the spring when it's all melted snow, and *that's* cold, boy. And there are things that live in the river, too, deadlier things than sharks."

Ennek didn't know if this was true. He'd never been beyond the walls of Praesidium, unless you counted an afternoon or two sailing in the bay or the one time Sopher had taken him to hunt deer.

He trailed Gory as the older boy stomped across the roof to the other side. Gory had a pocketful of pebbles, and he began dropping them over the edge onto the helmets of the guards below, pulling back out of sight when the guards looked up. "Here," he said, laughing and holding out a few small stones. "You try."

Ennek imagined the Chief's face if he found out. "No, thanks," he mumbled.

"Aw, c'mon."

Ennek found himself taking some of the smooth little things in his hand, then creeping to the railing. When the next guard walked by on his rounds, Ennek let go, and two pebbles plunked loudly off the man's head. Ennek crouched down, giggling.

"How about this?" Gory said. Now he was holding a larger chunk of stone, almost as big as his fist. It looked as if it had crumbled off the battlements.

"I'm not gonna drop that on someone's head!"

"Why not? They're wearing helmets. It's not like you're gonna kill anyone."

But Ennek shook his head, and Gory let the stone fall to his feet with a sizable *clomp*. A loud silence followed, Gory's full lips pulled up on one side, his lean hips cocked just so, one perfect eyebrow arched high.

"I went Under last month!" Ennek suddenly blurted.

Gory's eyes widened and then immediately narrowed. "You did not."

"I did! The Chief took Larkin to see and I was invited along." It wasn't quite far enough from the truth to be a lie.

Gory came very close to him, looked him up and down, and then leaned against the stone railing. He was trying for nonchalant but not quite managing, to Ennek's great delight. "What was it like?" Gory finally asked. Nodosus had no Under. Its worst criminals were simply hung, which was rather efficient but, the Chief had said, barbaric. Not to mention dangerous—a dead traitor could too easily become a martyr. But Nodosus's wizard was much less powerful than Praesidium's, as was fitting because Nodosus itself was much less powerful than the great polis to the west. Nodosus's wizard undoubtedly lacked the skill for Stasis.

Ennek looked at the way Gory's hair hung in his face, almost covering his eyes. He wondered what his own hair would look like if he allowed it to grow so long. Not the same, of course. Ennek's hair was thick and curly and nearly black. He imagined Gory's must feel very soft. "It was no big deal," he said.

"Oh?"

"Thelius showed us one of the prisoners. He was…. He looked kind of like a statue or… or a doll." That wasn't quite right, but it was as close as he could get. "And he was naked," he added in a near whisper.

"Really?" Gory's eyes shone in the cold moonlight.

"Really. He was in this sort of hammock thing. Thelius said their skin wears through if they're just left on the ground. Not that they'd feel it, but they would when they woke up."

"So you could do, like, anything to them, and they wouldn't know?"

"Yeah, I guess."

Gory chewed at his lip for a moment. "I want to see one!" he announced.

"Um, I guess your chief could ask mine."

"No. You know they'd never let me."

"Well, maybe someday when you're chief, you could—"

"That's a million years away, Ennek! I want to see now. Tonight."

Ennek swallowed. "No way."

Gory stood in front of him, stooping slightly so they were eye to eye. "Come on. Just a peek. We can go after everyone's asleep and nobody will ever know."

"But what if they found out?"

"They won't," Gory huffed. "Don't be a baby. I've snuck into tougher places than this plenty of times."

Ennek was skeptical about that. Besides, even if it was true, Gory had done his sneaking back home, where he was heir and the Chief had no authority. Ennek was going to say no again, was going to just turn away and go back inside, actually, when Gory stuck out his arm and clutched Ennek's shoulder with his tanned, man-sized hand. "Come on," Gory purred.

And to his own dismay, Ennek heard himself agreeing to meet his friend outside the dining hall in three hours.

KIM FIELDING is pleased every time someone calls her eclectic. Her books span a variety of genres, but all include authentic voices and unconventional heroes. She's a Rainbow Award and SARA Emma Merritt winner, a LAMBDA finalist, and a two-time Foreword INDIE finalist. She has migrated back and forth across the western two-thirds of the United States and currently lives in California, where she long ago ran out of bookshelf space. A university professor who dreams of being able to travel and write full-time, she also dreams of having two daughters who occasionally get off their phones, a husband who isn't obsessed with football, and a cat who doesn't wake her up at 4:00 a.m. Some dreams are more easily obtained than others.

Blogs: kfieldingwrites.com and www.goodreads.com/author/
show/4105707.Kim_Fielding/blog
Facebook: www.facebook.com/KFieldingWrites
Email: kim@kfieldingwrites.com
Twitter: @KFieldingWrites